Book Four of The Hidden Houses

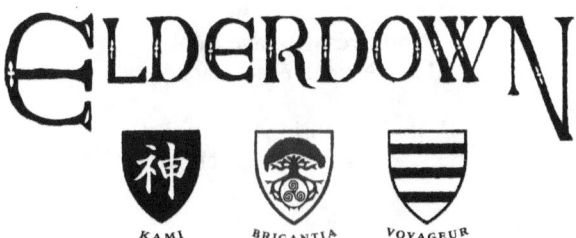

ELDERDOWN

KAMI   BRIGANTIA   VOYAGEUR

BY

Brendan Myers

NORTHWEST
PASSAGE
BOOKS

Elderdown
Book Four of The Hidden Houses

ISBN: 978-0-9939527-2-2

Published by
Northwest Passage Books
Gatineau, Quebec, Canada

For all enquiries, please visit
brendanmyers.net
fellwater.ca

Other titles in The Hidden Houses series:

Fellwater
Hallowstone
Clan Fianna
A Trick of The Light
The Seekers

Acknowledgements

Although funding for the editing and design of this book was sourced independently, I still wish to thank the many contributors to the campaign on Kickstarter.com, which paid for the production of the previous titles in the series. Among them, in particular, I wish to thank Ezekiel Zong-Han Azib, who inspired me to create one of the characters you shall read about here.

I thank my editor and designers, who believed in this project, and who did some really wonderful work for it. They made me feel like we were a team. I thank my friends MJ Patterson and Marie-Claude Dufour, who read early drafts of the text and who certified that it did not suck. I apologize to the friends, colleagues, and family members who had to tolerate my obsessed ramblings and strange mood swings during the writing process. We writers are all mad, you know.

Finally, and most importantly, I wish to thank all the readers of the previous books in the series, whose kind words of encouragement, and whose assistance with promoting the series, kept me going. Independent writers like myself depend on the support of the readers; I am more grateful than I can express.

Dedicated to everyone
who has ever lost something precious,
and started all over again.

BRIGANTIA

Ages ago, when the world was still new, ancient people wondered why they lived, and why they died, and why the world was made. They gazed into the waters, and fires, and stars, and their dreams, searching for the essence of things. They reasoned about their discoveries. They became the first philosophers.

Some of them discovered that knowledge is power. They became the first of the gods.

The descendants of the gods have lived alongside humanity since the beginning– but concealed in hundreds of secret havens, scattered across the earth. Organized into family dynasties called The Hidden Houses, they grew in strength, fought secret wars, and kept their traditions alive.

In the early twenty-first century, one such dynasty, the Roman-descended House DiAngelo, stretched out its arms over the other houses, and over the outside world.

Only one house resisted them: the Celtic-descended heroes of Clan Brigantia, who held the coveted freehold of Fellwater Grove.

They lost.

Miranda Brigand, chieftain of the Brigantians, gathered a band of refugees and dissenters, which they called The Fianna. Together they set out in search of a new home. With them came the scholar Eric Laflamme, an all-too-human outsider with no magic of his own, in a realm of fantastic creatures and mystical treasures. Having lost his lover and child to the war with the DiAngelo, he found comfort in the arms of the enigmatic voyageur, Ildicoe Brigand– herself another kind of exile, and possibly the last of her kind.

With bounties on their heads, and no place to call home, Miranda struggles to keep her clan united, and reclaim their stolen legacy.

And now, the conclusion.

~ 1 ~

"The scouts are back. Five columns of centurions approaching from the south, east, and west. Two columns mounted, armed with rifles. The other three on foot, carrying swords."

"How much time do we have?"

"About an hour."

Miranda Brigand opened a field telescope and studied the landscape surrounding Hallowstone village, from her perch on the castle's highest tower. In most directions, all appeared calm. A thick layer of ice from a recent winter storm blanketed all the trees, and reflected the blues and purples and reds of sunset. Some of the trees swayed in the wind. The ice that coated them crackled. To the north, the clouds were thickening, and a grey curtain of falling snow obscured the horizon. A brief northerly breeze tossed some of her ginger-red hair in her face. Beside her, the grey-haired and wizened master of the castle, Algernon Weatherby, folded his arms and sighed with worry.

"Any of their troops coming from the north?" asked Miranda.

"Apparently not," Algernon replied. "I think they're counting on the Wendigo and the bad weather to stop us escaping that way."

"What about the mounted units. What are they riding? Giant falcons again? Megastriders?"

"Horses."

Miranda allowed herself a chuckle. She put her telescope in a satchel that hung at her side, then drew her shawl closer around her neck and shoulders. Her heavy linen tunic, woolen leggings, and leather boots prepared her for action more than for the cold. The lines that creased her face had lengthened since last year. They did not show age; they showed a warrior's pride.

"Even so," said Algernon, "they outnumber us five-to-one, and we don't have enough time to re-supply. We do have time to evacuate the people and some of their valuables– it looks like we may have to abandon ship, at last."

Miranda silently studied the landscape for a moment longer. "Tell the warriors to gather in the castle courtyard, with their weapons."

"You have a plan?"

"I do. But you won't like it."

~ 2 ~

The first column of mounted centurions entered the village. Their captain carried the banner of House DiAngelo: red, with a white angel holding an hourglass. Beside him rode his lieutenant, holding a white banner that bore a trireme in full sail, silhouetted in front of the sun. The clop of their hooves cracked the ice on the cobblestones, but the noise was muffled by the snow on the cottage yards and rooftops. The captain ordered a halt, then dismounted. He planted his banner in the earth near the village gate, and walked ahead a short distance.

A wooden bucket rolled by with the wind, and landed in a nearby snowdrift. The captain shot it with his rifle, and it clattered away.

"Not a concealed grenade, after all," he muttered. Then to his lieutenant he said, "Secure the village gate, and the catacomb entrance beside it. Then tell Pollux he can bring his foot soldiers in."

"Sir!" the lieutenant saluted, as he turned his horse and trotted away. Captain Pollux appeared in his place a moment later, followed by a column of Roman soldiers armed with modern carbines.

"All right, you know what to do. The sooner we secure this place, the sooner we can get a hot meal," he told his men. They fanned into the village.

From a sentry tower on the castle wall, a little further than an arrow-shot away, Miranda watched the centurions explore the village. She made a snowball, crushed it into ice with her hands, and shot it with her sling-staff northward into the sky.

The curtain of snowfall shifted. Its waves of grey and white changed to a new rhythm, and its winds breathed in a new direction: southward, toward the castle and village. A blizzard was now on its way. Miranda smiled to see it approach.

From out of the blizzard there came a chestnut mare, impossibly galloping through the air, above the rooftops of the village. Miranda recognized it as a sign that her plan was now in motion. She pulled a large hood over her head, drawing it low on her brow. Her face faded into a shadow, leaving only two small points where her eyes reflected the white sheet of the sky. She climbed on to the railing of the watchtower and then leapt down, and landed on the horse as it passed by the tower. She steered it to the forest beyond the village, as three more teams of centurions marched in.

One of the soldiers below saw her and shouted the warning. "Bann-shee!"

The DiAngelo soldiers opened fire, though every bullet missed its mark. A perfectly-timed gust of wind, prompted by a gesture from the bann-shee, caused the soldiers to aim too high. Some lost their footing and fell into the snow. Pollux loaded a crossbow with a bolt twice as long as the crossbow itself, and with an arrowhead shaped like a clenched fist. He loosed it on his enemy. It never wavered in the wind, but the bann-shee vanished just before it reached her. It struck the upper floor of a brick house, and smashed a hole fit for a cannonball.

"What the hell! How did I miss!" Pollux howled.

From the left and the right, two more bann-shees rode on silver horses toward the centurion column. The arrows and sling-stones they loosed on the solders turned into flames as they fell. Some of the soldiers panicked, and ran to shelter behind trees. Others looked to their commander for orders.

"Into the village, there's more shelter there!" Captain Pollux barked.

They found shelter in the empty cottages just as the blizzard from the north arrived.

The four best warriors of the Fianna stood on the turrets of the castle, and the watchtowers on the walls. With their swords and spears raised they let out an angry, demanding battle-howl.

The blizzard replied by sending lightning bolts into the houses where the centurions sought shelter. Thunderclaps boomed across the sky. The few centurions still patrolling the village streets dropped their weapons to cover their ears.

Some of the lightning forks hit the cottages exactly where the defenders had concealed packages of gunpowder in the thatched roofs and the walls. The cottages exploded. Brick, stone, wood, and clay showered the streets, leaving behind heaps of burning rubble, some with the centurions inside them.

Carlo DiAngelo put down his binoculars and calculated in his head how much of his force might have just lost their lives. A grimace took over his face. Beside him, Kendrick McManus stuttered and gasped, searching for something to say. Behind them both, Paul Turner slowly shook his head with disbelief, and looked to Carlo for direction.

"We have to keep advancing," Paul implored, as he moved to Carlo's side.

Carlo grabbed Paul by his binoculars, almost pulling him off the horse. "This blizzard of theirs will kill half our soldiers from the cold alone. Then the bann-shees will pick off the rest."

"So what do we do?"

"We occupy the one building that they won't destroy the same way," Carlo said. "The castle."

"Why won't they destroy the castle?"

"Because it is the centre of this freehold's power. Whoever controls this castle controls how the Sources flow from here. And– controls who can touch them."

"It's almost certainly a trap," Kendrick complained.

"I know it's a trap," Carlo shot back. "That's why we spring it. We force Miranda to reveal her hand. Even with two of our platoons wounded and out, we still have three times the men."

"How do you know we have more men?" asked Paul.

"We have a spy in her camp. Do you think I planned an attack like this blind? Now move your men into the village and kill those *pezzi di merda*!"

Both Kendrick and Paul needed a moment to understand what Carlo had ordered them to do. Carlo quickly tired of their hesitation, and whipped Kendrick's horse to get him moving. Paul saw this, and didn't wait to be prodded next. Three remaining columns of soldiers entered Hallowstone Village. As the Bann-Shees and the Fianna battered them with burning sling-stones and arrows, the centurions formed a protective turtle-shell with their shields, and marched toward the courtyard of the castle. Paul loaded another of his fist-headed bolts into his crossbow, and fired it on the castle front doors, easily smashing them down.

The defenders on the courtyard walls withdrew. The centurions tentatively poked their heads out of their shield shell and, finding themselves no longer under attack, put their shields down. The interior of the castle appeared black and empty to the invaders.

"Another trap," Paul warned.

"It doesn't matter anymore," said Carlo. "We control the village. We will have the castle soon, no matter what they do. Then this entire hold will belong to us."

"Your collection will be complete," Kendrick grinned.

Carlo only glared at him.

"Right, let's do this," Paul said. He dismounted from his horse, and with a gesture he ordered three members of his team to follow him into the castle. He emerged a moment later. "The main hall is empty."

Kendrick turned to Carlo and said, "Maybe those bann-shees are the only ones left here."

"My spy assured me that–"

Carlo didn't finish, as one of his centurions flew out of the castle doors, and landed at the foot of Carlo's horse. Paul came running out of the castle next, and he hastily reloaded his crossbow from a pack of bolts on his horse. From the castle, a group of Wessex fighters, armed with rapiers and protected with gauntlets and metal breastplates, surged into the courtyard. From behind the centurions a team of Celtic warriors closed off their escape route. Their broadswords fell on the surprised DiAngelo centurions, cutting down the unprepared.

Carlo dismounted from his horse and sent it running with a smack to its hindquarters. Then he shouted at his soldiers: "Shield wall, now!"

The soldiers nearest him locked their shields into a protective ring, with Carlo and Kendrick in the centre.

"And into the castle!" Carlo ordered next. The ring of shielded centurions scuttled toward the castle, as the Wessex cavaliers and the Celtic warriors harried them.

"What if that's what they *want* us to do?" Kendrick shouted at Carlo.

"Then you go first!" Carlo replied, and he shoved Kendrick in the direction of the castle gates.

When most of the centurions had made it inside the castle, they built their shield-wall around the doors. Seeing them fortified there, Aeducan Brigand, the captain of the Celtic warriors, blew a whistle. The Celts and the Wessex cavaliers immediately fled the courtyard.

"Where are they going?" Paul said to Carlo.

Kendrick looked around the castle lobby, and realized exactly what trap they were in. "You said they wouldn't!" he marveled at Carlo.

Paul suddenly panicked. "Fuck me, they did!" he exclaimed.

Carlo quickly came to the same conclusion. He pushed two centurions out of his way, and ran out of the castle. Kendrick and Paul tried to follow.

Miranda, standing on a watchtower a short distance away, launched one of her flaming fairy-darts from her bow. It streaked into an open window just above the castle front doors, where it struck another package of concealed explosives.

The blast filled the entire ground floor of the castle with yellow-white heat and a deafening sonic boom. The blast wave shattered almost every window from the foundation to the upper towers. The ceiling of the front lobby collapsed upon the centurions sheltering there, burying most of them in bricks and rocks. Those few Romans who escaped the blast staggered into the courtyard, and collapsed on the cobblestones in pools of their own blood. Flames grew from the lower floor windows, and smoke filled the interior. The soldiers still trapped within coughed and struggled to escape, until the sound of their voices was overwhelmed by the sound of the burning castle around them.

Carlo turned to gaze on the smoke and rubble that filled the castle's main portal. Then he shook off his astonishment, and picked a rifle from one of the dead centurions.

Kendrick and Paul saw the Wessex cavaliers and the Celtic warriors running away from the castle toward the docks by the river. "Carlo, they're getting away!" Paul shouted.

"Let them go," Carlo said. "We have what we came for. Hallowstone is ours."

"Then let's search the village for any remaining traps."

Carlo checked the chamber of his rifle to see that it was loaded and ready. Then he said, "You do that, Master Turner. I will send the report to Il Duce."

As Paul left the courtyard, Kendrick said, "And just what kind of report will you send?"

Carlo smiled, and recited: "Hallowstone Castle and freehold captured for the New Renaissance. The retreating forces left extensive sabotage damage to the buildings, but nothing that cannot be repaired. Loss of fifty-five souls, including our brother Kendrick McManus of House Northumberland-Brigantia."

Kendrick turned and said, "Carlo, what do you—"

Before Kendrick could finish, Carlo pulled the trigger.

Captain Castor ran to Kendrick, and opened his clothes to get at the wound. Then he checked Kendrick's breath and pulse, and found none. He stood, and faced Carlo, and took a step back.

"What did you do that for!" he shouted.

"Such are the wages of sin," Carlo replied. "As for you, captain: I know you were only following orders. There is no sin upon you. But I can't have any witnesses, nonetheless."

Castor turned and ran. He did not get far.

~ 3 ~

From the roof of a nearby cottage, Miranda witnessed what Carlo had just done. She sat on the ridgepole and pulled her hood down, as she considered and dismissed and reconsidered a dozen or more explanations. The only thought that seemed to make sense was that she now had a chance to do something. She fitted a new arrow on her bowstring, and lined it up to loose it upon him.

She hesitated. Something in her fingers felt weak. She followed him with her eyes as he examined Kendrick's body, and wiped the fingerprints from his rifle using a handkerchief plucked from Kendrick's own pocket. She breathed on the arrowhead, and it blossomed into a small flame, ready to streak down and ignite whatever it touched. She held her breath to steady her body for the shot. Instead of letting the arrow go, she lowered her bow, and doused the flame in a patch of snow beside her.

The snowstorm parted slightly to give passage to a curraigh, which levitated in the air next to the cottage where Miranda perched. The bare winter branches of the wide oak tree which took the place of its mast and sail fluttered in the wind.

"Miranda, let's go!" shouted Ciara, who held the boat's rudder. Other warriors on board encouraged her with shouts and gestures to join them.

Miranda jumped into the boat, and Ciara steered it away. Two more similar ships joined it, and together they sailed into the oncoming storm.

~ 4 ~

"How long do you and your people wish to stay here?" said the wiry Algonquin elder, with the gentle but tired face. Although he and Miranda sat in a warm office, he was still wearing his winter coat and boots.

"Not long," Miranda replied. "A few days. We have some wounded with us; we'll move along when they are healed."

"When will they arrive?"

"They're already waiting outside."

George Medewiwin took another sip of his coffee and looked out the window as he spoke. "The DiAngelo are no friends of ours, I promise you that. But if you stay here too long, they will come here looking for you," he said.

"I know," Miranda conceded. "But they've taken Fellwater, and Hallowstone, and nearly all the important freeholds in this part of the world. They will come for you eventually, regardless of whether you help us or not."

George sighed, and said, "The Orenda Nation has always offered help to those who show respect."

Miranda showed her understanding by offering the elder a cloth pouch of tobacco, with her left hand. "It's only commercial tobacco, I'm sorry. But please accept it. As a sign of my gratitude."

George accepted Miranda's tobacco. He put some of it in his pipe to smoke, and put the rest into a seashell that sat on the desk beside him. He lit it and let it smolder for a moment, and then waved the smoke over his head and shoulders. He invited Miranda to do the same, which she did. When they finished this ritual, he motioned to Miranda to follow him. They left his office, walked through the school's corridors, and found the gymnasium.

"There might be space enough for you in here, and in some of the classrooms," he speculated. "But we will have to relocate you again, when the school re-opens in January."

The gym was only the size of a basketball court, although it also had a curtained stage at one end, and a climbing wall at the other. In the flickering of the old flourescent lights, Miranda could see a dozen banners for sports victories. A draft from the fire escape doors brought a slight chill to the air. To Miranda, it was the most welcoming sight she had seen in months. She opened the doors and waved to her clan, waiting in the parking lot. They entered, some limping, some leaning on crutches or on their friends' shoulders. One was carrying another in his arms. Others carried blankets, sleeping bags, tents, camp stoves, and backpacks over-stuffed with supplies. Moonlight streamed through the light snowfall, creating streams in the air between their shadows. Inside, they sat on exercise benches and classroom chairs, and the edge of the stage.

George knew most of them already, and greeted them warmly. "Good evening, Aeducan. Ciara. Síle. Welcome, everyone."

"Thank you for having us, Grandfather," said Miranda.

"He isn't really your grandfather, is he?" Finnbarr said to her.

Maread nudged him in the ribs. "It's a sign of honour."

"Welcome to my home, people of Clan Fianna," George said to them all, as they settled into a circle. He lit his pipe again and passed it to Algernon, seated at his left side. "I hope you find warmth and rest here. And I hope you don't mind me saying–how *interesting* it is, that you should come to the Orenda Nation in search of shelter, just as some of you did when you first came to this land, five hundred years ago."

Light laughter greeted George's words. He trusted his point was made, so he moved on. "Since we are here, I wonder if we might say a few words about what you plan to do, now that both Fellwater Grove and Hallowstone Castle have fallen."

Then he sat down again. At first, most of the Fianna looked to each other, waiting for someone else to begin. Algernon Weatherby stood first and said, "Miranda, I know you made the decision you thought was strategically correct. But you were right when you said I wouldn't like it. My home is destroyed. It didn't have to be. When we saw the centurions coming, all we had to do was retreat. We didn't have to– we didn't need to scuttle the village behind us."

Miranda stood and faced Algernon. "I apologise. Sincerely. But it seemed clear to me that if we stood and fought them straight up, they would have smashed us. If we retreated, they would have chased us into the winter, and hunted us down. As it is, they took Hallowstone, which they would have done anyway. You told me that, yourself. But we left it nearly useless to them. And we took down most of their soldiers with it. That's what winning looks like in a no-win situation." She sat down again.

"We could have just retreated," Algernon countered. "We had three of your flying boats. We opened a Seven-League-Door. Then we could have taken the castle back, some day."

"It would not have been the same," Miranda countered. "They would have twisted it to their purposes. Made it their own. Have you seen what they did to Fellwater?"

"Yes, I have," Algernon admitted unhappily.

"Anyway," Miranda continued, "we don't have the forces to take the castle back. We are no more than what you see here."

Algernon raised his voice almost to a shout. "Are you saying we should destroy all our last freeholds just to keep them out of enemy hands? Because I will not stand for that!"

Goerge Medewiwin stood. Since the Fianna were gathered in his space, he needed to do no more than that to bring quiet to the circle again. "Everyone, friends, all of you. We have the same problem, here. House DiAngelo has taken something, big or small, from all of us. They opened the Tartarus Gates deliberately, letting out all manner of monsters to attack everyone who refuses to join that gentlemen's club of theirs, their New Renaissance. We also know what is at stake here. If we are driven from our homes, if we lose these last few remaining places where we have lived in our own way since the beginning of things, then we'll become the same as everyone else. I suggest, that better than pointing fingers, we should tell our stories. When everyone has spoken, then perhaps we shall be of one mind, and we will know what to do."

Across the circle, Niall DeDannan stood up. "*Tá scéilín, mo chairde–* I have a story. My home in Rath Manannan has been taken from me," he said.

"Niall DeDannan!" George welcomed him. "Tell us your story."

"I was recently elected the chieftain of the DeDannans of Nova Scotia," Niall confirmed. "But it doesn't mean much. Beside Ciara and myself, there's only seven of us left who haven't joined Il Duce's New Renaissance."

"What happened?" Miranda asked.

"Just after my election, I went to visit our cousin clan in Galway," said Niall. "While I was there, a band of bastards calling themselves 'The Opposition Party' seized the gates of Rath Manannan. They locked me out. And now, the dolmen on our sacred hill has been painted in New Renaissance colours. Painted– did you catch that? As in: with paint."

Around the circle, angry words were whispered: "Painted? Painted! The bastards! What the hell! Sacrilege!"

A middle-aged, fierce-faced Hindi woman stood next. "I have more cause to be angry than any of you– Heathcliff tried to hold my daughter hostage!" Satya declared, as some faces nodded and remembered. Kuvira, her daughter, nestled closer to her father Ramanujan, when she heard her name spoken. "Well, for all that," Satya continued, "I'm not saying *we should go to war.*

But I am saying that we should do *something*. I'm too old for living on the road, like this."

"Satya, we have nowhere to go," her husband reminded her.

"I know," Satya acknowledged. "I just wanted to see if there's anyone else who has a better idea about what to do."

The next to stand was Ibrahim Nefzawi, a muscular West African man with a navy-blue turban, embroidered with stars and moons. "It seems to me, that we have two choices. We can become nomads. Wanderers, moving from one oasis to another, as we have been doing since the fall of Fellwater Grove. For that matter, as my house did, before we built the Songhai empire. Or– and I like this idea better– we can fight them! We can take a stand somewhere. Here, maybe. With the permission of our gracious host, of course."

Voices of both support and opposition grew from the assembly. George Medewiwin silenced them all by standing up again. "Let me remind you," he said, "that the shelter of this sacred place is open to everyone–," he looked at Ibrahim, "–who leaves his weapons behind."

The voices which supported Ibrahim now whispered of other places where they could go instead. Sovnhalla. Olorun's Hold. New Hexenfeld.

Ibrahim grew impatient. "Then let us not wait for them to bring the fight to us. Let us take the fight to them!" he exclaimed. "We don't have to conquer them. We only have to increase the pain on them, until they give us back our lands."

"They will never give you back your madrasa, Ibrahim!" said Aeducan. "They are a pack of prideful, self-absorbed shit-bags– they won't even acknowledge they did anything wrong. The only result that will come of attacking them is a quick and malicious counter-attack. Is that what you want?"

"I'm only saying, that these are our choices," Ibrahim explained. "Permanent nomadism, or guerrilla war."

The words 'guerrilla war' were repeated in the whispers around the circle.

A new voice from outside the circle said, "There is a third choice."

All eyes turned to see who had spoken. They saw an athletic woman, dressed for winter survival, with a colourful sash around the waist of her midnight-blue winter tunic, and two smaller sashes under her knees. She jumped down from the stage and drew close to the circle. Voices whispered her name: Ildicoe

Brigand. The lady-Voyageur. The one who broke open the gates of the underworld, and let out the monsters that destroyed Fellwater Grove.

Some of the warriors jumped to their feet and drew their weapons.

Síle MacBride stood and marched toward Ildicoe. "You traitor! You monster! My forest burned because of you!"

Ciara DeDannan joined Síle, shouting, "My Donall died because of you!"

Síle lurched for Ildicoe with a hockey stick. Miranda and Aeducan held her down. Ildicoe held out her hands to show she was unarmed, but the warriors continued their angry shouting. It abated only when George and Miranda stood in front of Ildicoe, and faced the assembly with hands held up to stop them.

"The *only* reasons I won't let these men kill you here and now," Miranda growled at Ildicoe, "is out of respect for Elder Medewiwin, and for the friendship you and I once had."

Ildicoe stepped out from behind George and said, "I did what had to be done. Just like you did, at Hallowstone, yesterday."

"Don't go there," Miranda warned her. Then she turned to Síle and said, "And you, put the stick down."

Síle dropped the hockey stick, but didn't take her eyes off Ildicoe.

Ciara said, "I will not sit in the same circle with her."

Ildicoe stepped forward. "I know that all of you think I'm the *bête noir* of the century–"

"Keep talking," Ciara sneered.

"–but I know a way to avoid an unwinnable war with the DiAngelo, *without* becoming nomads. Just hear me out, and then– and I'll go, and you won't have to see me again if you don't want to."

The assembly grew quiet. Most looked between Miranda and George for a decision.

Miranda said, "Two minutes. Speak."

Those who drew weapons on Ildicoe put them away and sat down. George remained on his feet, to remind everyone to keep the peace. Ildicoe took a tentative step forward.

"There's another place where we could all go. It's a freehold that belongs to House Voyageur. It's been abandoned for the last two years. It's almost as big as Fellwater Grove. It's a day's walk from the nearest paved road, so the outsiders won't find us. No one will. We would be safe there: it's defensible, mostly self-sustaining, and secret."

The first to respond to Ildicoe's suggestion was Ibrahim. "Why is it secret?" he asked.

"Because we Voyageurs are the only ones who know where it is."

Ramanujan Bhattacharya said, "Then why was it abandoned?"

Ildicoe shifted uncomfortably. "Because– well, we Voyageurs have always been one of the smaller houses– we didn't have enough people, when– around two years ago–"

Miranda realized what Ildicoe was trying to say. "It's been overrun by direcreatures, hasn't it?"

"Yes," Ildicoe admitted. Then she looked up again and said, "But with the warriors in this room, we could take it back. We could build our new home there."

"What do you mean *our* home?" Ciara seethed.

"Well, it's worth considering," Aeducan said.

Ciara rounded on Aeducan. "Don't tell me you *like* her idea! Look where it's coming from!"

"The merits and flaws of an idea have nothing to do with the speaker," Miranda reminded her.

"Thank you, Miranda," said Ildicoe.

"This doesn't mean I'm happy to see you," Miranda gritted back.

Ildicoe looked to the ground.

Aeducan said, "So, where is it?" he asked.

Síle and Ciara glowered coldly at him for his curiosity.

"It's in West Quebec," Ildicoe replied. "It's an island in a lake, surrounded by old mountains. A very peaceful, beautiful place. There were birds there, that came out only at night, that would sing together like a church choir. And each morning, the moment the first sunlight touched the earth, every green and growing thing would make a flower. Trees, grasses, bracken. Everything. We could make a new home there. Wouldn't that be better than living on the run? Or fighting a war that we can never win?"

"Sounds great," said Finnbarr, "except for the terrabiters spitting acid on everything."

Miranda ignored Finnbar and said, "I think I've heard enough."

"So, you'll come?" Ildicoe asked hopefully.

"We'll talk about it."

Ciara scowled at Miranda.

"I said we'll *talk* about it," Miranda re-asserted.

Ciara shook her head with disapproval, but let it pass.

"And now I think you better go," Miranda told Ildicoe.

Ildicoe nodded. "I'll say one last word. Elderdown. That's the name of it."

Whispers grew among the people again. "Elderdown? It's real? It's not just a legend?"

"And I'm the only one left who knows where it is," Ildicoe finished. "So if you want to meet me there, talk to Eric Laflamme. He knows how to reach me."

Ciara glowered at Ildicoe when she heard Eric's name. "We're not too sure we can trust *him*, either."

"He's the only man that *I* trust," Ildicoe declared. "Anyway, I've said all that I came to say. I hope that– I hope– well, I'll see you soon, maybe." Ildicoe pulled her hood over her head, put on her mittens, opened the fire escape doors, and braved the winter.

~ 5 ~

Most eyes around the circle looked to Miranda for a decision, or at least an opinion. Miranda cleared her throat and sad, "So, everyone, it appears we have *three* choices after all. To remain on the run. To fight to reclaim our former homelands. Or, to go to Elderdown, and start all over again."

"The decision is rightly yours, as the chieftain," said Ibrahim.

Miranda gave herself time to think. She looked over the faces of everyone in the circle: some hopeful, some anxious, some angry, and some tired. George was the only one who appeared patient.

"First we gather strength," she announced. "There are tools, weapons, and treasures, some of them lost since the mythic age, that we could use. Our enemies could find them useful, too. Let's find them first."

Aeducan, Maread, and Finnbarr agreed.

Miranda's confidence grew. "We are not the only ones that Carlo and company have persecuted. They've done far worse to others than they have done to us. Let's find those people. Let them know they're not alone. Let's invite them to join us."

Ibrahim, Satya, and Ramanujan joined the voices of approval. Ramanujan interjected with "Or maybe we should join them!"

"Whichever works," Miranda agreed with a laugh. Returning to her plan, she said, "Fellwater Grove was not only our home. It was also a name for a way of seeing things. A way of life. It was the standing-ground where we faced the world, with all its danger and unfairness and misery, and we found something in it we could call good and beautiful. It's the place where people from different clans, and different sources, could all come together. Not just to fight a common enemy. But to preserve the idea of a life of honour. Share our different ways of facing the same immensities, and thereby better understand each other. That idea did not die just because we are homeless. But without good soil, even the strongest of trees cannot grow. We need a place to call home again. It cannot be just anywhere– it has to be the kind of place where the best parts of our souls can come out and play. Yet as you all know, few such places remain. Fewer every year. Therefore, when we have grown strong enough, in arms and in allies–" Miranda paused, as the faces around her grew more expectant. They hoped she was about to announce the decision they wanted her to make. She unsheathed her sword and said, "We will take back Fellwater Grove!"

This produced the loudest and most enthusiastic show of support. The warriors got to their feet to cheer, and some of them brandished weapons in the air. Algernon, however, watched the cheering for a moment, then got up and left the circle. Some of his Wessex cavaliers followed him, into the school's hall.

When the assembly had settled down again, Aeducan and Maread approached Miranda. "I'm glad that you finally made a decision. I was getting tired of living on the run. In the Canadian winter!"

"Truth be told, so was I," Miranda agreed.

"Got some questions, though," said Aeducan. "How do you know that Carlo's people are out there, treasure-hunting?"

"Because I have a spy in their camp," Miranda grinned.

"Told you," Maread said to Aeducan, with a wink. Then she looked to Miranda. "And, umm, where exactly is Eric right now?" she asked.

Miranda perked her eyebrows. "Why do you ask?

"Just curious."

Miranda studied Maread's expression for a moment. "He's in a safe house," she explained. "After his video exposed the corruption in the Guardians organization, Carlo put out a contract on his life. Ten thousand clutches."

Maread bit her lip. "By the gods, that boy just doesn't get a day off."

Niall DeDannan joined the conversation. "Miranda, can I borrow these two warriors for a while? There's something at my old *rath* which we should steal. Call it the first weapon for your armory."

Miranda looked to Aeducan and Maread and said, "Interested?"

"If it gives Carlo a bloody nose, then I'll steal anything for you," said Aeducan.

Miranda smiled and said, "Take one of the curraighs, and be back in three days, if you can."

"You're gonna love it!" Niall promised.

Miranda turned to Satya and Ramu.

"I've a mission for you, too."

~ 6 ~

"Good morning Shinobi," Eric said to his handler.

"*Konnichiwa*, Eric-san, but that's not my real name," said Eric's handler with a smile.

"Then why not tell me your real name?"

"You don't know it, for your own protection."

Eric laughed. "Same conversation, different day."

Eric's safe house was a concrete-brick shed that had been converted into a studio apartment. It was tucked into the corner of the back garden of a mansion; Eric could only see the hanging ivy and some flowerbeds through his window. Most of the time, he only saw snowfall. He knew he was no longer in Fellwater, but as he had been brought to the safe house through a Seven League Door, he did not know anything else. Sometimes he wondered if he was still in Canada.

"I brought you some more movies today," said Shinobi, as he handed Eric a stack of DVD's. "All of it sci-fi and fantasy from the last ten years. Also a film of Wagner's Parsifal, from the Bayreuth Festival last year, just as you requested."

"What I really want," Eric lamented, "is to go for a walk outside. Honestly, a prisoner in a jail has more freedom than I do right now."

"The Guardians are everywhere, Eric. And since you posted that video, they all know your face, and they all hate you."

Eric began sorting the food delivery into the kitchen cupboards. "How long can you stay today? Want to split a beer?" he asked.

Shinobi accepted, and the two men sat down.

"I have some news that might interest you," said Shinobi. "Your old nemesis, Kendrick McManus, is dead."

Eric put down his beer. "Really? When? How?"

"Two days ago. He and your other old nemesis, Carlo DiAngelo, laid siege to Hallowstone Castle."

"Slow down– there was a battle at Hallowstone?"

"Half of the village was destroyed. The castle still stands, but the ground floor was gutted by an explosion. Kendrick was buried in a collapsed catacomb."

Eric contemplated his beer. "I suppose Hallowstone belongs to Carlo now."

Shinobi nodded. "It seems *all* the biggest freeholds in Canada belong to him. I wonder why he wants them. Simple greed, I suppose."

"No. Greed is not his motivation. He's a social reformer. He thinks that modern life is decadent and vulgar, and he wants to start a second– a second Renaissance–"

Eric's mind drifted. He pulled a file folder from a stack of boxes in the corner of the room, and rifled through it.

"What?" asked Shinobi.

"This!" said Eric, as he found what he was looking for: a photocopy of a Renaissance painting.

"I don't get it," said Shinobi.

"It's a copy of a painting that might have been made by Carlo himself, hundreds of years ago. It looks like *The Transfiguration of Christ* by Raphael. But different, see? That's Zeus in the centre, not Jesus. And on this ridge just below him, you've got Zeus' brothers Hades and Poseidon."

"If those are his brothers, why are they dead?"

"That's the million-dollar question."

Shinobi examined the picture a moment longer. "I still don't get it."

"You need to read this as if a man will die if you don't understand it," Eric explained. He pointed to the figure of Zeus. "That's Carlo in the centre. The angels on either side of him hold hourglasses– House DiAngelo's family crest. And that–" he pointed to the figure of Hades, "–is Kendrick."

"How do you know that's Kendrick?"

"Hades was lord of the underworld. And you said Kendrick's body was found–"

"–underground!" Shinobi realized.

"If my theory is right, someone else in Carlo's organization will soon meet his death by drowning."

Shinobi nodded. "Poseidon."

"This painting was stolen from its gallery back in the 70's," Eric said. "But I saw it in Carlo's basement, before the house burned down. That was back when he wanted Katie to play the role of this woman here, the oracle–" Eric pointed to one of the astonished onlookers below the ridge. Then he sat back in his chair, with the picture still in his hands, thinking.

"Carlo has a new prophet, now," Shinobi said. "Her name is Tricia Garvey. A musician from Newfoundland: she used to front a rock band called The Wild Men of Summer. I've seen her at the Guardian's public rallies. When she sings, the Shadow-Spell loses some of its force for a while. People spontaneously Awaken. I have to say, it's really something to see."

Eric digested this new information for a moment. Then he took a coloured marker and scribbled something on the picture.

"What are you doing?" asked the handler.

"If you can't let me out, then maybe you could deliver some mail for me?"

"Okay," Shinobi conceded. "Just be sure you don't say anything in your letters about where you are."

"That will be easy. I don't know where I am."

Eric sealed the picture in an envelope, and handed it to Shinobi. "Take this to Miranda. She'll know it's from me. Tell her she can put me to work as her intelligence analyst. Anyway, I need something more to *do* here."

Shinobi accepted the envelope. "I'll bring you a new video game next time, too."

"Couldn't we use your Seven League Door to go some place where no one would think to find me? Just for an afternoon?"

"I could take you to Japan, but you don't have the language."

Eric sighed. "And you don't have the time to translate."

"Same conversation, different day," Shinobi smiled. "See you tomorrow."

~ 7 ~

Shinobi barged through the office door without knocking first. He dismissed the secretary with a threatening glance and a jerk of his head toward the door. He sat on the desk, unfolded Eric's picture of Carlo's painting, and laid it on the blotter.

On the page, Eric had circled the figure of Zeus and written "Carlo" beside it. Next to the circled figure of Hades, he had written the name 'Kendrick'. Finally, beside the circle around Poseidon, he put three question marks.

"You see?" said Shinobi. "Carlo told everyone his plan, centuries ago. He hid it in plain sight. And now, he has the Guardians in his pocket, and the seven royal freeholds, and hundreds of lesser holds, *and* a new prophet. So he plans to dispose of the people with whom he has to share power. That may well include *you*."

"So it would appear," said Heathcliff Weatherby Wednesday. He paused in thought for a moment, then said, "Carlo and Kendrick and I are brothers, did you know?"

"No, I did not; aren't you all from different Houses?"

"We are," Heathcliff confirmed. "But when Kendrick and I were very small, Carlo's parents adopted us. All throughout my childhood I thought I was just as Roman as Big Nose here. But as it happened, after some investigating– an archive here, a records office there, a seer from House Delphi somewhere in the middle– it turned out my real ancestors were the Wessex-men. Germanic settlers of Anglia. Big-bearded, axe-wielding, heavy-drinking barbarians, you might say. You couldn't ask for people from more different from the DiAngelo: clean shaven, letter-writing, wine-sipping Romans. Kendrick, for his part, found his ancestors among Romanized Britons. He was half way between Carlo and I, you could say. But I still think of them both as my brothers. How could I not? We grew up together. We did everything together. We did everything–"

Heathcliff clutched his fist over his mouth and nose. Memories watered his eyes. He dropped the picture and took up in its place a framed black-and-white photo from his desk, of himself and Carlo and Kendrick as younger men, many years ago.

"Please accept my condolences for your loss– I don't know what else to say," said Shinobi. Heathcliff acknowledged it with a nod, without taking his eyes off the photo.

Shinobi added, "I think someone knows that the three of you are brothers, and I think that you might be the next to die. We should take this to Il Duce," Shinobi suggested.

Heathcliff thumped the framed photo on the desk. "You mean to confront our leader, and accuse my only living brother of plotting to kill me?"

"Nothing that confrontational. I think Il Duce should know there is a chance your brother Kendrick was murdered. He should know that Carlo may stand to benefit from his death. And to benefit from yours, should you be next. That is not proof of Carlo's guilt, but it is cause for suspicion. I would like the honour of reporting this theory to our leader personally."

Heathcliff considered the picture and its implications for a moment. Then he said, "I might be able to arrange it."

~ 8 ~

The boat drifted a kilometer from the shore. Its mast had no sail, and its stern flew no flag. A fisherman cast his line out to the sea, reeled it in, and cast it out again. The DiAngelo sentry on the rocky ledge of the peninsula put down his binoculars and made a note about it in his logbook. Then he returned to his poker game with the other sentries.

Evening became night. Scattered clouds loomed grey and then black, and the stars behind them struggled to shine. The fisherman bent down beneath the gunnels, out of sight.

Four shadows sat up and looked around. One shadow grasped the rudder. A second unfurled a flag on the stern: blue, with the figure of the harper standing in his curraigh. Needles and twigs peeled off from the mast, and then thickened and grew into branches. Leaves sprouted from their tips, and spread inward, until the tree was as thick as a summer oak in full foliage.

The oarsmen steered the boat toward the land. Just before the prow met the crests of the shore-waves, the keel lifted itself from the water. It flew above the pebbled beach, then over the rocky crags and lookouts where the DiAngelo sentries still played at cards, then over the fields of tall grass and spindly evergreens beyond.

The beam from a lighthouse went dark as the tree-boat approached. A technician climbed up to check his lamp: his back was turned as the boat passed over him. He banged his wrench on the lamp's metal casings. The lamp awakened again when the boat passed it by. The technician looked at his wrench and wondered if it was magic.

The peninsula was without trees: only tall grass and the occasional clump of gorse covered its thin black soil. Cottages of wood or plaster lay in the patches of flat ground. Further up the slope, the cottages gave way to artificial mounds, ringed with great kerbstones, some with sheep or goats grazing upon them. At the highest point on the peninsula stood the largest of the mounds, and on top of it stood a mighty portal dolmen: a wide and flat stone supported on three thin pillar stones. Easily as high as a house, the dolmen seemed to glow in the feeble starlight, as it had recently been painted: white for the pillars, gold for the roof. The DeDannan curraigh with the tree for a sail slowed just as it approached the dolmen. Three shadows fell from it and scurried into hidden corners in the rocky hillside. The fourth shadow looked down, to see that the three were safe and hidden. Then it grasped the rudder and the boat sped on its way.

The mound had a portal of its own: a decorated trilithon arch that opened to a shadowed passage into the earth. Two sentries sat on wooden chairs before it, warming themselves by a fire in a metal trash can. They shared a flask of whiskey between them.

One of the shadows from the boat crept behind them. It revealed a snake-blade dagger, which swiftly slit the throat of one of the guards. The shadow dashed away before the body hit the ground. The second sentry was about to shout the alarm but another shadow silenced him by grasping his head and twisting his neck.

A third sentry emerged from the passage in the mound. "Hey, dudes, have you got– what the hell!"

A third shadow fell behind him and pulled him into the darkness of the passage in the mound. A heartbeat later he sailed out again, cracked his skull on a stone, and made no complaint about it.

The three shadows gathered at the fire, and pulled their hoods down. Aeducan Brigand was the largest and most muscular of the them. He chuckled quietly as he surveyed the damage the team had done, pleased with himself for their success. Maread

Macbride shook her head and let her blonde dreadlocks fly around, then she grabbed Aeducan by his beard and pulled him close for a quick kiss. The third shadow was Niall DeDannan, who laughed with the others, although his brow furrowed; he was more surprised with how relaxed his companions were at the sight of the centurions at their feet.

"Welcome to Rath Manannan," he said, with outstretched arms and open hands. In a sing-song voice he added: "*Where the hills, they are hollow, and home to the fae*– I bet the outsiders would be disappointed if they found out the faeries were only people, all along."

Aeducan picked the flask of whiskey from the ground and said, "But some of the fairies have excellent taste in whiskey." He took a drink and passed it to Maread.

Niall picked up a rifle that hung on the back of a chair. "And in weapons."

"I still prefer swords," said Maread. "You don't have to reload them."

Aeducan frowned at the banners that stood on either side of the portal. On the left side hung the Guardians banner, with its black trireme and yellow sun. The banner of the DeDannans stood on the right, though it had been defaced by the letters "K" and "P" on either side of the harper.

"What do you think of this, Niall?" he asked.

"I'm trying not to," Niall replied.

Maread took off her cloak and was about to strip one of the sentries of his tabard for use as a disguise, but discovered it was too covered in blood.

Aeducan opened his field kit bag and said, "Here, I brought you a clean one."

Then they pulled the bodies of the sentries into hiding places, and searched their pockets and bags for ammunition. As they worked, Niall said, "We DeDannans were not much of a warrior clan. We were artists. Musicians. Poets."

"Egg-heads, you mean," said Aeducan.

"Sorcerers," Niall corrected him. "We perfected the only magic that's ever been proven to raise the dead."

"What magic is that?"

"Storytelling."

Maread chuckled.

"But the point I was getting to," Niall continued, "is that there aren't many weapons in the treasury."

"So– what are we stealing that's worth more than the lives of the three men we just killed?" said Maread.

"The *Dord Fian*."

Aeducan dropped his jaw and furrowed her brow. Maread dropped the belt she was buckling on, and strode up to Niall's face. "You had the Dord Fian, all this time, and you didn't tell us?" he growled.

"We had to keep it secret," said Niall. "Like I told you, we're not warriors. We had to have *something* we could use to defend ourselves, if we were ever attacked." When he saw Aeducan remained unconvinced, he said, "How do you think we pushed the Asatru into the sea, in the Battle of Clontarf?"

"You had Brigantians in the army."

"Well, we did. But we also had the Dord Fian."

Aeducan conceded the point. "All right. What does it do?"

Maread thought she knew. "It's a hunting horn, isn't it? The legends say it summons the warriors from the House of Donn the Old. It brings them back to life, to fight on your side."

Niall grinned. "We like that legend. What it really does is a little simpler. It gives you the strength of your ancestors, so you can fight as they did. Win, like they did."

"That could be damn handy in a scrap," said Aeducan, "as long as your clansfolk don't use it against the three of us before we steal it."

Maread said, "All right, let's pick who gets to stay out here and stand guard."

"I'll stand guard," said Niall. "I don't want to go in there, in case we have to fight anything."

"You have to go in there," said Maread. "You know the layout of the place."

"I suppose I do," he sighed.

Maread and Aeducan faced each other and shook their fists three times. On the third shake, Maread made paper and Aeducan made scissors.

"Damn," said Maread.

"Right then," said Aeducan. "Truth in our hearts."

"Strength in our arms," said Maread.

"Fulfillment of the oath," said Niall.

They bumped their fists together.

"Don't drink all the grog before we're back," said Aeducan, as he turned to enter the passage mound.

"Then you better get me a better sword," said Maread. She took a seat by the fire. Niall and Aeducan drew up their hoods and became shadows again, and disappeared into the passage mound.

~ 9 ~

The banner of the Nova Scotia Brigantians featured a green saltire on a white field, with the crest of the Brigantians inset in the centre. It flew on the ridgepole of a humble country farmhouse, giving the flaking paint and the crumbling bricks the air of a noble heritage.

"A lot of your people joined up with us, when Donall was chieftain of Fellwater," said Devon Willowtree, as she placed a well-stocked tea tray on the kitchen table. "They like it here now. And to be honest, I like having them here."

"I need them to help re-capture Fellwater Grove," said Miranda.

"I need them to protect New Scotland Farm from direcreatures. We never had many warriors here, until they joined us. Now I don't know how we got on without them."

"Let me talk to them. They know me. I'll tell them what's at stake, then they can make their own decision."

Neachtain the Healer, who until then had been cooking something on the range, sat next to Miranda. "I'm glad to see you again, Miranda. Really, I am. But I'll tell you right now, there's not much you could say to convince *me* to leave here. We have everything we ever had back in Fellwater– good food, good music, good jobs. Good company. But one thing we *don't* have, like we did back in Fellwater, is House DiAngelo constantly trying to kill us."

"They'll come for you here, soon enough," Miranda warned.

"If you can do something to delay that," said Devon, "then I'll consider sending the warriors to help you."

"I'll tell you what will impress them," said Neachtain. "Convince the head of a house that joined the DiAngelo, to join you instead."

Miranda sat back in her chair, with a mischevious smirk on her face. "All right, Devon: challenge accepted."

*

At a music pub in Hammertown, Gregory Morningfrost finished his first set of the evening, then jumped off the stage with surprise when Miranda sat by the bar.

"Miranda! Glad you came out to the show!" he grinned. "You know what I love the most about playing here? Everybody can see my antlers, and they think it's part of a costume. That's the Celtic Mist for you. Did you bring your guitar? Want to join me for the second set?"

"Not tonight," she said. "I need your help. Clan business."

Gregory ordered a Guinness for her, and a cider for himself. His beard and hair were neatly trimmed, his attire was sharp and businesslike, but the curved stag antlers that grew from his temples marked him as one of the Secret People.

"Carlo's people have chased us from one safe haven to another," he explained. "If you and your Fianna are planning to fight back, I'm with you."

"Wonderful!" Miranda exclaimed.

"The trouble is, I don't know how much good I'll be to you. I don't have my hounds right now," said Gregory.

"What happened to them?"

"Oh, they're just being puppies. A few nights ago they thought they saw some creature out of Tartarus. They ran off to attack it."

"So, can you call them back?"

"They usually come back on their own in a few days. They're almost as smart as people; I'm not really worried. But if you want them sooner, you'll have to help me find them."

*

In the monastery of Clan Columba, Brother Aidan the Wise received Miranda with open hands. "Welcome to Saint Columbanus Abbey. I assume you're here on clan business, and not to receive baptism?"

"You know me," she replied with an apologetic smile. "I wonder if we might have the help of your book."

"Why, Miranda! I'm delighted to hear that you're interested in the faith."

"Actually– the *other* book?"

Brother Aidan looked down at her over the tops of his glasses. "I renounced the warrior life a long time ago. This had better be for a *very* good cause."

"The recapture of Fellwater Grove."

Aiden sighed. "We have a contract with the New Renaissance, now. We provide wine to the Guardians Organization."

"You have a contract with them! Aidan! You know what they are!"

"We had to take it. Nothing against you or the allied clans, Miranda, but we need the money. People don't send their sons here for a Christian education, like they used to. And the youngest of the brothers here is fifty-five. If I was seen helping you, Carlo would cancel the contract immediately. And probably burn our vineyard to the ground."

"We'll make sure they don't know the book was yours, if that's what you need."

Aidan nodded. "I'd like some time to contemplate your request. By the way, it would help if you could find another buyer for our wine."

*

"Sure, I'll loan you the cauldron," said Marla St. David. She snapped her fingers, and her herald immediately departed to fetch it. Then she turned to Miranda again. "But if you're going to take it into battle– I'm sorry to have to say this, but if it gets damaged–"

"I understand, I agree," said Miranda. "Let me give you something of mine, in exchange. Something you can keep, if anything happens to the cauldron."

"The cup of Cormac the King," said Marla.

Miranda sighed, and rubbed her forehead, thinking of whether she could spare it. "I might need it to interrogate prisoners."

"My cauldron is unique in the world. If it is lost, there will never be another like it. Just like your cup."

Miranda conceded the point. "Very well. The cup of Cormac the King."

~ 10 ~

"We shall have potato samosas for the appetizer, cooked in olive oil and not vegetable oil. For the main course, we shall share a platter of tandoori masala with mutton and paratha, spiced with habanero peppers and a sprig of coriander. The coriander shall weigh no more than ten grams. And I myself will have a side-dish of deep-fried cicadas in poutine."

The waitress fumbled with her bill pad, then said, "Some of those things are not on the menu, sir. The cicadas– definitely not. Ew."

"Nonetheless, that's what I want. And be sure the cicada shells are thoroughly cracked open before you cook them. I hate picking those things out of my teeth. We will also have a bottle of DiAngelo Estates 2001 Sangiovese Red."

"I've never heard of that winery, sir."

"You have at least one bottle in the yoga studio, behind the building."

The waitress made an effort to be polite. "There's nothing I can do about that, sir. The studio is not part of the restaurant."

"Then get the manager."

The waitress left. Satya smiled at her husband.

"If that doesn't get his attention, Ramu, nothing will."

"I enjoyed that," said Ramanujan. "It's surprisingly fun, being an asshole."

Miranda grinned. "Don't enjoy it too much."

Miranda, Satya, and Ramanujan gazed around the dining room. Diwali candles still burned on most shelves and ledges, mixing easily with the Christmas lights in the windows. A bronze Ganesh statue in a niche in the wall seemed to glitter whenever someone walked by.

The manager appeared before them as if he materialized there when no one was looking. Dressed in a tailored suit and silk tie, a gold stud in one ear, and a Guardians pin on his lapel, he drummed his fingers on the back of an empty chair, and let the clicking of hidden claws speak for him.

"Raj Purana. *Namaste*," Miranda greeted him, with hands folded prayerfully.

"Get out of my restaurant," Raj Purana told them. His voice was crisp and controlled, but there was no hiding his ire.

"What are you going to do?" said Ramanujan. "Have the Guardians march us out at gunpoint? Just like last time, except with all these outsiders watching?"

"I'm surprised with you, Ramu," Raj Purana said. "Your wife is usually the excitable one. Now what are you doing here?"

Satya said, "We just wanted to say hello, and ask how are things at the ashram now that the Il Duce in charge."

Raj Purana blinked, but remained controlled. "Everything is fine."

"We would also like our things back," said Ramanujan. "You know, everything we had to leave behind when the Guardians forced us out."

"Your possessions have been redistributed," Raj Purana told them.

"And, we'd also like you to join our new Fianna," said Miranda.

Raj Purana paused, then leaned back and stifled his laughter. "Join the Fianna? Your Celtic clans are bog farmers, nothing more. Your greatest cultural achievement was a pile of rocks with a window. What can you possibly offer House Arjun?"

"Escape from the New Renaissance," said Miranda.

"Why would I want that?"

"Because you are no longer in control of your own house. You don't command the *kshatrias* anymore. You have no say in who may enter the hold, and who must leave. You don't manage the finances or any other common resources. Il Duce appointed some bureaucrat to do those things."

Ramanujan said, "All you do now is sign the paperwork. Probably with a rubber stamp."

Raj Purana let his smile subside. He looked up to the ceiling for a moment. Then he threw one leg over the back of the chair as he sat down. He leaned forward, so that their conversation would not be overheard. "How the fuck did you know that?" he said.

"Because that's what they do to everyone."

Raj Purana smiled and waved his finger at Ramanujan. "You're quite the gambler, coming in here."

"So you'll join us?" Miranda said.

Raj smirked at them. "What you need to understand about the New Renaissance," he explained, "is that their leader, Il Duce, is basically *right*. Look around my restaurant. What do you see?"

Ramanujan looked around. "Middle-aged businessmen closing a deal. The waitress trying to put herself through college. Two men on a date. Why, what do you see?"

"Children."

Satya and Ramanujan looked at each other. Miranda glared at the Raj.

"Children in need of a good bedtime story," the Raj continued. "Something to help them sleep at night, and give them something to do in the morning. Above all, something to keep them distracted."

"From what?"

"The fact that their lives are absolutely, completely, pointless."

Ramanujan gasped for words. Satya momentarily lost her breath. Miranda remained still; she had heard this line from New Renaissance believers before. She showed her disapproval with a cold glare.

"How can you say such a thing?" Satya exclaimed.

Raj ignored her question. "The New Renaissance is going to tell them a new story. A better story than the silliness they've been telling themselves about how the latest smart-phone or the next promotion at work will give their lives meaning. We're going to tell a story that will wake everybody up. I want to be part of that."

As he spoke, two muscular Hindi men wearing black T-shirts, leather jackets, and camouflage-pattern pants entered the restaurant and sat at the bar. The sitar player in the corner dropped a chord when they passed her. They each ordered a bottle of Tiger beer, and faced the table where Raj Purana sat with his unwelcome guests. Raj casually saluted them, and then smiled at the Bhattacharyas.

"What are they armed with," Miranda asked the Raj. "Daggers? Pistols?"

"Claws," Raj Purana repiled.

Under the table, Miranda pushed a fork into her hands, to use as a stabbing weapon in case she needed one.

"Very traditional of you," said Ramanujan. "But in the House Arjun that I remember, we preferred to reason with people before threatening them. What if we brought you evidence that the New Renaissance was behind the terror attack on Fellwater Grove?"

Raj Purana laughed. "I saw the Laflamme video. It's nothing but propaganda. And it's impossible to believe. As if an *outsider* could fall into Tartarus and then escape all by himself!"

Satya was losing her patience. "The New Renaissance is a cult, Raj! They keep slaves. They have a standing army. They even abducted our daughter– you remember Kuvira? Of course you do– you took part in her sacred thread ceremony. Heathcliff Weatherby tried to take her hostage. I was there– I saw it myself!"

"So your argument with the New Renaissance is personal, and not just business," Raj said dismissively.

"You're bloody right it's personal!" Satya shouted, as she thumped the table. The nearest restaurant patrons turned to look. They laughed uncomfortably among each other and returned to their meals.

"You can shout as loud as you like, Satya. I've already called the warriors to toss you both out of here, as soon as I walk away from this table," said Raj, and he nodded toward the two men who sat at the bar.

Miranda waved to the warriors. The men waved back. Then to Raj Purana she said, "But they don't really work for *you* anymore, do they?"

Raj Purana frowned, and looked to the ceiling again.

"Have you even *met* Il Duce?" Ramu asked.

"No, nobody has," said the Raj. "Well, I've met his messengers. But only three men have ever seen him in the flesh. Carlo and Heathcliff and Kendrick."

Satya was surprised to learn this. "So you don't really know who's in charge, do you?"

Ramanujan leaned back in his chair and quoted a sacred text: "Better is one's own law though poorly carried out, than the law of another followed perfectly."

The words jerked Raj's attention back to Ramanujan, and then to the warriors at the bar. "There's not much I can do for you, even if I wanted to," he admitted quietly.

Miranda understood. She wrote a phone number on a napkin and handed it to the Raj. "We have a few warriors on our side, too. If you want them to help you get out of here, call me."

Raj pocketed the napkin before the men at the bar saw it. He stood and said, "Enjoy your dinner."

The men at the bar stood and marched toward the table, but Raj waived them away. When they were gone, the Bhattacharyas let out heavy sighs of relief. Ramanujan loosened his tie; Satya let the bun out of her hair.

"We– whoa, we just– that was–"

"I know!"

"My dear, let me tell you how much I love you."

"I love you too. Mister Bond."

Miranda grinned at her friends. "I haven't seen either of you smile, in months."

The Bhattacharyas were too busy playing with each other's hands to reply. Miranda shrugged, and waved the waitress back to the table again. "Whatever they're having, put it on my tab."

~ 11 ~

Aeducan Brigand and Niall DeDannan crept down the passage, on their way to the subterranean areas of Rath Manannan. The only light came from the feeble penlights they carried; anything brighter, they reasoned, might give their presence away too soon.

Aeducan grimaced, and then lowered his light and continued walking. "So, where is the Dord Fian hidden?"

"In the treasury."

"And where's the treasury?"

"In the crypt."

"I should have guessed."

"And the crypt is underneath the Druid circle which is–"

The two men rounded a corner which brought them to the Rath Manannan great hall. Carved from the interior of the mountain, it was a wide circular cavern, with a high domed ceiling supported by thick pillars in a ring that resembled a massive stone circle. A crag in the ceiling was open to the sky, allowing starlight to shine down and illuminate a magnificent rowan tree that grew in a garden in the centre of the hall. More light came from a constellation of sea creatures that swam in the air around it: golden sunfish and chichlids and tetras, cyan-green jellyfish, shimmering electric eels, and a few muscular Atlantic salmon, all glowing with different colours and intensities of light.

"–well, as you can see," said Niall.

"Such an extraordinary thing," said Aeducan, as he stepped past one of the pillars. As his eyes adjusted to the sight, he saw that the glow in the trunk throbbed slightly at the base, as if the tree was breathing. Some of the branches were covered in red, as if washed with blood, and the skulls of various animals hung from the lower branches.

Niall grabbed Aeducan's shoulders and pulled him back to the wall. "Don't look directly at the tree," he warned. "You won't be able to look away again."

Following Niall's lead, the two thieves crept to one of the pillars and leaned their backs on it, and faced the passage from which they just emerged.

"When you look at a Druid's Tree, it gets into your head. You start seeing things. It inspires you to make music and art and sometimes prophesy. It intensifies your relationship with Nature, or with God, or whatever your Source might be. People Awaken just by looking at it. But if you look too long, it will overwhelm you with knowledge. You'll lose yourself; you might go mad; or you might *reveal* yourself, like all those poor sods in Tartarus."

"Not how I want to go," said Aeducan. From his kit pack, he retrieved a small mirror attached to a long rod. He extended it around the pillar to see what kind of opposition they might face.

"There's one of your druids," he reported. "If what you say is true, he'll stay looking at the tree and won't bother us."

Niall took the mirror, to see for himself. "That's not one of our druids," he said.

Aeducan took the mirror back and looked again. The figure approaching the tree wore a hooded white tabard. Chain-mail leggings glittered from underneath it. The figure broke off one of the tree's low-hanging branches, planted it in a pot of soil, and put the pot in a wooden crate. When the man turned to leave, Aeducan saw that his face was sheathed in a shining bronze mask.

"Shit! That's one of Il Duce's messengers!"

Niall took the mirror again and looked. "He took a cutting from the tree, didn't he? When I was chieftain, one of those fellas asked me to sell him one. I said no."

"Keep your mind on the mission," said Aeducan. "How do we get into the treasury from here?"

"The entrance is down a stairwell behind and underneath the tree," Niall informed him. "It will be locked. But I have the key."

"How many ways in or out of here?"

"Four others, besides the one we came in. Two in the common rooms, through that arch on the left. One in the chieftain's house, to the right. And one more, directly above us."

The two thieves pulled up their hoods and became shadows again. They crept around the edge of the space, dashed as fleet and wisp as birds, past the arch to the common room. They fell safely and silently into the stairwell that led to the treasury. There they discovered that a series of wires were strung across the door.

"Tripwires," Niall named them.

"Attached to booby-traps, or alarms?" Aeducan asked.

"Probably alarms," Niall guessed.

Aeducan released the safety catch on the rifle he took from one of the guards, muttered something about how swords are much more civilized than guns, and took a firing position at the top of the stairs. "You go in there and get the horn, while I cover you. Take my bag too, and fill it with something, for use as a decoy. Then we'll go out through the chieftain's room."

"Why not through the common room? There are more exits there."

"There are more people there, too."

"I wouldn't have thought of that," Niall said.

Aeducan tossed him the second rifle.

"I told you, I'm not a warrior," Niall complained.

"What do you think you've been doing here all night?" Aeducan countered.

Niall conceded the point with pursed lips. Then he put the key in the lock, counted down from three to one with his fingers, and opened the door.

As soon as the door touched one of the tripwires, an electric buzzer sounded somewhere in the common rooms. Angry voices started shouting, and heavy boots pounded the stone floors.

"Go!" Aeducan implored. Niall flung the door open all the way and dashed into the treasury. He ran past the stone crypts with their blank-eyed effigies, and the display cases of musical instruments and precious books standing between them.

At the far end of the treasury a statue of a druid, carved from the living rock of the earth, held a hunting horn. It was made from an ancient ox horn, with a long bronze loop attached to the small end, leading to the mouthpiece. Delicate filigree threads in gold and silver ornamented the horn with Celtic knotwork lines, and the shapes of warriors on the march. Niall didn't have time to admire it; he stuffed it into one of his bags.

Then he heard the pop of rifle fire coming from outside the crypt. He crouched low and grimaced; all hope of a stealthy operation left him. His breath and heartbeat quickened. He grabbed a wooden icon from a niche in the wall, where a coffin had been recently interred.

"Sorry, Dubhdarra," he said to the icon, as he stuffed it in the second bag.

Outside the treasury, the bodies of two centurions lay motionless near the foot of the druid's tree. Aeducan was aligning his rifle sight upon a third. Niall tossed him one of the bags.

"We have to split up!" Aeducan shouted. "You go out the common rooms, I'll get out some other way."

"We should stay together!" Niall objected.

Aeducan shot a third assailant who had come almost within range of Niall's head with a battle axe.

"More soldiers coming. We have a better chance if we force them to split up," Aeducan told him.

"Okay. The horn is in—" Niall started to say.

"Don't tell me!" Aeducan interrupted. "So they don't know either."

"You go out through the chieftain's house. The exit is easy to find. I'll go out through the common rooms. It's a labyrinth in there: it'll keep them guessing."

Five cables fell down through the cleft in the ceiling. Five Roman centurions, armed with carbines, slid down the cables. Niall turned and fired several shots at one of them; but being inexperienced with firearms, he didn't anticipate the recoil, and all his shots missed. Aeducan cooly lined up his sights and killed two soldiers with one round each, both before they reached the ground.

"How did you—" he started to say.

"Just run!" Aeducan bellowed at him. The two thieves immediately ran in separate directions. When Niall reached the common room, he paused to see if Aeducan made it safely to the chieftain's house. Aeducan was holding up the decoy bag and taunting the centurions.

"Hey, you Roman stiff-necked shit-sacks! I got your golden eagle!"

All three remaining centurions immediately ignored Niall and chased after Aeducan.

"He won't make it," Niall whispered. He fired some shots at the centurions. They missed again, but were enough to divert one of them away from Aeducan and toward himself, to give his captain a better chance.

When the third centurion came within fighting reach, Niall turned to defend himself. But the soldier was faster, and he saw his rifle fly from his hands. He backed away fearfully. The centurion stepped forward and took aim with his carbine, ready to fire.

Niall suddenly pointed toward the arch that led back to the Druid circle. "Look, it's Carlo!"

The centurion looked. Niall jumped behind him and twisted his head to a slightly new angle. The centurion's eyes filled with the sight of the tree. He lowered his weapon, walked toward the tree, and didn't notice Niall running away.

Niall dashed through the common room, jumping over couches and knocking over music stands and artist's easels as he ran. Some of the DeDannans, disturbed by the alarm and the gunfire, emerged from side rooms and the kitchen to see what was happening.

"Is that Niall?" some of them asked each other.

Niall pushed past them, shouting "Sorry! Excuse me! Sorry!"

He ran along the corridors and hallways until he reached an upward-climbing spiral staircase, which he knew led to the world above. Emerging to the surface again through another mound on a hill close to the one he entered, he looked for any sign of his companions.

Behind him, a guard shouted, "Hands up!"

Niall put up his hands and turned around. A centurion who had been guarding the exit now held him at gunpoint.

"Drop the bag!" the centurion ordered.

Niall dropped the bag. He looked up to the sky, then smiled, then laughed.

"What are you laughing at?" demanded the centurion. His answer came in the form of a heavy rock that fell out of the sky and clubbed him on the head. The soldier collapsed. Niall looked to see where the rock came from.

"Right behind you, Niall!" shouted Ciara, from the helm of the flying curraigh.

Meanwhile, Maread was sheltering behind the stone dolmen, watching another wave of centurions prepare to drop down the cables and enter the druid circle. As two centurions ran past her, one of them shouted, "Come on! Bravo Team is flushing the last of the animals out of the hole. We'll ambush him at the south exit."

Maread suddenly remembered she was wearing one of her enemy's uniforms. She slung her rifle over her shoulder and followed the centurions to the south exit. Arriving there, she saw two centurions with handguns waiting on each side of the door, and a third one on top of the mound, ready to attack Aeducan from above. Maread could see the shape of Aeducan's shadow just inside the passage. She subtly shook her head, to let him know not to rush out, then held up a finger to make him wait. Aeducan acknowledged with a salute. Maread pulled up the hood of the tabard, and boldly marched toward the centurions.

"You! Take position up top!" someone ordered her. She scrambled to the top of the mound, and took aim with her rifle.

After a moment, the centurion noticed that her rifle was actually pointed at him instead of at the passage. Then he noticed the blonde dreadlocks spilling out of her hood.

"Who the hell are you?" he said.

Maread pulled her hood down and whipped out her golden dreadlocks "I'm one of the animals!"

His moment of surprise gave Maread the half-second she needed to shoot him.

The two centurions below saw this, and immediately opened fire on her. She flipped away, to the far side of the mound, and out of their line of sight.

Inside the mound, Aeducan heard the fireworks and decided it was his moment to break free. He somersaulted ahead and let out a shot at the nearest Roman soldier. It struck his upper arm, disabling but not killing him. Aeducan dashed around to the far side of the mound, looking for Maread. He found her crouched low, with her rifle on the ground next to her, and her sword in her hand.

"Where's the getaway car?" said Aeducan.

"It's picking up Niall!" she said, and she pointed to the distance, where both could see Niall climbing inside Ciara's flying curraigh.

The third centurion from the ambush rounded the mound, and Aeducan was ready for him. He clubbed the soldier in the head with the stock of his rifle, then casually took the rifle out of the stunned centurion's hands. Maread fell upon him next: she circled around him and slit his throat from behind, then pushed him down the hill.

Thinking that the battle was over, Maread smiled at Aeducan. Her man stepped up and kissed her.

From the prow of her curraigh, Ciara frantically pointed at the mound. "Look out!"

Maread and Aeducan turned to see four more centurions emerging from the mound. As soon as they saw the Brigantians, they raised their rifles and took aim.

Maread swiftly stepped in front of her lover to take the first barrage.

When she fell, Aeducan and the nearest centurion faced each other, both with the same expression of shock on their faces.

Aeducan was the first to shake himself from it. He unsheathed his sword and decapitated the soldier who shot his lover, all in one swift swing. Then he charged, eyes bulging and hair flying. His body began to glow, softly at first, but in only a few heartbeats he was as bright as a fire: an effect of the Sources intensifying the abilities of those whose passions were aroused. Aeducan's passions were already beyond aroused. The next soldier to face him died before raising a weapon. He flung himself on the third, roaring with murder, and thrust his sword into the soldier's chest. But the sword blow bounced off the centurion's breastplate. The battering of bullets from the fourth soldier, which Aeducan had been ignoring, finally wore him down. He lost his balance and fell to one knee. The centurion stepped to one side to let him fall, smirked with superiority, and took aim for Aeducan's head.

Aeducan bowled himself forward and tackled him with his shoulder. They both fell to the ground. As they fell, Aeducan managed to stab his enemy in the neck with his sword. He gave himself a moment to confirm the kill, and catch his breath. Then he crawled to Maread, and touched her face. He lay down beside her, and wrapped her in his arms.

Niall and Ciara shrieked when they saw this. Niall jumped out of the curraigh and recklessly charged at the lone surviving centurion. At the same moment, the agent from Il Duce burst from the darkness of the mound, riding a black horse. The package containing the branch from the Druid's tree hung from a saddlebag. The centurion saw this, then lowered his rifle and dashed away. His only orders had been to buy his commander time.

"Fuck!" Niall screamed at his powerlessness.

Ciara dismounted from the curraigh, and sat on the ground beside Aeducan and Maread. She vibrated with shock.

Some of the DeDannans emerged from the mounds. "He took another cutting from the tree!" one of them breathlessly reported. Then she saw Aeducan and Maread.

"Are they–?"

Niall nodded, but did not speak.

"Niall, you were right about those New Renaissance people," said another DeDannan. "After they forced you out, they took over. There were soldiers on all the doors to the souterrain. We couldn't come and go from our own homes without explaining ourselves. And now this–" she gestured toward the two Brigantians, lying together, arm in arm, motionless and cold. "Well, we've decided: we want to join Miranda's alliance now. We will join the Fianna."

Niall put his hands on the shoulder of the one who spoke for the rest, and then hugged him. Then he opened his sack, and found he had been carrying the Dord Fiann, the whole time. He looked at Aeducan and said, "You knew that I had this, the whole time, didn't you?"

"That's the kind of man he was," Ciara told him.

Niall handed the horn to Ciara and said, "Take this to Miranda for me."

"You're not coming back with us?"

"I have to stay here, and– be chieftain." He turned to his clan and said, "These two warriors of Clan Brigantia– these two friends– I must see that their mortal remains reach the House of Donn the Old."

~ 12 ~

Snow and battering winds on the windows would not normally keep Eric awake at night. He sat by the window with the lights off, so he could open the curtains and watch the storm without much risk of anyone outside noticing his shed was occupied. His view gave him only a small rectangular sky, between the edges of three ivy-draped walls.

Three knocks sounded on his door. Ganga, his pet calico, awoke with the sound and turned her ears. Eric's breath quickened; this thoughts raced between which of his enemies might have discovered him. He picked up the emergency cellphone Miranda had given him, and held his thumb ready to speed-dial the panic number.

The door opened. Eric saw a snow-blown and sag-shouldered woman standing in the courtyard, backlit by a distant orange streetlight.

"Eric?" she asked.

Eric recognized her voice. He closed his phone. "Ildicoe? It's been months! Where did you go?"

"I am the most hated woman in all the Hidden World," she sobbed.

Eric ran outside to hug her.

"Even Miranda hates me– I can see it in the way she looks at me," she whimpered. "And maybe I deserve it, after what I did. There's no bounty on my head, like there is on yours, but there are people who would love to see me dead, all the same. You're the only one who has treated me with any kindness– can I stay here with you tonight?"

Eric nodded, and welcomed her into the safe house. He traded her snow-dampened coat for a dry blanket to throw over her shoulders. He put his arm over her, and let her fall into his embrace. She convulsed with the tears she had been suppressing.

When Eric thought she was ready to talk again, he asked, "Where were you all this time? Where did you go?"

"I suppose I can tell you now," she answered, as she dried her eyes. "I went looking for the other Voyageurs."

"Why didn't you tell me that before you left? I could have helped you."

"I was– I went looking for them in Tartarus. The chthonic prisons. The underworld. I couldn't have asked anyone to follow me there."

Eric nodded. "Then you were being compassionate, by not telling me."

Ildicoe touched his face. "I heard that you fell down there anyway. So you know what it's like."

Eric gasped her fingers, kissed them, and held them close to his heart. "I still have nightmares about it."

"So do I."

Eric looked down on the strange creature in his arms. He had seen her do things ordinary mortals cannot do, like run as fast as a jaguar, and merge into the shadows until she was almost invisible. He was one of the few who knew what she regarded as her deepest secret: and he unwrapped the scarf on her head and laid it to the side, to see that secret again. Yet for all the things that made her more than human, at this moment she lay in his arms, shaking and afraid, like an ordinary small girl. He caressed her face, dried her tears with his fingers, and guided her head into his shoulder, and hoped that his actions would answer her question.

She kissed him, and took him under the blanket on her shoulders, and kissed him again.

Eric coyly played with the buttons on her chemise. Ildicoe took his fingers and held them to her heart, to stop him undressing her.

"Tomorrow," she promised him. "For tonight, I need you to keep me safe and– and just hold me for a while."

Eric nodded, and understood. He flattened the futon that served as his bed, and built a nest of extra blankets and pillows for her. Then they lay down together, to share the kind of conversation that requires no words.

~ 13 ~

Morning brought a yellow glow to the safe house, as the sunlight diffused into the room from the rain-glossed wall outside the window. Ildicoe was awake and half-dressed, while Eric still slept. She sat on the windowsill, where she clipped a mirror to the curtain, so she could use both hands to comb her fingers through the feathers that grew in the place of her hair. With a soft brush she preened them, and with nail clippers she trimmed any that were broken. She traced her fingers down the back of her neck, and found that new pin feathers were growing there: the transformation was accelerating. Angrily, she plucked one of them out with her fingernails, and then pushed a finger on the wound, to stifle the blood. In her other hand she held the little feather up to her eyes, to contemplate it. A whimper attempted to escape her lips, but she tried to silence it, lest the sound of her feelings trouble Eric in his sleep.

Eric's hair was down, and his glasses were put away. It occurred to Ildicoe that she might be the only person to see him that way, just as he was the only person she allowed to see her feathers.

She closed the curtains. It made too much noise. Eric opened his eyes.

"Morning, love," she said. "Sorry to wake you."

Without his glasses, Ildicoe appeared to Eric surrounded by a soft aura of light and shadow. But he knew her by her shape. He smiled. "It's all right. Did you sleep well?"

"Mmmm, yes."

"There's cereal and coffee for breakfast. It's– it's all I have."

Ildicoe reached for the scarf she sometimes wore to conceal her feathers. Although Eric could only see a fuzzy moving shadow, he knew what she was doing. He sat up. "It's okay, Ildee. I like your feathers," he said.

"They're a disease," she said.

"They're not. They're uniquely yours. And they're beautiful."

Ildicoe stopped, and put the scarf down, and sat next to him. "My feathers– how do I say this? When we Awaken, we come to know the sources of reality more– more intimately, than other people. That much you already know. What you maybe don't know is: we *pay* for that knowledge with the permanent risk of turning into something that's– not human."

"Do you mean, like that tree in Miranda's back yard? She told me it was a man, once. It still has a human face."

"That tree *was* a man, once. Stephen Hobb was his name. I remember him. He sat at that place, overlooking the valley, long before the village was built there. He thought he saw the soul of the earth, surging up through the valley. He fell so in love with what he saw, that he let it seduce him, and absorb him. And now he is gone– well, he's not gone, but he's everywhere– he dispersed himself into the earth. Like a cup of water in the ocean. Like a single breath, in the wind. That's what it's like. The sources awaken you, then they entice you closer, enfold you, and *take* you. And it's blissful–oh! It's like coming home. But it's exactly like dying."

"Please tell me you're not dying, Ildee."

"I'm not dying, Eric. I'm– *changing*. That's the paradox of the Secret People: we have to touch the earth in the holds of the Hidden World. If we don't, then we lose our awakening, or we die. But if we stay too long, we change. I'm eventually going to look like one of the creatures that attacked the grove, last year. There are things I can do to slow the process down, but– but no one can stop it."

Eric touched her feathers, and gently traced them between his fingers. "You might be changing, but you're still human now."

Ildicoe pressed his hand against her neck, and kissed his wrist. She said, "Old Hobb's revelation was peaceful, but it doesn't happen that way to everyone. When it happens to me– oh Eric, everyone will fear and hate me, they'll want to throw me into Tartarus with the rest of the–"

Eric could easily see her state, and he pulled her into a protective embrace. Ildicoe pressed her eyes shut, and closed his hair into her fingers, pulling them, almost desperate to remember doing the same to her own hair, before she began to change.

"How did you know the right thing to say?" said Ildicoe.

"But I didn't say anything. I just hugged you."

"That's what I mean."

"Well, I was also– afraid of saying the wrong thing, and making you mad at me."

Ildicoe laughed.

"Besides," Eric said, "It's not for me to tell you the meaning of your experiences. You say you are transforming into some kind of animal. Well then, my job is to love you anyway."

Ildicoe hugged him again, tighter than before, and she squeezed the tears out of her eyes before Eric could see them.

When she released him, Eric said, "Besides, when you turn into a raven, maybe you can sit on my shoulder during my exams, and whisper answers in my ear–"

Ildicoe laughed again, longer, louder, and happier. She kissed him, and let the rest of her feelings go unspoken, trusting he already knew.

"I wonder what the rest of the clan will become," Eric speculated.

"Finnbarr will turn into a horse," Ildicoe laughed. "And I think he'd like it."

"Síle will become a flower. A daffodil, or a daisy."

"A daisy that bites people's heads off. Have you seen her get angry?"

"No, I haven't. Maybe I don't want to."

Ildicoe smiled. "Algernon will become a book in his own library," she imagined.

"And Miranda will become a tree. Just like her friend Old Hobb."

"Oh no, that's not her. Miranda will become a storm. The kind of storm that blows down everything. After that, she'll become a westerly wind, and a gentle rain," Then Ildicoe bounced off the bed, grabbed her scarf, and said, "Let's go for a walk."

Eric gulped with surprise before speaking. "Go for– a walk?"

"You've been stuck in this shit-hole since just after the battle of Fellwater. That was what– three months ago? Come on, we're going out."

"Ildiee, you know, those New Renaissance guys are looking to kill me. And what if Shinobi comes while we're still out?"

"We'll be back before he gets here," she reassured him. "And I found a way for you to walk out the door freely, with no one the wiser."

From her backpack she handed Eric a jewelry box. He opened it and found a small cloth pouch, embroidered with Kanji characters, attached to a silver chain.

"It's called an *omamori*," Ildicoe explained. "It's a traditional Japanese protection amulet, against evil spirits, bad luck."

"What is it really, then?"

"It's a protection amulet. Against the people like me. It intensifies the Shadow Spell around whoever's wearing it. So, someone with the Second Sight won't remember you, in the same way that the outsiders don't remember the Hidden World. They'll see you, but they won't *notice* you. And they'll forget seeing you as soon as they look away."

"A 'shadow spell' for outsiders," Eric mused.

"I'd like to say it will look good on you. But I won't remember it."

Eric considered this. "So that's the catch. As soon as I put it on, you won't know where I am anymore."

"I'll just have to trust that you're following me nearby. I'll pretend that you're my imaginary friend. It's the best I can do."

"There's no other way for me to escape this place unnoticed?"

"Well, we could take you out wearing my doppleface," she said. "You remember the mask that Siobhan used, to disguise herself as me? I still have it. What do you say– would you like to be me for a while?" Ildicoe caressed her own her hips and preened her feathers as she spoke.

Eric looked to the floor to hide his blush. "Not today."

"Oh, my man, you're a card," Ildicoe grinned, and she rewarded him with a quick kiss on his cheek. Then she wrote a street address on a slip of paper and said, "If we get separated, meet me here."

Eric looked at the paper. "This doesn't say what city I'm in."

Ildicoe was in a rush. "Don't lose that. Now get dressed. Time to go."

Eric got dressed. Ildicoe wrapped a red winter toque over her head, to hide her feathers. When they were both ready, Ildicoe kissed him one more time, and said, "Ready to go?"

"Ready," said Eric.

Ildicoe slipped the omamori over his head.

"It's surprisingly heavy," Eric observed. When he spoke, Ildicoe only looked around as if wondering where his voice was coming from, and then quickly lost interest in looking for it. She turned to the door and strolled outside, as if Eric hadn't spoken at all.

~ 14 ~

Eric slipped out the door behind her. She accidentally bumped into him as she closed the door. "Oh, sorry," she said. She did not make eye contact. By her expression, it seemed to Eric that she saw him there, but thought he was someone else, then instantly forgot him.

Eric fingered the *omamori*, intrigued by its effect. He stuffed it under his shirt, and followed her.

They walked along a snow-covered path beside the main house, and then to the public street. There Eric saw that his safe house was tucked behind a small mansion that had been converted into a Japanese cultural centre. Wooden wind chimes hung from the porch gables. Hand-painted kanji-characters decorated a large framed canvas beside the door. On a corner of the porch stood an incongruous banner-pole, with the angel and hourglass icon of the DiAngelo on the top, and the crest of the Guardians International organization on the banner.

"What's that doing there?" he wondered aloud, before remembering Ildicoe could not answer.

They came to a busier street, where Ildicoe flagged down a taxi. "The Museum of Civilization, in *Lac Des Fées*, sil vous plait," she told the driver, as she stepped inside. She made space for Eric to sit next to her, but did not appear to notice him slide into the seat next to her.

The taxi drove into the downtown. It passed various art-deco office blocks, and then three gothic cathedrals which Eric recognized instantly. He leaned out the window to admire the view and breathe fresh air.

Ildicoe leaned in front of him to close the window. Eric sighed.

"Lover's tiff, back there?" asked the driver.

"Oh, ha ha, no, we're fine," said Ildicoe. She looked in Eric's direction, although not exactly to his face, and said, "But close the window, please, love, it's cold out."

"Sorry," Eric said and closed the window, smiling. Ildicoe was trusting that he was there, even if she couldn't perceive him properly. The plan was working so far.

The taxi followed a road lined with more palatial buildings, a garden park, an art gallery, and an office block that looked like a submarine. It crossed a steel-truss bridge over a wide river, and then reached its destination: two yellow-white brick establishments whose organic curves and dome-capped roof made Eric wonder if the complex should have been a temple instead of a museum.

Ildicoe paid the taxi driver and stepped out. She entered the curatorial wing, ignoring a sign saying that it was off-limits to the public. A security guard asked to see her identification, and she showed him a small wooden amulet, painted in the colours of House Voyageur, which hung on a string around her neck. The guard waved her through.

"I'm with the band," said Eric, as he tried to follow.

The guard stopped him anyway. "Sir, this wing is off limits to the public."

Ildicoe showed her Voyageurs amulet to the guard again and said, "Let him through."

The guard waved them both through.

"How did you do that?" Eric asked.

Ildicoe didn't respond.

"Oh, right. You can't hear me."

Ildicoe led Eric down various halls, then down a stairway into the basement, and then through a solid iron storm door that opened into a cavern in the bedrock below. Water droplets echoed around them. Pebbles occasionally scattered beneath their feet. She took an oil lamp from a hook on the wall, tapped it three times, and the wick ignited into flame.

Eric took another lamp and tapped it the same way, but nothing happened. Ildicoe didn't see him take it, but she noticed its absence, and she quickly brandished a dagger and backed away, into the grotto.

"Whoever you are, get back!" she threatened.

"Ildee, it's me, look!" said Eric, as he took off the *omamori* and showed it to her.

Ildicoe sighed, relieved, and put her dagger away. "You really frightened me," she said. She took his lamp and tapped on its glass and blew into its vents, lighting it up.

"So, where are we?" Eric asked.

"We're in an old Voyageur supply depot," Ildicoe explained. "The museum was built on the site of one of our old field camps."

Eric traced his fingers along the walls as he followed Ildicoe down the cold stone corridor. He wondered how many others, over how many centuries, had done the same.

The corridor ended in a store room that Ildicoe unlocked with her amulet. She lit another lamp. "Well, here we are."

The room was lined with chests, boxes, and bags, of various materials and designs, some of which might have been here since the first Voyageurs, hundreds of years before. To the right of the entrance, two birchbark canoes sat on heavy shelves on the wall. Near them stood a stack of barrels containing whiskey, or pipe tobacco, or gunpowder. Next to them sat a pile of burlap sacks full of coffee beans and dried pemmican. A bookshelf held journals, accounting ledgers, and maps. On the wall directly across from the entryway, a Voyageurs banner hung from a craggy canoe paddle. On the floor just below it, arranged like an offering on an altar, was a wooden crate, with an alabaster vase on top, from which grew a white lily flower. Eric knelt down to look at it more closely. It perked up when he came close, unfolding its leaves and flowers. Ildicoe smiled to see it.

"Thank the gods. Our *petit fleur* still lives," she said.

"What does it live *on*?" said Eric. "There's no sunlight down here."

"It lives on hope," she said. "It lives only so long as there's at least two Voyageurs, somewhere in the world. That means, if you see it alive, you know you're not the only one left."

Eric looked at the flower again, and touched one of its leaves. "You're the only Voyageur I've ever met. Where are the others?"

"They could be anywhere," she said. "Our last sanctuary on Earth was a place called Elderdown. An island in a lake, not far north of here. Two years ago, a Tartarus rift opened near it. You wouldn't believe the things that came out. We were forced to flee. We scattered. I don't know where the others went."

Eric touched Ildico's arm. "Ildicoe. I– don't know what to say."

Ildicoe clasped his hand warmly. "I have *you* now, so I'm– I'm all right."

The wall to the right of the entryway held a rack of axes, daggers, and antique rifles. Barrels of gunpowder and musket shot lay near them. Ildicoe took one of the rifles and checked its chamber, and then polished it with a cloth from her pocket.

"These weapons are what I brought you here to see," she told Eric. "Ever since we were all forced out of Fellwater, I've– been thinking. Maybe– maybe we could go to Elderdown. We'll have to clear out whatever might have moved in. But– maybe– we could use these guns to do it."

Eric sat on a crate and considered Ildicoe's idea. "You know," he ventured carefully, "most of the Fianna blame you for what happened to Fellwater."

"It was those fucking DiAngelos tits who took it from us, wasn't it?" Ildicoe suddenly barked. "And it was Donall who signed a deal with the devil to let them in. I didn't do any of that!"

"Yes, I know," Eric quickly agreed. "I'm just telling you what people think. It was you, after all, who opened the Tartarus gate and let all the monsters out."

"I had to do it. I had to! There was no other way."

"I'm not disagreeing with you, Ildee. I'm just pointing out that you were the one who–"

Ildicoe looked away. Eric read in her posture that she didn't want to talk about it anymore, so he let it go. It occurred to him that someday she might ask him what he really thought of her choice. He hoped she would not ask him soon.

Ildicoe resumed polishing one of the rifles. "Our friends in the Fianna prefer spears, swords, weapons you need strength to use," she said. "We Voyageurs preferred rifles. We took these muskets, then we tinkered with the design. Eventually we had a decent breech-loading wheel-lock rifle, a hundred years before the outsiders invented one. Then we tinkered some more, and came up with this. You can put just about anything in the chamber– sand, wood chips, ice and snow– and it will still fire. Musket balls and gunpowder still work best, of course. But we never ran out of ammunition again. There should be enough of these for everyone in the Fianna. So– you go to Miranda– she's camping with the Orenda Nation right now, and– and tell her for me– tell her she can have all these guns, and anything else from here that she wants– if she takes the clan to Elderdown."

"I think I know why you're doing this," Eric said.

"It's big enough for all of us," Ildicoe continued. "Almost as big as Fellwater. And– and tell her that there's hunting game in the hills all around, and there's good fishing in the lake, and– we could rebuild the houses, and the watch towers, and– and–"

Eric stood, and took Ildicoe in his arms.

"It's okay. I'll tell her."

~ 15 ~

One entire wall of the apartment was stacked with folders and cardboard boxes, all filled with clippings from newspapers and magazines. The opposite wall was a floor-to-ceiling bulletin board, pinned full of more media clippings. Strings tied to push-pins connected some of the clippings to others; posted notes with frantic scribbling written in coloured markers provided a paranoid commentary.

"The Wild Huntsman? The dude with the antlers on his head? And the pack of demon dogs? Yeah, I think I've heard of him," said Harvard Willie.

Miranda looked to the shelves full of folders and boxes. A hand-scrawled note on the topmost shelf said, *Official Archive of the Mutual Monster Hunter And Freedom Fighter Network. Speak Truth To Power.*

"I wonder if you have a recent record in your archive of a sighting of the dogs, on their own, without the huntsman."

"Probably. Yes. I think there was such a sighting, just a few days ago. But you see the size of the archive. This could take a while."

Miranda understood what Willie was really saying. "You will accept payment in information, I assume?" she asked.

"What do you think I am? A sellout? Information is much more valuable to me than money," said Willie, as he cleared an empty pizza box from a chair and invited Miranda to sit. He accidentally spilled a can of lukewarm beer on the cushion. Miranda remained standing.

"Here's the address of a site on the dark web, where you'll find a video that I think will interest you," she said, as she held up a slip of paper.

Willie snatched the paper from Miranda's hands, entered the address into his laptop, and sat back to watch Eric's film of the direcreature attack on Fellwater Grove.

"Some of those guys with the guns, they're wearing the uniforms of those Guardians. I knew it! I told them I was on to them, but no, they wouldn't admit to anything on record, would they? The bastards! Well, see who's got the dirt on them now! Wait– what the hell are those creatures? Holy shit, they're big! Is that one puking up acid?"

"Willie? the Wild Huntsman?" said Miranda.

"Oh yeah. And his dogs," said Willie. But he did not take his eyes off the screen. "It's all real. I was right. I knew it! The Hollow Earth– Area 51– The Necronomicon– it's all real!"

Miranda cleared her throat to get his attention again. Willie turned in his seat and looked up at her. "How did you get this video? Were you part of that battle? Are you– are you one of them?"

Miranda grinned, raised a finger to her mouth to ask for secrecy, then she winked at him.

Willie dropped his coffee cup on the floor. "Who are you people! Are you even people? Are you even– human?"

"We are human, I assure you. Sometimes, all too human."

"Whoa, that's deep."

"And now– the information I need?"

Without looking, he reached into his archive and pulled out a file folder. "Here's everything I got on your pack of demon dogs. Last seen above the fork of the river near downtown Waldenshire. Heading northwest. Witnessed by at least four people. All of them lucky to be alive, if you ask me. The dogs are the souls of serial killers, condemned to hunt their own kind among the living. They're as big as bears, they're made of rage. Some say they can breathe fire. Take care of yourself, out there. But if you find them– bring me a photo?"

*

Miranda stood on a bridge over a frozen swamp in a small conservation park, with Harvard Willie's archive report in hand. On the ice below her, Gregory Morningfrost sat in the snow, in the middle of his pack of hounds. They jumped and yelped and licked his face in a frenzy of happiness. Gregory had a treat and a tussle for each of them, and a broad smile on his bearded face.

"So, your man thinks these cuddly little guys are as big as bears, and made of rage?" said Gregory.

"As you once said to me," Miranda replied. "That's the Celtic Mist for you."

Gregory grinned. "Now, you point us in the direction of Fellwater, and we'll take care of the bad guys for you."

*

Aidan read the headline on the newspaper: "Award-winning Niagara Winery Destroyed By Fire." Then he looked at Miranda and said, "You didn't have anything to do with this, did you?"

"Ask me no questions, I'll tell you no lies," Miranda grinned.

Aidan glared at her over the top of his glasses for a moment. Then he said, "It says here that House Sangiovese, whose vineyard is now a pile of ash, was the main supplier of wine to the Raj Purana restaurant chain."

"It was. And they need a new supplier now. Of course, I already mentioned your abbey."

"Isn't that chain owned by House Arjun? And isn't House Arjun part of the New Renaissance?"

"Their leader is having a change of heart, right now."

"And– you had nothing to do with that either?"

"Well, I might have helped."

Aidan smiled, and shook his head. "You Brigantians!"

"So, I can borrow your book?"

Aidan nodded. "It's yours." One of the monks brought it to her: it arrived in a richly ornamented wooden case. Inside was a more humble, leather-bound tome, with the title hand-painted in elegant calligraphy: *Leabhar Mhorrigan de Amhráin Cath.* Beneath the title was embossed the three ravens of House Corrigan.

Miranda stood, took the book in its case, and thanked him. As she turned to leave, Aidan said, "If any of the Fianna want to be baptised while they're here–?"

Miranda smiled again, and shook her head.

Aidan shrugged. "Just asking."

*

The Cup of Cormac the King sat on the table between Miranda and Marla St. David.

"Swear your oath that you will let me keep this chalice if my cauldron is damaged during your battle," said Marla. "If you promise false, the chalice will show me."

"By the gods of my people, I swear it," said Miranda.

The chalice remained still.

Marla smiled, and said, "I believe you will find the cauldron already delivered."

*

"This morning, I got a phone call from– of all people, Raj Purana!" said Devon. "He's offered me a complementary three-course dinner for two, with an open bar, at his restaurant in Halifax. He said it's a way of saying he'd like House Arjun and Clan Brigantia to be friends."

Across the Devon's kitchen table, Miranda smiled.

"I think I'll give the coupons to Neachtain and his new husband," she continued. "I can't really spare the time from the farm, if half of my warriors are going off to fight the DiAngelo."

~ 16 ~

Ildicoe handed her Voyageurs amulet to Eric and said, "Take this, so that you can get back in here again."

Eric took it, and hung it on his neck. "I seem to be wearing a lot of your jewelry now," he joked.

"Well, that one, I *know* looks good on you," she smiled.

"About the one that hides me from the Secret People," Eric proffered. "Where did you get it? How long have you had it?"

"Oh, that?" she laughed. "Umm– I've had it for a few days. It's only borrowed. I'll have to give it back pretty soon. It's best if I don't say anything more; these things are kind of taboo in our world."

They left the Voyageurs supply depot. When they reached the door that opened into the museum basement, she took his arms and held him for a moment, and said, "I love you, Eric. Do you understand me? Whatever happens, I want you to remember I love you."

Eric wanted to tell her he loved her too, and ask why she needed him to say he understood, but she slipped the *omamori* over his head before he finished speaking. Then she looked around for a moment as if she had dropped something, and then walked away. Eric had to dart past her before she accidentally locked him in the cavern.

When they reached the museum lobby, she stopped. Through the windows, they could now see several of the New Renaissance centurions wearing the red trenchcoats that they used when in public. A fourth man in a brown suit stood among them, facing away.

Ildicoe took a deep breath and held it in. As she did, her outline shimmered and faded slightly, and then her whole silhouette became foggy and translucent.

Forgot she could do that, Eric mused.

The fire alarm sounded. Eric assumed it was Ildicoe who set it off. As the hall began to fill with museum workers, Eric saw Ildicoe re-appear beside a washroom door, and then follow the growing crowd out of the building.

Eric picked a particularly tall and broad-shouldered man to walk behind. He stepped out, and hoped that the security guard wouldn't trouble him.

In the plaza between the museum's two wings, the workers mingled with the tourists and shivered in the January cold. The wail of a distant siren told them that a fire truck was on the way. Eric headed across the plaza, following the crowd, but keeping one eye on Ildicoe as best he could. The three trenchcoated centurions spotted her, and they weaved through crowd toward her. He could hear some of their conversation: "One suspect. Female. Red hat, blue coat. Moving to intercept."

Eric jogged after them, hoping that he might be able to provide some diversion, perhaps enough to help Ildicoe escape. But instead he saw one of them order the other two to stop. His cellphone rang. He answered it and listened for a moment, and then closed it again.

"Let the suspect go. We have new orders: The Ninth Legion is being called to Fellwater."

"All twelve hundred of us?" asked one of the other centurions.

The first soldier nodded. "It's time. The Magnum Opus is almost ready."

~ 17 ~

Eric arrived back at the safe house with only a few minutes to spare before his handler was scheduled to arrive. He frantically picked up the mess in the room, with special attention to anything that would show Shinobi that Ildicoe had spent the night there. With seconds to spare, he took off the *omamori* and the Voyageurs amulet and hid them in his pocket.

The door opened, exactly on time, and Shinobi appeared, looking as if he was out of breath from running.

"Good morning Shinobi," Eric said.

"*Konnichiwa*, Eric-san. But that's not my real name," said Shinobi, following the routine.

"What's chasing you?"

"It was me doing the chasing," Shinobi wheezed, as he threw his coat on the counter and fell on the futon. "I found out this morning someone stole something from the house. We got word that the thief was taking it to a dead-drop, and we were going to take it back. But– *dôshiyô*! The thief is fast."

"What was taken?" asked Eric, although he suspected he might already know.

"Just a little thing," said Shinobi. "What matters is that we're compromised. If the thief comes back for more, and finds *you* hiding here– we have to move you to a new safe house right away."

Eric immediately thought of Ildicoe, and the rendez-vous with her that he would miss. "What, are you moving me to a different city?"

"Best if I don't tell you. Grab your go bag. Forget about the cat."

"Forget my cat!" Eric protested. He began filling a backpack with some clothes and books. He flustered about the room, looking for things that he might have misplaced or lost. Shinobi kept his hand on the doorknob, ready to fling it open and run. When Eric came to his photocopies of Carlo's paintings, he said, "Do you know anything about The Magnum Opus?"

"Not much," said Shinobi. "It's some kind of experiment that they're planning. Something to do with the reason why they call themselves The New Renaissance. Something bigger than this cultural development stuff that they're always talking about. Why?"

"I met one of Il Duce's messengers last year. He said Phase Three was soon to begin."

Shinobi moved to the window and opened the curtains, to see that they were still unobserved. "Phase Two was the takeover of the biggest Hidden World freeholds in the country."

"So– the capture of Fellwater was part of a larger plan?" asked Eric.

"They took *my* holy ground, too," said Shinobi. "*Sakura No Tani*: The Valley of the Cherry Tree. It was the first place that House Kami settled when we came to Canada. Our little sheltered cove, on the coast of Vancouver Island. We had just bought our seventh fishing boat, when they came for us. We were finally feeling comfortable and happy."

"Why are they taking everybody's lands?"

"Don't know yet," Shinobi concluded. Then he shut the curtains and threw a blanket at Eric. "Okay, put this over your head, and follow me."

Eric took the blanket but put it aside. "Wait. I need to write another letter to Miranda."

"We don't have time right now," Shinobi urged.

"That's what the letter is about," Eric explained. "I don't know what Phase Three is, but I do know that they're beefing up security around Fellwater. That's the sign that Phase Three is going to begin, very soon."

"How did you know they were putting more soldiers in Fellwater?"

Eric didn't want to tell his handler that he had heard a centurion say so. "Isn't it obvious? Whatever their big plan is, Fellwater's the centre. With a little more information, I might be able to guess their timetable."

"I need to take you to a new safe house before we can do anything."

"Just take me to see Miranda."

"She's too far away." Shinobi had his hand on the doorknob, and was urging Eric to follow. Eric still wanted to wait for Ildicoe, but he had run out of ways to stall for time. He took the blanket, and followed Shinobi out of the safe house.

They reached the street, Eric risked a peek from under the blanket, to see if Ildicoe might be looking for him. Shinobi saw him do it, and put it down again. He pushed Eric into the back seat of the car.

"Okay, you can take the blanket off now, but try to keep your head down," said Shinobi.

When Eric saw that Shinobi was following the roadsigns that pointed to Highway 417 East, he realized he was being taken out of the city.

"We're going to Montreal, aren't we?" said Eric.

"I know another safe-house there. We can use it until we find something better."

Eric's heart beat faster, and his hands involuntarily pulled the blanket closer around his heart. Thoughts of Ildicoe, standing on some cold corner looking for him, filled his mind. Then he remembered the omamori, still in his pocket.

As Shinobi stopped the car at a red light, Eric quickly put on the amulet and jumped out of the car, running.

"*Dôshiyô!*" Shinobi cursed. "I left Eric back at the safe house! Wait a minute– no I didn't!" As he thought about this, a theory formed in his mind about why he might be confused. "*Dôshiyô, dôshiyô!* He has an *omamori*!"

~ 18 ~

Ildicoe's rendez-vous was a pedestrian bridge over a canal. It took Eric nearly an hour to find it and get there, as he didn't know the city, and he wasn't properly dressed for the winter. When he took off the *omamori* and let Ildicoe see him, she ran to his side and hugged him. "Let's get you a hot soup and warm you up. You must be freezing."

"I could murder a bowl of soup right now," said Eric. "But we can't stay here long. We're both 'wanted'."

"Exciting, isn't it?" Ildicoe grinned.

"You're wanted on *multiple* charges now," said Eric. He held up the *omamori* and said, "Because you stole this thing, didn't you?"

Ildicoe perked her eyebrows at him, but did not deny the charge.

"I went back to the safe house, so I wouldn't miss my meeting with Shinobi. He arrived all breathless, saying he had been chasing someone. 'The thief is fast', he said. Well, who else could he mean?"

Ildicoe could not suppress a small, proud smile. "I had to steal it, so that I could steal *you*," she said to him, and she held his face in her hands.

"So that I could talk to Miranda for you," Eric surmised. "It's all right. I don't mind being used by you. You're kinda cute."

Ildicoe grinned again. Eric loved the little space between her two front teeth. He kissed her.

"Miranda's sheltering with the Orenda Nation. We'll go there after we get a hot lunch."

"There's more now. At the museum, I heard two centurions talking. They said they're moving their entire legion to Fellwater. Twelve hundred soldiers. They said that Phase Three of the Magnum Opus was about to begin."

Ildicoe sat back in her chair, and swore under her breath. "The last time I saw Miranda, she was gathering allies to help her take Fellwater back. Twelve hundred soldiers– with those machine guns and those armoured cars with the huge wheels– Miranda's marching all of our friends into a death trap."

~ 19 ~

Miranda sat in the centre court of the Orenda school gymnasium, with a blanket over her shoulders to ward off the whistling draft from outside. Around her sat the various allies she had recruited over the last few days, and her best fighters.

"Our objectives, in order of importance, will be as follows," she related. "First, capture and hold all the gates of the grove. No one goes in, no one goes out, unless they surrender their weapons to us. Second objective: capture the highest ranking New Renaissance officer we can find, and hold him hostage. Hopefully we'll catch one of those faceless messengers from the big-boss-man himself. Third objective: drive all remaining centurions out of the grove."

Her listeners muttered with approval. Then Miranda noticed that Ciara wasn't listening. "Ciara, there's an important role for you in the coming battle. I need your attention."

Ciara looked up. "Sorry, Miranda. I was just thinking of– well, you know. How it came to this."

Miranda moved to sit beside her friend. "You're thinking of Donall."

Ciara nodded.

"He was a warrior," said Miranda, as she also drew close. "Warriors know they might die in the service. He accepted that. He died a warrior's death. I miss him too, but I'm proud of him."

"I know, but I just– I wish that–" Ciara said, but could not finish. She passed the Dord Fian to Niall, and covered her face in her hands.

Miranda touched Ciara's shoulder. "I'm sorry, Ciara," she said. Ciara threw her blanket off and hugged her. They held each other for a few heartbeats.

When Ciara let go, Miranda saw that most of the circle was watching her. She stood and addressed them. "Donall MacBride. Amergin DeDannan. Ghazwan Nefzawi. Aeducan Brigand. Maread MacBride. Katie and Tara Corrigan. People we loved. People who loved us. Perhaps they're watching us now, from wherever they are. Perhaps it gives them some comfort to know that we still love them. But let us not spend the whole night wringing our hands with grief. Let's do something to make them proud of us. Let's honour their lives by sticking it to the men who killed them!"

Some approving but tired sounds rose from the circle. Miranda was unsatisfied. She tapped Niall on the shoulder and said, "Niall, show us what Clan DeDannan brings to the battle."

Niall sniffled and rubbed his nose, then stood and held up his hunting horn for all to see. "This is the Dord Fian. The same treasure that once belonged to Fionn MacCumhall, the first great fighter to take the banner of Clan Fianna."

The warriors in the circle looked up. Miranda gestured to Niall that he should keep talking.

"The sound of this horn will fill each of you with the spirit of your ancestors," he said. "You'll fight stronger, faster, tougher, than ever before. That's what it does."

This made more warriors give Miranda and Niall their attention. The sounds of approval grew louder. Miranda pointed to Marla St. David next; she stood and addressed the crowd. "I have brought the famous Cauldron of Cerridwen. Any fighter who is injured, even if on the very edge of death, I shall bathe her in my cauldron, and she shall come out again whole and healthy, ready to go back to the fight!"

By now the warriors gathered in the circle understood what Miranda was doing. They cheered for Marla, and for Miranda, and they playfully punched each other.

Aidan the Wise stood next. "I have brought a book: *An Leabhar Mhorrigan de Amhráin Cath.* The Book of The Morrigan's Battle Songs. I shall recite from this horrible heathen book, and every enemy who hears me shall be full of terror. They'll cry for their mothers– they will wet themselves like children!"

Some of the warriors were on their feet now, as they cheered for Aidan the Wise, and for the battle they knew was about to begin.

Miranda pointed to Gregory Morningfrost next. "I bring to the battle my pack of fairy hounds," he said. "You've seen them– they grow as big as wolves when the battle-fury takes them. They will run among the enemy, tripping them up, knocking them down, tearing out the necks of the fallen!"

Excited by all the warrior chest-pounding, Ibrahim Nefzawi stood and said, "All those things that each of you said you will do: I will do them all myself!"

This drew the loudest celebratory laughter out of the audience. Everyone was on their feet, with weapons brandished, and shields bashing against shields.

"All right then!" Miranda shouted, to conclude. "Are we ready?"

Raaah! shouted the whole assembly.

"Then let's go home!"

With whoops and howls of both rage and delight, Miranda's army poured out of the gym through the fire escape, jumped into the waiting fleet of curraighs, and sailed into the night sky.

~ 20 ~

"We have to warn Miranda," said Eric. "Can you– maybe– open one of those doors that go from here to hundreds of miles away?" Eric asked.

"Actually, I don't know how to do that," Ildicoe told him.

"You don't? You're from a clan of explorers and traders. You specialize in long distance travel."

"We Voyageurs were always deep in the bush. No houses. No doors. Why don't you phone her?"

"Can't do that either," said Eric. "As soon as I turn it on, the Guardians will track the signal. And if I call her, they'll be listening."

"How does your phone do that without touching the Sources?" Ildicoe asked. Then she shook her head and said, "Never mind. We'll use a ghost messenger."

"What's that?"

"It's a Hiddenfolk thing. No time to explain. Do you have anything that Miranda gave you?"

"Yes, it's but back at the safe house– where Shinobi will be looking for you."

"We have to risk it," Ildicoe decided.

The safe house was a few minutes' of hard running from the pedestrian bridge. Eric was winded by the time they arrived; Ildicoe was still fresh, and in a rush. She unlocked the door by tapping on the keyhole; Eric had seen Miranda do this before, but did not know other Secret People were capable of the same trick. Inside the house, Ganga was unhappy to see them: her food bowl was empty, and her litterbox was full.

Eric found a book on the history of Roman Britain. "Here," he said, "Miranda gave me this, as a gift, a while ago."

"Perfect," said Ildicoe. She opened it to a page with an illustration of Cartimandua, Queen of the Brigantians. She set it on a small table, in front of the television.

"Your ghost messenger is a TV?" asked Eric.

"Any shiny surface will do."

Eric saw the page of the book Ildicoe had opened, and the illustration of the Celtic queen in her regalia. He asked, "Is Miranda descended from Queen Cartimandua? Or is she actually–"

"Not now, Eric, I have to concentrate."

With her hand on the illustration in the book, Ildicoe concentrated. "With any luck," she explained, "Miranda is some place near another shiny surface, and if she happens to glance at it, she'll see us reflected there, beside her."

"How will we know she has seen us?"

"We will see her reflected here."

"Can we talk to her? Or hold up signs or something?"

"I've heard stories about the most powerful Hiddenfolk using big mirrors to actually travel to each other. But the most I can do is try to speak to her, and hope she hears me."

~ 21 ~

On the crest of a low hill, three shadows lay in the snow, facing the ridge of Fellwater Grove. They surveyed the scene with field telescopes, and took notes and photographs. Then they crawled backwards down the hill, then ran through a cedar forest, until they came to a paved road and a children's playground. There they found several groups of serious women and men warmed their hands by camp fires.

A pack of dogs wandered among them, occasionally nuzzling someone in the hope of a friendly belly-rub or a share of the food. A tent stood in the middle of the scene. The vanguard brought their notes and photos to a table in the centre of this tent, where a tourist map of Fellwater conservation park had been laid out. Marker lines picked the location of the secret grove on the map. Miranda thanked the runners, and then addressed the captains and clan chiefs who surrounded her.

"All right, everyone," said Miranda. "Ibrahim and Morningfrost will form the eastern diversion flank. They will over-run the ridge, and come to ground close to the Well of Wisdom. Their job will be to get into the camp and create general mayhem."

"The dogs will love that," said Gregory.

"As soon as the east flank is inside, the DeDannans, led by Niall and Ciara, will lead the western diversion flank. They will scale the ridge with the trees, which Síle will bend into place to make the climb easier. Niall, you will sound the Dord Fiann when you reach the crest. With those two diversions in the field, the main force of Brigantians, and Ksatriyas, will assault the main gate as soon as they hear the horn. After that, the DeDannans will fall back and hold the gates, keeping them open for our warriors, and closed to theirs. Also, they will protect Brother Aidan, who will be chanting from the battle book, right here–" she pointed to a place on the map "–and they'll ferry any of our wounded back to Neachtain and Marla, who will have the healing cauldron, right here. The Brigantians and Ksatriyas will reach for their command centre. Best intel we have suggests it's in the stone circle, where they're building some kind of tower. Algernon's cavaliers will go after infrastructure targets: the electric power lines, the boat houses. We know there's at least one LAV-III in there: that's the army vehicle with the turret and the big wheels. The Wessex cavaliers will have to find it and put it out of commission, preferably before they point it at us. Questions?"

"Just one," said Finnbarr. "Did you put the Brigantians and Ksatriyas together because both their banners are yellow?"

Miranda gave Finnbarr a cold look.

Niall asked, "What kind of resistance can we expect?"

"Most DiAngelo centurions carry crossbows, and a steel gladius," said Miranda. "But we've seen them using Glock pistols and military-issue carbines. So I don't want anyone charging at them like it's 43 A.D. We'll have to move from one foxhole to another."

"What I mean," Niall clarified, "is– do you think that any of us will die?"

Everyone around the table paused; they all knew the answer, but no one wanted to say it.

"It's possible. Yes. Some of us may die."

Niall looked down to the table and mumbled something.

Miranda addressed the group again. "If resistance is too heavy, I will signal the retreat with a flare and three whistles. But if everyone trusts their mates and does their jobs, then we will all meet again in the feasting hall, and we'll drink their Roman wine until it's all gone."

Everyone around the table sounded their agreement and readiness, except for Ciara, who said nothing.

"Truth in our hearts," she said.

"Strength in our arms!" the others replied, with a happy roar.

"Fulfillment of the oath!"

"Yaa!"

They bumped their fists together, and then departed to join their various teams. As she left with them, Miranda noticed a flicker of movement, reflected on a teaspoon on the table. But she thought nothing of it, and followed Finnbarr and Síle to the Brigantian camp. Had she looked closer, she might have seen the silhouettes of Ildicoe and Eric, leaning into the image.

~ 22 ~

"Where is she!" Ildicoe bristled.

"Maybe she's too far away," Eric speculated.

"Quiet, please!"

Eric picked up Ganga and sat by the window. He decided to make himself useful by watching for Shinobi, or anyone else who might intrude. He saw a man emerge from the main house and fill a bird feeder. He had his back to the window, but Eric pulled the curtain anyway, leaving only a small wedge with which to see outside.

"I think she's not at the Orenda Nation anymore," said Ildicoe. "I can't be sure, but the colours and shapes are wrong. I think she's in Fellwater."

Then Eric saw Shinobi rush into the yard.

"He's here!" Eric warned.

The man with the birdseed waved to Shinobi, inviting him to talk. Eric used the delay to lock the door. He held the *omamori* in his hand, ready to put it on.

~ 23 ~

Niall faced the ridge that separated Fellwater Grove from the rest of the world. The cedar trees rustled in a slight breeze, blowing a thin breath of snow in his face. In his hand he held a pocket watch. Behind him stood a dozen women and men in DeDannan colours, with swords and shields ready, including Ciara, who was armed with a camera. Nearby, sitting in the branches of a tree and looking up to the sky, stood Síle MacBride.

"Just a few more minutes," said Niall, as he snapped the watch shut. "Are we ready for this?"

"They still know me," Síle whispered.

"The DiAngelo?"

"My trees, my forest. They sleep, in the winter. But they dream."

Niall looked at her for a long time. "These last few days, I haven't been able to sleep much at all."

Ciara smirked at him. "Battle jitters?" she asked.

"Something like that," Niall answered. "I keep thinking about Maread, and Aeducan. Did you know that Maread took a bullet for him? And before that, Aeducan got the centurions to chase *him*, instead of me, so I could escape. I don't know why. I've no special skills that others don't have, never said or done anything that changed anyone's life, never even had children. Never done anything that matters."

"You're the chief of Clan DeDannan," Ciara reminded him. "That matters."

"I was made the chief because no one else wanted the job. Then I was thrown out, almost right away. Worst chief in the history of our clan."

He stepped closer to the foot of the ridge, stretched out his arms, and jumped up and down. He looked up to Síle, who appeared to be entirely at peace.

"How can you be so relaxed?" he asked her. "I mean– these are the people who killed your sister Maread. I was there– I saw them do it. Why aren't you– I don't know– ranting and screaming at them?"

Síle dropped from the tree to the forest floor. Her movement was graceful and elegant, like swimming more than falling. He flesh was as delicate as moonlit snow. But her eyes were full of knives.

"I am drenched inside a with fire that no one else can see," she said.

Niall took a step away from her.

"But I am in my forest again," she added more gently. "It is always a good day, when I am in my forest."

Síle wandered a short distance away. Tree branches leaned aside for her, and folded themselves back as she passed.

"What do trees dream about?" Niall called after her.

Síle smiled at him. "Sunshine. Warm south winds. Birds on their branches. Spring rain. Why do you ask?"

Niall closed his eyes. "I suppose– I wanted to feel some calm before the storm," he said.

Ciara looked to Niall and asked, "Is it time?"

Niall checked his pocket watch again. It indicated three minutes until the battle was to begin.

"Ten seconds," he said.

Síle put her hands on the stones of the ridge, took a deep breath, and roared out a song of love and rage. Some of the DeDannans standing near her took a step away from her. Niall said to Ciara, "Is that bann-shee keening? Did you know she could do that?"

The trees nearest the foot of the ridge groaned in the earth. They leaned toward the ridge, and raised their branches into something like a natural ladder.

Niall jumped on one of the trees and raced its branches to the crest of the ridge.

"Niall! What the hell are you doing!" shouted Ciara.

Niall didn't respond. He reached the top of the ridge, and raised the Dord Fiann to his lips.

A sniper bullet from a DiAngelo sentry shot it out of his hands. It landed on the ground outside the grove, near Síle.

Ciara saw it fall. She grabbed one of the DeDannans and said, "Go tell Miranda– Niall just started the battle without us!"

~ 24 ~

Eric watched the doorknob rattle as Shinobi tried to enter. Then, through the curtain, he saw Shinobi enter the main house.

"He's probably getting the key," Eric said to Ildicoe. "Have you found Miranda yet?"

"Not yet. And keep your cat off me!"

~ 25 ~

Miranda was crouched in a hollow in the earth, a spear's throw from one of the main gates to the grove, surrounded by Brigantian warriors and Kshatriya fighters, when Ciara's runner arrived and told her what happened at the DeDannan flank.

"The fuck!" she blurted. The runner shrugged helplessly. Miranda took field binoculars from a scout and tried to see what was happening. She had no line of sight to Niall, but she saw some of the centurions running across the top of the ridge.

A glint in the light caught her attention. At first it appeared to be sunlight reflecting from an ice flow near the top of the ridge. Two human-like shapes seemed to step in front of it. One of them held up a hand, as if to warn Miranda away. Miranda put the binoculars down, and saw only an ice flow on the place where the two figures had been. She furrowed her brow, then looked through the binoculars again. The shapes were unclear, but they were nonetheless visible, and unmistakably pointing at her.

"I don't have time for omens," Miranda grunted. She turned to the warriors who surrounded her and said, "All right, we're moving the timetable up. Take your positions and prepare to attack. You–" she pointed to the runner, "–go tell Morningfrost to release the hounds."

The warriors crept forward to the last embankment before they came within range of the centurion's crossbows. Some held warhammers or battering rams, to bash the gates down; others held an assortment of swords, spears, and bows.

Miranda looked through the binoculars at the ridge again. More centurions had assembled on its crest, and most of them were loading crossbows.

"Why are there so many sentries?" Miranda wondered out loud.

~ 26 ~

Shinobi unlocked the door to the safe house and stepped inside. Ildicoe saw him, and shrieked with surprise. Shinobi reflexively snapped into a fighting posture. Two shining steel *sai* appeared in his hands. Ganga the cat hissed at him.

Eric bounced over to Ildicoe, and dropped the *omamori* over her head. Then he pushed her behind him.

"Wow– fuck– Shinobi, you scared me!" he said.

Shinobi maintained his fighting stance as he looked around the room. "Where's the *omamori*?"

"The what?" Eric asked.

"There's someone else in here," Shinobi declared, as he slowly moved along the circumference of the room, his back to the wall, his weapons ready to strike.

Across the room, where Shinobi could not see her, Ildicoe slid into the bathroom door. Eric moved to stand in front of her, and help keep her hidden.

"Shinobi, we have to get a message to Miranda," Eric pleaded. "If we don't– I don't know how many people will die."

"Eric, there's a ten thousand clutch price on your head. And there might be an assassin somewhere *in this room*. If you do not want to die, get behind me!"

"She's not an assassin. She's– my lover."

Shinobi lowered his weapons. "You have a lover?"

Ildicoe caught her breath, and put her hand on her heart.

"But never mind that," said Eric. "We need to find Miranda. Right now."

Shinobi's mind began putting things together. "Who exactly is she? Did she steal the *omamori*?"

"Shinobi, shut the fuck up, and listen!"

Eric's outburst startled Shinobi: he had never seen his charge lose his temper before.

"I left the safe house this morning. I'm sorry, I know it's dangerous, but I had to get out. I went to see her. We ran into some of the DiAngelo guys, and I heard them talking. The last phase of their Magnum Opus is almost ready, they said, and they're moving a legion of soldiers into Fellwater to protect it."

Shinobi stood still, and contemplated this news. He was still suspicious, but he put his weapons away. "There was an incident at the civilization museum this morning. Some centurions were there. I heard them say same thing."

Ildicoe whispered to Eric, "Ask him why he was there."

"Um, why were you there?" asked Eric.

Shinobi looked around the room again. "Threat assessment, and artifact recovery," he answered. "I told you: something was stolen this morning."

Ildicoe clutched the *omamori* in her fingers.

Eric finished his argument with what he hoped would be the clincher. "Miranda is preparing to attack the grove, to try and reclaim it for the Fianna. But she'll be outnumbered twenty-to-one. We have to warn her!"

"How do you know that? Did your girlfriend tell you? Is she still in the room?"

"No, I'm gone," Ildicoe whispered into Eric's ear.

"No, she's gone," Eric repeated. "Now, can you open one of those crazy doors that open to other doors? Please?"

Shinobi put his hand on the doorknob and the frame, concentrated quietly for a moment, and then said, "If Miranda asks, you make sure it's very clear that this was *not* my idea."

Moments later, Eric and Shinobi emerged from a concession stand building in the camping area of Fellwater Conservation Park. They ran toward the grove. Ildicoe followed.

~ 27 ~

From her field pack, Miranda took a bottle of wine, bit off the cork and took a sip, whispered something to the bottle, and then lobbed it into the air. It smashed on the rocks at the foot of the ridge. The rocks grumbled and shook, then parted, revealing the cleft in the ridge that led to the grove.

As soon as the crevasse was wide enough, Miranda blew a whistle: a sign to the Brigantians and Kshatriyas to storm the gate. They charged out of their trenches and over the snowbanks, fearless and fast, roaring their battle-cries and rattling their blades. Some of them were laughing. They were certain that victory lay less than a hundred meters away.

That was the moment Eric and Shinobi burst out of the bush, and crashed in the snow next to Miranda.

"Eric! The fuck are you doing here!"

"Miranda! You can't– the Ninth Legion!" Eric stammered.

"What about it?"

"They're here! In Fellwater!"

"How many of them?"

"All of them!"

Miranda sat up and turned toward the ridge. She saw a line of crimson-cloaked and bronze-armoured centurions on the crest of the ridge. They let loose a rainfall of crossbow bolts on the advancing attackers. The first wave of attackers immediately fell.

At a different breach of the ridge, Ciara reached the summit just in time to see more than a dozen centurions open fire on Niall DeDannan. He shook with the impact of the bullets as if he had been jolted with electricity. He fell off the ridge, dead before he hit the earth below.

At the third breach, Gregory and Ibrahim watched most of their proud hounds fall to a thick spray of machine-gun bullets hitting them from at least three directions at once.

Miranda blew her whistle three times and shouted, "Fall back! It's an ambush! Fall back!" She fired a flare gun into the sky, to signal the retreat to the diversion flanks.

Ibrahim and Gregory saw the flare when more than half their hounds was already dead. Gregory shot the nearest DiAngelo with an arrow that streaked into a yellow-red comet as soon as it was off his bowstring. It struck the ground near the centurion, and the explosion it created sent him and two of his companions flying. This gave him time to whistle his few remaining hounds back to his heel, and to scoop two of them into his arms and retreat. Ibrahim and his scimitar, almost as long as he was tall, kept anyone from getting too close as they dashed away.

Síle saw Miranda's flare just as she touched the mouthpiece of the Dord Fian to her lips. She ordered the DeDannans to retreat. For some of them, it was already too late.

At the front gate, the survivors of the first wave of crossbow fire managed to reach safety as the DiAngelo sentries reloaded. But they found themselves unable to retreat further, lest they expose themselves to the next wave of defensive fire from the ridge. Miranda saw riflemen now joining the crossbowmen, and other centurions taking position at ground level, just inside the gate itself. From her kit bag she took a small leather pouch, embossed with the sign of the bann-shee. She attached it to the fork of her sling-staff. Then she stood tall, although she entered every centurion's line of fire. She opened the leather pouch. A blast of winter wind surged from it, and Miranda struggled to hold the staff steady. The wind blew most of the centurions off their posts. Some remained standing, but they too struggled to keep their feet beneath them; they certainly could not fire at the same time. This gave Miranda's warriors the cover they needed to retreat. Some shouldered the weight of the wounded, some slapped the paralyzed to bring them back to their senses, some ran to save only themselves.

Miranda remained at her post, holding the majority of centurions back with the wind, until all her men were behind her. Then she closed the pouch, and surveyed the damage. Bodies of Brigantians, Ksatriyas, and a few centurions whom the wind had flung down, lay motionless around her. Red snow lay in patches, denser and darker as they lay closer to the foot of the ridge. The remnants of the wind creaked in the cedar trees. More centurions would soon arrive, she knew, and their counter-attack would be unforgiving. She followed the other survivors back to camp, where she ordered everyone into the flying curraighs, and into the sky.

On board the last curraigh to leave, she watched the land fall away beneath her. She kept her face as controlled as possible, as she did not want her friends to know what she was thinking.

~ 28 ~

They landed the curraighs near the school in the Orenda Nation territory. Ciara was the first to jump out and confront Miranda, shouting, "You said you had a spy in their camp! Why didn't you know we would be facing so many of them!"

"My spy isn't in Fellwater," Miranda claimed in her defense.

"So where is he!"

"Can't tell you that! Obviously!"

Síle, red-faced and almost too enraged to speak, collared Miranda next. "And how many people are dead because of that!" she shouted.

"I'm not the one who killed them!" Miranda pleaded.

"But you're the one who sent them into the fire!"

From another curraigh, Ibrahim and several of the allied clan leaders jumped into the angry exchange. "And why the hell did you start the battle three minutes before time?" he howled.

"That was Niall," Ciara informed them.

"Where is he? I'll kill him!"

"He's already dead."

"*Adjei!*" Ibrahim swore, as he stomped over to the nearest curraigh and slashed it with his scimitar.

Síle's anger was driven towards everyone and no-one. "Ciara, you picked up the battle-horn– why didn't you use it!"

"Because I saw the signal to retreat! You want to talk about who'se to blame? What about you, Aidan? Why didn't you open that book!"

"I saw the way the battle was going," said Aidan. "I did the most good by keeping this book safely *shut*. It speaks only of war and death, nothing else."

"We're already at war!" Miranda insisted. "We've been at war with the DiAngelo for months!"

"We've been at war with *somebody* for more than two thousand years," Aidan reminded her. "When will it end?"

Miranda snarled the answer. "It ends when they surrender or die."

"You can go back there if you want," said Gregory Morningfrost. "but I won't run face-first into that machine again. Only two of my dogs survived it. They won't survive another go. None of us will."

"But it's our home!" Miranda implored.

"It *was* our home, once," said Finnbarr. "It's not anymore. I think we need to face reality. The war is over, and we lost. Fellwater is gone."

A mix of tired and unhappy glances were traded around the ring, at the sound of Finnbarr's conclusion.

"That's a sign from the gods, if there ever was one," said Ciara. "Finnbarr the joker, talking straight about something."

"A sign of what," said Ibrahim.

"A sign that we all have a bigger problem," said Miranda. "If we can't find a new place to live– a place where the Mythic Age still holds– well, you know what will happen to us."

Eric had been watching the argument from his perch on the prow of one of the curraighs. He chose this moment to jump down and join it.

"I know such a place, where we could go," he said.

"What do you mean, 'we'?" Ciara scorned.

"Hear me out please," he asked. When he had everyone's attention, he said, "There's an island in a lake, in the mountains of west Quebec, that's a secret to everyone, even to the Hidden. I think you all know its name."

Several voices around the circle whispered, *Elderdown*.

"This was Ildicoe's idea, wasn't it?" said Ciara.

"Yeah, it was."

"That crazy crouton is even less trustworthy than you are," Ciara declared. To Finnbarr, who stood near her, she whispered, "Listen to him, talking like he's one of us."

Miranda silenced Ciara with a look. "He *is,*" she gruffed. "If he hadn't warned us that the grove was so well defended, maybe *all* of you would be dead right now. Eric was the one piece of good luck we had today."

Eric didn't expect anyone would speak of him that way. He couldn't think of how to reply.

Síle brought the conversation back to point. "We can't go to Elderdown. It's been overrun."

"Do you need weapons?" asked Eric. He showed them Ildicoe's amulet, and said, "I have the key to a stash of special rifles. Made by the Voyageurs; they don't need ammunition. And they're yours, and so is Elderdown itself, if you want it."

"We could have used those guns today," Ciara grumbled. "Why didn't you tell us about them before?"

"I didn't know about them before," Eric protested.

Across the circle, Finnbarr said to brother Aidan, "I don't think much of Ildicoe either, but going to Elderdown would be better than standing around here, freezing our dicks off."

"We shouldn't stay with the Orenda much longer," said Síle. "They've been kind to us. But we've taken too much from them already."

"Miranda, what do you think?" said Eric.

Miranda had been gazing in the direction of Fellwater Grove. She wrung her hands, then held her palm on her heart, then rubbed her eyes.

"Miranda?" Eric prompted her, one more time.

Miranda faced the group again. Her red-rimmed eyes glistened, and she dabbed them with her fingers before they spilled their tears. She said, "I don't see how my thoughts matter much. After what happened today– and after Hallowstone– I suppose some of you don't trust my leadership anymore."

"We trust you, Miranda, of course we do," said Síle.

Ciara, Ibrahim, and Eric made sounds of agreement. Everyone else, however, remained conspicuously silent. Miranda did not miss the divided opinion among her friends. She stretched her spine and raised her head, to summon her confidence, and to show that she was choosing her words with care.

"You've heard me say that Fellwater is not just a place, but also an idea. It's an idea that brought us here, to this moment, where we fight among ourselves for the right to point fingers of blame. If that's what you want to do, then all of you can point your fingers at me, and me alone. I'm the one you followed into battle. I'm the one who was so desperate for a victory I could not see we were not ready. I'm the one who insists on the need for good intel, and I went into battle without it. Perhaps it's only right, then, that I should carry the whole burden of today's failure."

Miranda's listeners looked at each other. Some who had been silent now bore the gaze of others like a weight. Some who had been supportive now grasped a heavier question.

The first to stand was Eric. "You can't be responsible for *everything*, Miranda. If I got to you sooner– if I found out about it sooner– Everyone's luck turns bad eventually. The only thing we can do about it, is hold someone's hand, and trundle on anyway."

Ciara stood and said, "I had the Dord Fian. Then I saw the flare, to signal the retreat. I could have used it anyway, to help more of us get away. I can't tell you why I didn't; I don't really know."

Brother Aidan rose to say, "I still think this book is dangerous. But I did promise to use it. I confess to the sin of breaking that promise."

Eric held up a waterskin and said, "Let's have a vote. If you want this Fianna to continue, with Miranda as our leader, then drink to her. If not, then pour your wine on the ground, or something. As for me, I vote for Miranda." He drank.

Finnbarr held up his canteen. "I'm for you too, Miranda. It's not your fault that the rest of us are such screw-ups," he said, and he drank. "Cheers."

Síle held up a clay chalice and toasted her friend. "Cartimandua!"

Others, hearing this, also toasted Miranda with her ancient name, some of them raising their voices to be heard above the rest. No one poured a drink on the ground. Miranda smiled, though she half-hid her face under her hair. She held out her hands, and everyone reached out to touch them. The chanting of her name gave way to cheering, and laughter, and some unexpected tears. Miranda thanked everyone personally by grasping their hands, until she came to Eric, whom she hugged.

"So, where shall we go from here?" said Eric, when she released him.

Miranda gave herself time to think. She looked to the fire in the centre of the circle, then to her companions.

"Elderdown," she said.

Scattered muttering greeted her decision. Some were glad that a decision was made at all; some remembered that the decision meant fighting creatures from Tartarus, and dealing with Ildicoe again.

"I know some of you don't trust her, after what she did last year," said Miranda. "But we can't stay here, and we have no where else to go. If any of you have a better idea, let's hear it now."

No one had a better idea.

Miranda looked to Eric and said, "You know how to find her?"

Eric said, "She's already there. And she gave me a map."

~ 29 ~

At the entrance of his command centre tent, Carlo dragged on his cigarette, and enjoyed the sight of his celebrating soldiers. To those who passed near him, he gave a smile and a victorious shake of his fist. When Shinobi came running, he smiled to see him, then grabbed his lapel and threw him into the tent.

"My lord, Master DiAngelo!" Shinobi complained.

"The reason I pay you," Carlo drawled, "is so that you will tell me about surprise attacks rather sooner than two minutes before they happen."

"Sir, I sent the warning as soon as I found out about it myself," Shinobi said.

"How long have you been infiltrating the Brigantians? Three months now? Four? That should be long enough to gain their trust. It is now quite reasonable for me to expect results."

"Sir, their attack was decided spontaneously. Very little planning. As I reported before, they do not have a coherent military policy. All they're doing is moving from one hold to another–"

"And each time I send a strike force to the place where you say they're hiding, I find that they've already moved on."

"I've never been wrong!"

"But you've never been helpful."

Carlo grabbed Shinobi's lapels again, and pushed him up against one of the beams that held up the tent walls. "I also hear that you made some very provocative allegations against me," he growled.

Now Shinobi began to shudder. "Sir, it was only a hunch. Only a way of looking at things–"

"You *see* too much, Shinobi. And not enough of what I pay you to look for."

Carlo flicked his cigarette aside, then gently drew his fingers down over Shinobi's eyes, closing them. He grinned, then pushed Shinobi to the floor again.

Shinobi stood, but bumped his head on a table as he did so. He touched his eyes. "Sir, what did you do? I can't open my eyes. I can't open my eyes!"

"I've given you a taste of the darkness that some day comes to us all," said Carlo.

"But how do you expect me to work for you if I can't see anything?"

"You still have ears. For the moment."

Shinobi tiptoed forward, his hands outstretched before him. He found the canvas walls of the tent, and from there he felt his way to the front flaps, and the winter outside.

Carlo watched him stumble into the camp, then turned his attention to the burlap sack on his table. He unwrapped it very slowly. Under the last layer he found the top of the glowing branch that had been cut from the Druid's Tree. He stared into it for a moment. Then he snapped his face away, rubbed his eyes, and wrapped the branch in its covering again.

~ 30 ~

Miranda took a small recce team, as she called it, to scout the location of Elderdown. She kept their flying curraighs low, just barely above the surface of the river ice, as they ventured north from the city of Lac Des Fées, in search of the island of Elderdown. The banks of the river sloped up in a wide shallow valley, where the dark peaks of evergreens on the rocky hills punctuated the grey-white blanket of snow-covered maples. A family of deer stood on one shore, and bounded back into the forest when the boats passed them by. In the prow of the lead vessel, a gentle but cold north-east breeze ruffled Miranda's hair, red in most of its length, yet growing white in its roots. But she did not take the protection of winter cloaks and wollen toques, as her companions had done. Nor did she join the song they sang to pass the time. She held the Dord Fian in her lap, and her thoughts moved over the wide cold country into which she was leading her people.

Eric had been cooking soup on a portable gas stove in the middle of the boat. He poured some into a coffee cup and brought it to Miranda.

"When you first came to this country, what was that like?" he asked.

Miranda grinned. "Hoping for an eyewitness account, for your Masters thesis?"

"I couldn't use anything you might tell me. No one would believe me. I just want to know."

Miranda drank her soup and remembered. "There were no glass towers, no highways, no cars. Just rivers and hills and trees. It was glorious."

"There were people, too," Eric suggested.

Miranda acknowledged it. "There were. Almost as many, back then, as there are now. I wouldn't say that life was better or worse, back then. But the frontiers of the immensities were closer. Fields and forests had no fences. Stars were not yet washed out by city lights. Your sense of *who you are* wasn't defined by a checklist on a computer. It was defined by your deeds, the friends you loved, the stories you told. You could walk for a day in any direction– people still walked that far, back then– and you'd come to a cliff top, a cave mouth, the ocean– the knife-edge of life and death– and there you found the answers."

"The answers? To what questions?"

From behind them, Finnbarr said, "Why'd the bloody chicken cross the feckin' road?"

Everyone on the boat laughed. Miranda wanted to be annoyed, but she couldn't hold back her own laughter.

"There you go," said Miranda. "Why did the chicken cross the road. Why do any of us do anything? Why does any of it matter?"

A new thought troubled Eric before he spoke again. "Curious to hear you speak that way about modern life. I've heard Carlo talk the same way."

Miranda rapped his arm. "Don't you compare me to him."

"It's just an observation," Eric defended himself. "He doesn't like modern life any better than you do. That's what his New Renaissance is about."

"House DiAngelo once controlled three of the largest holds in southwest Ontario. But a few years ago, they lost two of them. One became a block of upscale condos. The other, a lakeside amusement park. The third still stands– it's the one where they took you, last year. And now, like everyone else in the Hidden World, including us, they're scrambling for control of the last few holds that remain. I think Il Duce's New Renaissance is only a well-disguised bid for territorial conquest, nothing more."

Eric didn't wan to annoy her any more than he already had, so he changed the subject. "That reminds me– what do you think of my new theory about the painting? Any idea who Poseidon might be?"

"What– what do you mean?"

"You know, that painting that Carlo made. The one with Zeus instead of Christ. I sent you a letter about it, a while back. Shinobi said he would deliver it for me."

"Well, he hasn't, yet."

Eric perked his eyebrows at this news. Then Finnbarr slouched to the front of the boat to join them.

"Got another deep philosophical question for you," he said. "Are we there yet?"

Some childish guffaws came from Finnbarr's companions.

"I see you're already into the whiskey," Miranda smirked.

"We've been sailing up this river for hours. Couldn't wait."

Eric consulted his map. "Looks like we go round two more river bends, then we come to a lake, then we're there."

They rounded the last two river bends, and the ice beneath them widened into a frozen lake, bounded on its shores by steeper slopes and rougher cliffs, some draped with frozen waterfalls. Across the ice, just off the centre of the lake, rose the island of high hills, stepped fields, and towering rock pillars, some connected by wooden bridges. some capped with timber-frame cabins. Most astonishing to Eric: the island hovered above the lake, almost as high as the crests of the surrounding hills. Beneath it, dozens of rough stalactites gave shelter to hundreds of waterbird nests, and huge shards of ice.

Eric stood. His map dropped from his fingers.

Miranda enjoyed Eric's expression of awe. "Not too shabby, eh?" she kidded him.

"And it's ridiculous!" Eric said. "A flying island– It's wonderfully, gloriously, ridiculous!"

Ciara, who was piloting the lead curraigh, flew it higher, to give everyone time to take in the sight of their new home from all sides. Near the island's south shore, half-hidden in a scattering of winter-bare trees, stood what remained of the Voyageur's outpost: some log cabins, an outdoor blacksmith shop and carpentry shop, and a chapel with an iron brazier on the top of its steeple. Most buildings were clustered around a wide circular commons. Eric counted three open-air stone bastions near the edges of the island: a remnant of the days when it served as both trading post and minor garrison. Most of the buildings were damaged in some way: a collapsed roof, a torn-off door, a fire-blackened wall. A newly erected flagpole in the middle of the commons flew the banner of the Voyageurs: white, with three horizontal stripes in red, green, and blue. Beside it, Ildicoe jumped and waved, grinning and laughing, to welcome the Fianna, and to welcome her man.

They landed the curraigh near one of the bastions, and spread out as they walked toward the outpost. Their legs sunk up to their knees in the snow.

"So," said Ibrahim, when his voice came within reach, "this place is supposed to be overrun by Wendigo. Seems rather quiet, to me."

"It wasn't the Wendigo that drove us out," Ildicoe explained. "It was the kind of creature we thought we had left behind, back in France. But they followed us. We killed most of them, and locked the rest in a Tartarus cave. Two years ago, they broke out again. The outsiders call them *les loup-garou*."

"Werewolves?" said Eric.

"They're one part of our Hidden World that the myths of the outsiders got right. *Les loup-garou* were people, once. Like any of us."

"So, what else do the legends get right? Is it a disease?" Eric asked.

"Aye, and the full moon brings them out, and only silver bullets kill them," Finnbarr chortled.

Ildicoe rolled her eyes at Finnbarr, then turned back to Eric. "They're like any other direcreature in the Hidden World. They're people who stayed too long in a freehold of the mythic age, like this one. They stayed so long that the Sources changed them."

Miranda was thinking strategically. "So, how do they get up here? And how do we fight them?" she asked.

"They get up here by running and jumping, believe it or not. They can run so fast, you can't see them coming. They're not much affected by the full moon. Or silver bullets. But they do prefer to come out at night. Something to do with their eyes, after centuries in the chthonic prisons, deep underground: they can see in the dark much better than we can."

Miranda looked around. "The trading post looks like it might be a defensible place to stay the night. Let's get it ready before the sun goes down."

~ 31 ~

The least-damaged building in Elderdown was the trading post and warehouse, so Miranda decided to occupy it. She placed Finnbarr and Ibrahim in lookout positions where they could see anything approaching the post from the interior of the island. Then she and the others explored the other buildings, in search of any usable supplies left behind by the last inhabitants. They stripped a fire-damaged cabin of any planks and beams they could use to fortify their new foothold. They removed the trading post's front doors and replaced it with heavier ones from the chapel, and they installed wedges and beams so they could barricade it shut. Dismantling the chapel doors allowed them to move their curraigh inside, where it would be safer from wind and weather. They nailed blankets over the trading post windows as most the glass was broken, to stop the drafts and conceal their lights after nightfall. Finally, they got a fire going in an iron woodstove, and allowed themselves to warm up and get comfortable.

Later in the afternoon, the new inhabitants made an inventory of what was left in the warehouse store rooms: ration bags full of bread and pemmican which, as Ildicoe explained, had been enchanted by the Voyageurs to keep their contents dry and preserved for as long as they stayed closed.

"Mmm," said Finnbarr, as he chewed on the contents from one of them. "Still good. After two hundred years!"

"That's House Voyageur innovation," said Ildicoe, as she tapped the barrel that the pemmican came from. "Where other houses made shiny things, we made things you can actually use."

In a series of locked chambers and upper-floor platforms, they found barrels of gunpowder, crates of iron ingots, and bundles of wool and leather and furs. Some of these supplies were date-stamped as far into the past as the late 1700's. The history student in Eric wanted to admire them and study them: sometimes his sense of amazement would hold him in fascination, unable to touch anything he found, no matter how simple or humble it might be: a smoking pipe, a bone stitching awl, a pair of leather moccasins, a cracked wooden fiddle.

"These storerooms have been sealed for more than two hundred years!" he marveled. "We need to get an archaeologist in here."

"They're full of treasures, I know," Miranda told him, "but this isn't a museum. It's our new home."

"All right," Eric mumbled. He gave himself the job of taking inventory.

When night fell, the Fianna gathered in the trading post again, and lit oil lamps and tallow candles. They cooked another pot of soup on the woodburner, along with bread and pemmican from the ration bags they had found earlier that day. They sat on fur-trade bundles and shared a flask of whiskey.

"These rifles," said Ildicoe, as she handed one to each of the Fianna, "can fire almost anything that will fit in the chamber. So you never run out of ammunition. But don't rely on that– use these musket-ball cartridges first. That's what works best."

"I've never handled a gun in my life," said Ibrahim.

"Neither have I," said Eric.

Miranda examined her rifle carefully. "Hmmm. Looks like it's slow loading, break action. *Too* slow, if the enemy gets too close. Wish I had my old C-1A1. Great piece of kit, that was."

Ildicoe nodded. "I admit, they're not really made for combat. We mostly used them for hunting."

Miranda was still examining the rifle. "We're going to be fighting werewolves, not shooting deer."

"The musket-balls hit hard enough to slow down an allododger," Ildicoe explained. "But you'd need five or six shots for a kill. It helps if they're fired in a volley, all at once."

Eric asked, "What's an allododger?"

Finnbarr grinned at him. "If you saw one, you'd know."

Miranda sighed unhappily. "Right, so these guns might be good enough for base defence. But eventually we'll have to find where they're hiding, and drive them out. We can't bring the rest of the clan to the island until we know it's safe."

"If their den is somewhere on this island, then they must know that we're here by now," Eric suggested. "We made enough noise today. And left enough tracks in the snow."

"Ildicoe, can you tell us anything else about them, that will help us fight them?" asked Ibrahim.

"Not really," said Ildicoe. "Just that they're seven feet tall, very fast, very brutal– and very intelligent."

As each Fianna chose a window to keep watch, Eric said, "What about light?"

"Of course, our lights are telling them we're here," said Ciara. "Did you think we would leave them burning all night?"

"That's not what I mean. Ildee said they come out only in darkness, because of their eyes. Does that mean we might be able to blind them?"

"With what? A candle?"

"No, with–" then Eric switched on a heavy flashlight that he had in his backpack.

Miranda said, "Where did you get that?"

"I had it in the safe house. At night I wasn't supposed to turn the light on, in case the neighbours found out I was there. So I used this to read books under my bedcovers. Like I was seven years old again. I have lots of spare batteries–"

From across the room, Síle whispered, "Put it out!"

Eric put the flashlight out.

"Put everything out!" Síle quickly clarified. "I think there's something out there!"

"What about the door?" said Eric, as he saw the door was held shut by a flimsy metal hook, and not by the reinforcements they had prepared.

"No time!" Miranda replied.

The Fianna doused all the lights in the room, and crept to their positions by the windows again. Eric cringed as the floorboards creaked under his feet. He loaded a cartridge into his rifle, as Ildicoe showed him how to do, and he chose a window far from the door.

For a few heartbeats, no one heard any sound but the night breeze on the trees, and the creaking of the other cabins. Then they heard the light crush of snow beneath animal paws, then another step, then silence again, and then more steps, crossing the camp between the trading post and the chapel. Eric looked to Miranda, and to Ildicoe, for a sign of reassurance. Both had locked their eyes on chinks in the window that they had left open to use as gunports. Eric strained to see anything out his own window. All he could discern were shadows upon shadows, pricked by token slivers of starlight filtered through bare winter trees.

The crunch of the steps in the snow turned toward the cabin. Eric could not see the creature that created them, but soon he could hear its heavy breath, and then its curious sniffing around the building.

The sniffing sound moved to the foot of the wall just beneath Eric's window. Eric looked to his companions again. In the feeble glow from under the hatch of their woodstove he saw Síle gesture with her rifle, to encourage him to be ready with his own. Eric took aim, although he could not see what he was aiming at. He heard the shuffling of something heavy, and the digging of paws in the snow. For an instant, his peep-hole was half-filled with a black mass that might have been the shoulder of a mountain. Eric reflexively darted his head away, and pushed his back against the wall, and tried to hold his breath, so to stifle a gasp of fright.

The creature heard the thump of Eric's head on the wall. It barked and growled, and then bounded for the door. It sniffed and dug in the snow around the threshold, and then scratched the door itself. Finnbarr and Síle and Ciara dashed to a makeshift barricade behind a row of crates, and readied their rifles.

"Eric, you thick-head, you might have just killed us all!" Ciara hissed.

"Shhh!" her companions rebuked her. Eric only held up his hands apologetically.

The creature outside began punching the door. The walls shook with each blow. In the distance, all could hear the barking of a pack of wolves, attracted to the commotion. Miranda and Ibrahim, who were flanking the door, prepared themselves: Miranda pulled back the hammer on her rifle; Ibrahim grasped the handle of his scimitar.

The door burst open, bounced on the wall, and fell partially off its hinges. The creature that forced it open now stood before them: snarling and barking, covered with matted and scabrous black fur, and nearly too tall and too wide-shouldered to fit in the door. It stood on two legs like a man, but its muscular shoulders carried the head of a wolf, with yellow teeth bared and yellow eyes glowering.

Eric dropped his rifle.

The Fianna warriors opened fire.

The werewolf staggered back, and turned its shoulder to defend itself from the musket-fire. It howled long and loud, calling to its fellows to join the attack. As the Fianna reloaded, they could hear the distant pack change the tone of its howling. The werewolf took a few steps back from the door, then grasped the earth with all four claws, preparing to leap ahead.

Seeing the creature wounded gave to Eric some of his courage back. He had accidentally dropped his rifle too far away. His backpack was closer. He frantically dumped out its contents and took up his flashlight. He tumbled in front of the door, between the creature and the Fianna, landing on his shoulder, but at a good angle to shine his flashlight into the werewolf's face.

The werewolf covered its eyes with one of its front paws, and snarled again. This gave the Fianna enough time to finish reloading, and launch a second volley upon their attacker. Ibrahim dashed out of the warehouse and slashed at the creature with his scimitar, wounding it in the leg. The threefold effort of light, musket-fire, and steel, was enough to drive it limping away. But just to be sure, Miranda loosed some warning arrows into the snow behind it, so it would know what to expect if it turned around.

The Fianna cautiously moved out of the warehouse to watch it go, and to ensure it stayed away.

Eric examined the footprints the creature had left behind. "Did you see the size of that thing? Its paws are as big as frying pans!" he marveled.

Ciara said, "What the hell were you doing, Eric– knocking your head on the wall to tell it where we are! Then jumping in front of it where one of us might have shot you–"

"Eric's flashlight blinded that thing and gave us time to drive it off," Miranda reminded her. "And that was the *second* time this week that he saved your life."

Ciara had a rebuttal ready, but found she couldn't speak.

Miranda said, "That creature we drove off is going to come back, and bring its friends. We can't be fighting among ourselves."

"Fine," said Ciara. Then to Eric, she muttered a half-hearted "Sorry."

Ibrahim returned everyone's attention to the problem. "I don't know how many are still out there. But if we have to face a whole pack of them, a few guns and one flashlight won't be enough," he said.

Ildicoe looked to the steeple above the chapel and said, "I've an idea. I've been thinking about that brazier on top of the steeple."

"What about it?" asked Miranda.

"The last time I was here, it was a weathervane."

Eric reached the conclusion, and said, "So maybe the last Voyageurs put up a beacon, to keep the werewolves away."

"There's a few sacks of coal in the trading post," Finnbarr volunteered.

"Let's light it up and see what happens," said Miranda.

Ciara ran for the warehouse to get the coal. The brazier was only accessible from the roof of the chapel, so Eric and Ildicoe followed Ciara to the warehouse to get a ladder. Miranda and the others readied their rifles, and formed a protective circle around the chapel door. When Ciara was half-way up the ladder and carrying a sack of coal over her shoulder, everyone heard the barking and howling from a wolf pack, still far away, but coming closer.

"Here they come!" said Ibrahim, as he unsheathed his scimitar.

The first werewolf appeared on the roof of one of the cabins. Having leapt a long distance, it seemed to have fallen out of the sky. The Fianna turned to fire on it with their rifles, but it jumped out of the way just in time, and landed on the roof of the chapel. Ciara shrieked, and grasped her ladder tighter. The werewolf jumped toward her, and Ciara dropped the sack of coal to get out of its way. The werewolf landed on the ground on the other side of the commons, and then jumped into the sky again, to land somewhere in the darkness.

Finnbarr dropped his rifle, grabbed the sack of coal, and carried it up the ladder to Ciara, who by then had climbed on to the roof of the chapel. Another werewolf flew out of the darkness, skipped off the roof of the trading post, and smashed the ladder. Then it bounded back to the darkness again. Finnbarr found himself hanging from the gable of the roof by one hand, and holding the sack of coal with the other. The sack had been ripped open by a werewolf claw, and its contents were scattered on the snow.

"They know what we're doing!" shouted Miranda.

Eric rushed to the warehouse, brandishing his flashlight all around him, to get a second sack of coal. He emerged moments later with the sack, and a coil of rope. But the weight of the coal, and the depth of the snow, worked against him, and he tripped and fell. Ildicoe was closest to him, and she grabbed the rope and threw it up to Ciara. Then she turned and saw the yellow eyes of a third werewolf, near the edge of the commons. Its four paws dug into the snow, as it prepared to pounce.

Síle grabbed Finnbarr's discarded rifle, and fired it together with her own, one in each hand. The shots hit the creature just as it leapt ahead, causing it to crash into the chapel wall, where it broke the makeshift shutters. By then, Eric had righted himself after his fall, and he shone his flashlight into the creature's face. It howled painfully, and jumped away: and all heard the sound of it crashing into some bushes in the outer darkness.

Eric tied the sack of coal to the lower end of the rope. "Okay, pull it up!" he shouted to Ciara.

Ciara pulled. She got it on to the roof just as a werewolf shot past, attempting to cut it open again. But it missed, as it had to swerve itself to avoid being shot by a burning arrow from Miranda's bow.

Ciara ripped a small hole in the sack with her dagger, to empty the coal into the brazier. She had to stand on tiptoe to do it, as the brazier was almost too tall to reach, even as she balanced on the ridgepole of the chapel. Coal dust flew into her face, forcing her to cough and look away. She shrieked again, and dropped the sack on the roof, when another werewolf landed on the ridgepole at the opposite end of the roof.

"Just drop the bag in the brazier!" shouted Miranda.

Ciara saw that the werewolf on the roof was creeping toward her on all fours, and snarling hungrily. She looked down to Miranda, and saw that the chieftain was aiming at the brazier with her bow. The tip of her arrow was burning. The sight gave her some courage. She turned back to the werewolf, stern-faced and stubborn, and shouted, "You think you're strong and frightening? You should have seen my Donall. A thing like you took him from me. Now you and all your kind will pay me back!"

The werewolf leapt at her, just as she plunged the sack of coal into the brazier. All in the same moment, Ciara ducked out of the way, the werewolf leapt on top of the brazier, and Miranda's fairy dart planted itself in the sack.

The brazier exploded. Burning rocks flew in every direction. The werewolf took the force of the blast and landed in the middle of the commons, with its fur ablaze. It rolled itself in the snow to put the flames out, and then dashed into the darkness to join its pack, yipping and whimpering with defeat.

On the steeple, the fireball shrank to a bright and steady flame. Its yellow-red light was reflected in the eyes of the werewolves who lingered just past the tree line, or just inside the shadows of snowbanks. The Fianna fired a few warning shots at the lurkers, and they scampered off. Then they congratulated themselves with cheering and hugs and head-bumps. Some shouted tongue-in-cheek declarations of their warrior greatness, some pretended to warn the werewolves never to return. Eric was just glad to be alive, and he hooted with happiness, and hugged Ildicoe off her feet.

Ciara, lying almost face-down in the snow on the roof, let out a breath of relief. She slid down, to land in a snowbank beside Miranda.

"Are they gone?" she asked.

"I think for tonight," Miranda replied. "Best keep the beacon lit for a while, just to be sure."

Ciara began gathering the coal from the sack that had been torn open. Eric brought an empty sack from the trading post. "Can I help?" he asked.

"Sure, you've been a great help tonight," she sneered at him.

"Why? What did I do?" Eric complained.

Miranda stepped forward. "Eric was trying to make peace with you, Ciara. What is your problem with him?"

Ciara struggled to reply for a moment. Then she rounded on Ibrahim and said, "What about you– Aeducan's been dead less than two days, and you waltz right into the clan to take his place–"

Ibrahim held up his hands defensively, then turned to Miranda. "What is she talking about?" he pleaded to her.

"Ibrahim just got back from a mission I sent him on, where one of his brothers went missing in action, and the other tried to kill him," Miranda explained. "He's a good fighter. We need him. And he has no other family anymore."

Ciara stepped back, again finding herself floundering for words.

Miranda put her hands on Ciara's shoulders. "Everyone in the world carries a shadow the rest of us know nothing about," said Miranda. "There's no prize for carrying the darkest. And you don't have to carry yours alone."

Ciara shook her head. "I know you mean well, Miranda. But I learned a long time ago that no one cares about my feelings. Whenever I showed them, someone would tell me to snap out of it and grow up."

"Do you think that's what I'm telling you now?"

Ciara didn't expect Miranda to say that. As she grasped for words, Miranda hugged her.

Some of the other Fianna had wandered off to the edge of the commons, to pretend that Ciara's outburst wasn't happening. Hearing that she had calmed down, they wandered back. When Miranda saw them return, she released Ciara, and said, "We should take shifts on watch, tonight. Ildicoe, you and Eric will take first watch. Ciara and Síle, you're next. Finnbarr and Ibrahim will have third watch, until morning. Make sure the beacon stays lit until sunrise. And let's all try to keep warm."

Everyone slumped into the trading post and laid out haybales and fur sacks on the floor to serve as mattresses, and piled them with blankets. Miranda, however, leaned on a fence post and contemplated the distance.

"Aren't you taking a turn on watch, Miranda?" asked Eric.

"I'm going to follow those things, and maybe find their den."

~ 32 ~

Miranda carved a new path in the snow from the Voyageurs camp to the edge of the island. There she found a fallen log to sit on. The wind gently played with the ends of her hair. The uninterrupted dome of the sky opened above her: stars, in their many thousands, glittered for her. Below and all around, the hills gathered, solemn and dark, accented by the dim grey of the frozen lake and river below. From a pouch in her belt, Miranda produced three tallow candles, and she pushed them into the snow in front of her. With a quick breath, she lit the first one.

"Maread MacBride," she whispered.

She lit the second candle.

"Aeducan Brigand."

Then she lit the third.

"Niall DeDannan."

Three thin wisps of smoke drifted from the candles and into the valley before her.

"Thank you for sharing your lives with me– thank you for this earth, this island, this world. Thank you for being such good and beautiful people, and for being my friends."

Footsteps in the snow approached Miranda from behind. She turned to look, and saw her friends, standing nearby. Some held lanterns on the end of staves, some clasped their hands in prayer when they saw the candles.

"I knew you weren't really going where you said you were going," said Síle. "Your shape wasn't right. And you left your bann-shee hood behind."

Miranda gestured to them, that they should gather round. "I'm sorry, I just needed to talk to some old friends," she explained.

"Where are they now, Miranda?" asked Ciara. "Please tell me my Donall is in a better place."

"I have to tell you, my friend," said Miranda. "I hate it when people say someone's 'in a better place now.' Because *this world* is the better place. Not some other world, not some abstract heaven. This world, with its flowers and trees and mountains. This world, with all its people, living their lives, sharing friendship and love and happiness together. I want to live *here*, on this earth, among these people, in this world– this crazy, this lonely, this beautiful world."

Miranda's friends gathered closer to her. They touched her shoulder, and sat near her. Ciara fell into Miranda's lap, and hid her face. Ildicoe took off her toque and let her feathers unfurl. She leaned into Eric, and Eric held her. Ibrahim clapped his hand near his heart. Finnbarr revealed a flask of whiskey from his pocket, and he toasted the river, and poured the first dram on the earth before him, and then took a drink for himself. Síle sang a wordless lamentation. The wind stilled its breath, and the hills and stone towers that bounded the valley heard it, and acknowledged it with a distant echo.

~ 33 ~

In the morning, the sun fulfilled its daily promise to rise and brighten the world. The Fianna broke their fast on eggs, brown beans, and blood pudding.

"Now we've secured our base camp, we'll take a recce team out, expand the perimeter," said Miranda.

"I'm sorry if this is too soon to ask," said Finnbarr, "but when will you choose a new captain for the warriors?"

"I don't know that we really need one," Miranda sighed. "We are only seven, sitting around this fire. There's not many more still to come. And most of them aren't warriors."

"True enough," Finnbarr conceded.

"You were hoping for the job yourself?" Ibrahim grinned at him.

"I don't want to be war-captain," said Finnbarr. "I want to be Minister of Finance!"

"Ha! Well, if you can find two clutches to rub together, the job's yours."

"When you say 'clutches', do you mean fancy gold coins?" asked Eric.

"Yes. Why?"

"Because I found some, in a desk here in the trading post yesterday,"

Finnbarr laughed. "There you go! Now, Miranda, about that cabinet post."

Miranda grinned. "How many did you find?" she asked Eric.

"And why didn't you just steal them?" asked Finnbarr.

Eric chuckled. "Because, where would I spend them? And how would I explain to the police where I found them? And– I didn't find very many. The metal in them is probably worth a

few hundred bucks each, but that's not enough to buy everything
we need to rebuild this place."

"You can't spend them in an ordinary market anyway,"
Ibrahim explained. "They're enchanted, so that the outsiders
think they're worthless copper pennies."

"Then why can I see them?"

"You're enchanted too," Miranda explained. "That's a gift
your old girlfriend Katie gave you."

Eric glanced to the nearest window. Several times since her
death, he had seen her reflection on shiny surfaces, standing in
his place. But the glass in the trading post was too musty and
cracked to see anything more than a shadowy shape that may or
may not have been his own.

"What's more, the value of those coins is not just their
weight in gold," Ibrahim said, returning to the original point.
"It's also in goods and services that you can't buy with the
outsider's money."

"So, we can use these coins to buy favours from the other
Hidden Houses?" Eric asked him.

"Favours you couldn't get any other way," Ibrahim
confirmed. "Favours like the lordship of a freehold. Or
someone's assassination."

Eric shuddered.

"Someone might have paid these to the last tenants of
Elderdown, in exchange for possession of the island," Miranda
speculated.

"Someone paid my brother with coins like these to kill a
defenceless old man," said Ibrahim. "The weight of the coins–
well, the thing to remember is: when you flash this kind of cash,
it is never for the good."

"You're probably safe, here in Elderdown, Eric," Ildicoe
reassured him. She stood behind him and rubbed his shoulders
and said, "Anyone who would want to kill you will have to get
through us."

Eric took her hand and kissed it. Ildicoe smiled.

"Eric, Ildee, I've a job for you both," said Miranda. "I want
you to figure out what happened here. Why Elderdown was
abandoned. Why they would leave money like that behind. I'm
sure the werewolves were not the *only* reason."

"If there is another reason, we'll find it," Eric promised.

"The rest of us can strap on snowshoes and hike around for a
while," said Miranda, with a girlish grin. "What does that old

poem say: 'Who knows what we'll find, and who knows what will change when we find it.' Then she winked at her companions and said, "Come on. This will be fun."

~ 34 ~

On a wall near the front door of the trading post, Eric was distracted by a map of Voyageur trading posts and canoe routes. The lines began in Montreal and extended south to Louisiana, and west to Alberta, Yukon, and Montana. He noted some locations that he hadn't heard of before, which he presumed belonged to the Secret People, and so would have been unknown outside the Hidden World. In a nearby desk, he found a small stack of documents which, unlike most everything else, were computer-printed instead of handwritten. The date on the folder that contained them was only three years old. He opened it to find a letter from Carlo DiAngelo, addressed to an Etienne LaChase.

Across the room, Ildicoe was opening up old barrels, wooden chests, and cloth sacks. "What's that?" she asked him, when she saw him pause over the papers.

"It's a contract, between the Voyageurs of Lac Des Fées, and the New Renaissance" said Eric. "Looks like the same contract they offered everybody: swear allegiance to Il Duce, and in exchange get better protection from the monsters."

"Did they sign it?"

Eric flipped to the page at the end. "No," he reported.

"Then we can bet the attack on this place wasn't accidental," she concluded.

"If that's true, why didn't the DiAngelo come to occupy the place when the Voyageurs left?"

"Two possibilities that I can think of. One: they think it's too dangerous here. Werewolves, and such. And two: there's nothing here that they want."

"Maybe they found what they wanted somewhere else."

"In Fellwater," Ildicoe whispered.

"That's what I was thinking, too."

Eric looked at the map on the wall, and drew an X on the spot where Fellwater Grove belonged. He stared at it for a while, concentrating intently.

"What is it?" Ildicoe asked him.

"This contract came with a sales pitch. A list of other territories that Il Duce claimed to already possess, at the time. They're on the map. And look how they're arranged. There's Hallowstone–," Eric marked it on the map, "–on the east side of Lake Superior. Here's Elderdown, in west Quebec. There are some smaller places around Ontario, like that temple in Royal Wyndham. A few in the States: the finger lakes of New York, west Pensylvania, the thumb of Michigan."

As he spoke, he marked each place on the map with another X. Ildicoe looked at the pattern they created, and asked him, "What do you make of it?"

"Look at where Fellwater is. Almost in the middle."

As Eric drew lines connecting each of the peripheral points to Fellwater, Ildicoe considered his discovery. "But this list is three years old. He's got places in thirteen countries now, and Fellwater might not be in the middle anymore. Rath Manannan is in Nova Scotia. Shinobi's old place is on Vancouver Island."

"I bet he has more possessions surrounding Fellwater, than anywhere else."

Ildicoe was curious now. "There might be a way to find out. Miranda said she has a spy in their camp. We could ask him. Or her, or whoever."

Eric stepped back from the map and looked out the window, to consider a new thought. "There are two more conclusions we can draw from all this. The first is that there's something special about Fellwater. Maybe it's going to be the centre of whatever he's planning. Maybe it's where he wants the big event to happen."

"Could be," Ildicoe smiled. "What's the second?"

"It's the obvious one, at least to me," Eric called it. "This contract is proof that they know about this place. Our location might not be secret, after all."

~ 35 ~

With the snowshoes they found in the trading post tied to their boots, and with travel packs and weapons slung over their shoulders, five Fianna tramped across the snowy fields of the island. They soon found the landscape wouldn't give them a simple path. Steep rocky slopes, small canyons and chasms, and persistent thickets of trees, forced them to meander. Síle often wandered away from the group, following her Second Sight toward one fancy, and then another. Her companions were content to follow her, although Ibrahim sometimes complained about it.

"We're not staying on mission," he said.

"We don't really have a mission," Miranda reminded him. "We're just exploring, for the sake of exploring. When was the last time you did that?"

"When we had money to spare, which we never do," Ibrahim replied with a grumble.

"We have something better, and we have it abundantly. We have *time*," Miranda grinned.

Finnbarr playfully thumped Ibrahim in the shoulder. "Come on, mate. You gotta admit that freezing our asses off, here on this island in the middle of nowhere, is much more fun than eating a hot meal and sleeping in a proper bed."

Ibrahim smirked at Finnbarr.

The explorers passed over fields of snow and sheltered valleys, some wide and open to the sky, some narrow and sheltered from winter winds by rock faces or tall trees. They spotted deer and rabbit tracks, and the tracks of their predators. Sometimes they spotted in the distance an exotic thing found only in the Hidden World: two-headed eagles, grandmother trees, florescent elk. In a narrow valley, full of aspens and alders, they unstrapped their snowshoes and stopped for bread and coffee in the lee of a pillar stone that stretched taller than the trees. They made smalltalk about the size of the island, and what forces might be keeping it in the air, and whether it might be possible to fly it around the earth. Somewhere in this conversation, Síle dropped her coffee thermos and wandered away, without putting her snowshoes back on. Her steps alighted on the surface of the snow without sinking in.

"Where's she going this time?" Ibrahim complained.

"Ever since we left the camp, something has been bothering me," Síle explained. "Something feels out of place."

"Isn't it obvious? The people who used to live here were driven out by werewolves," said Finnbarr.

"That's not it. There's something else, and I think it's close now," Síle whispered, and she stepped on.

Ibrahim looked to Finnbarr and said, "She was awakened as a small child, wasn't she?"

"She was nine years old," Finnbarr confirmed.

"That explains the weirdness."

Miranda said, "Boys, let her be. I don't understand her half the time either, but she's right more often than she's wrong. I've learned to trust her." Then she followed Síle, although she sank in the snow, and had to retreat to put her snowshoes back on.

They followed Síle to a small knoll, a short distance away. Síle shook her head at it.

"Whatever's wrong with the island, it's in there," she whispered.

Emerging from under the snow, on the top of the knoll, they saw a Roman banner pole, crowned with a cast-bronze icon of an angel holding an hourglass.

"So, they found this place," said Ibrahim.

"But why plant their flag here?" asked Ciara. "Why not back at the camp?"

They dug the banner out of the snow, using their snowshoes as shovels, to find out. Eventually they discovered the headstone of a grave.

"Etienne LaChase," Miranda read the French inscription. "It seems this man was leader of the expedition that discovered this island. He was also the engineer who raised it from the lake, to keep it safe from the outsiders. Died only two years ago."

"Then the DiAngelo paid their respects by planting their flag on his grave," said Finnbarr. He reached out his hand, to pull the banner out. Síle stopped him.

"Wait– don't touch it!" Síle warned. When Finnbarr looked to her for a reason, Síle said, "It's– *doing* something."

Miranda crouched down near the banner pole. She touched the soil packed around its base, although this caused Síle to made a slightly panicked intake of breath. Then she stood and said, "Síle's right. This banner is interfering with the way the Sources comes through, around here."

Ibrahim knelt down beside her, and put his own hand on the soil around the banner's base. Then he stood and said, "I know what this is. We used to do something like this in the days of the Songhai, when all we had were scattered oases in the desert. It's a way of gathering the *ashé* from many small holds, so you can treat them all as if they are one, much-larger hold."

Miranda stood again, and examined the banner-pole closer than before, while heeding Síle's warning not to touch it. "So this is a ley-line marker," she named it.

"How does it work?" asked Ciara.

"There will be two markers like this, to complete the line," Ibrahim explained. "One in the vassal hold, the other in the lord's hold. Pull one of the markers out, and the bond between the two holds will break. But whoever is at the other end will instantly know we're here."

Finnbarr said, "Then we'll have to find out where the other end of the line is."

Miranda smirked at him. "That's not very hard to guess."

~ 36 ~

That evening, back in the trading post, Miranda stood beside Eric, and the other Fianna stood behind them, as they all studied the map on the wall. Following a discussion among themselves about which freeholds in the Hidden World had declared for the New Renaissance, Eric had drawn more points on the map, and more lines connecting them. The resulting shape resembled a spider's web, with Fellwater Grove in the centre.

"So, while we were distracted, our enemy built an invisible empire," Miranda concluded.

"But why Fellwater?" asked Eric. "They have a freehold of their own, only twenty kilometers to the south. Domus Eleutherios. They could have made *that* the centre of their network. Or, anywhere else in the world."

"Maybe because Fellwater is bigger, and older," suggested Finnbarr.

"It has the Well of Wisdom," said Síle.

"It's also in the countryside, not the middle of a city," Ildicoe speculated. "So it might be easier for them to hide whatever they're doing."

"My spy told me they were building some kind of structure on the site of our old stone circle," said Miranda.

"Probably the convergence point for all these ley lines," Ibrahim reasoned. "The really important question is– what does Il Duce want to *do* with this empire?"

As the Fianna discussed among themselves what they thought the answer to Ibrahim's question might be, Miranda stared at the map, silently, thoughtfully. Eric noticed her silence, and said, "I want to go there and find out."

Miranda looked at Eric with calculating eyes. "You're joking. You're not joking."

"I'm not," he said. "I was stuck in the safe house with nothing to do, for months."

"Staying inside, doing nothing, probably kept you alive," Miranda reminded him.

"Staying here in Elderdown might not be any safer. Carlo's people know about this place."

Miranda took his shoulders in her hands. "Eric, you've saved our lives twice in as many days. You called for a vote of confidence in me, that kept the clan together. You've already done a lot for us. Now stay here, stay safe. In the outside world there will be more eyes looking for you. There's none looking for you here."

"I'll be all right, Miranda. I've got a thing that Ildee gave me, that keeps me safe. We've already used it; we know it works."

"Ah, so that's who stole the *omamori*," she said. "My agent was looking for it."

Ildicoe smiled. "I can neither confirm nor deny."

"Besides," Eric added, "Ildee and I were talking about it: some of the clan aren't too happy with having me here. Or Ildee, for that matter. They still blame us for what happened last year. Might be helpful to get us out of the way for a while, too."

Ciara made an unhappy cussing sound. Then she looked out a window, and hoped that no one looked at her.

Miranda decided Eric was right. "In that case, I'm giving you both a job to do. Go to Fellwater, find the ley-line marker that connects to Elderdown, and break it. Actually– break as many as you can, to hide the fact that we're here, and to put a dent in their empire. I'll have you co-ordinate with my agent. He should be able to smuggle you in and out."

Eric looked to Ildicoe for an opinion.

"*C'est bon, pour moi,*" she said.

"Tomorrow morning, take the flying boat to the safe house. And Ciara, I'd like you to go with them," said Miranda. When Ciara pretended not to hear, Miranda added, "You can sort out your differences with those two, on the way. I want peace between you by the time you get back. And while you're there, pick up the rest of the clan from Orenda Country, and bring them here."

Ciara rolled her eyes and said, "Whatever you want."

Eric picked up the purse of gold clutches and brought them to Ciara. "Maybe you could take those coins with you."

"You trying to *buy* your way into my good books?" she scorned.

I just thought– you could use them to get some supplies for the camp," Eric explained. "You know. Food, fuel, building materials. There might be people in the Hidden World who sell such things. And we have lots of work to do here."

Miranda nodded. "It's a good idea, Ciara."

Ciara acquiesced. Eric handed her the leather purse, and she took it without meeting his eyes, then left the cabin.

Eric returned to Miranda. "So, who is this spy of yours. How do we find him."

Miranda smiled. "You probably already know who he is."

~ 37 ~

No one spoke as Ciara piloted the curraigh away from Elderdown, with Eric and Ildicoe on board. When they turned the first bend around the river, and Elderdown was out of sight, Eric sat next to Ciara.

"Want to talk about it?" he asked.

Ciara looked at him for a long time, and then said, "I suppose I should apologize to you," she said.

"It's all good," said Eric. "I know what it's like to be angry at everybody, for something that isn't anyone's fault."

Ciara smiled softly, then shifted closer to him. "Tell me about Katie," she asked. "I never met her."

Eric didn't expect this. "Well– she was– she was a vet student when I met her, but then she ran out of money so she quit university and got a job at a bank–"

"No, I mean, tell me what she meant to you."

"Okay," Eric said. His mind sifted through the last few years of his life, to choose a story, and to try and understand Ciara's question. When he was ready, he said, "She was my first love. She was my partner, my treasure, my red-haired disaster, my ransom to fortune. But I was also afraid of her; sometimes I wanted to possess her, sometimes run away from her. Is that normal? I don't know. But I think that if love could become a person, it would look like her."

In the front of the curraigh, not quite beyond the range of Eric's voice, Ildicoe shifted in her seat, and wrapped her cloak around her more tightly.

"Then she became the mother of your child," Ciara said.

"I was just getting to like the idea of being a family man, when they were both taken away from me."

"Do you still miss them?" Ciara asked him.

"Every day. You know, I still see Katie's image reflected in things like mirrors or windows. But not as often as I used to. It's like she's moving on. But sometimes, it's also like she's only gone on a trip, and she'll be home any day."

"Do you still love her?"

Eric looked to Ildicoe before answering. She was sitting in the front of the curraigh, facing away from him, watching the scenery pass by.

"It's been less than a year. It's still hard for me to talk about it. I'm trying to move on. I'm with Ildicoe now, and–"

"But– are you still in love with her?"

"Every day," he whispered. "If I had anything to regret, it would be that I didn't tell her that, often enough. I thought she wouldn't want to hear it; and I thought there'd be more time. I was wrong about that: there is only the time you have, there's never any more."

"Thank you," she whispered. "Miranda was right, to remind me that I'm not the only one."

"I miss Donall, too." Eric offered. "He was a friend. He helped us get Tara back, after Carlo and his mother kidnapped her."

"He told me," Ciara confirmed. "He was good like that. To everyone." She gestured toward Ildicoe and said, "I'm glad to see you've fallen in love again. Seeing the two of you, it's like a sign, that maybe I could fall in love again someday, too. Now go on up there, don't let your lady get ideas about *us*."

Eric smiled, hugged Ciara, then moved to sit near Ildicoe. He put his hand on her knee, to show his affection. Ildicoe patted his hand, then turned her attention back to the passing scenery.

Behind them, Ciara glared at Ildicoe. Her smile disappeared. Her gaze became critical, and calculating.

~ 38 ~

Ciara dropped Eric and Ildicoe in the courtyard behind the Japanese cultural centre. They slipped into the safe house, while Ciara remained on guard outside, to ensure they weren't noticed. When the they were safe, she waved at them, and sailed away.

"Ganga!" Eric exclaimed, when his cat bounded on to the kitchen counter to see him. Eric picked up his pet and cuddled her.

"Eric, what were you and Ciara talking about?" Ildicoe asked him.

Eric did not expect Ildicoe's question. "When do you mean?"

"In the boat, on our way here."

"She apologized for being horrible to me."

"Was that all?"

"She wanted to know about Katie. I suppose you heard everything," Eric asked.

"Yeah, I did," she confirmed with a sigh. "You say you're over her, but you're not, are you?" When Eric tried to object, she said, "It's okay– it's understandable– it's been less than a year."

"I haven't been to see her grave since last summer, because of Carlo's bounty. I probably won't be able to go there on the anniversary."

Ildicoe bit her bottom lip as she raised the courage to ask a difficult question. "I need to know something, Eric: where do I stand, in your world? Am I just your– how do people call it these days– your rebound girl? Who am I, to you?"

Eric took her hands to answer. But a knock on the door stole the moment from him. Ildicoe immediately jumped up and dashed for the bathroom, the only obvious place in the room where she could hide.

The door opened, and Shinobi stepped in. He was dressed in his usual turtleneck and sport-coat ensemble, but added a pair of sunglasses.

"*Konnichiwa*, Eric-san," he said, with a slight bow. "And I trust your ladyfriend is with you?"

Ildicoe stepped out of the bathroom. Her scarf was back in its place, wrapped around her head. "How did you know I was here?" she asked. "I heard that some Hiddenfolk can see through walls–"

"Nothing so esoteric as that. Miranda told me to expect you." Ildicoe grinned sheepishly.

"So you're her agent. I should have guessed it would be you," said Eric.

"I've been asked to insert you into Fellwater Grove. But there's been a new development, that will make the mission much more dangerous. At least for me."

"What's that?"

Shinobi removed his sunglasses and said, "I may need you to show me the way."

Ildicoe moved closer to look into Shinobi's eyes. They were open, but the pupil was cloudy, and the whites were bloodshot and sore.

"*Calise!* Did someone *do* this to you?" Ildicoe exclaimed.

Shinobi deflected her question with a wave of his hand. "It was not unexpected," he said.

"We could ask Neachtain the Healer to look at you–"

"No," Shinobi declined. "If Carlo learns my eyesight was restored, he'll only take something else from me."

"There must be something we can do for you."

"Allow me to do my part for your mission," Shinobi told her, as he put his sunglasses back on. "If, of course, you can tell me what it is."

Eric and Ildicoe saw that Shinobi wanted to get back to business.

"We think that House DiAngelo has built a complex network of ley-lines, with Fellwater at the centre," said Eric. "We are going to find and destroy the centre of that network."

Ildicoe added, "The markers would look like Roman-style banner poles, like the one you have on the front porch of your cultural centre."

Shinobi perked an eyebrow. "It's a ley-marker? I thought it was just a sign of my sensei's politics. That must be why he told us not to move it."

Eric gave Shinobi a quizzical look; he thought it odd that Shinobi would not have known that his sanctuary was part of the New Renaissance empire. But he decided he had more important questions. "There must be a place somewhere in the grove where all these ley lines come together. Any ideas?" he asked.

"The temple, probably," Shinobi suggested. "There's a banner hanging in almost every window. One for every house and every hold that pledged allegiance to Il Duce. The temple is still under construction, but that won't make it easier to get inside."

"What kind of security have they got in there?" asked Eric.

"It's pretty heavy," Shinobi said unhappily. "There are lookout posts on the ridge every thirty meters, with floodlights to watch for anything approaching by air, and ballistas to shoot it down. The main gate is guarded at all times by a squad of six. They change the guard every ninety minutes, like clockwork:

sixteen shifts a day. They check all comers for identification badges, and they don't just refuse people who don't have one. They imprison them in the caverns under the ridge."

Eric thought some more. "The Ninth Legion is camped in the grove," he recalled. "That's a lot of bellies to feed. How do their supplies get in?"

"A galley from Domus Eleutherios arrives once a day."

"Maybe we could stow ourselves on board."

"I still think it's too risky. Both of you are wanted people. Especially you, Eric. Some very talented assassins are looking for you. They refer to you as 'the Rabbit', by the way."

"The Rabbit? Why?"

"Because you outran their foxes."

Ildicoe grinned. "I think that's a compliment," she said, as she stroked Eric's ears.

Eric smiled, then returned to the problem at hand. "But security won't be as tight in Domus Eleutherios. And no one will be looking for us there. You must have one of those badges you mentioned, right? Could we use it to make forgeries?"

"I do have one that we can copy. I can get you some centurion uniforms, too. Though neither of those will help you if anyone knows your faces."

Ildicoe sighed. "Shinobi, I don't get you. You're supposed to be our inside man, right? You're supposed to help sneak us inside. Why are you being so difficult?"

"Because there's no way to do it. No way, without breaking my cover. Unless I hand you over to Carlo for the bounty. He would welcome you into the grove with open arms if we did that. Then he'd kill you right away."

Eric said, "There's always another way."

"I don't see it."

The three sat silently looking at each other for a moment.

"How many ways are there to get inside a secure location?" said Eric, thinking aloud to break the tension. "There's only three, right? There's brute force, which we can't do because Miranda already tried it. There's sneak-in-the-back-door-at-midnight, which Shinobi won't do because he thinks it's too risky. Then there's Trojan Horse, in which we get the guards to *invite* us inside."

"What do you have in mind?" said Shinobi.

Eric thought some more, and then said, "When I was taken to Domus Eleutherios last year, they took me in a windowless carriage, that could also fly."

"I've seen those," Shinobi confirmed. "They use them to transport prisoners."

"Do you think you could get your hands on one?"

"What do you have in mind?" said Shinobi, skeptically.

"Something like this: we find one of those carriages, load it on to the galley that brings supplies to the grove, and tell the guards that it contains a secret gift for Il Duce– something they need to put in the temple they're building. Then, in the middle of the night, Ildee and I sneak out, pull up all the ley-markers, sneak back in again. Then you tell the guards you have to take the carriage somewhere else. To Carlo's mansion in town, maybe. But once we're out of sight of the grove, we go back to Elderdown instead."

Ildicoe said, "You're proposing a Trojan horse-drawn carriage. Love it!"

"I don't know, I still think it's risky." Shinobi groaned. "What if you get caught while you are in the temple?"

"That's where I can help," said Ildicoe, "I have your *omamori*." She took it from her pocket to show to Shinobi.

"Are you the one who stole it?" asked Shinobi.

"People keep asking me that," smiled Ildicoe.

"My sensei was very angry when it went missing," Shinobi told her.

"It will be returned. Eventually."

Shinobi accepted this with a grimace. Then he said, "But that will help only one of you."

"Eric can use it. I have my own way to avoid being seen," said Ildicoe.

"So, Shinobi," said Eric, "can you get us one of those carriages?"

Shinobi grinned. "Eric-san, I think we have a plan."

"It's going to be risky," said Ildicoe.

Eric touched Ildicoe's arm affectionately, saying, "Yes. But apparently I'm a rabbit. So it's going to be fun."

~ 39 ~

Shinobi left Eric and Ildicoe in a picnic pavilion in Fellwater conservation park, where they could keep warm, as well as keep hidden. They decided it was safe enough since no one was using it in the wintertime. He picked them up again a few hours later, at nightfall, with one of the DiAngelo carriages.

"I couldn't get one with no windows," he apologised. "But if you keep your heads down when we get close, and use your omamori, then you should be fine."

The window in the carriage was barely the size of a mail slot, and a wire mesh prevented it from being used as one.

"Maybe we can get a quick look at the place, this way," said Eric.

As they climbed inside, Shinobi removed his winter coat, revealing that he was wearing a tuxedo beneath it. He put on a bow tie, and then a ceremonial robe resembling a graduation gown. The badge of the Guardians was embroidered into both breasts. Eric studied it for a moment.

"Shinobi, what is your position in the Guardians organization?" he asked.

"I'm a regional co-ordinator," he replied. "Just above a local chapter president, just below the likes of Carlo and Heathcliff. It's the uniform, isn't it?"

"It's certainly not the uniform of a foot soldier."

"It's camouflage," Shinobi grinned. "A good ninja doesn't always wear black. He wears whatever will help him blend in, wherever he is."

Eric nodded, then got into the carriage.

When they were underway, he whispered to Ildicoe, "He's really high ranking with them."

"But he's on our side, right?" Ildicoe replied.

"I hope so," said Eric. "But it seems to me, you'd have be *very* loyal to *them,* to be promoted that high up."

"Relax, love," said Ildicoe. "He could have betrayed you months ago, when you were first taken to the safe house. He wouldn't do it now."

Eric sat back, and folded his fingers under his nose, as he thought about it.

At the main gate to Fellwater Grove, Shinobi halted the carriage, jumped down, and saluted the sentries.

"Magnum Opus Facimus," he said.

"Avete, Il Duce!" the sentry replied with a sharp salute. He looked into the carriage and said, "Lord Sanchin-Goju, we were not expecting you until tomorrow. I'll have to notify the duty officer."

"No need," said Shinobi. He opened a wallet and showed something to the sentry. Eric and Ildicoe could not tell what it was, as Shinobi's back was turned to them.

Whatever it was, it made the sentry blink and look twice. "Open the gate!" he ordered.

"Shouldn't we check inside the carriage first?" said another sentry. Shinobi showed the wallet to him, and the second sentry immediately apologised and opened the gate.

Eric and Ildicoe shared worried glances. "I think he might be higher up in the organization than he let on," Eric whispered.

The carriage entered the cleft in the ridge, and then emerged into the grove. Ildicoe and Eric could see how the DiAngelo had transformed it. Each side of the path was covered in the maroon tents of the New Renaissance army, all in precisely-aligned rows and columns. Each column was signposted with section and platoon numbers; some were further decorated with mascots or mottos. Every tenth row was made wider, to allow space for cooking pits and training rings. As they moved along, they saw the remains of the Brigantian Great Hall. Only a few of its sturdiest posts still stood, but they were fire-blackened, and leaning on strange angles. Where the central feasting hall had been, there now stood a row of portable toilets. Further down, they got a quick glimpse of the path that led to the well of wisdom. It was now buried under a small heap of stones.

"That's what they think of us," Ildicoe said.

The temple was built on the site where the stone circle once stood. Although unfinished and half-caged in scaffolding, it was already impressively tall. From a rectangular ground floor of Roman columns and square portals, there rose a series of rotundas, capped at the top with a dome surrounded by a golden icon of an angel holding an hourglass. A tall banner pole stood between the columns on every level, decked with the symbols of more houses, clans, and holds, than Eric had time to count.

"There's no way we will take them down without being seen," said Eric.

"Get comfortable then," said Ildicoe. "We may need to stay in this box until very late at night."

Eric grinned. "If our relationship can survive us being locked in a box together for a few hours, then it can survive anything."

Ildicoe kissed him, and then said, "But you don't have to wait in here with me the whole time. Take the *omamori* with you, just in case."

Shinobi drove the carriage to the side of the temple still covered in scaffolding. He parked it inside the columns of the stoa, where it would be unobtrusive, although not entirely hidden. He jumped down from the driver's bench, and whispered to Eric and Ildicoe through the window: "I can't get you inside the temple. I'm sorry, but this is the best I can do."

"Shinobi, how do we get out of here?" asked Eric.

Shinobi was already out of sight: with the help of a passing centurion he unhitched the horses from the carriage. Eric didn't want to risk calling out loud to him, in case anyone else heard him. He slumped back in his seat, careful not to rock the carriage. He looked out the window on the other side, to see where Shinobi went. Between the scaffolding bars and the stone pillars of the temple he could see very little. A trio of soldiers walked by, gave the carriage a passing glance, which caused Eric's heart to leap. Then they kept going; from what he could hear of their voices, they were more interested in finding somewhere to stay warm, where they could drink the night away.

Ildicoe searched the edges of both doors with her fingers. "See if you can find a latch or a hook or something," she said. Eric brushed his fingers over every surface on the opposite door, but found nothing.

"I've seen you do that magic thing where you open locked doors. Can you do this here?" asked Eric.

Ildicoe tapped quietly on the place where she thought the latch might be, but nothing happened. She tapped a bit more frantically up and down the frame, but the door remained firmly shut.

"I can't," she whispered. "Something's in the way. I think they put some kind of ward on it."

Eric rattled the doorknob again, and then sat back. "Ildee," he whispered, "I think we've been betrayed!"

~ 40 ~

As Miranda shoveled the snow off the paths, Ciara's flying curraigh returned. It was full of passengers; some sat in the trees that grew in the place of the mast. Behind it, several more shadows emerged from the clouds. These soon resolved themselves into the shapes of similar flying boats, with more passengers. Miranda, and the other Fianna who were nearby, ran to greet the arrivals.

Ciara touched the ground, and Miranda looked to her for an explanation.

"I'm sorry, but I just couldn't turn these people away," she explained. "It seems the Hidden World has a new religion, and it's called the New Renaissance. Everyone has to convert, or leave the empire." Then Ciara handed Miranda a leaflet. "Whenever anybody says anything critical about them, within days they paper the walls with these flyers."

Miranda read the first few lines of the text. One line aroused her ire, and she read it out loud: "*The New Renaissance welcomes all Hiddenfolk, no matter their language or their customs, so long as you agree to live in accord with our laws, and do your part to realize our Great Work.*"

"As far as I'm concerned, it's an eviction notice," said Ciara.

As the other boats landed, Miranda greeted everyone, but evaluated those she didn't know with a critical eye.

"Elderdown is barely more than a campsite, right now," Miranda told Ciara. "We don't have anywhere to house all these people."

"We brought all the supplies we could carry," said Ciara. "Eric gave me only eighteen clutches, but they went a long way, surprisingly."

The Bhattacharya family stepped out of the next boat to land, along with several others from House Arjun. They unloaded tents, as well as bundles of blankets and winter clothes. Miranda came over to help.

"Is Raj Purana coming?" she asked.

Ramanujan shook his head. "Him? Haha! The only thing he respects is power. He would have sided with us if we won back Fellwater. But since we didn't, he changed his allegiance again."

"Right," Miranda acknowledged.

The next boat carried several familiar, tired faces. Marla St. David stepped out and looked around, and pulled her shawl tighter. Before Miranda could say hello, Marla said, "They knew I had lent you my cauldron. I don't know how, but they knew! So they took the Cup of Cormac, saying it was a 'material accessory to terrorism.' Can you believe it!"

"They'll use it on their prisoners, no doubt," Miranda grumbled.

Gregory Morningfrost and his hounds jumped out next.

"Morningfrost! So good to–" she started to greet him. She noticed he had only two of his hounds with him. His shoulders were slumped, and his eyes never looked up. He and his hounds walked directly to the trading post, to warm up and find some food.

The last to touch the ground was Algernon Weatherby, accompanied by several of his Wessex cavaliers. "I still don't think much of your gambit at Hallowstone," he said. Then he sighed, and added, "But we have no where else to go."

Some hours later, several new tents had been erected around the camp, and some of the cabins were rigged with temporary repairs to make them at least minimally inhabitable. As the sun dropped behind the hills, the beacon on the chapel was lit, and a night watch schedule had been established. The Fianna retreated to the warmth of the trading post, for a meal of hot beef and barley stew.

"Our strategic situation is not as bad as some of you may think," Miranda told everyone. "We have twenty-five of these Voyageur rifles now, and enough shot and gunpowder for about a thousand shells. We still have assets like the Dord Fiann, and the healing cauldron. We are a much smaller force now, than we were just a few days ago. But a smaller force is a nimbler force: we can move faster, and go to places a bigger force cannot. We can make quick, precision strikes. Then retreat to the shadows again. We know our enemy strength now, too. Therefore we can make a better plan."

"A plan to do what," said Finnbarr.

"What do you mean, 'to do what'? To take back Fellwater. Obviously."

"You want us to fight a guerella war?"

"We Celts basically *invented* guerella war," said Miranda. "We invented it to fight the Romans all over Britain. Then to fight the Normans, in Britain *and* in Ireland. Then the Vikings. Then the English in 1916– sorry, Algernon."

Algernon smiled, and rolled his eyes, and let it pass.

"We must really suck at it, because we've never defeated anyone that way," Finnbarr snarked.

"But we're still *here,*" Miranda insisted. "Nobody has ever wiped us out. We've always survived. And more than that, we've always prospered, flourished, succeeded in life in every important way."

"Yah," Finnbarr pretended to agree. He gestured around the room and said, "Our new home here is quite the palace."

Rumbles of quiet sardonic laughter greeted Finnbarr's remarks.

"Elderdown is not Fellwater, nor is it Hallowstone, but I'll say this much," said Algernon, as he rose to his feet. "It's spacious, defensible, mostly secret, and it carries a certain rustic charm. With a little bit of work, fixing up the cabins and such, planting gardens in the spring, I think we could be quite comfortable here."

Algernon looked around to see if his idea had any support, and found that it did. The cold and tired faces of the Fianna looked to him now, and to each other, making quiet sounds of agreement and relief.

"What are you saying, Algernon?" said Miranda. "Do you want to stay here? In this winter? And with a pack of werewolves always circling around us?"

"Even so, I think we're better off here than anywhere else," Algernon replied.

Finnbarr said, "Staying here, like he said, kinda beats fighting a guerrilla war that we know we cannot win. And we're on a flying island. That definitely doesn't suck."

Síle leaned forward. "For once, I think I agree with Finnbarr. Sure, I miss the old stamping ground, the same as you do. But this island is– lonely. I think it *wants* us to live here. I think we could make a new home here."

Miranda turned to Ciara. "The DiAngelo took Rath Manannan, too. Wouldn't you like to punish them for it?"

"Sure I would," said Ciara. "But we've told you many times, we DeDannans are not warriors."

"Yes you are," Miranda tried to encourage them. "I've seen you go into battle. Bravely. Effectively."

"I'm a getaway car driver," said Ciara. "That's about as close to warrior as I get."

Miranda turned to the Bhattacharyas next. "What do *you* think?"

Satya said, "I want to hit them back as badly as you do. But not tonight. Tonight, I just want something for my family to eat, and some place warm for us to sleep."

Miranda pursed her lips and looked around some more. All eyes were upon her.

"Well, as your elected chieftain, I think what we need to do is fortify this camp, then prepare a strike team too–"

Algernon interrupted her. "Miranda, what are you doing?"

His words silenced the room. Miranda locked her eyes to Algernon's, and attempted to force him to retract his question by power of her look alone. He only stared back.

"Why don't we talk about this again in the morning," he said, attempting to make peace.

"We need to talk about it *now*," Miranda insisted. "The longer we wait, the deeper they dig in. The harder it will be to dig them out."

"Let it go, Miranda," said Algernon. "I had to let go of Hallowstone, for you. Ciara had to let go of Rath Manannan. Now you have to let go of Fellwater, for us. For all of us."

Miranda looked around the room, and saw that everyone appeared to agree with Algernon. She closed her eyes and ran her fingers through her hair, and breathed deeply.

"I'm taking first watch tonight," she gruffed. She put on her coat, added a shawl to her shoulders to break the wind, and left.

~ 41 ~

In the icy darkness of the locked carriage, Eric and Ildicoe pulled their arms inside the sleeves of their coats, and tried to keep warm. Ildicoe nestled herself into Eric's shoulder, and Eric leaned his head on her hat and kissed the top of her head.

"Do you think we'll be here all night?" asked Eric.

"I doubt it," said Ildicoe. "Shinobi is probably claiming the bounty on your head right now. That will bring Carlo running."

"I still have the *omamori*," said Eric. "You can still turn yourself invisible, right?"

"I can, but it's not much help if Carlo already knows we're here."

Four soldiers approached. Three of them moved to the back of the carriage, to push it ahead. The fourth took the horse hitch, to steer it as he pulled. From what little Eric and Ildicoe could tell through the small window, they were being taken inside the temple.

They heard a soldier behind the carriage ask, "Anybody know what's in this?"

The soldier at the front said, "You can open it and find out, but you know what will happen if you do."

"We keep bringing weird shit in here, and no one tells us what it's for," another centurion complained.

"We'll find out soon enough."

Eric recognized the voice of Paul Turner. He mouthed the words *I know him!* to Ildicoe. Ildicoe held her finger to her mouth, to signal for quiet. Eric opened his coat enough to be able to put the *omamori* over his head, if he needed to.

The carriage stopped when it reached the main front portal of the temple. Eric and Ildicoe heard the sound of heavy chains falling to the ground; it was Paul unlocking the temple doors. The soldiers pushed the carriage into the temple and parked it near the portal, then they left.

The two prisoners waited for a few breaths, before peeking out through the window again. They could see only shadows, and the vague shapes of some boxes of building supplies. The only light came from torches or candles, somewhere out of their field of view.

"Something's very strange here," said Ildicoe.

"Is it the fact that we're locked in a nineteenth century carriage, in a second-century Roman temple, here in the twenty-first century?"

Ildicoe gave him a friendly slap on the wrist. "Silly! No, it's something to do with what the Sources feel like in here."

"What do you mean?"

"It's hard to explain. It's something you have to experience to understand."

"Miranda once told me that Fellwater and the other freeholds are places where the sources of reality come through more strongly."

"Yes– and that's what feels strange to me right now. Fellwater has always been a place of power, but mostly for only *one* of the sources: the earth. Here, I'm feeling *all four* of them. And stronger than I've ever known them, anywhere else."

"Perhaps it's a consequence of all those ley lines, coming together here," Eric speculated.

Ildicoe didn't fully hear him. Her attention was fixed upon something intangible. She pulled her toque off, and her feathers bristled and rose up. A dim glow emanated from her flesh. She walked her fingers over Eric's shoulders as she spoke. "I feel like– I feel like a sunrise, I feel like a storm wind. I feel like taking you, *having* you, right here in this carriage–!"

Eric kissed her fingers, and then said, "Maybe we should do that *after* we get out of here."

Ildicoe laughed, and kissed him anyway. Then she looked at the door, inhaled, and held her breath. She tapped the door of the carriage lightly with two fingers. Its frame shattered, and the door flew across the space, and clattered on the opposite wall. Ildicoe emerged from the carriage and slowly turned around, to take in the new surroundings. Eric stepped out next, and looked up.

The carriage sat in an alcove along the side of the temple, next to a tower of scaffolding. Forklift skids carrying bricks and sacks of powdered concrete lay up against the wall. Eric followed Ildicoe into the main chamber, where he saw where the light was coming from: a wrought-iron brazier, fixed in the place in the temple where a statue of a god would normally go. Standing taller than Eric or Ildicoe, it was ornamented by figures representing various Roman gods. Offerings had been placed around it: locked chests, ancient books and scrolls, figurines and statuary of gold and jade and marble, the skulls or taxidermied heads of fantastic animals, and a potted tree cutting which glowed dimly with its own light. Around the circumference of the brazier, a ring with polished brass letters spelled out the motto: FIAT LUX.

"How good is your Latin, Eric?" asked Ildicoe.

"Sucks," he replied. "But anyone who studied history knows those words. 'Fiat Lux': Let There Be Light."

"Let there be light," Ildicoe repeated.

"This place is astonishing," Eric whispered, as he explored it some more. He was about to ask Ildicoe something about it, but he stopped at the sight of her fingers, which glowed brightly from just beneath her flesh. A similar glow emerged in her heart, her eyes, and her feet. She had thrown off her winter coat, despite that the temple was almost as cold as the winter outside; and she too was engrossed in the sight of her glowing fingers.

"Ildee, what's happening to you?" he asked, with a tremor of fear.

Ildicoe looked at him, as if she noticed his presence for the first time.

"Eric?" she said. Acknowledging his presence changed her world; the glow in her fingertips faded away.

"Is that normal for you?" Eric asked.

"No, it's not," she said, as she looked at her fingers and wondered why they looked normal again.

"Did it hurt?"

"No, it felt fine. It felt strange– but good. Like my hands were no longer mine, but that they belonged to something greater–"

The portal to the temple opened, and Paul Turner entered. Eric and Ildicoe rounded to him. A dagger appeared in Ildicoe's fighting hand. Paul strode forward confidently. Within moments of his entry, his centurion armour began to shine with a hazy golden glow. His carbine was slung over his shoulder, but his hand was on the strap, ready to swing it into a firing position.

"Shinobi said the carriage contained ten thousand clutches," he said. "So I wondered why we were told to bring it here, instead of to headquarters. Now I know."

"That's the value of the bounty on my head?" Eric asked.

Paul laughed. "With both of you here, maybe I'll get twice as much!" He took a two-way radio from his belt and was about to speak to someone with it, when Ildicoe darted forward, as fast as a raven in flight, and knocked it from his hands.

Paul immediately slung his firearm into an offensive position and let loose a volley of bullets in her direction. Ildicoe had already sped past him; Paul's bullets hit the stone columns and ricoched in various directions. Everyone ducked behind the nearest shelter and covered their heads.

"You noticed what this temple does to you, eh? How it makes you more powerful? It does the same to *me*, too!" he shouted. He dropped his firearm and drew a shortsword from his belt, and lunged for Ildicoe. Though she was now perched on the railing of the rotunda above, Paul was able to leap high enough, and land just beside her. She blocked his first sword slash with her dagger, then flipped in the air, over his head, and attempted to slit his throat from behind. But she missed, as Paul spun around in time, and connected the back of his fist with her temple, sending her sprawling into the wall. He lunged for her with his sword a second time, intent to pierce her breast. She leapt up and out of the way, and caught the railing of the next level of the rotunda.

Eric, watching this, wanted to help, but the two Hiddenfolk were moving so fast that sometimes he could not see them clearly.

"Eric! The mission!" Ildicoe shouted.

"Right!" said Eric, and he scaled the scaffolding to the first level of the rotunda. In each niche between the columns there was a stained glass window, which Eric could easily unlock. The ley-line banner poles were hanging just outside each window. He pulled open the nearest window and yanked its banner-pole inside, broke it over his knee, threw it to the floor below, and moved to the next niche.

"Eric, no!" shouted Paul, and he immediately disengaged from chasing Ildicoe around the room, to charge at Eric. Ildicoe swooped down in front of Paul just in time to trip him before he got too close to Eric. Paul fell off the rotunda's edge and landed on the carriage, breaking its roof. He staggered for a moment, and then blasted the carriage fragments away from him with a sweeping gesture. He jumped to the rotunda again, where Eric had broken three more banner-poles.

"I can't let you do this, Eric! If for no other reason: Carlo will have my head!" Paul howled. Then he stormed toward on, brandishing his sword high. Ildicoe flung one of the carriage wheels at Paul, which forced him to disengage from Eric to dodge it. Eric ducked behind the nearest column to avoid being hit by it as well. Then it occurred to him that he had an advantage over Paul that he wasn't using.

"Ildee, put out the lights!" he shouted.

Ildicoe made a grasping gesture with her hand. Some of the windows in the temple broke, as a cold breeze forced itself into the temple. The fire in the brazier shrank, then became mere glowing embers. The temple now lay in darkness: only a faint light from the campfires outside filtered into the space through the windows and diffused on the floor.

Eric put on his *omamori*. Ildicoe looked puzzled at first, as from her point of view Eric had fallen into a shadow, out of sight, and then out of mind. She stepped into the nearest alcove, mindful of the crunch of glass beneath her feet, and melted into the shadows.

Paul swing his sword from one point to another. "Where are you?" he howled. From behind him, he heard the sound of another window opening, and another banner-pole breaking, and landing on the floor below. He dashed toward it, but found only the wake of the cool wind where Eric might once have stood. He swung his sword around him again, but it sliced only air. He jumped to the floor again, found his carbine, and shouted "Come out! Come out or I'll shoot at everything!"

"You'll only kill *yourself* that way," Ildicoe crooned into his ear. Paul swung toward the sound of her voice and opened fire. His bullets rebounded in a hundred different directions, forcing him to crouch down and cover his head, and hope nothing hit him. When the last bullet-bounce ended, he stood again and howled, "What do you people want anyway!"

One of Eric's broken banner-poles fell on him from above and struck his shoulder. Paul fired in the direction he thought it came from, but succeeded only in smashing a window.

From outside the temple came the thumping of armoured fists on the portal, and the voices of soldiers demanding to know what was happening inside.

Paul looked at his armour. The golden sheen that had glowed there earlier was fading away. Another broken banner-pole hit the floor near him, and his hero-light dimmed a little more. He understood what was happening.

"You won't stop us by doing this! You might slow us down, but you won't stop us!"

Eric was perched on the third tier of the rotunda, where he felt safe enough to remove the *omamori* so that he could talk to Paul. "Stop you from doing what, anyway?"

Paul took aim with his carbine but did not fire, as he still couldn't clearly see his target. "You already know what the Great Work is all about. Hell, I once *told* you what it's about. And the world needs it! If you were smart, you would be on *our* side."

"You told me already? When?"

"Oh for the love of God, Eric, I shouldn't have to tell you twice."

Eric crawled along the rotunda, careful to stay just out of Paul's line of sight. He was reaching for the last remaining banner-pole, which he noted carried the banner of the Voyageurs. He reached up and unlatched the window, and pulled it into the temple. Paul saw the change in the light, and took aim.

More fists banged on the door from outside. Paul hesitated. Then he lowered his weapon, and moved to the door.

"Everything's fine in here," he shouted at the door. "It's just some kind of moth attracted to the flame. Tell Heathcliff and Carlo I got it under control."

The banging on the door ceased. "Better have it cleaned up before Caro gets here," said one of the soldiers.

Paul was relieved. Eric leaned over the railing to see what Paul had done.

"Still there, Eric?" Paul shouted. "I just saved your life. Hope you're grateful. Now why don't you make a deal with me."

"Hard to make a deal with a man who's shooting at me," Eric countered.

"You want to get out of here alive? I can make that happen. For you and your girlfriend."

"You want to claim the bounty on me for yourself, right? Can't let you do that either."

"I can smuggle you out of the grove. Take you safely all the way to Royal Wyndham, or New Berlin, or wherever you want to go. I can do that for you."

"What would you want in return?"

"You'll have to tell me where the rest of the Brigantians are hiding."

"Don't be ridiculous. I'm not telling you that."

"There's an even bigger bounty on Miranda, than there is on you. Fifty thousand clutches. We can split it between us."

Ildicoe alighted on the edge of the rotunda beside Eric. She was shaking her head, urging Eric not to take the deal.

"How do I know you won't just turn me in for ten thousand more?" Eric shouted.

"I suppose you don't," said Paul. Then he un-shouldered his carbine and slowly laid it on the floor beside him. "But look. As a show of good faith. I'm putting my weapon down. You can come out of hiding, I won't do anything."

Eric saw that Paul was holding his hands up, showing he was unarmed. Eric stood.

"There you are!" said Paul. "How did you disappear like that– you're not a Hiddenfolk."

"I'm the rabbit," said Eric.

Paul laughed. "Owning your reputation, eh? Listen. Carlo hates Miranda much more than he hates you. I'm willing to bet half my share of her bounty that he'll lift the price on your head if you give her up yourself."

"Why would I do that? She's one of my best friends."

"One-half of Miranda's bounty. That's twenty-five thousand. You could buy the lordship of a small hold of your own, with that kind of coin."

Ildicoe emerged from a shadow near Eric, and settled behind him, just out of Paul's sight. "Eric, what are you doing?" she whispered.

Paul could hear the whispering. "Is that the Voyageur behind you?" he said. "Eric, my friend, you have the worst taste in women."

"What the hell does that mean?"

"Think about it. Katie was an impulsive man-eating screw-up who never considered the consequences of her actions. Siobhan was only using you to get into the Hidden World, and she was still dating me at the same time and didn't tell you. Or me. And Ildicoe disappears for months without telling you where she goes, and she hasn't even told you her real name!"

Eric looked at Ildicoe. "This isn't the first time I've heard that. What *is* your real name?" he asked her.

Ildicoe shook her head defensively. "Eric, he's keeping you talking so that reinforcements can arrive!" she warned him.

Now Eric looked back and forth between Ildicoe and Paul.

"We don't have time for this. Let's finish the mission and go!" Ildicoe pleaded.

"What mission?" shouted Paul.

"Eric, please!" she begged him.

Eric studied Ildicoe's face. It seemed to him that she had more feathers on her head now: the longest ones had grown longer, and the line where they ended had creeped lower down the back of her neck. But in the darkness, it was hard to tell. Then he saw movement from outside the window. Lights, torches, and the glint of armour approached the temple. Eric looked down and said, "No deal, Paul!"

"I had to try," Paul smiled. Then he somersaulted to the side, picking up his gun on the way, and fired on them.

Ildicoe was already out a window and jumping to the snowy earth below. Eric sheltered from the bullets by flattening himself on the ledge. Carefully, he slipped the *omamori* over his head again, and waited until the bullets stopped flying. He crawled to a different window for his escape, where he could climb to the ground on the scaffolding. By the time Eric's shoes hit the snow, Ildicoe had raced away toward the boathouses on the river bank.

Some of the advancing centurions were running after her, although they had no hope of catching her. Eric trusted that Ildicoe's ability to run, and to vanish into shadows, would keep her safe. He also trusted the *omamori* to hide him from the centurions; he smiled to himself, as he imagined walking out the main gate as casually as on a holiday stroll, while hundreds of soldiers were looking for him. But that which kept him safe also made it impossible for Ildicoe to find him. Still, he felt it best to go to the village, as he was sure Ildicoe would not come looking for him inside the grove. He hiked toward the nearest ramp leading to the boardwalks on the ridge, intending to escape the grove by climbing down its face. He kept to the well-trod paths, to make it harder for anyone to follow his footprints in the snow.

A figure in a heavy hooded cloak, who moved with the aid of a walking stick, broke away from the centurions who were searching the temple, and followed him.

Once Eric was on the hiking trails of the conservation park, he started to run. When he came to the first fork in the trail, he saw a crow's feather, stuck upright in the snow, just a few yards down one of the forks.

Eric picked the feather up on his way, to make sure no one else would follow it, and moved on. At various intervals, sometimes where the path bent, or where a shortcut through the bush might be made, he found more feathers stuck in the snow for him to follow. Finally, near the fence line that separated Fellwater's conservation park from the village, Eric found a rough map of the village drawn in the snow, with a feather stuck on a line representing a downtown street.

Eric knew the spot. He erased the map, and made for the Carriage House, one of the village's pubs.

As he walked along, he said out loud in case Ildicoe was hiding nearby: "This is quite a risk she's taking– to put such an obvious sign where anyone chasing her would find it."

A dozen yards off the trail, where Eric didn't look, the cloaked figure sat still, willing himself to appear like another shadow in the forest. When he saw Eric erase the cypher and move along, he pulled himself to his feet with his walking stick, and resumed the chase.

He left behind the corpse of a dead crow, with most of the feathers on its wings plucked.

~ 42 ~

Eric was almost within reach of the Carriage House front doors when he heard a voice from behind him.

"Eric Laflamme! Turn around!"

Eric turned to see Nicholas Brogger pull down the hood of his cloak.

"Nice bit of bling you got there," said Nicholas, as he pointed to the *omamori* with his walking stick.

"Aren't you one of them? How is it– you can see me?"

"It only works on the Awakened. And I'm definitely *not* one of those. Carlo's made that *very* clear to me."

Eric looked up and down the street, hoping for a sign that Ildicoe might be nearby.

"Don't bother running," said Nicholas. He flashed his jacket open just enough to show Eric that he was carrying a handgun. "And don't count on your half-breed girlfriend coming to help you. Because as long as you wear that chain–"

Nicholas didn't have to finish the sentence. Eric looked around again, this time to see if anyone else saw Nicholas flash his gun. But it was too late at night; no one else was on the street, but for a few locals heading home from the pub.

Eric said, "So, how did you know I was here?"

"Actually, I didn't know I'd find *you*, at first," said Nicholas. "We knew that Ildicoe stole the *omamori*. So they brought me in to keep an eye on the temple, in case she tried to sneak in."

"So, how did you know she was the thief who took it?"

"We caught her on camera. You've got a lot of questions, for a dead man."

"If I'm a dead man, then there's no harm answering them."

Nicholas chuckled. "You're a funny one. Talking as if you expect one of the gods to fall out of the sky and save you, any minute now. But it won't happen. Not as long as you wear that talisman."

Eric looked at the *omamori* around his neck, then took a step back from Nicholas. He moved to take the talisman off, but Nicholas stopped him.

"Keep it on you," he warned, as he put his hand inside his jacket to cock the hammer of his gun.

Eric put his hands up again.

Nicholas then took a whiskey flask from inside his coat and drank from it. "Tell me, Eric. Are you religious?" he asked, as he closed the flask and tossed it to Eric.

Eric caught the flask but did not drink. "Why should you care?" he said.

"In case you wanted a minute to make peace with your God. Now walk with me down to the bridge." When Eric did not move, he added, "Eric, there's an easy way and a hard way to do this. And I don't care which one you prefer. I'll get the money for your bounty either way."

Eric led the way to a pedestrian bridge that connected downtown Fellwater, on the north bank of the river, to a parking lot and an empty industrial property on the south bank. When he reached the middle of the bridge, he looked around, and touched the amulet Ildicoe had given him, and looked up to the sky.

Nicholas held his gun up, aimed for Eric's heart. But he did not fire.

When Eric had waited long enough for Nicholas to shoot, but found himself still alive, he dropped his hands, and perked an eyebrow. "You know, what you said just now, about a thief getting caught on camera? It reminded me of something. Fellwater is a tourist town. We've got a row of shops on Mill street, and another row of shops on the boardwalk below, and an LCBO across the river."

"So?"

"So this place is covered in security cameras."

Nicholas pursed his lips.

"Now why would you want to shoot a man, with all these eyes watching you?" said Eric, as he stood up straighter.

"Because I'm not afraid of the cameras," said Nicholas, with a grin.

"No, that's not it," said Eric, as he grew bolder. "The answer is that you don't really want to shoot me, do you? You just want to be *seen* as the one who caught me."

"Take off the *omamori*," Nicholas ordered.

Eric didn't move. "Another question for you," he continued. "Why the walking-stick? You didn't limp like that when I first met you. It was only after you were assigned to keep Katie prisoner, and she got away from you."

"I was injured in a battle with some– things– from out of Tartarus."

"Nope. Don't like that answer either. Because you're basically an office worker, right? An all-purpose gopher with a law degree? I'd say that you're limping because someone *punished* you for letting Katie escape."

Nicholas drew his gun and pointed it at Eric's heart. "Give me the *omamori*!" he ordered again.

"Oh, you want it now? That must mean I'm right," Eric smirked.

"Fuck you, Eric."

"As soon as I take this off, your DiAngelo friends will know that I'm here. But that's what you really want, isn't it? You want them to see you're the one who caught me, so you can get back in Carlo's good books again."

"I could still shoot you, and claim the bounty! You're worth a lot of money, you!"

Eric waved at a nearby security camera and said, "How will you spend that money in jail?"

Nicholas had run out of comebacks. He aimed the gun at Eric's face, cocked the hammer, and gritted his teeth. Then he dropped the gun and leapt forward, grasping at the *omamori* around Eric's neck.

Eric easily stepped out of the way, tripped Nicholas on his weak leg, and watched him fall face-first into the snow.

Two of the DiAngelo centurions appeared. "Nicholas! What the hell are you doing?"

"It's Eric Laflamme! Eric Laflamme!" Nicholas shouted desperately. "Follow his footsteps in the snow! There! It's him!"

The centurions looked, saw nothing, and then picked Nicholas up from the snow. "You've really lost it, haven't you, buddy?" said one of them.

The other said, "I hear that you were once outsmarted by an eleven-year-old girl!"

Nicholas twisted his head toward Eric, as much as the centurion's grip on his arms would allow. His eyes bulged, and his face grew red. "I'll kill you, Eric! I'll find you again, and I'll kill you!" he screamed.

Eric had already turned his back on Nicholas and was walking away, toward the Carriage House.

~ 43 ~

Eric chose a seat in the pub that gave him a good view of the front door. He kept the *omamori* around his neck, in case Nicholas convinced the centurions to look for him there. He took a notebook from his coat, and sketched a diagram of Carlo's painting, to pass the time. He was half way through his beer when Ildicoe entered the pub, and looked around. Eric took off the charm and stood up, so she would find him.

"Glad you're safe," she said. "But you left a rather obvious trail for me. Those soldiers followed it right here. And why did you set fire to the temple?"

"What? The temple's on fire?" Eric appeared honestly surprised.

"The centurions are saying that we did it. *I* didn't do it. Did you?"

"I was too busy running for my life."

Ildicoe decided to accept his explanation. She took his hands and kissed them. "Well. With all those bullets flying, anything could have happened. The important thing is: mission accomplished."

"Mission accomplished!" Eric agreed. A waiter arrived with Ildicoe's beer, and they toasted each other.

Eric showed her the sketch he had been drawing. "While waiting here for you, I got to thinking about something Paul said to us tonight. Remember how I asked him what the New Renaissance is all about, and he said he already told me? I've been trying to think of every conversation I've had with him since he joined up with Carlo. I'm trying to put it together with everything else that's happened in the last few days. We heard them say the final phase of their Great Work was almost done, and they assigned an entire legion to protect it. We also discovered their ley line network—"

"—and we broke it," Ildicoe added with a grin.

"We did," Eric happily agreed, as he clinked his beer glass with hers. "We also know that someone killed Kendrick McManus, and that this painting— you remember it from Carlo's rooms in Domus Eleutherios? It practically prophesized the manner of his death. By the way, I showed this to Shinobi. He said he would bring it to Miranda, but he didn't."

"Now we know why. He's a double agent," said Ildicoe.

"I keep thinking that the answer is right here in my hands, but I don't know how to see it," Eric complained.

"Maybe you need someone else to look at it for a while," Ildicoe suggested, as she took his sketchbook and studied it herself. "Let me see what I can see."

Eric took another swig from his beer, and watched Ildicoe think about his drawing. He said, "Your feathers have grown, haven't they?"

Ildicoe's feathers were at that moment mostly hidden beneath a curly brown wig and a knitted woolen beret. She lifted the wig hair on the back of her neck enough to show Eric that he was right. "They're half way down my spine, now. It happened in the temple tonight. Because of all those ley-lines coming in, I think. It's hard to explain. It's like— it's like I was standing in a hundred golden temples at once, and all of them flowing with beauty and knowledge and love, flowing in from all over the world. Never felt anything like it before."

"So, you're saying a freehold is like a generator, and the ley lines are like a hundred generators all series-linked together?"

"I don't know what that means. But I'll say this: with all those places of power coming together, acting as one, everything in my heart and soul felt– I don't know– *magnified*. My thoughts, my desires, my love, my anger, my dreams. And–" she pulled on one of her feathers, "–my changes."

"I'm sorry, Ildee."

"It's all right," Ildicoe replied, although her glance to the floor told Eric it wasn't.

Eric squeezed her hand lovingly. Then he took a gulp of his beer, and looked around the pub for a while, and then back to Ildicoe. He said, "Tell me again the word you used for what's happening to you."

"Revelation. Why do you ask?"

"Because– why *that* word, instead of a simpler word like 'changing'?"

"We call it revelation because– the way we change reveals something about how that person relates to the sources. Whether the relationship is healthy, or whether it's damaged or corrupted."

"Interesting."

"Interesting–why?"

"Because it's also the name of that painting," Eric said, as he pointed to his sketch.

"So this painting is about Carlo's relationship with the sources?" Ildicoe concluded.

"That, or it's what he wants us to *think* it is," Then Eric's eyes wandered around the room, as his mind busily assembled new connections. His voice reported his thoughts as they came to him: "Something's been right in front of us, all along, and we haven't seen it. Something they're not really hiding; but they're drawing attention away from it. I can figure this out. I just need to start with the right question."

"Here's a question: why did Carlo name this painting Revelation?"

"Good one. Let's start there. Why the word Revelation. It's a word for something revealed, something brought out from hiding, out from behind shadows and curtains and closed doors. Also the name of the final book of the Bible. Why that name. Because they plan to reveal something. Next question: what does he plan to reveal?"

"The Magnum Opus."

"Right. So, next question: what is it? It's Latin for 'The Great Work'. A concept from mediaeval alchemy. The process of creating a philosopher's stone. A stone that turns lead into gold. That's a transformation– The title of the original painting– *transfiguration*! A word for something *changed*, something turned into something new."

"Like Stephen Hobb: a man turned into a tree."

"Yes, exactly! And this painting: in Raphael's original, it's a man turned into a god. What do gods do? They create things. Make laws. Work miracles. Talk to prophets– revelation again. What else? You said Revelation has to do with your relationships with the sources of reality. There were four of them, right?"

"The earth, the soul, the mind, and the sciences," Ildicoe reminded him.

"Right. Now, how do all these pieces fit together. Think! What transfiguration would reveal a relationship to those sources– what would reveal the *truth* about the sources, to everyone. Is that the right question? No, it's not. Start again. Who will do the revealing? The Guardians. A word for the Golden Race in Hesiod's *Theogony*. Also the name of the ruling class in Plato's *Republic*. But they're a front group for something else. Something called The New Renaissance. From the Italian: *Rinascita*, and *rinaschimento,* words for rebirth, renewal. A synonym for Revelation, perhaps? Especially since some kind of transformation is involved? What are the Guardians rebirthing? The Great Work. That takes us back to the beginning. New question: what is keeping the Great Work hidden? What are the shadows that– oh! Oh no! I know what it is! Oh, they really have been telling us all along, but we didn't hear them. But now, I have it! The Revelation– The Great Work– I know what it is!"

Ildicoe leaned closer. "So what is it?"

Eric was still too excited to answer directly, and he continued ranting. "I know why they took over Fellwater, built the ley lines, and the public front company, and the recruitment drive, and all of it. Ildee, if I'm right, if they succeed, if they finish what they're doing, it's going to change the world! The whole world! Everything!"

"Eric, you're making no sense. Talk to me."

"The Hidden World, Ildee! He plans to reveal your world. To everyone. He's trying to *banish*–

~ 44 ~

–The Shadow Spell," Carlo DiAngelo drawled, as he drew breath on his cigarette. "It was the *magnum opus* of its time. Awakened-folk from more than a thousand freeholds, all over the world, concentrating their wills to common purpose. Summoning and stirring the wellsprings of reality itself, calling them forth toward one clear and singular end: to hide the last remnants of the Mythic Age from unawakened minds. Its lands, its treasures, its people: all hidden. An extraordinary accomplishment, I cannot deny. But now that ancient enchantment hangs over us like a permanent shroud between the earth and the sun. It's the reason we are called *secret people*, when we should be called *mortal gods*."

"It's our protection," said Shinobi. "The outsiders outnumber us by almost a million to one. They'd overwhelm us if they knew we were here. Probably hunt us down, too– you know how they fear and hate the things they don't understand!"

"Oh yes, I know what outsiders are like," Carlo said. "Yet they need our leadership. The Guardians Organization is much more than a simple recruiting tool for the New Renaissance. When the outsiders finally collapse their world under the weight of their own ridiculousness, our guardians will swoop down and restore stability and dignity. Their day of calamity is coming, I have no doubt. Some of them actually look forward to it. My proposition is, why *wait* for it? With the shadow-spell overthrown, the people will see us for who we really are. They will see a vision of reality more just, and more glorious, than the sham they're living now. They will welcome our leadership."

"I don't think humanity *deserves* our leadership," said Heathcliff. "I think they need a farmer. Better yet, a jailor."

"They need a savior," Carlo corrected him. "They're demanding one. They're crying for one. Their movies and television, and even their comic books, are all about super-human men who come out of nowhere and save the world. Even their biggest religions positively *celebrate* the idea that they cannot save themselves, they have to wait for a Messiah. They'll take nearly anybody who sounds like he believes in himself: preachers, rock stars, politicians, anyone. Oh, they say they want freedom, oh yes, they're good at that. They built a space robot and named it 'Freedom'. But look at the way they actually choose to live. All over the world, they're trading in their freedom in exchange for security and stability. They accept as perfectly normal all those cameras watching them, in shops, and public parks, and even their own computers. They welcome all those laws designed to ruin a man's life for stepping one toe out of line. It makes them feel safe. Clearly, then, looking not at their words but at the evidence of their lives, the people don't want freedom. They want someone a hero who can can keep the bogeyman away."

"I've been saying that for years," said Heathcliff. "If the people want to vote for a bogeyman, then I want to be–"

"But let me remind you that ours is not an exercise in simple greed," Carlo interrupted. "We must take power not for the sake of power, but for the sake of advancing civilization. It is a responsibility. It is a sacred duty."

"We've had this conversation already, Carlo," Heathcliff said. "And I'm still not convinced. You say 'Look at the evidence'– but the evidence shows us men squabbling like rabid dogs over trifles from the master's table. Men committing secret murder in the night, for a debt of thirty silvers. That's humanity, in a nutshell."

"Secret murder is in fact what I wanted to talk to Il Duce about," said Shinobi. He showed Carlo and Heathcliff the copy of The Revelation, with Eric's notes. "Someone in our organization must know that you two are brothers. Now that Kendrick is dead, one of the two of you is next. And the killer intends to usurp the survivor."

Carlo took the picture and studied it for a moment. "I agreed to hear your theory against my better judgment. Before, I thought it was impossible. Now I think it's just ridiculous. Who's notes are written here?"

"Mine, sir," said Shinobi.

Carlo crushed his cigarette into the paper, and then crumpled it into a ball and tossed it aside. "Kendrick was killed in action, during the siege of Hallowstone, that's all. There is no conspiracy. No need to speak to the boss."

"I don't see why not," said Heathcliff. "Let the man present this theory to The Man directly, and let him make up his own mind."

"You and I can report this theory to Il Duce ourselves. But I think you already know what he will say."

Heathcliff nodded. "I suppose I do."

"I have often wondered," said Shinobi, "why the two of you, and Kendrick before his unfortunate passing, were the only ones allowed private audiences with our leader."

"He is very old, very private, and he does not trust easily. And–" Heathcliff glanced to Carlo, who nodded approvingly, "–his enlightenment has revealed itself upon his mortal coil."

Shinobi nodded. "I see."

Heathcliff laughed. "With those eyes? No, you don't."

"It is not that he is ashamed," Carlo continued. "Rather, he does not wish for rumours about his physical condition to interfere with the reception of his message."

"But since, as you point out, I cannot see," said Shinobi, "therefore it is impossible for me to be distracted by his condition."

"Here's a clever one," Heathcliff chuckled. "We should be promoting him, not dismissing him."

Carlo remained impassive. "Nevertheless, after tonight's terrorist attack, I cannot recommend a private audience. We need to develop tighter security measures first. It seems that a fortified rampart and a thousand soldiers is not enough to protect our most strategic asset."

"The ley line network?" Shinobi speculated.

Carlo nodded. He opened the tent flap to look at the temple. The flames from a fire licked out of its ground-level windows, and smoke poured from its upper floors.

"Rebuilding it will take months," Carlo muttered. Then he shut the tent with an angry slap. "Will no one rid me of this meddling– damn him! Raise the bounty on him to thirty-thousand clutches. The same for his woman. Somebody somewhere, hunt him down and put him away!"

"Yes, sir," said Shinobi. He stood up and bowed, and unfolded a white cane to assist him as he left the tent.

"I have noted your enthusiasm for meeting the boss," Heathcliff said to Shinobi. "So if you're the one who brings us Eric's head, you'll get the bounty *and* your chance to meet him."

Carlo added, "Perhaps even your chance to *see* him."

Shinobi contemplated this offer. Then he bowed lower than before, and said, "Magnum Opus Facimus."

Heathcliff stood and replied, "Avete, Il Duce."

Carlo merely lit another cigarette, and opened the flap in the tent, to contemplate again the fire burning in the temple.

~ 45 ~

Eric jumped down from the flying curraigh before it touched the ground in the Elderdown camp. He threw handfuls of happy snow in the air over his head.

"So good to be here!" he shouted, and then he turned to throw snowballs at Ildicoe, who had jumped down behind him. Ildicoe swore at him with laughter, and launched a few snowballs of her own right back.

Ciara was chopping wood with Algernon at the time they arrived. When she saw them, she paused, and dropped her mouth open. She handed the axe to Algernon and left.

Miranda emerged from the trading post. "Eric! Ildee! I wasn't expecting you for days!"

"Mission accomplished! And I am very glad to be out of there and back here," Eric exclaimed, and he tossed a snowball at Miranda.

"Then I am glad to have you back," Miranda grinned.

Eric stepped closer to her, and dropped his next snowball on the ground. "You might not be so happy when we tell you what we know."

Some hours later, all the Fianna sat around the woodburner in the trading post, digesting the story that Eric narrated to them. They stared at the glow of the fire, barely blinking, barely moving. Their meals of bannock and pemmican lay forgotten in their hands, and the whistling of the draft in leaking windows passed unheard in the silence.

"Somebody, say something!" Finnbarr pleaded. "It's too quiet, I can't take it."

"What is there to say?" said Miranda.

"Well– to start– is it even *possible*?" asked Finnbarr.

"What one man has made, another can destroy," said Algernon.

"Besides that: nothing lasts forever. Not the veil of Maya; not the Hidden World; not even us," said Satya.

"But how will we protect our lands from outsiders?" said Ibrahim.

"What if the outsiders find the chthonic prisons, and break them open again?" said Satya Bhattacharya.

"What if their scientists try to *study* us?" said Gregory, as he gripped his antlers in his hands.

"What if they find out that their fairies and angels and gods were only *us*, all along– what if they *don't like* the truth?" said Síle.

"What if– what if– we can finally walk among them and not have to pretend anymore?" said Ciara.

This turned everyone's eyes her way, and stopped all other questions.

"With the shadow spell gone, we won't have to live double lives," she continued. "The lifting of the spell will give us freedom. We could get regular jobs, we could buy houses, we could travel, and we wouldn't have to pretend to be something we're *not*. It's like, we could rejoin the human race!"

"Lots of hiddenfolk have jobs and houses and things," said Eric. "You yourself were a lawyer, once. When has the Celtic Mist ever stopped you from doing what you want?"

"Eric, you're an outsider, you wouldn't understand," Ciara dismissed him.

"He's not an outsider, not anymore," Ildicoe defended him.

"He's not Awakened either, and never will be," Ciara countered.

"I get that this is a big deal for all of you," Eric said. "Or I'm trying to. But if you're angry about it, don't take it out on me. I had nothing to do with it. I'm just the guy who figured it out."

"Don't be so selfish, Eric," Ciara told him. "This isn't about you. It's about the end of the Shadow Spell. The end of *hiding*. I think it's brilliant. There used to be *one* world, you know, and we were all part of it. Then they cast that spell, and we split the world in half, and gave the outsiders the bigger part."

"We got the better part," said Finnbarr. "We got the flying island."

"That may be, but still, we locked ourselves in the smaller part. Now we live like prisoners in our own homes. But if we lift the Shadow Spell, we unite the world again. Imagine what we could do, Miranda! You have often said that your clan swears by hero-values like courage, friendship, and honour. The lifting of the shadow-spell is your chance to teach those values to a world that has mostly forgotten them."

"The Mist *protects* those values," Miranda replied. "It ensures there's at least one place left on earth where you can live a hero's life."

"What is a hero's life, in the twenty-first century, anyway?" asked Finnbarr. "Is it even possible to live a hero's life anymore?

We battle monsters from the underworld all day, then feast and drink all night. It's a fun life, but it's all a joke, really. The monsters we fight all day don't threaten the end of the world anymore. They're just as much a joke as we are."

"A joke, Finnbarr?" Miranda scorned him. "We fight to keep the people outside our world safe from dangers they will never know about. It's a serious responsibility. And it's an honour."

"There's no heroism among the outsiders anymore, either," Finnbarr continued. "We fight for honour and glory. They fight for parking spaces."

"There's lots of heroes among the outsiders," Miranda reminded him. "Nellie McClung. Rosa Parks."

"Look, I'm just calling it like I see it," said Finnbarr. "We Hiddenfolk like to think we're so enlightened. But Awakening to the truth about the universe didn't make us any better or worse as human beings than we were before. Instead it made us into the leftovers of history. While we were playing hero-games in the Hidden World, the outsiders built rockets and walked on the moon!" Finnbarr had to raise his voice to be heard over the whispered comments that his words provoked. "I just think it doesn't matter whether the Celtic Mist stands or falls. The Mythic Age is over. It's been over for centuries. That's the one thing the DiAngelo understand properly, which we don't. Their only mistake is thinking you can bring it back. You can't. It's gone. We are all that's left of it. The modern world is going to overtake us and absorb us one of these days, Celtic Mist or not. Even *we*, hiding up here on a flying island, have a member of the boring old modern world sitting among us–" Finnbarr pointed at Eric, "–drinking our beer, shagging our women–"

"For God's sake, Finn!" Ildicoe scolded him.

"–figuring out our enemy's plans, and showing us how useless we are," he finished.

Miranda silenced him with a cold glare.

"That's what makes the lifting of the shadow-spell an opportunity," said Ciara. "Not just for big and rich houses like the DiAngelo, but for *everyone* in the Hidden World. Even us."

Algernon cleared his throat, and said, "I agree."

"You agree!" Miranda blurted.

"I've always thought the shadow-spell entirely paradoxical," Algernon explained. "The outsiders' ignorance of our world is reinforced by the very nature of our world, because of that spell. It may be good for us to have one less absurdity in our lives."

"You are missing something very important," Miranda sternly reminded them. "The man trying to part the Mist is Carlo Maliguida DiAngelo."

"It doesn't matter whose plan this is. It only matters that the spell is ending," said Ciara.

"In this case, it *does* matter. Carlo has always spoken of the outsiders with contempt. He thinks he knows what's good for them better than they do. He thinks they're not smart enough to live their own lives. With the Mist out of his way, who knows what he'll do to them."

"I concede that Il Duce's New Renaissance would be a curse for humanity," said Algernon. "But I remind you that Carlo is not the only one who would benefit from the end of the shadow-spell. All of us will benefit."

"For my part, I just kinda wanna see what will happen," said Finnbarr.

"I will tell you what will happen," said Ramanujan. His words attracted attention, since he had said little up to then. "As it stands, the Veil of Maya creates two words: one for us, and one for them, and very little traffic in between. Were the Veil to part, it would create two *political castes*: one for us, and one for them, with not even the smallest trickle of traffic in between. For we are descended from the gods, and they are not. It is a categorical distinction. We will have intrinsic advantages over them, that none of them could ever gain. Not even in theory. Ours would be the class of the stronger, the faster, the longer-lived. Theirs would be the class of the weaker, the slower, the disadvantaged in every way. The Veil of Maya prevents us from oppressing them."

"Thank you Ramu," said Miranda. "I thought I was arguing this side by myself."

"The class divide you speak of would be quite immaterial," Algernon offered. "The Outsiders would still be many, and we Hiddenfolk would still be few. Their advantage of sheer numbers was the reason the spell was cast in the first place."

"It's not a question of numbers, it's a question of power," said Ramanujan. "We will still have more of it, and they will still have less, no matter that they outnumber us a million to one. The question we need to ask is not whether the fall of the Veil of Maya will be good for us, the few here in this room. The question is whether we can trust the DiAngelo with the power they will suddenly possess."

"And the answer is, we cannot," said Satya. "My father was the first of his line to get an education. His father before him played as a child in cattle fields and garbage pits. The landlords and law-men drove by in carriages so clean you could eat off the leather seats. They would look at us as if we did not exist. Or they would laugh at us, and tell us it was our laziness and our stupidity that kept us poor. When my family joined the Hidden World, our grandfather had us swear an oath, that we would never become like them, no matter the gifts given us by the gods. The question is, can we trust *everyone* in the Hidden World to make such an oath? The answer is, no, we cannot."

"I'm on your side too, Miranda," said Ibrahim. "I certainly trust everyone in this room, with the kind of power we're talking about. But I do not trust the DiAngelo. Never will."

"Neither do I," said Síle, as she walked across the room to sit beside her chieftain. "What they did to my forest in Fellwater, they will do to everyone. I cannot bear the thought."

Miranda smiled to see her newfound supporters. She put what she felt was the winning argument before her critics: "A man who gains enough power soon comes to want only one thing: *more* power. Over centuries of history, I've never seen a single exception. What House DiAngelo did to all the Hidden World– fake emergencies, election rigging, kangaroo courts, identity theft, persecution of their critics– they will do the same to corporations, governments, whole nations, everyone! Can you imagine!"

Algernon leaned forward on his stool and said, "I should like to hear the opinion of the only person in this room qualified to speak on behalf of the outsiders. Master Laflamme, if you would give us your mind."

Eric stood up to speak. "I should tell you I'm not an unbiased observer here. Carlo held me prisoner, he tortured me– he killed my lover, and our child. As far as I'm concerned, nothing he does is for the good."

"But what do you think of the shadow spell, in principle?" Algernon insisted. "Do you think it protects humanity and the Secret People from each other? Or do you think it keeps humanity unaware of things they have a right to know? If we cannot trust our enemies with power, how can we be sure that we will not become the same as our enemies, if *we* take power instead? It seems to me, that those are the questions we need to ask. Eric, as the only outsider here– and I apologise for drawing attention to that fact– what are your thoughts? Do you think people have a right to a safe and happy ignorance? Or might bringing enlightenment to the masses be worth the risk of letting a new form of evil loose upon the world?"

Eric sighed and took of his glasses to clean them on his shirt, while scrambling in his mind for an answer. "Those are rather big questions, Algernon. I don't know that I can answer them on the spot, like this."

"Your answer will help us decide whether we should continue sabotaging Carlo's efforts, or whether we should leave him to his work. And that is something we should decide sooner, not later. Certainly before he rebuilds his ley-lines."

"If you put it that way, you already know what my vote will be."

"Of course we do. It's personal for you," Ciara accused.

"It has nothing to do with me personally," Eric countered. "Look: I'm a scholar, I love knowledge. I think it would be great if more people knew about the Hidden World. With no magical curtains and no mystical shadows and lights, the world would be exactly what it appears to be. Anyone could see it for themselves. And I have to ask: would that be so bad?"

The listeners who understood him best bristled with irritation.

"But Carlo and Heathcliff and that faceless leader of theirs– they can't be trusted," Eric concluded. "If we leave them alone, they'll only rebuild. Soon enough they'll be stronger than before. Then they'll come for us again."

Síle said, "I vote that we keep fighting them– and I freely admit it's personal for me. It should be personal for all of you, too."

Ciara said, "I vote that we leave them be, fortify this camp, and just– try to live our lives."

Miranda stood and said, "If we're going to vote on anything, then I want secret ballot. I don't want this question to divide us. The camp is not in a fit state to house us for the winter; and there's a werewolf pack prowling outside every night. Whatever else we do, we have to stay united to survive."

Ciara shook her head. "If we're going to stay together, then we shouldn't have secrets from each other. I want to know where we stand."

"*Secret* ballots," Miranda insisted, "and I want an oath from each of you that everyone will commit themselves to the result. I want no one to punish anyone for voting differently than themselves."

"Nobody here would do that," Ciara objected.

"Remember what happened to Niall DeDannan?"

Ciara sighed, and sat down. "Whatever you want, then," she said.

"I will count the ballots myself, and I will cast no vote of my own, unless there's a tie," she added, to give people confidence in the results. She took some scrap sheets of paper from a balance-book in the trading post desk, and handed them out. "The ballot question is: *Shall we continue to fight House DiAngelo?* Write yes, or no, on your ballot, then fold it and put it in this basket. I'll write your names on this ledger when you do, so that nobody votes twice."

"You're really serious about this," Algernon observed.

"We've had nothing but arguments among ourselves since since we were forced to leave Fellwater. I've had enough. I want some peace in our time now," she said to him.

The Fianna took their ballots, passed an inkwell and a quill around their circle, and wrote their decisions.

A few minutes later, Miranda sat at the trading counter, with the ballots open in front of her. She held her forehead in her hands, and rested her elbows on the counter. When she decided she had kept the others waiting long enough, she turned to them and said, "I have the result now. The vote was seventeen votes to eleven votes, with one spoiled ballot. A majority for– for the 'No' side."

The news was received with gladness and relief by most everyone. Ciara smiled and clapped. Finnbarr laughed and banged his spoon on his soup bowl. Síle shunted over to the nearest window and rested her head on the glass. Eric and Ildicoe looked at each other, shook their heads, then hugged each other. Miranda scooped up the ballots and tossed them into the woodburner, then sat beside it and gazed into its flames.

Algernon, who had been shaking hands with Finnbarr and Ciara, saw Miranda's posture and decided to sit next to her. "I gather that's not the decision you wanted."

"To say the least," she replied.

"It's not all bad," Algernon tried to be consoling. "We've been fighting the DiAngelo for many years. Now we don't have to anymore. We can build up Elderdown, make it into a new home for all of us, and have your peace in our time."

Miranda nodded, and patted his shoulder to show him she was committed to the group's decision. Then she gazed into the fire again, and watched the paper ballots curl up and blacken as they burned.

~ 46 ~

The following day, Miranda returned to Etienne LaChase's grave. She uprooted the DiAngelo banner that had been planted there, and tossed it on the ground.

"Elderdown belongs to us now," she said to the clan, who had followed her there. They applauded her.

For the rest of the winter, the flying boats went out from the island every morning. They returned every afternoon, laid low with the treasures of lumber yards, grocers, textile mills, and fuel stations. The walls of the weakest cabins were torn down; the planks and posts re-purposed as scaffolds for the repair of the stronger, or else chopped into fuel for the beacon on the chapel. Paths in the snow were shoveled and cleared; after the first week, the circle between the chapel and the trading post was entirely open. On the evenings and nights that were not too cold, the Fianna cooked their evening dinners in a fire pit in its centre, where more of them could sit around it and enjoy the warmth and the company.

New cabins rose up. New paths were cut in the snow to the bastions and the island interior. New hedges were built around the camp to break the wind. A rope bridge connected the island to the mainland. Fishing huts appeared on the ice. Storms were weathered with the clan bundling up in the trading post, lest unfinished cabins collapse in the wind or under the weight of heavy snowfalls. Nights of deep cold were endured with pots of hot soup to eat and tea to drink, and the heaviest blankets they could find or make, hanging over their shoulders or weighing down their beds. The lovers among them covered each other with their bodies.

In better weather, the blacksmith shop, fed with old iron from the warehouse and new coal from the daily supply runs, clanged to life. Algernon claimed it as his own, saying that it was his family's craft before they became scholars. He soon moved his tent beside it, and took to working late into the night. In the carpentry shop he repaired the fiddle Eric had found in the trading post. When asked why he didn't first work on more practical things for winter survival, he said, "When we finish building this island, we'll have a celebration, and I'm already looking forward to it. This fiddle is a sign that we shall do more than merely survive."

Gregory Morningfrost set out every day into the woods that surrounded the lake below, with his two dogs and with one of the Voyageur rifles on his back. He returned each evening with a brace of ducks or beavers or wild turkeys tied up at their feet, or with a white-tailed deer on his shoulders. His return was always greeted with celebration. Finnbarr, making fun of imaginary barbarians, hunched his shoulders and jut out his jaw, saying, "We ate well today. It has been a good day." Soon this statement became a motto of pride: the Fianna used it at the end of every evening meal.

Ildicoe and Eric took to the carpentry shop. The first thing they made was a frame for the banner of the Voyageurs, which they could hang on the wall of the chapel. The place of the altar was taken by a standing stone, about waist-high, set into the earth; the chapel was built around it.

"The early Jesuits used this as a mass-stone," Ildicoe explained. "But when we Voyageurs awakened, we kept it here, as an aid for when we seek the presence of the sources. That was even before we lifted the island above the lake." She placed the lily in its alabaster vase upon it. Each day that passed, the little stalk grew slightly taller. On the day the first patch of grass was revealed by the warm spring sunshine, the flower unfolded.

By the spring, the supply boats needed to go out less often, and they returned with goods intended for more than mere survival, such as books, and musical instruments, and wine. Algernon forged a collection of carving tools in his blacksmith shop, and Ciara used them to cut the shapes of flowers and tree foliage into the posts of all the buildings, and then paint them in cheerful summer colours.

Satya and Ramanujan happened upon Síle staring intently at one of the cabins. "I'm trying to teach myself how to open a Seven League Door," Síle explained. "But it's not working. There's too many of them. Doors, that is."

"What about the clouds, then?" said Ramanujan. "There's only one of them. One cloud, broken into fragments, and spread around the world. Just like we are all fragments of one mind."

While the Bhattacharyas argued that proposition, Síle contemplated the clouds for the rest of the day. Later that evening she asked Miranda, "Could you fly one of our ships into one side of a cloud, and then out another– hundreds of miles away?"

"If you can, then you will have invented a new way to travel!" Miranda praised her.

The Bhattacharyas debated each other about whether this new form of travel was invented or discovered.

In the trading post, Eric gathered scraps of various fabrics left over from the curtains and bedding they had made, and sewed them together into a new banner. As he explained to the clan, "It's black, because we're all outsiders here. There's this sword, because we began as a warrior clan; overlaid on the sword there's the Dord Fian, to show some continuity with other clans that have called themselves Fianna, over the years. And finally the sword and the horn are surrounded by these nine circles– in heraldry they're called rondels– one for each of the clans that we came from. And one more, for outsiders like me."

"It's perfect," said Algernon.

They raised new banner-poles on each side of the path from the rope bridge to the commons, one for each clan that someone in the Fianna had come from, or left behind. On the highest flagpole, they raised Eric's new banner.

"We've built a good thing here, my friend," said Algernon to Miranda, as they admired the new flag, and the work everyone had done to build the camp.

Miranda smiled, and patted his shoulder agreeably. But she moved away from him and the others, to sit by the edge of the island, and gaze at Fellwater, far beyond the horizon.

~ 47 ~

When the last patches of snow were only small banks in the shadows, and the trees revealed the first buds and flowers of spring, they raised a Maypole in the centre of the camp. Miranda summoned the clan to the dance with a blast from the Dord Fiann. Each dancer took a ribbon, tied to the top of the pole; then a child sitting on Algernon's shoulders crowned the pole with a wreath. A core of musicians struck up a dancing rhythm: first the fox-headed Wessex fiddlers; then blue-painted Brigantian drummers and harpers; then Arjun singers and chanters; finally the DeDannan wild men on horns and rattles of every kind. Someone handed Eric a pair of drumsticks and put him in front of a bass drum. He played it timidly at first, but soon his hair was down, as his arms pounded it like a Celt. When the dance finished, he saw a red-haired woman, reflected in his place in the trading post's windows, moving as he did. He kissed his fingers and opened them to her. She did the same to him.

A "goddess", really Síle in a mask and costume, emerged from the chapel, to a reception of cheers and laughter. She tossed bread rolls into the dancer's waiting hands. They broke them open, poured butter and olive oil on them, and ate; Ciara found in hers a single gold coin baked into its heart. She cheered excitedly, and held it up for everyone to see. They declared her the Queen of the May, and put the wreath on her head, and showered her with leaves and flower petals.

Some of the men gathered in a lineup and laughingly called out, "Time to choose your May Laddie!" and "Pick me, I'm the best fighter!" and "Choose me, I'm the best looking!" and "Don't choose him, he snores!"

Eric stood apart the lineup, but Ildicoe took his drum away and put him in the line.

"But what if she picks me?" Eric asked, worriedly.

"Relax, Eric, it's all part of the game," Ildicoe reassured him. He smiled, and took a place in the line. Immediately, the other men pretended to jeer him: "Don't pick Eric, he's a nerd!" and "Don't pick him, his hair is too long!" and "You can't choose him, he has glasses!"

None of them mentioned that Eric was an outsider. He smiled.

Ciara stood before each of them, one by one. To the first man she said, "Why should I choose you, Ibrahim Nefzawi?"

"Because of all the men here, I'm the best fighter, and the best poet, and I fixed the cabin you sleep in!" he boasted. Some of the men nearest him slapped his shoulders and congratulated him.

"Why should I choose you, Gregory Morningfrost?"

"Because everybody eats the food I bring to camp, everybody dances to the music I make, and I have the cleanest beard."

"And the best antlers!" someone called out, and Gregory grinned.

"Why should I choose you, Finnbarr MacBride?"

"Because I'm the Stallion of Elderdown!" he shouted, as everyone laughed.

"Why should I choose you, Algernon Weatherby?"

Algernon gave her a tired smile. "Oh dear girl, do not choose me. I am far too old."

"Why are you in the lineup then?"

"Tradition!"

More laughter, especially from Ciara herself. She kissed him on the cheek before moving on.

"Síle DeDannan, what are you doing in the line?"

"I'm breaking tradition!"

This elicited the loudest laughter yet. Some of the audience encouraged Ciara to pick Síle precisely because it would break tradition. Ciara giggled, kissed Síle's cheek, but moved on.

"Why should I choose you, Eric LaFlamme?"

Eric hesitated, and looked around. He saw Ildicoe urging him to say something. "Um, because– because I just finished my master's degree?" he said.

This produced some good-natured moans of disappointment from his peers. "That's not heroic! Doesn't even compare! There was no killing involved! What a nerd!"

"What? I even snuck in and out of the university for the thesis defense, and none of Carlo's assassins found me," Eric complained, which made them pretend to disapprove all the more noisily.

"For a man who says he's not a warrior, you know how to boast like one!" said Miranda, proudly.

Ciara took the May Laddie crown and placed it on Eric's head. "A thinking man. That's who I want for my Laddie."

From the side, Ildicoe added, "It helps that he's handsome, too!"

The men surrounded Eric and slapped his shoulders. "Hail, the May Laddie! Good luck with the May Queen!" they cheered. They lifted Eric and Ciara on their shoulders and carried them around the camp. At the foot of the chapel, Miranda handed a bottle of wine to Eric, and a chalice to Ciara.

"We'll be two minutes. Or, maybe an hour," Ciara winked. Then she pulled Eric into the chapel and shut the doors.

Outside, the Fianna laughed and cracked ribald jokes about what they might do during that hour, and hailed them King and Queen again. Morningfrost took up his bouzouki and played a love song for them.

~ 48 ~

Inside the chapel, Eric asked, "So, Ciara, what do we do now?"

"You pour the wine into this chalice–" she opened the wine and poured it as she spoke, "then you take your dagger and hold it between your palms as if you're praying, and then dip the blade into the chalice, like this–"

When Eric's dagger was immersed in the wine, his eyes met Ciara's. He shuddered.

"Hail the May Laddie," she whispered.

Eric wanted to withdraw his dagger, but his muscles wouldn't allow it. He smiled, more from self-consciousness than from anything else. He said, "This isn't the way it was done in ancient times, is it?"

"Oh no, not at all," Ciara confirmed, with a wink. "Back then, we would have done much more than bless a chalice of wine." She held herself close to him just long enough to be uncomfortable, then stepped back, and let him lift his dagger up and away again. She poured some of the wine on the altar stone as she whispered a prayer, and then turned back to him and smiled.

Eric closed his eyes and breathed again. He dried the dagger on the fringe of his tunic. "So why did you choose me? I thought you didn't like me," he asked.

"I was angry with you for a long time, Eric. I blamed you for what happened to Donall. But we've been working together here, rebuilding Elderdown; you've left me alone; and I've seen the kind of man you are. I needed everyone to know that we are okay with each other now. I needed *you* to know that, most of all."

Eric nodded. "We are," he said. "And I like you. But I'm already committed to Ildee," said Eric, as he carefully backed away.

"I know you are," she said. "But is she committed to you?"

"Yes, she is– where are you going with this?"

"The other reason I chose you for the Laddie was to get you alone in here for a moment, to tell you something I just found out about her. It's very important, and very secret." She leaned close to Eric again and whispered, "Ildicoe is a spy."

"No, she isn't!" Eric chortled.

"Then why did she run away from you? Twice, no less! Where did she go? She's never told anyone."

"She told *me*, actually. She came here to Elderdown. And found it empty. So she went looking for the other Voyageurs."

"She went to meet her contacts in House DiAngelo. She broke open the Tartarus prison last year because she was *ordered* to do so."

"Why are you telling me this? I thought you didn't like me."

"As I said, I've seen who you are. I've seen how much you love our Ildee. But she is not who she appears to be. Eventually she'll betray us. She'll probably start with you, because you're worth thirty-thousand clutches to her."

"It's– hard to believe. Ildiee already had lots of chances to betray me– all of us– if she wanted to. How do you know she's a spy?"

"Because, as you know, Miranda had a spy in Fellwater, watching the DiAngelo– and it was my job, as the summoner, to handle his messages."

Eric turned away for a moment, to contemplate Ciara's argument.

"I'm sorry, Eric," Ciara told him. "But that's how it is. Now, the whole clan is just outside, waiting for us to come out. Put on your festival-face, and let's go." Then she grinned, and pinched his cheek, and walked away.

They emerged from the chapel, to the applause and delight of the others.

"So why did you close the doors? Did you bless the wine, or did you 'bless the wine'?" cracked Finnbarr. Ildicoe smirked and elbowed him in the ribs.

Eric turned slightly red, but smiled; Ciara laughed. Eric and Ciara took the chalice to everyone in turn, to give them a sip of the wine. When they were done, the Fianna cheered for them, and declared that the coming year would surely be full of all good things. As the ceremony ended, the Fianna went about putting together the biggest feast they had shared since they first landed on the island. By the time the sun was setting, the island's meadows had sprung up with flowers.

~ 49 ~

That evening, as the Fianna sat about the fire, their bellies full of food, and their heads full of mead and wine, Ciara followed Ildicoe back to her cabin. When Ildicoe had removed the beret and the wig that kept her feathers hidden, Ciara shut the door, just loud enough to be startling.

"Ciara! What are–"

"I should never have closed the door on the chapel with no one but Eric in there with me."

Ildicoe reached for the nearest scarf, to tie over her feathers. "Why not?" she asked.

"Because of what he did in there."

"He wouldn't have done anything."

Ciara walked around the cabin, and traced her fingers on some of the scarves and hats that hung on pegs on the wall, and the small collection of wigs that sat on wooden dowls on a desk.

"He didn't touch me, if that's what you mean," said Ciara, "but he wanted to. I could tell."

"Not my Eric," Ildicoe insisted. "Not my man."

"You think not? Less than a year ago, he buried a woman who meant more to him than you do. And besides that, when you ran away without telling him where you were going or how long you would be gone–"

"–I told him, when I got back," Ildicoe informed her.

"–Eric accepted an invitation from another woman, for an evening of what you might call adult entertainment." Ciara stated, without interruption.

"I know," said Ildicoe. "He and I have already argued that out, and forgiven each other. A long time ago."

"And now that he's at peace with you, he's ready to let you go," Ciara said. She combed her fingers through the almond-coloured waves of her hair, and said, "He wants a natural woman now."

Ildicoe silently gaped at Ciara. One of her hands involuntarily reached for her feathers.

"We all know how you are changing," Ciara told her. "There's no point in hiding it. Eric won't say it because he knows you love him, and he doesn't want to hurt you. But in his heart he's already moved on. You should move on too. Set him down gently. While you can both still be friends."

On that note, Ciara tossed her hair over her shoulder, and left the cabin.

~ 50 ~

The cheerful sun that rose in its fairy-tale blue sky did nothing to cheer Ildicoe's mood. Most everyone else, however, brightened along with it, and went to work smiling. Ciara went singing.

As Miranda dug weeds in a vegetable garden, and covered her elbows and knees with soil, she saw a chariot pulled by two horses flying up the river valley toward the island. She walked to the edge to get a closer look. When she recognized the armour that the chariot-driver wore, she ran to the trading post and got her bow and quiver of arrows.

Eric was sitting on the front porch of a nearby cabin, reading a book, when Miranda ran by. "What is it?" she asked.

"I think it's a scout from everyone's favourite Italian clan," she informed him. "He's probably coming to reclaim Elderdown with a new ley-line. My spy told me they're almost finished rebuilding their network."

"Who is your spy? Is it Shinobi? Because he definitely cannot be trusted."

"It's best if I don't say. Just in case someone captures you and sells you for the bounty." When Eric showed her a worried look, she added, "Don't worry, I got your six. It won't happen without a fight."

Eric smiled, and looked down, modestly. Then he gestured toward the flags that lined the avenue from the commons to the rope bridge. "As soon as that chariot gets close enough, they'll see that we've fixed up the place," he noted.

Miranda suddenly quick-marched toward the commons. "Then they'll turn around and come back with an army. Shit! Tell the warriors to get the boats in the air. We need to capture them!"

As she ran for the nearest bastion, where the boats were kept, Eric ran back to the camp to convey Miranda's orders. He found Ciara near the trading post, talking to Síle.

"Get the boats in the air! The DiAngelo are here!"

Ciara and Síle saw the chariot, and sprinted to the bastions. They found Ibrahim, Ildicoe, and Finnbarr, on the way, and pressed them into service. Miranda's curraigh was already airborne, when Ciara's boat took off with Ibrahim and Finnbarr, armed with Ildicoe's rifles. Ildicoe brought the third boat into the chase, with Síle in the front, armed with bow and arrow.

As Miranda predicted, the chariot driver saw what was coming at him, and turned around to make an escape.

"Fire warning shots!" Miranda ordered.

When the charioteer heard the first shots burst around him, he turned and saw the boats darting into the clouds and out of them again at different places. He twisted and banked and spiraled around, to make it harder for the Fianna to catch him. But inside the space of a few heartbeats, Miranda's boat was on top of him, and Ildicoe and Ciara had flanked him. Then Miranda recognized the driver and passenger.

"Turner! Shinobi! Put the chariot on the ground, unless you want to die!"

Paul obliged by steering the chariot downward, then jumping out and vanishing into shadow before he hit the ground.

"I thought only Ildee could do that," said Ciara.

"Capture his chariot," Miranda told her. "If it goes home empty, they'll know something's wrong."

Ciara swung her boat close enough to the chariot to allow Ibrahim to jump into it. When he did, he landed on Shinobi. The two men wrestled with each other: Ibrahim working hard to control the chariot, and Shinobi struggling to throw Ibrahim out. The chariot car knocked side to side, grazing tree branches and bouncing off the rocky cliffsides. The pinnacle of a pine tree got caught the axel, which sharply jolted the chariot to half its speed before it broke away. The two wrestlers crashed to the front of the car. One of the horses broke its tethers and galloped off.

The chariot slowed enough for Ildicoe's curraigh to catch up. Síle, perched in the prow, launched a fairy dart from her bow: it became a spurt of flame as it streaked through the air, and it snapped the tethers holding the second horse. The horse bolted away, and the chariot crashed to the earth.

Shinobi managed to escape Ibrahim's grip and leap away before the chariot struck the ground. He tumbled into a ball and landed solidly on his feet. He gave himself a heartbeat to spot Paul, then ran into the forest.

Ciara and Ildicoe took their boats to round up the two horses. When they were caught, and their bridles roped to the boats, the two pilots landed in the nearest clearing to meet with the other Fianna.

Miranda inspected the damaged chariot, and found a banner-pole, broken from the fall, and a DiAngelo banner folded in a satchel.

Ildicoe looked around for any sign of where the charioteers might have gone. "They could be anywhere now. We'd need an army to find them."

"We have an army," said Miranda. "We have a whole forest full of soldiers."

Miranda sat on the earth and touched the palms of her hands to the soil. She closed her eyes. Branches on nearby trees fluttered in a newly rising breeze. The sounds of insects and birds changed: quieter, yet more alert, and tense. After a few breaths, a flock of sparrows and robins passed overhead. Soon it was joined by crows and ravens, then a few hawks and kestrels, first in pairs and small bands, then in a wide flood of wings and excited cries. Next followed the rangers of the ground: chipmunks and squirrels, then a flock of rabbits, then a family of deer. The seekers spread into the forest where they were soon heard and not seen.

Finnbarr asked, "How did you do that?"

Miranda opened her eyes, and leaned back on a nearby tree. She looked to the sky and smiled. "When you take the time to know someone, and treat them with kindness, they're much more likely to do you a favour when you ask."

"But so many, all at once!" Síle marveled. "That must have taken half the life out of you!"

Miranda closed her eyes again and said, "The land will want this favour returned someday, no doubt."

The wings above and the stampede below grew louder again. Their prey crashed through the ferns and undergrowth, tripping on rocks and whipped by low-hanging branches. They fell directly into the waiting arms of the Fianna. Once captured, the flood of wings and claws circled around, saw that the job was done, and dispersed.

Paul threw up his hands. "All right, you win, I surrender," he shrugged. "But I'll tell you right now, holding us hostage won't do you any good. Someone will eventually come looking for us."

"Oh, boil your head!" Miranda scorned him. She motioned to her companions to take the hostages away. "Put them in the store rooms in the trading post, and nail the doors closed."

When Paul and Shinobi were bundled into a curraigh, Síle noticed that Miranda remained seated on the earth.

"Not coming?" she asked.

"In a moment," Miranda replied.

When the others were gone, Miranda leaned on a tree and sighed with exhaustion. A few bees hummed past. A breeze rustled some of the dead leaves from the previous autumn. She closed her eyes and enjoyed the smell of all the pine and spruce oil carried on the air.

She felt an itch on her scalp. She combed her fingers through her hair to find the source of it, and pulled out a few spruce needles. Then she let the needles slip to the ground, when she noticed a greyish discolouration on her fingers. Her nails had become rough, and brown. She pulled off her boots and socks, and found the same condition affecting her feet and toes.

She let her hands collapse to her sides, and she looked up to a crow that had alighted on a branch nearby.

"So, it's come to me, now," she said to the crow. "Well. I should have known this would happen eventually. Life is only a ripple in river that flows ever on to the sea." Then she stood and shouted, "But I'm not finished with it yet!"

~ 51 ~

Eric saw the flying boats return to the camp, carrying two prisoners, bound at the wrists and ankles. When he noticed Miranda was missing, he ran to meet them. "What happened? Where's Miranda?" he shouted.

"She's coming later. We need to clear out a store room in the trading post," Síle told him.

Eric saw who the two prisoners were, and he laughed.

A store rooms in the trading post was emptied. With Eric and Ildicoe's help, Síle shut Paul and Shinobi into it, and nailed the door closed. Eric and Ildicoe volunteered to stand guard over them for a while.

"You should have taken my offer, Eric. Stayed with the Guardians," said Paul.

"I like these people better," Eric replied.

"You won't get anything in exchange for releasing us," Paul warned. "Carlo will say we were captured because we were weak. He won't take us back."

"That's a clever way to say we may as well let you go," Ildicoe scorned him.

"You might as well," Paul smirked.

Eric looked to Ildicoe and rolled his eyes. He turned to Shinobi. "Why haven't you said anything?"

Shinobi was sitting in a lotus posture in a corner, meditating, and giving no acknowledgment of their presence.

"What the hell's wrong with you!" Ildicoe shouted at him.

"He has no reason to cooperate," Paul said. "Besides. He can't even see you. Witness what our dear leader does to people who fail him," Paul explained.

Eric said, "So, Shinobi, if that is your real name. How long have you been a double agent?"

Shinobi did not move.

"Forget about him, Eric," Ildicoe recommended. "He won't talk to you. He thinks he's being spiritual, by staying silent. He's actually being a *putain!*"

Miranda plodded into the light, with her head down. She was adjusting a pair of leather gloves on her hands.

"There you are!" exclaimed Ildicoe. "They said you stayed on the mainland for a while? Are you all right?"

"I'm grand so," Miranda answered. "Now, I'd like to see our prisoners."

"They're all yours," said Eric, and he let Miranda sit in his chair.

Shinobi said, "Eric, the carriage was–"

"Shut your gob," Miranda ordered him.

Shinobi stopped, and resumed his meditation.

"The longer we hold you," said Miranda. "the more likely they'll send someone after you."

"No, they won't," Paul interjected.

"I said shut it!" Miranda barked at him. "When your boss discovers you didn't plant his banner on our island, he'll send someone else to do it. You're going to tell me how long until that happens."

"I don't have to tell you anything," Paul defied her.

"Then you can stay here until you starve," Miranda shrugged dismissively, and she got up to walk away.

"Hey, aren't we protected by the Geneva Convention, or something?"

"Your own leader says we Hiddenfolk are *above* human laws," Miranda scornfully reminded him.

"All right, I get it, all right," Paul conceded. Then he shifted his posture, attempting to sit up straighter. "You know, the damage you did to our ley lines actually did us a favour," he taunted her. "It gave us time to recruit more people. Our empire has more clans now. Thanks to you!"

Eric sighed. "Knew that would happen," he whispered to Ildicoe.

Miranda picked up a crowbar and marched back to Paul. She held it where he could see it, as she contemplated how to respond to him. Paul scuttled into a corner of his cell.

"There's no reason to hurt me, or do anything to me," he whimpered. "Not like last time. And anyway, I don't have anything you want. I'm only a foot soldier."

"You've been Carlo's war captain ever since you were Awakened," she retorted.

"I was," Paul said. "But when he finds out you held me prisoner like this, he won't take me back. He'll do to me what he did to Shinobi, here."

"Then you have no reason to be loyal to him anymore."

Paul shifted toward her. "If you let me out tonight, I can go back there, and no one will suspect anything. I'll keep my old job. I'll turn spy for you. We both win."

Miranda smiled. "I remember from our last meeting that you're fond of making deals."

"I'll make any deal you want, if you will let me out of here. *And* I'll be your spy."

"You're rather quick to turn on your master. I don't know that I can trust someone whose loyalties are so flexible."

Paul sat back again. "Carlo and the others– they're planning something really big, really soon. And I don't know that I want to be part of it anyway."

"The lifting of the Celtic Mist," Eric said.

"You figured that out, eh? I used to be all gung-ho for it. But in the last few months, I've been standing on guard in front of closed-door meetings with some very-well-dressed people, who almost always end up in the news a few days later. Know what I mean? And, too many to be coincidence. They say it will be worth it in the end. But I don't know. There's even a rumour going around that Kendrick didn't die the way they said he did. That there was a bullet hole in his chest."

Miranda contemplated this news. She said, "In fact he was murdered by Carlo. I saw him do it myself."

Paul digested this news. But a breath later, his earnestness was quickly replaced by a smirk. "I have no reason to believe you," he said.

"I have no reason to make a deal with you." Miranda walked away again.

"Wait! Wait– just– tell me what you're offering."

Miranda turned back to him and said, "You're afraid of something, and it's still not me. Interesting."

"That's not it!" Paul insisted. "It's that– I need a way out."

"You'll be in that box a long while if you don't cooperate."

"I mean, a way out of the New Renaissance! A way out, that doesn't involve Carlo putting a bounty on my head. Or having me thrown in Tartarus– you know what happens to people who spend too much time down there! I need a way to start over."

"I'm still not sure I can trust you, so–" Miranda paused in thought for a moment. Then she jammed the crowbar into the door, and ripped off the planks that held it shut.

"Take Shinobi outside," she ordered Eric and Ildicoe.

"Miranda, what are you doing?"

"Do it, please?"

Eric and Ildicoe shrugged at each other. Then they picked up Shinobi by his armpits and took him away.

When they were gone, Miranda pulled her chair forward and put her face very close to Paul's. "Now, Paul, we're alone. Haven't you always wanted to get me alone?"

"Not like this."

Miranda smiled, and then adopted a businesslike tone. "The deal I'm offering is as follows. You will tell me where Il Duce meets with his messengers and generals. I'll ask Shinobi the same questions. And I won't allow you to talk to each other. If you both tell me something different, I will keep you here until you get your stories straight. If you both tell me the *same* answer, I'll send someone to check it out. And if we find you both spoke the truth, I will let you both go. If it turns out you both told me the same lie, then I will feed you to the werewolves."

Paul "What! That's– that's insane!"

"It's one way to be sure you tell me the truth."

"But what if Shinobi doesn't know? Then we'll both be stuck here until we starve!"

"He knows," Miranda assured him.

"What if I tell you what I *believe* to be true, but it turns out I was wrong?"

"Your boss Carlo is one of the few men allowed to speak directly to Il Duce, is that right?"

"Yes," Paul reluctantly admitted.

"Then you *do* know where he is. Take all the time you need to think about it."

As Miranda stepped away, Paul tried one last argument. "Or I could just sit here and wait until Carlo notices I didn't report in. He'll send an army to destroy this place. He'll take you all prisoners. You will find yourself kneeling before him in less time than you think!"

Miranda marched back to his cell door. "I would rather see half the world burned in a fire storm before I take anyone as my lord and master!"

Paul remembered what Miranda did to Hallowstone, and he believed her.

"He moves around," said Paul. "He doesn't stay in the same place for more than a few days. He lives on board a galley that never comes to land."

"Then where is that galley right now," Miranda demanded.

Paul wrung his hands and shook his head, and looked at her.

~ 52 ~

Outside, Eric and Ildicoe took Shinobi behind the trading post, where they were mostly out of sight of the rest of the camp.

"You know, I trusted you, Shinobi!" Eric growled, as Ildicoe pushed him to the ground. "You were the only person I was allowed to talk to, for months. I did everything you asked of me, while buried in that safe house of yours. Were you waiting for the right moment to sell me to Carlo? And the one time, the *only* time, I asked you to do a favour for me– just to deliver a letter to Miranda– you didn't do it. Why?"

Shinobi said nothing.

"He's not worth your time, Eric," said Ildicoe.

Eric persisted. "And– that night at the temple in Fellwater– why did you lock Ildee and me in the carriage?"

Shinobi perked his head up. "I did not lock you in the carriage," he grunted.

"He speaks!" Ildicoe scorned.

"But it *was* locked!" Eric insisted. "Were you handing us over for the bounty?"

"I am not interested in Il Duce's money," Shinobi replied.

"He must have offered you *something*–"

"I am not who you think I am!" Shinobi swore.

"Now that's the first thing you've said that I actually believe."

"I told you– I'm not the one who picked the carriage. Carlo had taken my eyes from me, so I had to ask for help from–"

Shinobi was interrupted by Miranda's arrival. She grabbed him by the back of his neck and led him away from the camp.

"Don't follow us," Miranda grunted to Eric and Ildicoe. Then she and her captive marched into the trees, where the darkness quickly covered them.

"I think she's leaving him out for the werewolves," Ildicoe said, with a slight tremor of surprise in her voice.

"She wouldn't do that," said Eric.

"I once saw her threaten to cut off Paul Turner's leg with a tourniquet. She is not who you think she is, either."

Eric tried to pretend he didn't here that. "Maybe she's just going to frighten him for a while, to get information from him," he offered.

"Eric, you've known Miranda for only about– what, a year? I've known her for more than two hundred. Most of the time, she is what she appears to be. Fun-loving, honourable, generous. But she's also a Celt. And the Celts can hold a grudge for decades."

Eric leaned on a tree, folded his arms, and looked to the place in the darkness where Miranda disappeared. He pursed his lips for a moment, contemplating his next words, while Ildicoe looked at him, and similarly searched her mind for what to say.

"Ildee– are *you* who you say you are?"

Ildicoe put her shoulders back and perked an eyebrow. "No one knows me better than you, Eric."

"But all those times you went away–"

"I told you, I went looking for the other Voyageurs. In the underworld."

The two lovers looked at each other. Eric softened, and nodded, his hand on his heart. After a heartbeat, Ildicoe looked away.

"Eric, you never did answer my question," Ildicoe eventually said. "Who am I, to you? When you look at me, what do you see?"

Eric remembered that she had asked him a similar question last year. His answer, back then, won her love. Today, he knew the same answer wouldn't work: not for her, nor for him.

"You're wondering if I'm still in love with Katie?" he asked.

"I know you are," she replied. "But are you also in love with me?"

Eric sighed. "I guess I'm no good at *saying* so, am I?"

"Say it now."

Eric collected his thoughts to answer carefully: he knew Ildicoe wanted to hear more than just the words. "Ildicoe Brigand, I love you. I see you sometimes as one so different from myself, that I fear I could never understand you, or that you wouldn't want me. Other times I see you as everything I'm not, but secretly wish that I was. Now, as you know, I don't believe in soul mates. But I do believe in people. People who come together and lift each other up. Make each other into better people than they could ever be on their own. That's who we are, I think. And that is why I love you."

Ildicoe listened and contemplated his words. Her heart beat slightly faster. Eric saw this, and moved closer, to invite her into his arms. She dropped his hands. "So, now that I helped you let go of Katie, you're going to let go of me, too?"

"That's not what I'm saying," Eric complained.

"Then what were you doing that night with Livia?"

Eric's breath held in his throat. "Look, you disappeared for months. I didn't know where you were. I didn't know if you were coming back. Did you know that I went looking for you? Everyone I met told me you didn't want to be found!"

Ildicoe's heart beat heavier again. "No, I didn't know that. But what about yesterday, in the chapel, with Ciara? Why did you shut the door? What were you talking about in there?"

Eric searched for an answer that she would find acceptable, but which didn't reveal what Ciara had actually said. "I thought that was the custom," he answered. "The May Queen and the Laddie are supposed to do it in private. Aren't they?"

"Back in the Middle Ages, maybe. Not today. You didn't– actually–"

"No, no," Eric reassured her. "We used the dagger and the chalice."

Ildicoe smiled, but her expression told Eric she was still troubled.

"You've wanted a chance to talk about this for a while now, haven't you?" he asked her.

"For weeks, yes," she admitted. Then she turned her back to him, took off her hat, unclasped the barrettes that held her wig in place, and dropped them all on the grass. She opened her corset and chemise, and let them slip down, so that Eric could see the feathers on her head were now growing all the way down her spine.

"Do you still think I'm beautiful?" she asked, without turning around.

"I do; I always will," Eric answered. He stepped forward to touch them, but Ildicoe pulled her chemise back over her shoulders.

"But you're not going to want me forever," she said.

"Ildee–!"

"It's true, Eric. Someday soon these things will spread again, and change me completely. You won't recognize me when you see me. It affects the mind too; so I might not recognize you. It might happen all at once. You'll think that I ran away again. Everything about me will be so changed, it will be as if I died."

"You're not dying, Ildee. You're just changing."

"But that's what it feels like! Like I'm dying. You need to think about me as if I had Alzheimer's, or cancer, or– I don't know what to call it. Hiddenfolk disease. You've already had one girlfriend die in front of you. And a child. I can't ask you to watch that happen again. Not when you have most of your life still in front of you. It wouldn't be fair."

Eric reached to her again, but his hand hesitated. His fingers closed, and moved away.

"Ildicoe, I think that we should–"

Footsteps in the forest interrupted Eric's thought. Miranda emerged from the darkness.

"What happened to Shinobi?" Eric asked her. "Is he still out there?"

Miranda said, "No."

Eric and Ildicoe looked at each other. Eric's eyes widened; Ildicoe covered her mouth with her fingers.

"I have another mission for both of you," Miranda told them. "It might be the most important and the most dangerous thing I will ever ask you to do."

"What is it?" asked Eric.

"We can't talk here. Follow me to my cabin."

As they walked, Ildicoe fell a few steps behind Miranda, and said to Eric, "What were you about to say we should do?"

Eric plodded ahead a few steps before speaking. "Nothing. Just nothing."

~ 53 ~

Miranda's cabin walls hung with long sheets of variously coloured fabrics and curtains, and lit with lines of Christmas tree lights. It was barely large enough for a fireplace, a desk, a bed, and a chair. Her two guests managed to find space on the floor near the fire, while she paced to the door and back as she spoke.

"It has to be the both of you on this mission, because you can move about the Hidden World undetected, like no one else. And you work so well together."

Ildicoe looked to Eric, while Eric looked to the floor.

"But I need you both to swear on your honour that you will never tell anyone about this mission," Miranda warned them. "In fact if you're caught, I'll have to deny that I sent you."

"Of course," Eric and Ildicoe both agreed. "Yes."

Miranda continued pacing around the cabin. She rubbed her eyes, and combed her fingers through her hair, and leaned her forehead into the wall, then paced to the door and back again. She tried to introduce the mission, then she would stop, and rub her temples, and begin again.

"Why don't you sit down?" Eric suggested. He and Ildicoe made room for her between them.

Miranda sat down. "The mission is this. We have a chance to face our enemy directly, and finally know him."

"Who do you mean? We already know Heathcliff, and Carlo, and–" said Ildicoe.

"No, I mean the man they answer to. He's never shown his face; we don't even know his name. All we know is his title."

"Il Duce," whispered Ildicoe.

"The very man," Miranda confirmed. "Paul and Shinobi gave me some very valuable intel tonight. They say that Il Duce lives in a fleet of Roman galleys that never come to land. Always on the move. But in two days, his fleet will arrive at the site of a public rally for the Guardians organization. Il Duce will watch the rally from above."

"So where's the rally?"

Miranda smirked as she spoke; Eric and Ildicoe could not tell if she meant amusement or frustration. "Parliament Hill," she reported.

Eric whistled. "It'll be full of people. Hundreds of security cameras, too. We won't be able to get anywhere near him."

"You don't have to get near him," said Miranda. She handed Eric a small leather sack, about the size of his hand, and said, "All I want you to do is hide this somewhere on his galley."

Eric opened the sack. "It's just a broken stone," he observed.

"It's a finderstone," Miranda clarified. "Broken in half. You put that piece on Il Duce's galley. I keep the other piece, and I use it to follow him."

"To *follow* him?"

"That's right."

Eric paused before saying, "A few months ago we all voted *against* this sort of thing. The clan doesn't want to fight anymore. They want to finish building their homes here, and then just live their lives."

Miranda nodded. "But soon they will discover that Paul failed to reclaim Elderdown for their empire. Then they'll send a larger force. I want plenty of warning before that happens."

"That makes sense," Ildicoe said.

Miranda took her bow from its rack on the wall, and rubbed it down with an oiled cloth. "The clan may not want to fight anymore," she said. "But *someone* still has to. They'll understand this, soon enough. Until then, you two shall be my special-ops team. My secret weapons. My daggers in the dark."

Eric and Ildicoe looked at each other, with pursed lips, and perked eyebrows.

~ 54 ~

Shinobi washed his face in the water of a large iron cauldron. Occasionally he would grimace or groan, as the water caused his eyes pain. He splashed more water on his face anyway.

"That's probably enough," said Marla St. David, who sat by a dinner table nearby. "The healing usually needs only a few minutes."

With his eyes still closed, he reached for a towel, and dried his face. Then he turned his eyes to the fireplace, and he saw it.

With outstretched hands, and a growing grin, he stepped closer to the fire, and whispered. "How beautiful– such colours, such elegant movement– how beautiful to *see*!"

Marla said, "Miranda told me not to ask who you are, or how you arrived on the island. But I heard that two of Carlo's agents were captured here today– please tell me you're not one of them."

"I assure you madam, I am loyal to House Kami, and to those my House are sworn to protect. No one else," said Shinobi.

"So, can I ask who you are sworn to protect?"

"Not the DiAngelo, I'll say that much."

Marla nodded. "Glad to hear that, at least."

Shinobi folded the towel and laid it on the back of a chair, near the fireplace. "I'm so sorry for troubling you tonight. I'll never forget the good you've done me here."

He bowed smartly to her, then marched out of the cabin and looked to the stars. He stretched out his arms, turned around in a circle, and laughed.

~ 55 ~

The city was at work.

Engines groaned ahead on green lights and grumbled to a stop on red. Horns blared at anything that fell out of step. The rattle of jackhammers and the sear of angle-grinders flooded over the traffic in some places; in others, the blare of muzak from a shopfront or a streetside vendor owned the air. Metcalfe Street flowed one-way, from south to north, like the history of the world. It began with simple houses, in the shadow of the Museum of Nature's stately battlements, then swept past the many transepts of antique apartment blocks, to the glass and steel skyscrapers of the shadowed apse, and finally to the gothic arches of Parliament itself at the altar. Along the way, hundreds of lawyers, government professionals, petitioners of every kind, all vested in silk ties or high heels, charged ahead from offices to coffee bars to parking lots.

Only when the sun aligned with its length could daylight reach between its northern towers and touch the floor. Today, at that hour, the long shadows of Il Duce's galleys pitted the street and kept it dark. They floated among the towers, along parallel streets and side alleys, swift and quiet as scattered clouds on a lazy day, entirely unknown to the mass below. Their only sound was the fluttering of their sails, and of the flags of House DiAngelo that flew from their masts and sterns. The rectangular glass windows of the office towers reflected their curved organic lines, but only in hard and fragmented squares of steel blue or cloud grey. The largest of the ships was almost as wide as the street. It carried in its midsection a complete Italian villa, richly ornamented with arches, caryatids, and frescoes. From its prow,

Carlo and Heathcliff looked down: Carlo with the ends of his lips curled in victorious pleasure; Heathcliff, with his arms folded and his brow concerned.

"One thing I will miss, when the Great Work is done," said Carlo, "is entering big cities like this, with not a single soul beneath us aware of our presence at all. How all these people's lives are about to change. How they have no idea."

Heathcliff waved to the tower that housed the Business Development Bank of Canada, and said, "There are men in these towers who can move mountains with a word, no less than the gods once did. It's not magic. It's economics: the most powerful force of nature known to mortal man. Do you really think we will be able to control it, when the Work is done?"

"Oh yes," Carlo grinned. "When the Shadow-Spell disappears, time-shares of access to the Sources will become a tradable security. A scarce resource, in high demand. And we will have a near-monopoly on supply."

"Curious to hear you say that. I thought you weren't interested in money."

"I'm interested in justice. Money is a means to that end. Only a fool thinks it's an end in itself."

"Ha! And the world is composed of fools, isn't it?" Heathcliff chuckled agreeably.

Carlo leaned on the railing of the ship and looked to the city below. "We'll take the smartest, the strongest, and the best of them, and we'll bring them to our temple, where they will see world as it was when the gods were still young. They'll see the foolishness of their culture, and the necessity of our leadership. Instead of competing for money or fame, they'll compete for greatness, and a place at our side. The weak shall no longer shackle the strong. But the strong will take care of everyone. It's we who know their needs better than they do, after all. You won't recognize this country when we're finished with it. But it will be the way the gods always intended."

When the galley reached the corner of Metcalfe and Wellington streets, it turned west, and skirted the edge of the grass on Parliament Hill. Below, a gaggle of hippies launched out of a city bus, carrying *djembes* and congas, wearing beards and sandals. They joined a growing crowd that moved to the front steps of Parliament, for the Guardian's rally.

Heathcliff nodded toward them and said, "What about the rest of humanity? There's a risk that when the shadow falls, they'll discover that–"

"Of course, there's that risk. But it will be easy to control them. Because we already do."

A rambunctious host of people gathered by the foot of Parliament, jumping and dancing along to the rock rhythms bursting from a temporary stage at the top of the stairs. Many in the crowd waved the flag of the Guardians; many more held home-made protest signs demanding that the Guardians Organization receive tax-exempt status as an official religion.

The only motionless figure in the throng was the band's lead singer, who held herself almost perfectly still; her ankles crossed, her wrists leaning on her microphone stand, her voice crooning the lyrics of a modern rock anthem. A yellow-white aura radiated from her flesh and hair: the hero-light, that only the Awakened could create, and which all others would never remember having seen. In a large ornamental urn behind her stood a tree sapling, no taller than herself, glowing with a similar aura. As Carlo and Heathcliff watched, a few people in the audience spontaneously lit up with a hero-light of their own. Whenever that happened, handlers dressed in priestly robes and hooded tabards took them to an unmarked tent at the edge of the grass.

"We should have thought of this centuries ago," said Carlo.

The galley sailed alongside Parliament's West Block building. The crew extended a gangway to its roof.

Heathcliff said, "I better go. I hope you have a good view of the rally." Then he stepped down the gangway and entered the tower through a maintenance door on the roof. Moments later, he emerged through the building's front doors, and strolled to the edge of the stage. His outfit had changed: he now wore a cherry-red suit, with a maroon bow tie, and a grad gown patterned with images borrowed from ancient Greek pottery. He smiled and shook hands with those nearest to him, and he doffed his top hat and bowed whenever someone commented on his outfit. When the band finished the song, he took the microphone from the singer. The crowd erupted in cheers for him. Someone started chanting "Magnum Opus Facimus! Magnum Opus Facimus!" When most of the crowd had joined the chant, Heathcliff replied with "Avete, Il Duce!" The crowd responded with happy screams, and a vigorous chant of "Avete, Il Duce! Avete, Il Duce!"

"Friends, thank you so much for coming today. It's so wonderful to see so many of you, here in the nation's capital. Since we took this show on the road, we've been to many wonderful places, and met many amazing people. But the people we love the most, and always come back to, are right here in downtown Oh-Town!"

The audience roared their approval for this. Many shouted out that they loved Heathcliff too. More flags emblazoned with the brand of the Guardians Organization appeared over their heads.

Above, on the deck of the galley, Carlo smirked. "He says that everywhere we go, and they fall for it every time."

~ 56 ~

From inside a parked tour bus on Wellington Street, Eric and Ildicoe had an excellent view of the rally, and of Heathcliff's arrival.

"The tree on the stage glows like the one in Rath Manannan," Ildicoe observed.

"It doesn't look healthy. The leaves are turning brown."

"If it *is* a cutting from the Druid's Tree, it won't survive long. It needs to be planted in sacred earth, not in a pot. Oh– if you get too close to it, don't look directly at it."

"Why not?"

"You won't be able to look away."

Eric looked to the sky, and saw the fleet of Roman galleys converging around the square. "So, Il Duce's in one of those ships," he said.

"That one, I bet," said Ildicoe, pointing to the one with the Italian villa on its deck, moored to Parliament's West Block.

Eric had Miranda's field telescope, and he studied the galley. "It looks like Carlo's the only one on deck."

"Getting on board should be easy for you, with your talisman," said Ildicoe.

"The hard part will be getting through the crowd below," Eric noted. "This talisman won't help me if Nicholas is there."

Ildicoe borrowed the telescope and studied the crowd, looking for Nicholas, or anyone else who might be a problem. Finding no one, she closed the telescope and smiled.

"If we stay to the edge of the hill, we should be fine. Let's go."

~ 57 ~

With the rally underway, the lane that surrounded the grass of Parliament Hill was less crowded. A small group of people clustered around the Centennial Flame; another small group took photographs of each other with various monumental buildings in the background. Eric and Ildicoe pulled hoods over their heads, and kept their eyes fixed on their destination.

From the stage on the front steps of the Centre Block, Heathcliff's excited voice held the attention of the crowd.

"The Guardians have always stood up for justice. But what is justice, really?" he crooned. "That's one of mankind's oldest questions. There are thousands of answers, but they all eventually arrive at the same conclusion. Justice is what you get when the world is ruled by the right kind of leader. Nearly everyone agrees about that– what people *disagree* about is exactly who or what the right kind of leader truly is. Is he an elected president? Is he an hereditary king? Is he a capitalist? A socialist? Or even a communist? People say no one knows. We Guardians, however: we've figured this out, haven't we?"

The crowd enthusiastically answered him: "It's the artists! The dreamers! The creative people! It's us!"

"That's right. The enlightened ones. The Awakened. We shall soon see the day when the stone the builders rejected shall become the corner stone. But wait! There are still some among you who *doubt*. Still a few skeptics, still a few cynics, even among those who have been with us since the beginning. I can see them, hanging around the edges."

Eric suddenly wondered if Heathcliff could see him.

"You can always tell the disbelievers," Heathcliff continued. "They're the ones with the blinders on. The coloured glasses–" Heathcliff donned a pair of clownish neon-green sunglasses, three times too big for his face, "–that filter out what they don't want to see, and hold them back from their own success. Which would be nothing of anyone else's concern, if only they weren't holding back the rest of us with them. So as we rally here to demand our rights, let's look around, and see if you can spot any *greyfaces* in the crowd! Look around, you'll see them, pretending they're too cool for this. Look around!"

"There's one!" shouted someone close to Eric. The cluster of people nearest the accuser began chanting "Greyface, greyface, greyface!"

"Bring him up here to the stage," Heathcliff ordered.

Eric saw six people roughly grab a young man with a sports logo on his hat and a panicked expression on his face. "Greyface, greyface!" they shouted at him, as they pulled him deeper into the crowd.

"There's another one right there," Heathcliff laughed, as he pointed at someone else in the crowd. "He's still thinking he can merely watch without getting involved. Freeloader and wallflower– bring him up to the stage!"

Those nearest the man Heathcliff singled out pointed at him and shouted "Greyface, greyface!" More pairs of hands grabbed him and lifted him off his feet, to carry him to the front of the rally.

Next Heathcliff selected two women who were declining the gift of a Guardian's flag. "And what about that pair of greyfaces, right over there! Still attached to their ignorance. Looking down their noses at us. Let's educate them!"

The two women grasped each others hands and tried to walk away. But a line of uniformed bodies blocked their path. Within seconds, they were herded to the front of the stage, where hundreds of people could point at them. The chant of "Greyface, greyface!" grew louder with each new victim dropped at Heathcliff's feet.

Still wearing his green sunglasses, Heathcliff held his microphone high and sang, "God, I love my job!"

Eric didn't want to be the next greyface. He took Ildicoe's hand and picked up their walking pace. Ildicoe pulled her hood down further over her head. They pushed their way through the stragglers on the edge of the crowd, many of whom tried to tag them as greyfaces and draw them back into the square. Ildicoe put her head own and ran; Eric pushed a few people out of his way as he followed. One person managed to grasp Ildicoe's wrist and slow her down. Eric freed her by threatening her captor with his dagger. They reached the curb of the laneway that surrounded the grass of Parliament Hill, just across from West Block. From this vantage they saw a team of riot police on horseback trotting toward the hill. The nearest Guardians shouted warnings: "The cops are here, the cops are here!"

On the stage, an aid whispered something into Heathcliff's ear. He acknowledged it, then took off the glasses and addressed the crowd again. "Friends, let us remember that we are exercising our constitutional right to peaceful assembly. Let us recite our Guardians Code, so that the brave men in blue over there, and these sadly misguided people here, can know who we truly are."

The chanting of "Greyface" subsided, as most people in the crowd held hands with whoever was standing nearest. A new chant, led by Heathcliff, flowed from them: "We pledge ourselves to the Great Work. Of building the Beautiful City. And to the wisdom and justice for which she stands—"

As the crowd recited its oath of loyalty to Il Duce, Eric and Ildicoe reached the steps of the office block where Carlo's galley was moored. They turned back to look at the crowd one last time. Some of the Guardians delivered a particularly rebellious "greyface" to the police; they arrested him for participating in an unlawful assembly.

"But you're supposed to protect *me* from *them!*" the man howled.

"Valeo, Il Duce!" the officer replied, as he cuffed the protester and helped him into the back of a squad car.

"Let's keep moving," Eric recommended to Ildicoe, and she followed him into West Block. Inside, they let themselves breathe normally again, and tried to relax. Ildicoe found a decorative brass plaque that was shiny enough that she could discretely adjust the wig that concealed her feathers. Eric leaned on the wall nearby, and looked out a nearby window. The view of the rally was obstructed by cars and trees. Most people in the lobby were going about their business as if nothing unusual was happening outside at all.

A commissionaire approached Eric and Ildicoe and said, "May I help you?"

Ildicoe said, "Yes, sir, thank you, could you tell us how to get on the roof of this building?"

"Do you have a security pass?"

"What's that?"

Eric stepped to the side and said, "The roof of a building like this is usually off limits to the public."

"How was I to know that? I don't leave the Hidden World very often," Ildicoe said. She showed the commissionaire her Voyageurs amulet and said, "Which way to the roof?"

The commissionaire, with a slightly dazed look in his eye, said, "The stairwell, just down the hall."

As they walked away, Eric looked back and saw the commissionaire shake himself. "Is that some kind of Secret People mind control device?" Eric asked.

"Not exactly. We Voyageurs helped create the Commissionaires, but thanks to the Shadow Spell they only remember it when they see our badge."

"That's going to change if Carlo gets his way."

"Haven't decided what I think of that, yet. Come, let's hurry."

They took the stairwell that led to the roof. Once they were outside again, they hid behind some tarpaulin sheets on a construction scaffold, and spied on the Roman galley moored on the edge.

"Looks like there's only one centurion on the gangway," said Ildicoe. "And Carlo has gone back inside."

"They're probably counting on the shadow-spell to keep intruders out," Eric guessed.

"It won't keep us out," Ildicoe winked. She stood and walked toward the ship.

"Ildee, what are you–" Eric hissed, but he stopped himself in case the centurion could hear him. The soldier noticed Ildicoe right away, and raised his carbine to ward her off.

"Stop right there, or I'll– holy shit, aren't you–"

From Eric's point of view, it appeared that Ildicoe took the centurion's face in her hands, whispered something to him, and then slung his arm over her shoulder as they walked together on to the galley into the villa on its midship. As Eric watched, Ciara's warning about Ildicoe came to his mind.

A moment later, Ildicoe emerged from the villa and walked down the gangway again. "Come on, Eric, let's go!"

"How did you get rid of the guard so easily? Do you know him, or something?" he said to her.

"No, I just knew what to say to him," she replied.

"What– like, a pass word, or a call sign, or–"

"Eric, we don't have much time!"

Eric took the omamori from his pocket and considered putting it on in order to hide, not from Carlo, but from Ildicoe. Then he looked down, and saw that Heathcliff was introducing another entertainer to the stage. He followed her on to the galley and into the villa.

They passed through a narrow vestibule into a cloistered atrium, open to the sky above, with portals along its sides leading to various rooms. Caryatids and busts of characters in Roman history stood wherever there was a space for one. Climbing vines grew from large pots in the corners. Directly across from the vestibule, and above an arch with two double doors, there stood a tall square tower.

"Where is everybody?" asked Eric.

"What do you mean?"

"If this is where Il Duce himself holds his court, wouldn't you expect more people? More security, for one thing. And secretaries, lawyers, communications people. But instead, there's nobody."

He opened a nearby door off the atrium. It led to a kitchen, equipped well enough to feed the ships crew, but everything was put in its shelf or hanging hook, as if nothing had been used since the last spring cleaning.

"Something's not right," he said.

Through the doors below the tower, Ildicoe could hear the sound of Carlo's voice, arguing with someone. She waved to Eric to join her; they crept closer to try to hear more.

"No, you have already been told, no. The answer isn't any different just because it's a different day. Our timetable is not open for negotiation," Carlo said.

"Do you have any idea how hard it will be to change *my* timetable?" said a female voice.

Carlo's argument continued. "Some of the people you answer to are rallying in front of the Peace Tower at this very moment. If you cannot deliver your promise on time, you'll have that rally camped on your front door every day, and all night, until you deliver," he insisted.

"I want to speak with the boss," demanded the second voice. "I should be negotiating directly with him, and not with his messenger."

"Il Duce does not receive unscheduled visitors."

"He doesn't receive visitors at all. That's the problem."

"No one comes to the boss. The boss comes to you. And only in his own time."

"But he's only just upstairs, isn't he? If I'm going to hand him the kind of power he wants, then I want to meet him."

Ildicoe nudged Eric. "Il Duce is in that tower!" she exclaimed. Eric looked. He couldn't see anyone up there.

The doors beneath the tower opened. Ildicoe gasped in surprise, then ducked behind a column. She inhaled and held her breath, and her form faded into shadow. A door opened and closed; Eric assumed that's where Ildicoe went to hide and observe. Eric tripped over a clay urn in his rush to hide with her. By the time he righted it, Ildicoe had shut herself in a kitchen. He fumbled with the omamori in his pocket, and got it over his head just as Carlo entered the atrium.

Carlo was accompanied by a middle-aged woman with short blonde hair and an unflattering business suit.

"Everyone will get to meet him soon enough," Carlo muttered. "You will have to be patient, just like everyone else."

"You still need me to make your Magnum Opus legal," said the woman. "And my request is not unreasonable."

"I could have you *disenchanted*, and accomplish my goals without you," Carlo threatened.

The woman regarded him for a moment. She tapped her heel on the marble floor, to give herself time to think. Then she said, "Good day, Mr. DiAngelo."

"Good day, Madam Smallfoot. Until next time."

Eric suddenly remembered who the woman was.

The woman left the galley. Carlo watched them go, then noticed the urn that Eric had tripped on was out of place. He set it back where it belonged, and looked around the atrium carefully. Eric grasped the *omamori*, and held his breath, as Carlo looked directly at him.

A moment later, Carlo shrugged off his suspicion, and returned to the tower. Eric removed the omamori, and Ildicoe emerged from the kitchen.

"That was Edith Smallfoot!" said Eric.

"Who?"

"A federal politician," Eric explained. "I've seen her in the news recently."

"She's one of us, too. One of the Hidden. Did you see that?" Ildicoe observed.

"No, I didn't. But I wouldn't have. I'm not– you know."

Ildicoe acknowledged this with a nod, but she touched his arm, to reassure him. Eric patted her hand, then brushed it away.

"Let's just plant the finderstone and get the hell out of here," she said.

Eric buried the finderstone in the soil of one of the potted trees in the atrium. "It still bothers me that there's hardly anyone on board. Just Carlo, and one guard. Something's not right. I want to look around."

They crept to the double doors through which Carlo had gone. Beyond it they found a small chamber with a steep wooden staircase, leading to the tower above, and the under-deck below. Eric peeked into the underdeck, and saw a single centurion, possibly the same one who had been guarding the gangway, sitting on one of the crates and leaned on the wall. Eric grasped his *omamori*, ready to put it on if the centurion turned around. The galley shuddered, and tilted slightly to one side. Eric and Ildicoe steadied themselves on the railing of the stair. Beneath them, the centurion fell off his crate, and a beer bottle in his hands dumped its contents on the floor.

"Good job with him," Eric grinned to Ildicoe.

"It wasn't hard, really," Ildicoe grinned back.

The galley righted itself, and the two intruders continued exploring. Behind the stairs they found an elegant office, with a writing desk and several chairs for guests in the centre. A laptop computer on the desk played a slide show of Renaissance art photographs, for its screen-saver. The walls were lined with glass cabinets containing books and framed photographs. Light entered from small scrim-curtained windows along the ceiling. Between the cabinets, the pine-paneled walls carried a collection of Venetian carnival masks.

"I've seen these masks before," said Eric. "In the basement of Carlo's mansion, back in Fellwater."

"They're dopplefaces. Perfect disguises." said Ildicoe.

Eric found among them three gold-plated, bejeweled masks clustered on the far wall, behind the desk. "Il Duce's messengers use these ones. So do those New Renaissance judges," he said. He took one off the wall and examined it more closely. His mind returned to the trial he endured in the fall of the previous year, where he was almost convicted of crimes he didn't commit. The thought of stealing one tempted him.

"Best to put them back," Ildicoe advised. "Their absence will be noticed right away."

The galley shifted and tilted again.

"What's happening!" Eric wondered. He steadied himself with a nearby cabinet, then put the mask back on the wall. A paper envelope on the desk slid to the floor. Ildicoe picked it up and read the label: "K.P. Timetable. Counter-Proposal. And a file number, and today's date."

She opened the file and found a series of documents with government letterhead. "*Tabernac!* Eric, that politician we saw was the Minster of Foreign Affairs!"

Eric whistled, impressed. "And you say she's one of the Hiddenfolk now?"

Ildicoe nodded. "It seems they are Awakening people in order to control them. Imagine that: enlightenment itself as a weapon of oppression."

"Let's take that envelope with us and study it later. Carlo would have thrown it out anyway. He won't miss it."

Ildicoe nodded; Eric put the envelope in his coat pocket.

"And– I think we've been here long enough, now. Let's go," said Ildicoe.

As they left the office, Eric looked up the stairs leading into the tower. Ildicoe took his hand and led him into the atrium. But Eric's attention remained on the tower.

"Wait, Ildee," he said.

Ildicoe shook her head. "Eric, it's too dangerous. It's probably a trap."

"You think so?"

"That might explain why it was so easy for us to get here."

Eric kept his eyes looking up. "I want to find out who he is. We don't have to confront him. Just get his photograph, maybe. We might never get this chance again."

Ildicoe sighed, and conceded the point. "Keep your talisman ready, in case you have to escape quickly."

"If that happens, I'll meet you at the safe house."

Ildicoe nodded. Then they climbed the steps into the heart of the tower. Eric cringed with each creak of the floorboards beneath his steps. A trap door lay at the top of the stair. There was no way to open it without alerting anyone who may already be up there. They paused, and looked at each other. The galley tilted to one side again. From above, they heard the sound of something shifting around.

"I'll go first," said Ildicoe. She held her breath. Her form faded into a shadow. She crept up the stairs, pushed the trapdoor open as narrowly as possible, and slid into the chamber at the top of the tower.

A moment later, she opened the trapdoor widely, and then climbed down the stair again. She made no effort to hide. She looked at Eric, sighed, and shook her head.

"What?" asked Eric.

"There was– the tower's empty. Nobody here," Ildicoe told him.

"No one?"

"See for yourself."

Eric pulled on his hair for a moment. "I don't understand. We heard Carlo say his boss was up there."

"Maybe he lied," Ildicoe speculated. "Maybe this galley is only a decoy."

Eric looked away, through the atrium and toward the front door of the villa. There were still some areas that he hadn't searched, but he now believed he didn't have to. He glowered at Ildicoe and said, "Or– maybe– the reason he's not up there is because this ship is a trap. Not for both of us. Only for me."

The force of Eric's gaze made Ildicoe step bak from him. "What do you mean?" she asked.

"I've been thinking. Maybe the reason there was only one guard on this ship, and maybe the reason you sweet-talked him into letting us on board so easily, is because he knew you were coming."

"Eric, make sense."

"Just like the locked carriage back at Fellwater. Maybe *you* were the one who locked it, so that when Carlo arrived, he could pay you the bounty for my capture right away."

"That's– Eric that's ridiculous!"

"Maybe as soon as I go up those stairs and into the tower to see for myself, I'll find a dozen soldiers waiting to arrest me. And Nicholas will be right there, to point out where I am, so I can't use the talisman to hide."

Ildicoe turned around in a circle, frustrated and shocked by Eric's words. She pulled off her wig and threw it at him. "Is it because of the way I'm changing? Is this your way of breaking up with me, and making it seem like my fault?"

"Ildee, your feathers have nothing to do with it."

"These *things* growing on my head are my most important secrets, Eric. This is the one part of my life where I'm honestly terrified of what might happen to me. I need a boyfriend I can trust as I change, and I need him to trust me in return."

"But how can I?" Eric retorted, as he threw her wig back at her. "This might be the *second* time you've led me into a trap."

"Eric, I'm not conspiring against you. I love you!"

This silenced Eric's argument.

"But I know you don't love me anymore," Ildicoe continued. "And it's all right. I suppose I can't expect a man like you to love me for who I really am. Not the way I'm changing. I'm Hiddenfolk– I could never possibly be what you imagine I am, or want me to be."

Eric sniffled before speaking. "So, now, this is your way of breaking up with me?"

"Since it's obvious that you don't love me anymore."

Eric stepped closer to her. He saw that he had hurt her, and wanted to make amends. "But I *do*, Ildee," he said.

"You just accused me of being a spy. So, no, you don't."

Eric sniffled again, and rubbed his temples. "Look, I'm scared too. I'm scared that some bounty hunter will find me and turn me in. I'm scared that there's something wrong with this galley– I don't know why there's nobody here, and I don't like not knowing things. I trusted Shinobi for months, but he turned out to be a spy. Then Ciara told me–"

Ildicoe looked away. "I don't think you can talk your way out of this one, Eric."

"So what do you want me to do?"

Ildicoe gritted her teeth as she spoke. "I want you to go up those stairs and into the tower. You'll see there's *nobody* waiting to arrest you. Will that be enough to prove whatever you want me to prove?"

"It will," Eric agreed.

"Go on, then. See for yourself."

Eric moved to the foot of the stairs, and paused to give Ildicoe time to come with him. She remained where she was.

"I hope you're right, Ildee. I really do," he said. He slipped the omamori over his head, and pushed open the trap door.

The top chamber in the tower was, indeed, empty of people. A table stood in the centre, with maps and writing instruments. Nearby, a GPS device had fallen to the floor. Looking out the open windows, Eric saw Carlo and Heathcliff standing together on the galley's prow, deep in discussion with each other. He did not see any soldiers.

Eric leaned his head on the wall, and tried to swallow a wave of weakness that enervated his muscles. "Oh, I am a shitbag," he whispered to himself. "I've just done to Ildee what Carlo did to me. Accused her of a crime she didn't commit. What's wrong with me?"

Looking around again, Eric saw that the galley had left its mooring by the office block, and was now gently sailing over the Rideau canal, toward the river. The fleet of smaller galleys followed.

"Shit!"

He dashed back down the stairs and into the atrium, and tore off his omamori. "Ildiee, they've set sail again. We can't get off–"

Then Eric noticed that Ildicoe was gone. He checked in all the doors leading off. One opened to a set of stairs leading to the galley's wheel house, just above the vestibule. Others led to the kitchen, another office, and a shrine to the Roman god Jupiter. But Ildicoe was gone.

~ 58 ~

Ildicoe ran across the grass of Parliament Hill, away from West Block. She jumped across Wellington Street, sprinting fast enough to dodge the oncoming traffic, and skidded to a stop in the outdoor patio of a restaurant. Ciara was waiting for her there.

"It's done," said Ildicoe. "But they're heading down the river. Eric is still on board."

Ciara nodded. She took out her cell phone, picked a number from the address book, and called it. "Miranda? It's done. The finderstone is in place." When she heard Miranda acknowledge this, she hung up.

Ildicoe twitched slightly. "Why didn't you tell her about Eric?"

"He's a big boy, he can take care of himself."

~ 59 ~

Miranda sat on the pinnacle of the National Art Gallery's glass tower; a position that gave her a perfect view of the DiAngelo ships as they left Parliament Hill and followed the river. She acknowledged Ciara's message, then turned off her cellphone and dropped it beside her. She produced the other half of the finderstone from a pouch on her belt. It hung from the end of a short chain, and spun around, so that its broken face pointed in the direction of Carlo's galley.

"I should have known it would be the biggest one," she whispered to herself. She stood, and pulled her Bann-Shee hood over her head, inhaled sharply, and reached out with grasping hands, one toward a nearby cloud, the other toward Carlo's galley.

The cloud began to crackle and spit with electricity.

~ 60 ~

On board the galley, Eric climbed down the tower stairs, and sat on the bottom step. He put the *omamori* back on, just in case Carlo or Heathcliff came in. Then he retreated to the office in the back of the villa, and locked the door behind him. He sat in a chair, and contemplated his new situation.

He looked at the three golden masks on the far wall. "According to Shinobi, only three people were ever allowed to speak to Il Duce directly," he mused aloud.

In a cabinet near them, he saw a framed photo of Carlo and two other young men. He had seen this picture last year, also in Carlo's mansion, he recalled. Carlo must have taken it out before the house burned down, along with all these other things. Eric took it out of the cabinet and looked at it more closely. This time, he recognized the other two men beside Carlo: Heathcliff. Kendrick. As he put the picture back in its cabinet, he noticed the masks on the wall again. Eric's mind raced. *Carlo said the messengers wear masks so that you never know when the messenger is really the boss-man himself. He also said Il Duce might be someone I already know. Might have been the man himself as the chief judge at that trial. But Carlo and Heathcliff were there, so it can't be one of them. And it can't be Kendrick because a messenger came with him to the rail tunnel, where he was arrested. Well, it could be Kendrick, if that messenger wasn't the man himself– no, it can't be him, because he's dead now. Who else? A woman– Livia Julia, maybe? No, can't be her; Kendrick was poisoning her to keep her at home. Who else, then? Paul? Nicholas? No, they're not smart enough. Is it someone I don't know? Was Carlo wrong about that? Maybe, but– oh! Oh! Now that's a possibility! How smooth! And now that I think of it, how obvious. I'm such an idiot for not seeing it sooner. Need more evidence, to be certain. But I think–*

I think I know who Il Duce is.

~ 61 ~

Miranda exhaled. A lightning bolt arced from the cloud and struck the galley. Thunder blasted the sky, and shook every window in the downtown core. Fragments of wood and stone erupted from the side of the galley where the bolt struck it, leaving behind a charred and blackened hole. Smaller sparks chased each other around its hull, and sputtered away.

Inside the office, Eric screamed involuntarily, mostly from surprise than from pain. He climbed under the desk and covered his ears. Some of the cabinets fell over, as the ship jolted to the side.

At the restaurant patio, Ciara and Ildicoe heard the thunder, and jumped to their feet. "Thunder that loud, on a mostly sunny day?" Ciara mused.

"Hiddenfolk battle-spells," Ildicoe named it. The two of them ran down the street, toward the canal and then the riverside paths, to find out what was happening.

~ 62 ~

On the main deck of the galley, Carlo and Heathcliff fell to their feet. Carlo opened his cell phone and shouted into it, "All captains, protect the flagship! Move in closer! Find whoever's doing this!"

Heathcliff crawled to the gunwales and looked around the city and the river banks below. He spotted the Bann-Shee standing on the art gallery, and pointed her out to Carlo. "It's Miranda!" he shouted.

Carlo looked, and saw. "Get inside the villa. We'll be safer there."

They ran into the villa, slammed the door behind them, and ran for the office.

"Why did you lock the office?" Carlo demanded.

"I didn't!"

Carlo grimaced at him, then kicked the door down.

Eric saw them enter. He trusted his *omamori* to keep him hidden, but he crawled behind a cabinet that had shifted out of place when the lightning bolt hit the ship.

"I told you we should have brought more security on board with us," Heathcliff said Carlo.

"Miranda is not a serious threat anymore," Carlo scoffed.

"She could destroy this ship, with us on board!" Heathcliff countered.

"But she can't stop what we're doing. The Work almost runs by itself now. Victory is inevitable."

A second thunderclap boomed; a second lightning bolt struck the galley. It ripped a hole in the wall of the villa, near the atrium. More sparks danced across the hull. A sickening feeling gripped the stomachs of everyone on board, as the ship lost altitude.

"Where's the damned pilot!" Carlo shouted. He struggled out of the office and found the lone centurion guard at the foot of the stairs in the galley hold below. He climbed down for a closer look.

"Is he there? Is he dead?" asked Heathcliff.

Carlo felt the soldier's neck and wrist for a pulse. Then he checked to see what Heathcliff's line of sight was. Seeing he was sufficiently hidden, Carlo took the man's head in his hands, and swiftly twisted his neck.

"He's dead," Carlo confirmed. Then he took out his cellphone again. "Captain Pollux: can you see the damage to the flagship?"

Pollux's voice came through the phone: "The second strike hit your atrium, and ripped a hole straight through to the bottom. Sorry sir, but as soon as you hit the water, you'll sink."

Eric, hearing where the lightning bolt struck, realized that the lightning was following the finderstone.

"Bring your ship alongside when we crash, so you can pick us up," Carlo ordered Pollux. "All other captains: stay close. One of you has to take the next hit, so that Il Duce can get off this ship safely."

"Carlo–," said Heathcliff, as they returned to the office, "When they rescue us, they'll find out that Il Duce's not really here."

Eric, still hiding behind a cabinet, moved out as far as he thought was safe, to better hear how Carlo would respond.

"No, they won't," said Carlo. "We'll tell them he escaped on his own. They don't need to see him to believe what we say about him. That's the beauty of followers who have faith."

The ship lurched again. Carlo, Heathcliff, and Eric reached for the nearest wall to steady themselves.

"I think we just hit the river," said Heathcliff. "Let's get outside. I don't want to be trapped in here when it fills with water."

"I'll take the messenger masks. We can't let them go down with the ship."

Carlo picked up a briefcase from the floor where it had fallen, and put the three golden masks in it. Then from a hidden pocket in the same case, he took out an antique wheel-lock pistol.

Heathcliff reached the threshold of the office when he heard Carlo cocking the hammer on the pistol. He turned around. "What are you doing, Carlo?"

"As I told you a moment ago: the Work almost runs by itself now."

"So?"

"That means it doesn't need you anymore."

Heathcliff glared at Carlo for a moment, and then began to laugh. "You're funny!" he said. "Because that means it doesn't need *you*, either!"

Carlo chuckled along with his brother. "But it still needs Il Duce."

"He has served us well, hasn't he? The myth of the mysterious leader, all knowing, and wise, and perfect."

"He has, indeed," Carlo grinned. Carlo took a brush from the briefcase and cleaned the barrel of his pistol. "We've been telling each other that story for a long time now, haven't we?"

"Like that time when we were kids, just after your father adopted Kendrick and me," said Heathcliff. "We liked to pretend that our real father was someone else, and that he'd come for us the next day. He'd take us to his secret empire, where each of us would have a kingdom of our own."

Carlo put the brush away and loaded a bullet down the pistol's muzzle. "And nobody would ever tell us what to do, ever again."

Across the room, Eric's eyes widened. He looked at Carlo and Heathcliff, then at the framed photo of the three young men that sat in a nearby display case.

"We're almost finished turning our fantasy into reality," Heathcliff mused. "Did you see the size of the rally today? That was the biggest one yet."

"I did see it," Carlo smiled, as he loaded a small cartridge of gunpowder into the pistol's pan. "I wonder if you remember:

there was another part of that story we used to tell. The part about how the day came when the father died. And the three brothers couldn't agree on which of them should replace him as king. For a while, they ruled together, as a triumvirate, just as in the days of the old Roman Republic. The first ruled the earth, the second ruled the sky, and the third ruled the sea."

"Just like Hades and Jupiter and Poseidon," Heathcliff named them.

"But the realms of earth and sea were so badly managed that they *fell*, and the outsiders took over."

Heathcliff began laughing again, although a touch of strain entered his voice. "I recall that part of the story differently."

Carlo polished the pistol with a silken cloth as he spoke. "I remember it *perfectly.* I was *there* when it happened. It goes like this. A foreign army invaded the realms of earth and sea, when their princes were too busy feasting in their castles to notice. That invading army carried weapons that the brothers had never seen before: weapons like shopping malls, theme parks, televisions. And all of it disposable! Well, the third brother resolved that no such new modern army would invade *his* realm, in the sky. But an intelligent strategist never attacks a stronger force head-on. Instead he seduces his enemies. He gives them wine and music. He builds temples for their gods. He lets his enemy think he's a friend. Eventually, his enemy grew to love him, and they made him their king. After all, why fight and destroy your enemy, when you can rule him instead?"

Heathcliff kept his smile on his face, but his eyes on Carlo's pistol. "What became of the other two brothers?"

"Oh, for a time the three worked together, in this new kind of soft-power war," Carlo said, as he tested all the moving parts of his pistol. "but the brother who ruled the sky soon realised that his other two brothers would soon want more power. One of them would eventually betray the other two. It is the natural way of things. The only thing to do about it is move against one's enemies, before they move against you."

Heathcliff chuckled. "Funny story," he said.

"Did I frighten you?" Carlo grinned.

"Oh yes," Heathcliff laughed. "Even after all these years, you can still get to me. But it's all meant in fun, right? All just a joke, right?"

"That's right, Heathcliff. The truth is that the brother who ruled the earth died in a cave-in, beneath a castle. And the brother who ruled the sea died in a sinking ship."

Heathcliff's smile disappeared. "Carlo, what really happened to Kendrick?" he asked.

"I killed him, of course."

Heathcliff's mouth gaped open, and then curled into laughter again. "Oh, Carlo, you pantaloon! You had me believing you were going to shoot me next! Or leave me to drown here, when this ship goes under."

"That's why there's no guards on this ship. No witnesses. And a suspect with an impeccable reputation; no one would believe that I did it. The perfect crime."

Heathcliff laughed. Carlo laughed. Heathcliff laughed louder. Carlo shot him.

Heathcliff staggered back into a wall, and slunk to the floor. "What– what is this!" he struggled to say.

"It's your payment for your years of incompetent service, and lackluster loyalty. Anyway, you would have done the same to me," Carlo explained cooly. He put the pistol back in his briefcase, along with a few more documents that he decided to save, and finally his laptop computer. He paused at the threshold as he was leaving, to look upon his adopted younger brother, and satisfy himself that the bullet had done its work. Then he marched out of the office.

Eric crept closer to Heathcliff. He took off the *omamori*, and let himself be seen.

"Eric! How did– how did you get here?" Heathcliff stammered.

"What just happened, Heathcliff? Why did Carlo do that?"

"I don't know–" said Heathcliff. He touched the wound on his heart, looked at the blood on his fingers, and said, "This– isn't happening."

Eric paused for a moment. Given their history, he had no reason to like Heathcliff, nor do him any favours. Yet Heathcliff was no longer the charismatic schemer and deceiver that Eric once knew. He looked upon his former enemy and chose to see him as a simple man, lonely and suffering and confused, no more and no less than anyone else.

"Is there anything on this ship we can use to help you? A first aid kit? A cellphone, to call for help? A magic healing potion?"

Heathcliff didn't seem to hear. "I was supposed to live forever–" he wheezed. Then he said no more.

Eric sat back. Then he brushed his fingers over Heathcliff's face, closing the eyes.

Water began to seep into the room from under the floorboards. Eric stood, put his *omamori* back on, and ran out of the room, then out of the villa.

Another of the DiAngelo galleys floated nearby; Carlo stood on the deck. Its crew had just withdrawn the gangplank. Several other galleys hovered in the air above. Beyond that, Eric saw a low-hanging cloud illuminated from within, and crackling with electricity.

Eric dashed back into the villa's atrium. The tree in which he had hidden the finderstone was on fire. By this time the water in the galley was as high as his ankles, so he kicked the tree on its side, to put out its flames, before digging through its soil to retrieve the finderstone. When he got it free, he splashed his way into the tower, and up the stairs to its highest platform. From there, he contemplated for a moment throwing the finderstone on to the galley that rescued Carlo. Above him, he saw a cloud crackling with sparks, and glowing pink in its core. He turned around, and threw the finderstone as far away from all the boats as he could. It splashed into the river, just as the cloud unleashed its angriest shaft of hot lightning. The bolt hit the river at the place where the finderstone splashed down. Its thunderclap hit the galley like a wave, forcing Eric off his feet. Lesser bolts forked across the water from the point of impact, reaching the docks and the moored pleasure craft on both shores of the river. Eric squeezed himself out the tower windows just in time to avoid being trapped in it by the rising waters. He clambered on to the roof, jumped into the river, and swam for the shore.

~ 63 ~

On the roof of the art gallery, Miranda admired the sight of Il Duce's sinking ship. But she wondered why her third volley of lightning struck the water. She launched herself into the air, running as though upon an unseen track, and came to the ground on the shore of the river, near to where the galley went down.

Eric also come to the shore not far away. He crawled on to the jetty of a rowing club boat-launch. He saw Miranda, so he took off the *omamori*, he shouted her name. Then he lay flat on his back, exhausted.

Miranda ran to him as soon as she saw him. "Eric! Eric! What are you doing here?"

"I was– still on board the boat, when it was hit by lightning," he wheezed.

Miranda looked at the place in the river where the galley went down. A few bubbles were still trickling to the surface. "Why didn't you plant the finderstone and get off the boat right away?"

"Ildicoe and I had an argument, then she left."

"What? You had a fight in the middle of a mission!"

"And then the boat took off before I could escape."

Miranda pointed an accusing finger at him as she spoke. "You and Ildee had a mission! When you're in the field the mission comes first. It comes before your feelings; it comes before your lives. You save your big emotional scenes for when the mission's over."

"It was a long time coming, and we--"

"I don't want to hear it," she dismissed him with a tired wave of her hand. "Now, did you accomplish the mission or not?"

Eric propped himself up on an elbow. "We planted the finderstone in the galley, and then–Miranda, does it do anything else besides let you follow it?" he asked.

"No, that's all it does. Why do you ask?"

"Because the lightning went straight for it. With me still on board."

Miranda looked away. "Who else was on board, when the ship sailed off?" she asked him.

"Carlo and Heathcliff, and one soldier."

"I saw Carlo escaped– did you see what happened to the others?"

"Heathcliff is dead," Eric reported.

Miranda smirked, but shook her head. "Fair trade for the lives they took from us."

"It wasn't the lightning that killed him. It was Carlo. Shot him in the heart."

Miranda's smile vanished. She looked to the river. "He killed Kendrick, too. What's his game?" she wondered aloud.

"Miranda, I still need to know," Eric insisted. "When I planted the finderstone, was I just painting a target for you?"

Miranda's mind was still on Eric's news. She contemplated the bubbles rising from the galley's underwater grave. Then she stood, and helped Eric to his feet. "I'm sorry you had to go through all that. I'm glad you're all right. Let's find Ildee, and get you both home," she said.

"I don't think Ildee's coming back, either," said Eric.

Miranda sighed. "Sure she is. So you had a lover's quarrel? She loves you well; she'll surely be back soon."

"Not this time," Eric lamented. "Not this time."

~ 64 ~

On a roadside above the rowing club, Ildicoe and Ciara watched Miranda ministering to Eric.

"See," said Ciara, "Eric wants a real woman, now. And it looks like she wants him, too."

Ildicoe looked, and nodded slowly. "I hope he's happy with his choices," she said.

"Best if you leave them alone for a while," Ciara advised. "In fact I would steer clear of Elderdown entirely, for a few days. Besides. The whole clan thinks that you're a spy."

Ildicoe turned sharply on Ciara. "Why do they think that! Who would tell them such a thing!"

Ciara only looked at Ildicoe. A smile grew on the corners of her mouth.

"Ciara! You didn't!"

"You were always running off, without telling anyone where you were going, or how long you would be gone. What did you expect us to think?"

"I was searching for the other Voyageurs. They had fallen into the chthonic prisons. I couldn't ask anyone to come with me down there."

Ciara paused. She knew of the dangers of the chthonic prisons, and the kind of bravery needed to survive them. In her eyes Ildicoe now seemed a little stronger, a little wiser, and even a little taller, than she appeared to be a moment before. She stepped back. Then she swallowed these feelings and said, "You know what? I don't believe you. And neither will anyone else. We all know what's happening to you. The fact you try to hide it means you're hiding something else, as well. No one wants you around anymore. No one trusts you. Not even your man Eric; not

177

anymore. As far as the whole clan is concerned, you are one of
them."

Ildicoe sputtered with venom for a moment, then said,
"Ciara! What are– what have I ever done to you?"

Ciara's expression grew more stern. "You are the reason we
lost Fellwater. You are the reason my Donall MacBride was
killed. You– and that outsider boyfriend of yours. And now I've
taken from you what you took from me."

As Ciara laughed at her, Ildicoe backed away. She threw off
her beret and her wig; her feathers raised themselves up, like a
black aura surrounding her head.

"I gave you a new home!" she howled. "A place where we
could all be safe. I worked with you for months to build it and
defend it. I saved your fucking life when we were attacked. Yet
you still treat me as if I don't belong. In my own home! Tell me,
Ciara, why am I not good enough for you? Why is nothing I do
ever good enough for you? What do I have to do? What do you
want me to do?"

Ciara only continued laughing.

Ildicoe screamed.

The volume of her voice shattered the windows of the nearest
buildings. Ciara covered her head, to protect herself from shards
of flying glass. Then Ildicoe started running. Ciara crouched
down, low to the ground, certain she was about to be attacked.
But Ildicoe ran into the air, and across the river. As Ciara
watched, Ildicoe vanished into the forested hills that surrounded
the city of Lac Des Fées.

~ 65 ~

That evening, Eric sat on a wooden stool near the fire in the
centre of the Elderdown commons. In front of him sat a short
bench, upon which he had carefully laid out the contents of the
envelope he stole from Carlo's office on the galley. Waterlogged
and fragile, the ink ran down in long lines on most pages,
making much of it illegible. Some of the pages were ripped from
Eric's attempt to peel them apart.

Around him, a small cluster of people peered over his work.
They shone flashlights on the pages as Eric laid them out, and
pointed at lines they thought were clear enough to read, and
debated what they might mean.

Outside Eric's cluster lay another ring of people. They clambered around each other, waved their hands and arms in each other's faces, shouted bloody curses, swore ill-considered oaths, and stomped away with indignation only to return a moment later with another point to score. "We voted *against* fighting them!" "I'm only mad that she didn't pick me to come with her!" "What gave Miranda the right to take this into her own hands?" "We should hit them again, tonight, while they regroup!" "I want another vote– I demand another vote!"

When Eric read the last page in the dossier, he almost accidentally ripped it in half. His mouth hung open.

"It's happening in three days," he whispered.

Then he looked up, and noticed the fracas around him for the first time. He stood on his stool, held up the leaf of paper, and shouted, "I have their timetable! They're lifting the Shadow Spell in three days!"

No one heard him. He shouted again: "Three days!" Still with no response.

Someone shoved another person into Eric's stool. Eric fell to the ground. The sheet in his hand ripped apart, and most of it floated into the fire, where it was quickly eaten by the flames. Eric got up and pushed his way through the crowd toward Miranda, who was hotly debating something with Algernon.

"Not now, Eric," she scolded him.

"But look!" he said, and he showed her what remained of the last page of the New Renaissance timetable.

"Not now, I said! We've got a war to fight, here!"

Algernon waved an angry finger in Miranda's face. "No, we don't. Only *you* do," he chastised her.

"We'll all be fighting it soon enough. You know that," she retorted.

"We'll be fighting it because you started it!"

"I didn't start it– *they* did, when they demanded we swear allegiance to them!"

"You dropped three lightning bolts on Il Duce himself!"

When Eric heard that, he pushed himself between Miranda and Algernon. "You mean– the galley was attacked by *you*?"

"I didn't know you were still on board!" Miranda apologized.

"You told me you only wanted to follow them, not kill them."

Miranda scowled. "I needed a spotter, to paint my target. *Without* knowing why. So that if you were caught, you'd still be innocent. I was protecting you."

"Your 'protection' almost got me killed!" Eric shouted.

"I promise you, I didn't know you were on board," Miranda repeated.

Eric backed away from her, and then marched out of the circle, to the edge of the commons. He turned to look at the Fianna, fighting among themselves, and thought about whether he still wanted to be among them.

A thumbing noise, like boots scraping on a rickety wooden rooftop, reached him. A swift cold wind followed it. Eric looked up. He saw Ildicoe, with her feathers raised sharply, standing on the ridgepole of the chapel. She waved her hand toward the burning beacon at the top of the steeple. A cool wind whipped around it. Then its fire burned low, and extinguished, leaving only a few faint embers and a thick river of ash and smoke in the air.

"Ildee?" he called to her.

Ildicoe saw him, but turned away. She swept her hand toward the fire in the centre of the commons. It too was smothered under a breath of cold air.

The Fianna stopped pummeling each other and looked around. Some of them noticed Ildicoe on the chapel roof, and they pointed her out to the others. Ildicoe stared back at them for a moment. Then she ran off, into the darkness.

"Why the hell would she do that?" asked Miranda. "She knows that if the beacon fires go out–"

"–then the werewolves can attack," Ciara finished for him. "That's exactly why she did it."

Miranda stepped toward Ciara. "And why would she want that?"

"Because– because–" Ciara stammered in reply. Her attention was drawn to the frontier of darkness outside the camp. A pair of eyes, yellow and large and hungry, had appeared there; as the Fianna watched, more such eyes appeared, and surrounded the camp.

Miranda saw the eyes. She slowly turned her head toward Ciara. Her face was gaping with awe at what was about to happen. Ciara covered her mouth with his fingers. Then she pointed into the darkness. Miranda looked where she was pointing, just in time to dodge the charge of a black and grey haired animal, easily twice her size. It landed in the centre of the smoking fire pit, sending ash and charred coals and the last glowing embers flying into the commons. Those nearest the fire pit were covered in hot ash and embers. The arms they raised to shield themselves were no protection. Then the creature leapt onward. Its front paw swiped at Finnbarr as it rushed passed him, knocking his hastily-drawn sword from his hand and leaving him with a vicious scar across his forearm. Then the creature vanished back into the darkness.

"Werewolves!"

More of the massive animals charged through the commons. Weapons appeared in the hands of the Fianna: swords, two-handed spears, rapiers. Claws the length of daggers unsheathed in the paws of the werewolves. Rifles fired blindly, toward wherever the barking and growling seemed to come from: sometimes the shooter would hear the yipping of an animal he wounded, but more often he heard the growling of an animal he missed.

"Someone get these fires lit again!" Miranda ordered.

But the swift attacks of the fast-leaping werewolves prevented most from obeying, or even hearing, Miranda's order. In twos and threes, the creatures pounced into the commons, lashed out to break someone's weapons or to tumble someone to the ground, then leapt back into the darkness again. Sometimes one or two of the Fianna would chase them, only to be flung back into the commons by unseen arms. Often they would land on a companion, and bowl him down into a blood-spattered heap.

Miranda pulled an arrow from a quiver at her hip. She tightened its head in her fist and whispered something into it, then shot the arrow directly above her, into the sky. When it reached the height of its range it exploded, and the fireball kept burning, and floated slowly to the earth. The commons was now illuminated by a dim but serviceable orange glow: just enough to fight by, if not quite enough to keep the werewolves away.

"Form up in front of the chapel!" Miranda howled. "Blades in the front. Rifles in the back. Noncombatants: relight the beacons. Do it now!"

Only Eric heeded her voice. He piled some firewood into his arms and ran with them to the chapel. The other Fianna were still crouched on the ground to avoid being hit by the next wave of werewolf attacks. Miranda grabbed Finnbarr by the collar and pulled him where she wanted him, in a position by the chapel doors. Then she did the same to Ibrahim, and Síle, and the other front-line fighters.

Two more werewolves flung themselves into the commons. This time, the light from Miranda's flare gave the fighters just enough warning to be ready. A volley of bullets and arrows pelted the two creatures. One of them tripped and crashed into a cabin, destroying its front wall. The other yipped in pain, and viciously reared up to tackle the first fighter it could reach. But the sharp ends of three Brigantian spears lanced into its chest. It ploughed into the Fianna's shield wall, more from its momentum than from any calculated force. It struck its head on the chapel's foundation stones, and did not move again. The creature that fell into the cabin was back on its feet now, and leapt ahead to swipe at the trio that killed its partner. Ibrahim's scimitar was faster: he chopped the creature's right arm clean off at the elbow. It rolled into a ball and tried to regain its balance. The sight of the stump of its arm infuriated it, and it raised itself to its hind feet and howled into the sky.

"He's calling the rest of them here!" shouted a panicked Algernon.

"Get the beacon lit!" Miranda shouted back.

By this time, the riflemen had reloaded their weapons. They cut the creature's howl with a second battering of bullets. It fell backward, groaning and writhing, but then it seemed to chuckle. It had lived long enough to summon its companions: all could hear their answering howls in the darkness beyond the camp.

Ciara darted out of the protective circle of the Fianna fighters. In the dim light of the flare above, some blood spatter on her clothes was clearly visible. She picked a sword from a fallen Wessex cavalier, and then shouted Ildicoe's name.

"Ciara, what the fucking hell are you doing!" Miranda called out.

"We have to find her! She's the one who put out the beacons– broke open the underworld and let out all the– We have to make her pay!"

Miranda lauched a second flare into the sky, to try to create more light with which to protect Ciara. "Come back here– you'll be killed!" she shouted.

Ciara pointed at Eric and said, "This is your fault anyway!"

"My fault!" Eric gasped.

"None of this would have happened if you didn't try to blackmail my Donall!"

"Heathcliff did that, not me!" Eric objected.

"You're the one who delivered the package for him!" Ciara shot back. "Then after that you're the one who lost Fellwater for us because you ran off to the woods with Kendrick's wife!"

"You want to punish me for that, for the rest of my life?" Eric hollered. "isn't it enough that Carlo put me through hell and back– the actual underworld!– *and* that he put a price on my head!"

"No, it's not," Ciara growled.

Miranda stepped forward in Eric's defence. "It was Donall, not Eric, who signed the contract with the DiAngelo."

"Donall is dead because of him!" Ciara howled back, with her sword pointed at Eric.

"Is that what this is really about, Ciara?" asked Eric. "Not me, but Donall?"

"How would you know what it feels like to watch your lover die, right in front of you!" Ciara spat at him.

"I know *exactly* what that feels like," Eric spat back.

Ciara stammered and stepped back, as she tried to think of how to respond to Eric's dark reminder.

"Eric is not responsible for Donall's death," Miranda told her.

"Yes, he is– and so is that grotty French girl he's been sleeping with!" Ciara cried. She pointed her blade at Eric again. "Was Katie's body even cold yet before you jumped into bed with her?"

"Ciara, what the fuck!" Eric snapped back.

"It's not fair!" Ciara continued. "Your Katie died and you got another girl right away, but my Donall died and I got no one– it's not fair!"

"You're right, it's not fair," Miranda agreed, to calm Ciara down. "But you want to debate this now, when there's a pack of werewolves attacking the camp?"

Ciara was unconsolable. "I can't take it anymore!" she cried. "I can't stand watching him win, while I keep losing."

"What do you want me to do about it, Ciara?"

"I want Eric gone! Ildicoe, too. And I want them both to think no one will ever love them again. I want them to cry themselves to sleep every night–"

"Is that why you told me she's a spy for Carlo?" Eric demanded.

"Ciara, you didn't!" Miranda scolded her.

"I did!" Ciara proudly admitted. "And for all we know, maybe she is. Think about it: she hasn't even told anyone her real name!"

"And what did you tell her about us!" Miranda wanted to know.

"I told her nothing she didn't already believe about herself."

"Did she put out the fires just now because of you?" Eric said. "Are we fighting these werewolves because of *you*?"

"Don't you pin that on me!"

"Then what about that carriage that Ildee and I were stuck in. Are you the one who locked it with us still inside?"

Without admitting guilt, Ciara said, "And then you escaped. See– it's not fair."

"What happened to you, Ciara?" Miranda asked. "We've been friends for years. You're better than this. You're honourable. Rational. Sensible! This isn't like you!"

"It's more like Carlo," Eric muttered.

Ciara heard him. She pointed her sword at him again and said, "How dare you! How *dare* you accuse me of being like him! I *know* who I am. I will *never* be like him. I am only doing what I have the natural right to do–!"

Eric interrupted her to step forward and shout: "Ciara, behind you!"

Ciara looked behind her, just as a werewolf flashed into the commons, easily disarmed her, and flashed out again. A second creature swooped in and swiped at her legs, throwing her to the ground. As she sat up, a third pounced upon her, pinning her down.

Some of the riflemen took aim, but Miranda pushed their barrels out of the way. "Don't! You might hit her. Let me," she warned them. She already had an arrow on her bow: she lined up her shot and loosed it on the werewolf. But at the same moment it flew, her second flare hit the ground, and darkened to a smoking ember.

The last thing anyone saw before the light disappeared was the werewolf leaping high into the air, out of the line of Miranda's arrow shot.

A piercing, ear-numbing wail seared the darkness, and then there was silence.

"Ciara?" "Ciara!" "What happened–" "Are you–" "Is she–?" the Fianna whispered among themselves.

Miranda launched another flare into the sky. When its light filled the commons, the Fianna saw Ciara, somewhat further away than before, lying on her side, with her back facing the others. Those who knew her best stepped closer. They saw her roll on to her back. They saw Miranda's arrow lanced through her throat.

"Ciara!" whispered Miranda. "Oh, Ciara, I've killed you, I've killed you, I've killed–"

She sat on the ground. Her hands trembled, her mouth hung open as she repeated her lament, her eyes blinked rapidly, her breath stopped in her throat.

On the roof of the chapel, the beacon fire lit up again. The Fianna looked to see who had done it, and they saw Paul Turner sitting on the roof. Although his hands were still tied at the wrist, he managed to light a cigarette.

"You people are fucked up," he remarked.

"Turner, what the hell are you doing up there!" Algernon shouted at him.

Paul smirked and shrugged his shoulders. "Everybody was watching the werewolves. Nobody watching me. So I thought I'd make my escape."

As the commons brightened under the light of the beacon, the Fianna heard a few growls and barks from the last remaining werewolves, scrambling to get out of the light. Some of the Wessex riflemen opened fire, more to chase them away than to hurt them.

Miranda's closest friends, Eric among them, gathered around her. No one spoke. When Algernon moved in to close Ciara's eyes, Miranda grabbed his wrists and threw him to the side. When Eric attempted the same, she hissed at him. No one else moved closer again.

Miranda turned her eyes to the sky. From the west, she saw a flying curraigh, with a yew tree in the place of its mast, floating toward Elderdown. No one was on board. Those who surrounded her looked where she was looking, and saw it. Some gasped; some took a step away from it; some touched their hands to their hearts and lips and foreheads, in salute; some merely stared in away.

"It's the Night Ferry," Síle named it, "from the house of Donn the Old."

Finnbarr looked on Ciara's silent face and said, "What do we do about this? We can't– we can't *blame* anyone for her death. I don't know what to do."

Eric said, "Then maybe we don't do anything."

"But we have to punish *someone* for things like this. It's our way!"

Eric shook his head. "Then we have to find *another* way. Because we can't go on like this. There has to be– there has to be– another way."

Miranda cradled Ciara in her arms, and carried her out of the camp.

"What do we do now?" asked Síle.

As Miranda left the camp, most eyes looked around the camp in search of someone else who had an answer. Eric looked up to the approaching ferry from the House of Donn the Old, and he gulped. Then he stood up and stretched his spine, and said, "I've an idea. All fighters: form up an honour guard."

The Brigantian warriors looked at each other; some of them shrugged, others nodded. They unsheathed their swords and held them front and centre, hilts to their breasts and points down, and marched into formation on Miranda's right side. Some of the Wessex riflemen looked to Algernon for a cue; Algernon nodded, so the riflemen shouldered their arms and marched on Miranda's left. Morningfrost took his position at the head of the procession, and played a dirge on his bagpipes.

The night ferry landed in a clearing outside the commons, just off the path to the rope-bridge and the mainland. Miranda gently placed Ciara's body on board, and stepped away. Eric placed his dagger in the boat, beside her. Those who weren't in the honour guard picked some of the nearby nocturnal flowers, to lay on Ciara's side, or at her feet.

Miranda sat on the grass, looked up to Eric and said, "Eric, I need a moment."

"But the werewolves?" Eric asked.

"I'll be all right. Just go. Please?" she whispered.

Eric put his hand on her shoulder for a moment. She squeezed it, to reassure him. Then he turned to the warriors. "Honour party: I don't know– dismissed?"

The warriors turned around, in unison, then marched in perfect lock-step back to the commons.

Eric watched them go for a moment. Then he looked to Miranda again.

"I'll be fine," she said.

Eric nodded, and followed the warriors back to the commons.

He did not reach half way there when Miranda jumped to her feet, ran to him, and hugged him.

"You're right, Eric," she said. "We have to find another way."

The ferry hovered high again, turned around, and drifted back to the west, toward a cloud formation that might have had a small cottage on its edge. Its stone walls were dark; its thatch roof was steeped high, and its wide and thin windows glowed warmly. In the darkness, the cottage might have been only cloud, and the glow of its windows might have been only stars.

~ 66 ~

Back at the Elderdown camp, Eric returned to the documents he had stolen from Carlo's galley. Deciphering them gave him something to do. Beside him sat Finnbarr and Síle, equally anxious for distraction. Across the bench from him sat Paul Turner, whose interest in the document was more than passing. Ropes had been tied around his wrists. But because he lit the beacon that banished the werewolves, no one treated him like a prisoner anymore.

"The Minister of Foreign Affairs! I knew we were well connected, but not *this* well connected." Paul remarked.

Miranda sat on a stump on the other side of the fire. No one sat near her. She held a long stick in her hand, and she poked the fire with it whenever she heard someone whisper her name.

Around the camp, most voices were sombre. Eric could hear them list names of people who had done one thing or another, to contribute to the long chain of events that had just culminated in the evening's tragedy. But he lifted his head when he heard Satya Bhatacharya say, "It's all the fault of that DiAngelo *bakrichod*– what's his name? Il Duce!"

Eric stood. "Everyone: I've something to tell you. There is no Il Duce. There never was."

This got everyone's attention. Silence befell the camp.

"He was only a story, nothing more. A story about a wise and perfect king, who lives in a castle in the clouds, and who promised to return at our time of greatest need, to save us from ourselves. We all believed this story because we wanted to. Because there's no such perfect king here on earth. Even we who didn't want to be ruled by him, believed in him. We wanted to believe our enemy was a worthy foe. But he isn't. He's just a fairy tale. That's all he ever was."

"How do you know?" asked Satya.

"Politics is theatre, right? So I looked behind the curtain," he said, as he held up the *omamori*. When he saw that most people recognized it, he continued. "I've been using this talisman to avoid Carlo's assassins. And to sneak into Il Duce's throne room. That's how Ildee and I stole this dossier. While I was there, I saw Carlo and his brother Heathcliff– did you know they were foster brothers?– I heard them talk about Il Duce like he was an imaginary friend from their childhood. And I went up to the top of the tower. No one was there."

"Then who were those messengers? And the judges? If there's no Il Duce, then who's really in charge?" asked various voices in the commons.

"The three of them together, taking turns," Eric answered. "Carlo, and Heathcliff, and Kendrick. Three brothers, in fact. They took turns playing the role."

"You sure about that?" asked Paul.

"Haven't you noticed that when one of those messengers comes by, you never see all three of them together?"

Paul thought about it for a while. "Well, that must be why they never let me go up the tower to see the boss for myself," said Paul.

The Fianna marveled about this new information. New whispers outpaced the old.

"But didn't you say Heathcliff is dead?" asked Ibrahim.

"I did," Eric confirmed. "I saw Carlo murder him."

"Kendrick is dead, too," said Miranda. "So that leaves Carlo in charge of the whole thing, by himself."

"Well, then the day he plans to part the Veil must be pretty soon," said Satya.

"Three days," Eric reported. "That's what I was trying to tell everyone before the werewolves came and– well, before."

A few people looked over to Miranda; she pretended to ignore them.

Paul said, "Three days seems about right, to me. We're planning massive rallies in all the loyalist holds in three days. All the outsider Guardians, all the star-eyes–"

"Star-eyes?"

"People we Awakened in the last twelve months. Still new to the Hidden World– kids with stars in their eyes. We've been raising up as many as possible, mostly using the water that we got from your well. Thousand of them. We need them to help with the spell-breaking effort."

"Thousands? How profoundly irresponsible!" said Algernon. "Each year, there's fewer places on earth left to us. What will happen to all those new people when there's not enough room for them to touch the sources? They might lose their Awakening. They may even die!"

"They'll have a very strong incentive to conquer more holds for the New Renaissance," Paul told them.

"So that's his plan for what happens *after* he breaks the spell," Algernon speculated. "More expansion. More conquest."

Paul nodded grimly. "And we won't just exile those who won't pledge their loyalty. We'll have them disenchanted."

This news elicited gasps of anger and shock from everyone.

"It makes sense," Paul explained. "Like my lord Weatherby said: there won't be enough room for everyone anymore."

"Would you stop saying 'we'!" Ibrahim chastised him. "You say you want *out* of their house. But you talk as if you're still *in*."

"Old habits," Paul shrugged.

Algernon looked to Eric and said, "Does the timetable say anything else?"

"It does," said Eric. "Though it's hard to read. The letters K and P keep coming up. That's the cypher for the 'Kallipolis', the new kind of society they want to build."

"It's more than that," said Paul. "It's also the name of a new kind of government. I bet that's why you saw Carlo talking to the Minister of Foreign Affairs. They're going to declare all the holds in the ley-line network the sovereign territory of a new state. A Vatican City, but for Hiddenfolk."

"With House DiAngelo as the royal family, I'm sure," said Satya.

"*Bismillah!*" Ibrahim swore. "Can you imagine what will happen if they got their hands on state power? They'll raise armies. They'll print their own money. They'll have a seat at the U.N."

"We already raise armies," said Paul.

"We have to *do* something," said Ibrahim.

"Why don't we just *let* them break the spell? I still kind of want to see what'll happen," Finnbarr snickered.

Síle swatted him. "Don't be stupid, Finnbarr."

Ibrahim said, "We have to fight them. We have to raise an army."

"We tried that already," Algernon reminded him.

"So this time we raise a bigger army," Satya suggested. "It won't be hard to do. The DiAngelo have been pushing people out of their freeholds up and down the country. There might be lots of angry warriors out there willing to join us."

"It's not a question of how many warriors we can get. It's a question of strategy, and efficient use of resources, and timing."

"So what do you suggest? Marching up to their doors and surrendering?"

"I didn't say that."

"You may as well have. Suppose we lay down our weapons: they will never lay down theirs. The moment we show anything resembling weakness, they'll call down fire from heaven upon us."

Miranda threw her poker into the fire, then stood and stretched out her arms, addressing everyone. "Who here wants to be the next to die?" she beseeched them. "Do you, Ibrahim? Finnbarr, what about you? Because that's what will happen if we carry on like we always have. We take far too much pride in our ability to kill. And not nearly enough in our ability to think. Or to build. Or to love. So we trapped ourselves in a spiral of hate and fear and death. Someone has to be the first to say: that's enough. I'm done. I'm not playing that game ever again. I'm going to find another way."

"But Miranda, there is no other way!" Finnbarr insisted.

"There is *always* another way," Miranda countered angrily. "And we have to find it."

Silence befell the camp again. Most of the Fianna looked to the fire, or to the ground. Finnbarr said, "I wouldn't know where to look."

"I think I know someone who could help," she said. "But I'll need some time. Give me two days– can you do that for me? Two days?"

"The DiAngelo are going to break the spell in *three*," Algernon reminded her.

"I'll be back before sunset on the second day," she promised. "I'll be back with a plan."

They watched her board one of the Brigantian flying curraighs, and sail into the sky, where a cloud enveloped her, and took her away.

~ 67 ~

The grass in the back garden of Miranda's cottage had not been cut. The brown and muddy leaves of last year's autumn still covered most of the ground. Everything was slick and glistening with the remains of a recent rain. She made her way to the foot of the yard, and to old Hobb, the oak tree.

His branches sprouted new buds for spring leaves, but his bark had grown greyer and more creviced than Miranda remembered. His pitted face seemed downcast, like a man dreaming of a long-lost love.

She laid out a wooden bowl in his roots, and shared some whiskey into it, as she often did when she sat in his shade. She waited for the usual signs that Old Hobb might be listening: a bird alighting on a branch, a rustle of leaves in a well-timed gust of wind. But no such sign appeared. All things in the garden were still and silent. Miranda wondered if Hobb was waiting for something, or if perhaps he was angry with her for being away for so long.

"I killed a friend yesterday," she confided in him. "Ciara DeDannan. You remember her. Donall's partner. Young. Smart. Pretty. Everyone loved her. And I killed her. You must understand: I was aiming for– and it jumped out of the way, just in time. Who knew those things could move so fast! She had a wonderful life, waiting for her. And I took it away. It was an accident– I swear by earth and sky, it was an *accident*!"

The garden remained still: no wind, no change in the light, no sound. Miranda shifted her seating posture uncomfortably.

"We lost a lot of good people this year," she continued. "And all their deaths were preventable. I had a chance to kill the man who started the war. I had a good arrow on my bow, and a clear line of sight. His death would have changed everything for the better. It would have been *right* to kill him– no one would have judged me for it. There's many who would have thanked me! But I didn't take the shot. I don't know why."

This news, as important as it seemed to her, also provoked no apparent response from her friend.

"That's not true. I do know why. Because I didn't want to kill him– I wanted to *hurt* him. It's what he *deserves*, for what he did to us! I wanted to make him feel *pain*! I wanted him to– no, that's not the reason. I should know by now that I cannot lie to you."

She sat back, leaning on her arms. She studied the morning clouds: the only natural movement in her field of view. The sounds of the village coming to life began to enter the garden: cars starting up, doors opening and closing, dogs barking, radios tuning into the news. Old Hobb did not move.

"I didn't mean to kill her!" she hollered. "She was my friend– I was trying to save her life!"

A small flock of robins in the neighbour's yard flew away, startled at the sound of Miranda's shouting. Old Hobb did not move.

"Now Carlo is going to part the Mist in only two day's time," she said. Her voice cracked with stress. "With the power he'll possess, he'll keep us on the run forever. And I promised my friends that I would have a plan. But I have *no* plan. No plan at all. I don't know what to do."

A grey squirrel came into the yard. It saw Miranda, and it ran away again. Miranda scowled. Old Hobb did not move.

"Think of what will happen to *you*, old Hobb, when he succeeds. Because it looks like he will. Imagine– the outsiders will treat you like a tourist attraction. They'll turn my house into a gift shop. They'll stand beside you and take pictures of themselves. They'll cut off your branches for souvenirs. They'll carve their names on your face. Maybe, if you're lucky, a team of scientists will analyze your DNA and cross-breed your acorns with an eggplant!"

Miranda picked up the bowl of whiskey and threw it at him. The whiskey splashed over Old Hobb's cheeks and forehead, and the bowl bounced away.

Even still, Old Hobb did not move.

"Can't you hear me anymore? Can't you see me?"

A low rumbling sound came from high above her. She looked up to see the sign of Old Hobb's acknowledgement that she was expecting, but saw only the silver flash and the vapor trail of a passing airplane. Miranda leaned back, picked an acorn off the ground, and tossed it at a squirrel, to chase it away. She scratched her head, and combed her fingers through her hair. More spruce needles fell. The dark grey tinge on her fingers had spread to her hands and wrists, and had become coarse to the touch. She examined them closely for a moment. In the dim light and cool air of the dawn, they looked and felt like someone else's hands; the thought held her breath in her throat. Her heart beat heavier, and her eyes welled with salt and water. She untied the laces on her boots and threw them away, and then she peeled off her socks. The same greyish stiffness had taken the flesh of her feet, and crept part way up to her calves.

She looked at Old Hobb again. "And now, what happened to you, is happening to me," she trembled. She pulled her shawl tighter over her arms. Then she laughed. She did not know why she was laughing: it seemed wrong to laugh while her eyes were bedewed with tears. She rubbed them, though that did not dry them. And she looked at her hands again, and shook her head, until the laughter spent her, and left her as it found her.

The last of the neighbour's cars drove away. Somewhere out of sight, a sparrow greeted the morning. A gentle breeze stirred her hair. The sun parted the clouds and filled the garden, and Old Hobb brightened.

Miranda felt the change in the light more than she saw it.

"It's been a long time since I came out here just to sit with you, isn't it?" she said to him. "Not to complain about anything, not to bring the news, not to ask for advice or for help. Just to sit with you, and watch the sun rise."

She sat up straighter, stretched out her fingers and touched the earth. The zoom of every mosquito and dragonfly in the yard, and the fleet of the clouds above, filled her ears. She closed her eyes, to listen to deeper sounds. She heard the nearby river dance over the rocks and splash upon its banks, and pour itself through distant lakes, and finally into the ocean. She felt every green and growing thing between her and the horizon turn and face the sun. She felt the heavy rumbling of the earth, as it turned from night to day, as it orbited the sun, and as the sun flew ever onward through space.

She opened her eyes again, and said, "You were right to say nothing, my friend. All you had to do was be here. And now, I know what to do."

~ 68 ~

Miranda marched to the front of her cottage. Someone had planted a DiAngelo banner in her front flowerbed. She scowled at it, then uprooted it and brought it inside. She folded it respectfully, laid it on her dining table, and leaned the banner-pole by the door.

"That will get someone's attention," she said.

The air in her cottage had grown stale in her absence. Dust covered the bookshelves, furniture, and floor. The draft from the woodburning stove was thin, but in the time she was away it was enough to spread an apron of ash on the floor. She toured the space, partly to see if anything had been stolen, but mostly to reclaim the feeling that this was, indeed, her home.

She rummaged around her bedroom and found a pair of striped knee-socks, and a pair of purple silk gloves that extended past her elbows. They made for a strange combination with her Brigantian tunic and sash. But she felt not yet ready to show her new hands and feet to the guest she was expecting. Then she put the kettle on for tea, and waited.

By the time the tea was ready to drink, someone kicked her door open. Shinobi barged into the room. His sword was drawn.

Miranda held up a bowl of tea in both her hands, and offered it to him.

Shinobi smiled with relief, and put away his sword. "I was told the ley line was broken here. How did you know the boss would send *me* to fix it?"

"Carlo wouldn't come personally for a hold as small as my cottage," she told him. "I gambled that you would volunteer for the job."

Shinobi unbuckled his sword belt and laid it aside, accepted Miranda's offer of tea, and sat in the guest chair by the fire.

"Have they figured out that you're not blind anymore?" she asked him.

"I don't think so. I keep the sunglasses on, and I still use the white cane. It's interesting to see what people do when they think I'm not watching."

"I need you to do something that might require you to break your cover," Miranda said, more seriously. "Very simply: if there is *anyone* in Fellwater Grove who you trust, anyone you think has a good mind and a good heart, no matter their clan: smuggle them out of the grove. And do it *before* Carlo breaks the shadow-spell."

"You're planning something, aren't you?" he grinned.

"I am."

Shinobi traced his fingers along the edge of his tea bowl. "It's about time. For far too long, I have been gracious and polite in the face of evil men. I smiled whenever I saw them. I called them my friends. And my heart almost died, every time. What kept me alive was the thought of the day when I could draw my blade against their master, and finally show them all who I really am."

Miranda sighed. "Then I'm sorry to have to tell you this, but their master is not who we thought he was. The intel on this is five-by-five. And I have to ask *you* to stay out of the Grove, as well."

Shinobi set down his tea. "Let me remind you of the promise you made. I agreed to be your agent for only one reason: the chance to kill the man who took *Sakura No Tani*. If you're planning something else now, I will not help you anymore."

"I'm planning a different kind of satisfaction," Miranda assured him. "And I hope you will agree, a better one. For all of us."

~ 69 ~

Ildicoe hiked along the sandy shoulder of the country road leading out of Royal Wyndham. Whenever she thought the driver of a passing car felt right, she held out her thumb. With her weather-worn trousers, her dirt-smeared chemise and Salonnière corset, and Eric's green trenchcoat, she looked like someone who didn't care what she was wearing. A woolen beret was a token effort to hide her feathers: they fanned out underneath it anyway. The flowers painted on the shaft of her boots were only vaguely visible under the dust kicked up by the passing cars.

A Range Rover passed her in the oncoming lane. It turned around at a nearby intersection, and came toward her. Sensing that the driver was one of the Secret People, she put out her thumb. It stopped to pick her up.

"Thanks for saving my life," she said, as she climbed into the passenger seat.

The driver lowered her Bann-Shee hood and let herself be seen.

"*Merdu!*" Ildicoe blurted. She pulled on the door handle, ready to jump out. But Miranda placed a hand on her arm.

"Ildee, please! I only want to talk to you."

Ildicoe threw open the door anyway, and tried to shake off Miranda's grip. Then she saw the state of Miranda's hands. She relaxed.

"You too?" she said.

Miranda nodded. She cut her car's engine, and got out.

There was a creek bed nearby, and they walked to where it ran through a culvert under the road. Miranda found a rock on the edge of the water to sit on. Ildicoe sat beside her and took her hands, to give them a closer look.

"How long have you known about this?" she asked.

"Not long," Miranda replied. "A few days."

"My feathers go all the way down my spine, now," Ildicoe told her. "And across my shoulders, too."

"On me, it's just my hands and feet, so far. And some needles in my hair."

"Is this what happens to all of us?"

"Most of us. That's why there's so few as old as I am."

Ildicoe broached her next question carefully. "How old are you, really?"

Miranda smiled, although she looked to the passing water. "Old enough," she said.

"I discovered a way to slow the process down," Ildicoe offered. "It worked for me, for a few decades. It isn't a cure, but– but all you have to do is–"

"It's okay, Ildicoe. I'm going to let the revelation happen."

Ildicoe stood up again. "No, no, you can't!" she spurted, much to her own surprise.

"Yes, I can, and it's all right," Miranda reassured her.

"You can't. Because– You're the one we all count on to stay grounded and centered when everyone else is losing their shit– you're the one who always knows what to do–"

"Actually, most of the time, I make it up as I was going along," Miranda explained.

Ildicoe didn't hear that as she ranted on. "You're the one who helped me to Awaken, and you found a place for me among the Voyageurs. You're the only one who knows the name I was born with. I can't imagine life without you. And now, after what I did yesterday– You often say that once an adventure begins you can't go home until it's over. But they'll never let me go back home. I'm sure of it."

"About that–"

"I was just so angry!" Ildicoe shouted. "You should have heard what Ciara said to me. After all I did for her. And for the whole clan!"

"Ciara is dead," Miranda informed her.

"She's *what!*"

Miranda met Ildicoe's eyes, and didn't need to repeat herself.

Ildicoe sat on a fallen tree trunk, and dropped her beret on the ground beside her. She covered her heart with her hands.

"The werewolves?" she asked.

"No," said Miranda. "One of my arrows."

This did not give Ildicoe much relief. "Still, if I hadn't put out the beacon–"

"If a lot of things hadn't happened," Miranda finished for her. "Ildicoe, please realize that I am more like you than you think. I've made mistakes worse than yours, in my time."

"Worse than opening a Tartarus gate? Worse than–"

"–killing a friend?"

Ildicoe softened.

"I was a queen, back in old Albion," Miranda confided. "I made the laws. I fought the wars. I took the best of the spoils. I had my choice of the boys, too. And now, my royal hall is this culvert, under this road. That should tell you everything."

Ildicoe looked at the culvert. Its edges were decayed and rusting. A logjam of driftwood at its mouth trapped a small mass of dead leaves, white foam, and discarded plastic bottles.

"What is more," Miranda continued, "You are a better person than you think you are. Courageous, persevering, hard working. Deeply loving. Honest about your failings. Exactly the sort of person I would want to replace me, when my time arrives."

"I could never replace you," Ildicoe said. "No one could."

"But soon, someone will have to."

"The clan won't have me back, after what I did. I've hurt everyone I care about. I feel like I should crawl under the road over there, and never come out. Let the change take me. That way I'll never hurt anyone again. I'm sure that's what the clan wants me to do. And maybe they're right. Maybe I don't deserve to go back."

Miranda took Ildicoe's hands. "I have seen the way out for all of us. Even for you. Something's going to happen in two days: something that will change everything. And you have a part to play."

"What is it? Whatever it is, I'll do it."

Miranda opened a satchel took from it an antique wooden chalice. Ildicoe recognized it with awe.

"I can't accept that," she said.

"Yes, you can," said Miranda, as she placed it in Ildicoe's hands. "And you must. Your part will be to gather the clan, tomorrow morning, and bring them to Fellwater. Now, the timing will have to be right: you must gather them *after* I finish my part of the plan, but *before* anyone else comes to occupy the grove. Which they will– there being so few places like it left in the world. Take this finderstone–" Miranda handed Ildicoe a small leather pouch, containing the stone, "–and I will give the other half to Síle, so you can find each other. Show the clan the chalice, tell them what I told you, so that they will trust you. Bring them home– but only after it's safe again. If you can show the clan you are the good person that I know you can be, then everyone can go home. All of us can finally go home."

Ildicoe accepted the chalice. "What will your part be?" she asked. "What's going to happen?"

Miranda said, "You'll see."

~ 70 ~

Algernon Weatherby stood on one of the rock pillars on Elderdown Island. High enough to crest the trees, but low enough to remain unnoticed from a distance, it offered an excellent view of the river, and of the hilltops that flanked the valley. He scanned the vista to the south with a field telescope.

"No sign of her," he said.

Eric, standing near him, said, "She said she'd be back in two days. She never breaks her promises."

"It's already the morning of the second day," Algernon reminded him. "She had better come back with a plan that will work in less than twenty-four hours. Because that's all we have left."

~ 71 ~

A small cloud moved among larger ones, blown by a different wind than the rest. Its shadow rose and fell with the contours of the land. When it neared the centre of the peninsula of Rath Manannan, its bottom thinned, and the hull of a Brigantian curraigh slipped gently down. The leaves on its tree were full grown for spring, and a few birds perched to its branches. From its stern flew the saffron-yellow flag of the Brigantians, with its black tree, and the triskele in its roots. Miranda stood at the helm.

As the curraigh passed over the crevice in the earth that marked the centre of the hold, she pulled her bann-shee hood over her head, leapt from the bow, and let herself fall. She controlled her dive with a cluster of raven's feathers that she held in each hand. She fell through the crevice and landed on the stones of the Druid's Tree chamber.

The tree was covered in a tarpaulin tent. Its glow was dimmer, and the tinkle of windchimes that normally pervaded the air was silent. A DiAngelo centurion, sitting at a security checkpoint nearby, dropped the tablet computer he was playing with, and reached for his rifle. The Bann-Shee jumped into the air and landed both her feet on his weapon, kicking it out of his grasp. The surprised soldier and ran down the passage that lead up to the surface, shouting for help all the way.

Miranda lowered her hood and contemplated the tent that covered the tree. She cut some of the knots and ropes with a dagger, and pulled the tent away. There she saw the tree: seemingly threadbare, for the many branches that had been cut away. Its leaves were small and pale and few. The glowing fairy-fish that surrounded it were trapped in glass balls that hung from chains or rods attached to an elaborate scaffold. A DiAngelo banner had been planted in the tree's roots. Miranda stepped in to remove it, but found that it was bolted directly to the tree. She sat beside it, and put her hand on a nearby root. The tree's glowing pulsed like a breath, but slowly, as if each beat was a struggle.

Miranda inhaled deeply, held her breath for a moment, and then unleashed from her heart a chilling Bann-Shee wail. Her voice echoed everywhere in the chamber, and down all the connected passages and portals. The soldiers stationed outside, as they armed themselves and crept down the cavern toward her, stopped and had second thoughts about engaging their intruder. Then the many glass cages that imprisoned the tree's attendants shattered, and the fairy-fish swam free. They clustered and spiraled around the tree, and pecked at its bark for the small morsels of food it once gave them, but found precious little. The scattered music of windchimes returned to the air, but it too was feeble. Only the older, lower chimes sounded.

A branch from the tree bent toward Miranda. From it hung a small cluster of berries. A salmon nudged the berries toward her with its head. Miranda understood. She picked the berries from the branch, and wrapped them carefully in a cloth.

The glow from the core of the tree subsided. The fairy-fish drifted upward, and spiraled through the crevice in the cavern ceiling, and moved out of sight. Miranda looked into the pouch where she placed the berries. A delicate gleam still flickered there: but it was now the last source of light in the chamber. Only the smoky sunbeams from outside, passing through the crevice above, illuminated the now darkened body of the Druid's Tree, and the fragments of glass on the floor.

The sound of shouting and stampeding feet reached her from one of the passages behind her. Miranda tied the pouch to her belt, and pulled her bann-shee hood back over her head. When three soldiers ran into the chamber, she was already prepared for them.

Their rifles quickly clattered to the floor as her spear-play disarmed them. One of them produced a pistol and took aim: Miranda whipped around and broke his arm, caught the gun, and pointed it straight back at him. He stepped back. His companions drew sidearms of their own.

Miranda fired the pistol in the air above them. The bullet dislodged a boulder from the ceiling, near the crevice that opened to the sky. The soldiers turned to watch it crash to the ground. Then they looked up, fearful of another collapse in the ceiling. The bann-shee took the chance to escape down the passage. When another boulder fell and broke into fragments and dust on the floor, the centurions ran after her, not to catch her, but to save themselves.

They emerged to the world above in time to see the Bann-Shee leap into the air, tumbling head over heels, and land safely on the deck of her Brigantian curraigh. It ascended to the sky. One centurion raised his pistol at it, but before he could fire the boat was enveloped in a cloud, and away.

~ 72 ~

"It's near mid-day," complained Ibrahim, as he stood by the shore of the island and looked to the south.

"She'll be here," Eric promised.

"I'm sure she will keep her promise if she can," Ibrahim acknowledged. "But it may be time to discuss what we should do if she cannot."

"Give her more time," Eric said. "The sun hasn't set. The second day isn't over."

Ibrahim only grunted in reply, and borrowed Eric's telescope to scan the horizon again.

*

In the garden of his monastery's cloister, Brother Aidan The Wise read the letter handed to him by the green-skinned troll in the Canada Post uniform. He stood in quiet thought for a moment, while his monastic brothers curiously gathered around him.

"Miranda Brigand writes to say we need to go somewhere safe, outside the monastery, from sundown tonight until sundown tomorrow," he told them. "She didn't say why."

One of the brothers said, "Isn't that the same time when Carlo asked us to hang his banner in the chapel, and pray for him?"

"It is," said Aidan. "Curiously, Miranda also says we *should* go ahead and raise Carlo's banner. Though she also says we must stay away from Fellwater. And, away from any of the holds connected to Carlo's empire. I don't like this. It doesn't seem like her."

Aidan paid a silver clutch to the postal troll, and handed the letter to the novices, so they could read it themselves. By the time they finished, Aidan had his hooded neck-wrap on his shoulders, and his walking stick in his hand.

"I'm going to see what she's doing for myself," he explained. "While I'm away, hang the banner, then head into town and check yourselves into a hotel. You can pray for Carlo *there*."

*

Devon Willowtree handed the letter to Neachtain, and put up her feet and took another sip of her wine. When Neachtain finished reading it, he looked at her, and sighed.

"She's not asking us to *do* anything," he ventured.

"Other than leave our hold undefended for an entire day," Devon replied. "After that embarrassing defeat she gave us last winter, I'm not doing her any favours anymore. I'm staying right here."

She looked to the Nova Scotia Brigantian banner, which flew from the roof of her horse barn. "Tell the ambassador from

House DiAngelo he can fly his flag from the roof now. I'm done with Miranda."

*

Raj Purana crumpled up the letter and threw it toward the corner of his office. Then he smiled, and took a pair of iron fighting-claws from his desk drawer and put them in his fists.

"Nice of her to tell me where she is," he told the postal troll, "so I can collect the bounty on her head."

~ 73 ~

Evening came to Elderdown. The sun still shined upon the island, but it was low in the west. The Fianna gathered by the fire pit in the centre of their camp, to start cooking dinner. Síle wandered to the edge of the camp and began twirling around in a circle. Finnbarr and the others saw her, and gathered around.

"Again? What now?" said Finnbarr.

"Something's happening, something's happening," she sang.

Satya ran to her, grasped her hands to steady her balance, then grasped her face to steady her vision. "What are you seeing? It's all right– you're safe. What do you see?"

"A gathering. In Fellwater."

"More soldiers?" asked Algernon.

"No," Síle reported. "A gathering of shadows, but also of lights. A ring of clouds. But also stars. And in the center– is it a man? No, it's not a man. It's a child. No, it's not a child. I can't quite see. It's a– ah– ahhhhh–"

Satya patted her cheeks to break Síle's trance. Síle steadied herself, then rubbed her eyes. "I'm okay now," she reassured Satya.

"So they're coming on by themselves now, are they?" said Ramanujan.

"That hasn't happened since I was a girl," Síle said, as she returned to the fire pit and sat down. "But it feels different this time. The world feels troubled. Like waves suddenly rolling on calm water. Like there's a storm coming."

Algernon looked south-west, the approximate direction to Fellwater Grove. "A side-effect of Carlo's spell-breaking, I'd wager," he said. Síle nodded, to show she agreed.

Finnbarr turned to Paul Turner, who was sitting by himself at the fire pit. "I thought you told us it's all happening tomorrow."

"Tomorrow morning at sunrise," Paul confirmed. "But I'm sure he's getting ready tonight. Still wanna see what will happen?"

Finnbarr pursed his lips and sighed. He wandered a few steps away, and looked to the setting sun, then to his friends around the fire pit, then to the south. He saw no sign of Miranda's return. He drank deeply from his mead horn. Then he stood up and threw it on the ground. The dregs from his horn splashed on the hot rocks around the fire, and hissed as they evaporated away.

"This is bullshit!" he announced. "I'm taking one of the boats, and going to Fellwater. Right now. Anyone who wants to come with me: gear up, and let's go."

"There's an entire army stationed there!" Eric reminded him, as he moved to stand in Finnbarr's way.

"I know that," Finnbarr bit back. "And I don't care. I'm sick of sitting around."

"They'll kill you."

"Better to die fighting than to live under a false peace!"

"I'm with you, Finn," said Ibrahim. "If Carlo wants to tear down the shadow-spell and destroy our world, then I won't have it said that I did nothing to stop him."

"But this is suicide!"

Finnbarr grabbed Eric's collar and pushed him to the wall of the chapel. "I don't care if I live one more day or a hundred more years. As long as Carlo dies," he snapped.

Then Finnbarr and Ibrahim pushed past him and marched for the boats. Across the camp, Eric saw Síle buckling a weapons belt around her waist. He ran to her. But before he could say anything, she said, "You think I'm nothing but a daydreaming babe-in-the-woods?"

Eric turned to Satya and Ramanujan, who were strapping armour on each other. "Why are *you* going? You're not warriors!"

"We are now," Satya told him.

Eric turned to Algernon. "Can't you convince these people to wait a little while?"

"We've waited long enough," Algernon grunted, as he loaded a fresh cartridge of gunpowder into a rifle.

Morningfrost and his two hounds trotted past. He looked to Eric and said, "You coming?"

Eric only stood and watched his friends climb into the Brigantian curraighs. The boats lifted off from their berths in the old fortress bastions, one by one, and sailed toward the setting sun. They faded into the long thin clouds, and out of sight.

Paul Turner trundled over to stand by Eric's side. "Well my friend," he grinned, "Mom and Dad are away; we have the house to ourselves. Want to order pizza, maybe invite some girls over—?"

Eric only shook his head and walked back to the fire.

That was when a cloud somewhere behind them darkened, as Miranda's curraigh emerged from it.

When she landed and stepped off, she looked around, and her face grew stern. "Where is everybody?"

Paul grinned, and said, "Well, they're not on the island."

"They're in the boats," Eric told her. "They're going to Fellwater. They just left, a minute ago."

"The idiots!" Miranda howled. "They couldn't have held on for one fucking minute!"

"I tried to make them wait," Eric pleaded. But Miranda wasn't listening. She looked to the southwest, the direction she surmised they followed. Then she looked to the Fianna banner, blowing on the flagpole. She turned to Paul.

"Your DiAngelo colours are in storage in the trading post. Go run it up this flagpole."

"Seriously?" Paul chortled. "That will connect Elderdown to Carlo's empire."

"That's part of the plan," she told him.

"If you say so," Paul said, as he ran into the trading post.

To Eric, who was giving her a puzzled look, Miranda gave the pouch containing the berries from the Druid's Tree. "Take this, and don't let anyone know you have it."

"What is it?"

"A packet of seeds from a very special tree," she said, as she lowered the Fianna flag and folded it. "You're going to plant them in the floor of Carlo's temple."

Eric's eyes grew. He stepped back from Miranda. "What, the one in Fellwater? The one surrounded by more than a thousand—"

"That one," Miranda said. "You're the only one I can ask to do this because–" she paused, as she sighed and looked away. "Because you won't be affected by what's going to happen."

Eric looked at Miranda. Her shoulders sagged. Her feet shifted. Her eyes darted from one point on the horizon to another.

"You're scared of something," Eric observed. "And it's not Carlo's army."

Miranda shook her head. But Eric didn't believe her. He gently took one of her hands. She closed her eyes as she let him remove her purple glove. Her skin was grey, dry, and rough to the touch. Eric's eyes widened for a moment when he saw it. Then he clasped both her hands together in his, and said, "When it's over, what will happen to you?"

Miranda looked into his eyes, and stroked his face, and said nothing.

Eric understood. "Well then, when do we go?" he asked.

Turner raised the DiAngelo banner on the flagpole, and discretely cleared his throat.

"We go now," said Miranda.

She ordered Paul into her curraigh with a waive of her pointing finger, then climbed in and took the rudder. Eric jumped in after her.

She lowered the Fianna banner from the mast, and raised her old Brigantian flag in its place. Eric nodded, and smiled; he saw it as Miranda's way of telling the clan, and telling the world, that her mission was hers alone.

The boat lifted itself into the sky, found a cloud that seemed right, and disappeared into it.

The last limb of the sun fell behind the hills to the west.

~ 74 ~

Carlo's temple was now complete. A stately tower of Roman arches and pillars rose from its sonorous foundation, to the wide dome on its summit. In each window hung a banner from a hold that had joined the New Renaissance empire. On the top of the steeple flew the banner of the Kallipolis itself: the red field, angel, and hourglass of the DiAngelo, quartered with the white field and black trireme of the Guardians. All around, the soldiers of the DiAngelo army gathered in clear-cut ranks and files, though they were at ease: they talked and drank and laughed, and took pictures of each other with the tower in the background. A V.I.P. area had been roped off near the temple's front portal, where a collection of well-suited politicians and financiers toasted each other with long champagne flutes, and nibbled on hors d'oeuvres served by women dressed as priestesses.

Carlo himself stood just outside the tent that served as his command centre, admiring the completed temple, and ignoring the crowd. He drew breath on his cigarette and closed his eyes as he exhaled.

"Moments like this come round only once, maybe twice, in a lucky man's lifetime," he said.

"You must be especially lucky to be at the centre of it all," said Shinobi.

"You might think *yourself* especially lucky, to be standing by my side at this moment. But as for me, luck had nothing to do with it. I made this happen."

"You and your brothers, together," Shinobi reminded him. "It's too bad they couldn't be here with you, to share this victory."

"Heathcliff and Kendrick were good men. But they were always too enthusiastic about the crumbs my father dropped from the table," Carlo drawled. Then he walked away.

Shinobi gave himself one breath of time to hide his disgust, then followed Carlo. "There's a rumour among the men that Il Duce himself will speak to us, directly, tonight," he asked.

"Persistent, are we?" Carlo answered, as he took off his suit jacket and shirt, and replaced it with the undergarment of a Roman senatorial toga, handed to him by an aid. "There's another rumour I've heard, which says that your loyalties are not where you say they are."

"Sir?"

Carlo controlled his temper before speaking. "If I understand correctly, there are two kinds of warriors in House Kami. One kind is the Samurai: they serve the lord of a noble house, they are loyal to the death, and they fight with honour. The other is the Ninja: they come from the peasantry, they're experts at infiltration, and they fight dirty. You, my lord Sanchin-Goju of house Kami, are not a Samurai."

"Sir, I have been your faithful agent ever since the freehold of *Sakura No Tani* joined the New Renaissance. I have infiltrated the house of your enemies, the Brigantians, and reliably followed their movements for you. I have asked for nothing in return but the honour of speaking directly to our lord Il Duce."

Carlo rolled his eyes. "Well then, I'll tell you something about him, that my brothers and I kept secret."

"Yes?"

Carlo wrapped the toga shawl around his waist and over his shoulder, with the help of an assistant. When the outfit was complete, he said, "Il Duce never liked wearing those messenger masks."

Carlo butted out his cigarette on the canvas wall of the tent, then flicked it toward Shinobi's face. Shinobi flinched, just a split-moment before it bounced off his sunglasses.

Carlo nodded, a smirk growing on one side of his face. "That's what I thought," he said.

Shinobi's mouth dropped open. He took a step back and looked around, expecting be lynched. But Carlo merely turned away, and accepted a gold laurel wreath from an assistant, which he placed on his head like a crown. Then he marched away, followed by his honour-guard.

Shinobi watched him depart. He thought about Carlo's remark about the messenger masks. It did not take him long to understand them. He took off his sunglasses, and his eyes widened.

He looked around, and saw that he was now alone. He ducked down to a better-concealed position at the side of the tent, and took off his sunglasses. He withdrew a small blow-dart tube from a pocket in his jacket, inserted a poisoned needle into it, and took aim for Carlo.

At the same moment, Captain Pollux emerged from behind the tent, and clubbed Shinobi in the head with the hilt of his sword.

~ 75 ~

Miranda finished cleaning the ash from the floor surrounding the woodburning stove in her cottage. Then she stood, silent, pensive, and alone, looking around, hoping to see any remaining domestic tasks that she could use to delay her appointment with her own plan. She took a clean cloth and toured her shelves, and dusted off the things which prompted a pleasing memory.

There's my commission as an officer in the Princess Louise regiment. There's my license to practice midwifery. The cup from my last spot of tea, before I left, seven months ago. The lamp where they hid a listening bug– is it still there? Yes, there it is, on the floor, right where I crushed it. Good. What else? Some old candlesticks, hand-forged. A ticking alarm clock, long since stopped. My guitar. My mead-making kit. And seven hundred books, covering this wall, floor to ceiling, end to end. All these things: the detritus of my life. A queen's haul of treasures; a flea-market of trash. Such a fine line between them.

She dressed herself in her saffron-yellow Brigantian tunic, kilt, and body armour. She twisted warrior-braids into her hair. She donned thin leather gloves and heavy leather gauntlets, to conceal the change upon her hands and arms; and a pair of solid boots with mid-height heels, to conceal the same which had now spread to her knees. At last she added her heavy linen shawl, and fixed it in place with an iron brooch, because it reminded her of home.

She stepped on to the back deck, and carefully closed the glass doors behind her. She laid a new bottle of whiskey by Old Hobb's roots, and stayed by him for a while.

Eric, patiently waiting on her deck, discretely cleared his throat, and called her name. She touched Old Hobb's lowest branch, then looked to Eric.

"Ready to go?" he asked.

"No," she said, with a little smile. She handed him the keys to her Range Rover and said, "How about you?"

"No," he said. "But it's time."

"Any last questions?"

Eric stood. "Are you *really* Queen Cartimandua– are you really two thousand years old? Or are you just a descendent of hers?"

Miranda laughed. "That's your last question?"

"Well, what I really want to ask is: can't we find another way to do this? But I already know what you'll say to that."

Miranda smiled. She took his hands, drew him close, and whispered something in his ear. Eric took a step back, as his mouth dropped, and his eyes boggled.

Miranda kept his hands held tightly in hers. "It's all right, Eric. For all the life I've lived, for all the things I've been and done, my proudest days were when good hearts like yours became my friends."

Miranda kissed his forehead, and hugged him.

Paul Taylor came around the corner of the cottage, saw them, and whistled. "Nice one, mate. But isn't she kind of old for you?"

Miranda let Eric go, then marched over to Paul, grabbed his arm, and dragged him toward the cottage, and pushed him roughly against the wall. With one arm holding him there, she tapped on the frame of the door with her other hand, then opened it. The interior of her cottage had become the interior of Eric's apartment. She shoved Paul inside.

"Stay there!" she ordered him. "Don't come out until this time tomorrow."

"What the fuck, Miranda! Pushing me through a seven-league-door? Take a joke!" he complained, when he saw where he was.

"I'm saving your life, you jammy bastard. You can thank me later."

She slammed the door shut, and locked it. She gave herself one last breath of time to look at Eric, and register a wordless apology for the interruption. Eric nodded, to show he understood.

"All right," said Eric. "Let's go."

~ 76 ~

Fellwater conservation park was empty of tourists and campers. Signs at all the entrances said that the whole park had been reserved for a private event. No one, therefore, noticed the small fleet of Celtic curraighs which fell from the clouds and landed on the edge of the same children's playground where they had set up their base of attack, that previous winter. The Fianna jumped to the ground as soon as the boats were low enough. Then they darted to the tree line, and leaned their backs on any shelter they could find, and plotted.

"No point in assigning objectives and diversions this time," said Finnbarr. "And I'm not much of a strategist anyway. I like fighting. That's what I'm here to do."

Nods and grunts of agreement rose from his companions.

"We should open multiple battle-fronts anyway, for maximum surprise and distraction," said Algernon.

"Okay, then, uhh–" Finnbarr looked around, took mental stock of his companions, and opened his hands, as if at a loss for plans. "How about this: Everybody do the same thing they were

going to do last time. Those without much combat experience–
Algernon, Satya, Ramu– can form a rearguard by the boats.
Keep the escape route clear. Sound good?"

When the warriors sounded their agreement, Finnbarr said,
"Truth in our hearts."

"Strength in our arms!" the warriors responded.

"Fulfillment of–"

Síle, who had been peeking over the gunnels of the boats,
interrupted the moment: "They found us!"

A trio of pickup trucks drove up to the boats, and a team of
DiAngelo centurions piled out of them. They quickly created a
line of rifles, and took aim.

"Stand up and drop your weapons!" Captain Pollux shouted
to the Fianna. Then he clicked the button on a radio attached to
his shoulder. "Sir, hostiles sighted near the south-west sector–"

"Sick of this shit," muttered Ibrahim.

"Me too," Finnbarr agreed.

Síle bent down on one knee and touched the earth with the
flat of her hand. She whispered something into the soil. A
heartbeat later, the grass nearest the DiAngelo soldiers began to
stretch and grow around their ankles, then around their lower
legs, then up to their knees. When the centurions realized what
was happening, most of them were already immobilized. Some
of them dropped their rifles and drew knives, to cut themselves
free.

Finnbarr leaped over the hull of his curraigh. He sank his
sword into the chest of the centurion he landed on.

The rest of the Fianna howled with rage and joy, and
followed him. The battle began.

~ 77 ~

Two shadows hopped over the fence that marked the line
between the village and the conservation park. They mixed with
the shadows of trees and rocky ledges, and crept along paths so
familiar and loved that they needed no lamp to guide them in the
dark. First the path skirted the edge of the gorge, where a simple
metal bar spanning a line of rough stone cairns was enough to
keep the unwary from falling to the river below. Then the
shadows came to a sinkhole in the earth, where stairs set in the
stone led to a lower plateau, closer to the river's edge. They
moved among old cedars that clung to the rocks with roots like

gnarled hands; along crusty narrow ledges where the path gave them only a wall to one side and an unprotected abyss on the other; then to a rustic stair that returned them to the higher plateau, and the clear path to the ridge that bounded a sacred grove. The sounds of a battle grew as they approached. The two shadows paused, and perceived, then moved again: one toward the ridge; the other toward the battle.

~ 78 ~

The centurions around the Fianna's feet lay dead. The Fianna stood among them, some with one foot on the bodies of the slain, like proud predators standing over their prey.

"That was exciting!" said Ramu, who stood over a fallen centurion of his own. Smoke still drifted from the barrel of the rifle in his hands.

"That was the easy part," said Algernon.

A voice on Captain Pollux's radio demanded a report. Finnbarr picked it up. "All hostiles terminated. Area secure. Everybody take five."

"Is that you, Pollux? Who is this?"

Finnbarr crushed the radio in his fist and threw it away. "Can't stand talking to those people," he said.

"That was damned stupid," said Algernon. "Now they'll send reinforcements."

Síle said, "They'll have to open the gate to do that."

Algernon thought about that for a heartbeat. Then he understood Síle's meaning. "Ah, you've done this before," he grinned.

"It only works if we move fast," said Finnbarr.

Ibrahim climbed into one of the boats. "Then I'll take this boat and crash it through the main gate. The rest of you come in after me. Then it's a straight race to Carlo. Whoever kills him wins. Sound like a plan?"

Finnbarr put his hand on the gunnels of the curraigh. "My boat. So I crash the gate," he told Ibrahim.

"You want to argue about this *now?*"

Finnbarr relented. Ibrahim reached out his hand to help Finnbarr into the boat. "Our names and stories will be remembered forever, no matter who is at the helm of this boat. And no matter how it ends," he said.

Finnbarr accepted Ibrahim's helping hand. "I think you might be a better man, than me," he said.

Ibrahim grasped the rudder of the boat, lifted it no higher than the canopy of the trees, and sped it toward the gate of Fellwater Grove.

A shadow arrived at the scene of the battle. She saw the Fianna charge toward their destiny, and she held her hand on her heart. Then she moved on, from one shadow to another, following.

~ 79 ~

Carlo rode on a white horse from his tent, along the torch-lit cobblestone avenue, lined on both sides by the ranks of his people. Before him he held a lance, and the banner of his house draped from it. The many followers who lined each side of the avenue held out their own flags and banners, hoping theirs would touch Carlo's. All around him, voices chanted the salute: "Magnum Opus Facimus! Avete, Il Duce!" Yet his face remained stern, stone-cold, and grim.

Arriving at the temple, he spurred his horse to a gallop, and raced in a circle around it. When he completed the circuit, he dismounted on to a platform that stood before the front portal. There he raised his arms to his followers. They raised their arms to him, their hands open, receptive, and ecstatic.

He calmed the cheering with a gentle wave of his hands, and took his place behind the podium. Before he uttered his first word, a section of the crowd near the gate was disturbed by the din of soldiers scrambling for their weapons and shouting orders at each other. Carlo looked to see what was happening. Most of the crowd looked with him.

Finnbarr's curraigh smashed through the cleft in the ridge, sending the splinters of the gate flying like shrapnel into the defending DiAngelo sentries. The boat skidded to the ground, as those nearest scrambled out of the way. Some who tripped as they ran were crushed beneath its keel. Finnbarr perched on the prow, sword in hand.

"Hello Fellwater" he shouted happily. "How many Romans does it take to screw in a lightbulb!"

The soldiers on the nearest watch post immediately grabbed their weapons and ran to the attack.

"It takes only one to Go Fuck Yourself!"

The soldiers opened fire. Finnbarr ducked under the gunwale of the boat just in time to avoid the first volley.

At the same moment, Síle blew the Dord Fiann. Its note resonated all over Fellwater Grove, as one by one the trees and stones answered its call. The centurions looked at each other and wondered what was happening. Some clutched their ears, as the sound grew loud enough to cause them pain. Blood trickled from their noses.

The Fianna charged into the field.

Caught by surprise again, the first line of DiAngelo centurions fell to the Fianna's bayonets and blades. They shielded their eyes from the Fianna's hero-light, radiating with the note from the Dord Fiann. But the second line of centurions were prepared. They raised their carbines and opened fire, although the Fianna's hero-light made it hard for them to aim. The Fianna took most of them down with the same ease that they defeated the first line. Then they fell back to the mouth of the gate, and formed a defensive line of their own.

A second flying curraigh shot out of the cleft in the ridge. This one, with Morningfrost at the helm, and Ibrahim in the prow, aimed for the tower. Though the soldiers at the gate fired upon it as it passed over their heads, it neither slowed nor deterred from its path.

Carlo, watching passively from a safe distance, only scowled. When the boat was less than it's own length away from him, he stretched out his hand to it, made a fist, and slammed his fist into his other hand. The boat immediately fell out of the air and smashed upon the cobblestones of the avenue. Its crew spilled on to the ground, injured and flat-footed and, in some cases, unarmed. Carlo smirked at them.

As they regrouped, the audience pounced on them. Ibrahim and Morningfrost managed to beat down the first to reach them, but soon found themselves so absurdly outnumbered that they lost their weapons, and then their footing on the ground. Even as they writhed and cursed and kicked their defiance, the crowd seized their arms and legs and carried them away.

Carlo smiled again, and laughed, and applauded his followers.

He did not notice the shadow slip around the temple from behind, and slide in through a broken ground-floor window.

~ 80 ~

Inside the temple, Eric looked around. A cluster of mirrors hung from the centre of the ceiling, apparently angled to catch the sunrise through the windows and focus it on the bowl of the brazier, so that it would be illuminated from all sides. As the east horizon was brightening, the brazier was already appearing to glow.

"Let there be light, indeed," he marveled.

He untied a pickaxe from its holster on his back, and hacked the stones at the foundation of the brazier.

I hope these stones aren't ten feet thick! he thought.

~ 81 ~

Ildicoe unlocked Eric's apartment door and stepped inside. Paul Turner whipped around from behind her, pushed her against the wall, and pointed his crossbow in her face.

"What are you doing here?" Paul accused her.

"This is my house!" she angrily replied.

"Eric's house," Paul corrected her.

"I took it over when Eric went into hiding," Ildicoe explained. "Now what are *you* doing here! In my house."

"Miranda put me here. Said I had to stay out of the Hidden World until tomorrow."

Ildicoe glared at him for a moment. "Any idea why?" she asked.

"None at all," he admitted. "Just that she's going to the grove. That's where all the fun is happening tonight. I'm sorry to miss it. But I have a feeling that there will be profit in the chaos that follows."

"The– chaos? What do you mean?"

"Didn't you hear? Carlo's taking down the shadow spell tonight."

Ildicoe looked out the window, as she grasped this thought, and drew the conclusions. "She's gone to stop him!" She looked at the finderstone in her hand.

"You should stay where you are," said Paul, as he took her finderstone away, and raised his crossbow to her face again.

Ildicoe decided it was safest to comply, for the moment. "What do you want with me?"

"I don't want you. I want the bounty on you. And then I want to get the hell out of Dodge."

~ 82 ~

At Fellwater Grove, the Fianna retreated to the shelter of the cleft in the ridge, where the main gate used to be. Any centurion who ventured into their line of sight was shot at; but any Fianna who stepped out received the same welcome.

"Remind me whose idea this was!" Síle shouted at Finnbarr.

Finnbarr fired a few shots for effect, just to keep the centurions away. "If I die, and you live, you can say it was mine."

The shots from the centurions ceased. A great wind fell from above the ridge, blowing the shards of the gate into the faces of the centurions, and blowing the centurions themselves on to their backs. Síle and Finnbarr stepped out cautiously, and looked around. The wind widened their foothold in the grove, and put down any DiAngelo soldier who got in its way. Síle looked up, and saw that the wind came from the top of the ridge, and from a small leather pouch, slung on the forks of a sling-staff, carried by a figure she was very happy to see.

"Miranda!" she cried.

Carlo saw her too. "All Centurions, stand down," he ordered. When the soldiers nearest him made confused faces, he said, "Cartimandua belongs to me."

Miranda leapt off the ridge and landed in a ring of dust on the path below. She marched toward the temple. Carlo stepped off the platform to greet her.

"I believe the last time we met, face to face, man to man," Carlo smirked at her, "we were just on the other side of that gate. I came to recover something an associate of yours stole from me. How sublime to meet you again, in the same place, but with the tables turned."

"That is not why I am here," Miranda replied.

Carlo perked an eyebrow. "You have come here to kill me?"

"No."

Carlo looked to his audience, to see if any of them were growing as confused as he was. "But you have come to stop me from breaking the shadow-spell. No? Yes, of course you have. You're much too late for that. I have a hundred hidden holds in my empire. And hundreds– and thousands!– of souls in every

215

one of them. All praying, invoking, wishing, turning their wills toward a singular great work. My work. The sun will rise, in mere moments. Light will fill the temple. From there it will spread across my empire and around the world. The light that banishes shadows. The light that will set us all free."

"Whose freedom? Everyone's, or just yours?" Miranda questioned him.

"I did this for you, too, Brigantian!" Carlo barked at her. "The shadow-spell imprisons all of us. It's time the world knew who we really are."

"Who are you, Carlo Maliguida DiAngelo? When you banish the Shadow-Spell, what do you think the world will see?"

"Do not lecture *me* in theology: I *know* who I am. A direct descendent and heir to the throne of the Father of All, great Jupiter himself. I am the New Sun– made in the image of God!"

"Made in the image of God– you think you're the only one?" Miranda mocked him.

Carlo's eyes flared with controlled anger. "You want to see who I really am?" he mocked her. Then he tore off the shoulder-throw of his toga, and ripped open the chest of his shirt.

From his back two magnificent angel wings unfurled. His hero-light glowed from them. He stretched out his arms to heaven, and cried out to the world: "I am the New Sun!"

The host of soldiers, supporters, and allies who filled Fellwater grove erupted with cheers. Carlo smirked at Miranda, then opened his hands to receive the people's adulation. He turned his back on Miranda and walked to the temple. His hero-light intensified as he drew closer to it.

Reaching a stage built on the steps to the temple's grand portal, he proclaimed to the host: "The days of our exile in the shadows is almost over. Justice shall return to the world! Let there be one lord! One king!"

The host chanted the salute "Valeo, Il Duce! Valeo, Il Duce!"

Miranda remained severe. She followed him to the foot of the temple, then leapt into the air and landed a heavy kick on the centre of his chest. Carlo fell to the earth again, but his hero light remained undimmed. He drew a sword from behind his back, and brandished it at her. The sword blade ignited in flames.

"You cannot take this victory away from me, Cartimandua," Carlo mocked her. "I have gathered more power to my soul than any man alive has ever done. When the sun rises, I will step into the light, and make it mine. The shadow-spell will fall, and the world shall fear the gods again!"

Sunlight touched the top of the tower. The first limb of the sun peeked over the ridge, to the east. The clouds directly above the tower parted. A small space appeared there, open to the sky above. They began to spiral around the tower, slowly at first, but their dance spread outward as the clouds turned faster.

Miranda sprinted toward the temple. Carlo roared, and lashed out with his sword to block her. Miranda deflected the sword with a hastily-drawn blade of her own. Sparks flew in her face; she squeezed her eyes shut reflexively. Her momentary blindness gave Carlo the split second he needed to swing his sword around again and slash at her from behind. His blow sent her sprawling to the ground, her hair in a tangle, her sword out of reach.

As the sun rose higher in the east, more of the temple spire shone with its light. The first rays entered the uppermost windows. There they struck the mirrors that guided it down to the brazier in the centre of the temple floor. The logs stacked in the brazier's fire bowl instantly ignited. Within the space of a heartbeat, the whole interior of the temple glowed with the blessing of the sun. Seeing this, the host of the Hiddenfolk celebrated the end of the shadow-spell. Weapons were brandished. Strangers hugged each other. Dancing prevailed. Tears were shed.

The Fianna, by contrast, lowered their weapons, gazed upon Carlo's work, and despaired.

~ 83 ~

Ildicoe sat on the couch. Paul sat on a chair facing her, with his crossbow in one hand, the television controller in the other, and a bowl of popcorn on the floor in front of him.

"Why doesn't Eric get the country music channel?" Paul complained, as he scrolled up and down the stations. Ildicoe rolled her eyes.

Then he dropped the controller, and the crossbow. His heart began beating a little faster. The picture on the television screen distorted with momentary interference. Paul stood up to look out the window, but found his legs slightly weakened. He sat down again. Ildicoe, similarly, had rolled on to the floor.

"You felt that too?" she asked him.

"The sun must be up, in Fellwater Grove, now," Paul surmised. "The light is filling the temple, and spreading along the ley lines to all the holds in the New Renaissance empire. The Shadow-Spell is breaking. Miranda and Eric couldn't stop him–"

"What do you mean– Eric's there too?"

"Miranda gave him a special job to do. Break into the temple, or something. But he must have failed. You felt that tremor just now? It can only mean that Carlo's winning."

Ildicoe looked out the window, and saw the sky brightening from sunrise orange to early morning cyan.

"Have you thought about why Miranda didn't want us to be there?" Ildicoe asked him.

"No. Why should I care what she wants."

"And if you think Carlo's winning, don't you want to be there to share his victory?"

Paul glared at her. "What are you playing at, Ildicoe?"

"It's not like Miranda's holding you here against her will."

"Good point," he said. "But I'm not having you follow me after I leave. There's a roll of duct tape in the kitchen closet: tie yourself up."

Ildicoe found the duct tape and gave it to him. He guided her to a kitchen chair, with the tip of his crossbow bolt pointed at her heart. He sat her down, then tore off a length of duct tape to cover her mouth.

It was the chance Ildicoe needed to bash his nose with her forehead, and jab her knee between his legs.

As he crumpled backward, Ildicoe punched Paul in the head to knock him unconscious. She wrapped his arms and legs in a cocoon of duct tape. Then she zipped her boots back on. She looked at the finderstone, which sat on Eric's desk. She picked it up and considered whether to pursue the Voyageurs.

She ran, into the sky, toward Fellwater Grove.

~ 84 ~

Carlo felt the wave of power from the temple wash over him, and he steadied himself on the podium, recovering quickly. He stood over Miranda, sword in both his hands. He raised it up, hilt above his head, tip poised over Miranda's heart.

Finnbarr, Síle, and Ibrahim dashed to the scene in time to defend Miranda. They drew their weapons, then sniggered uncomfortably at the sight of Carlo's wings.

"They look awesome, I'll give you that," Finnbarr mocked him. "But they make for an easy target, too." Then he waved his hands at his sides to make fun of them.

Carlo therefore swing at Finnbarr first. The three warriors snapped their minds back to the fighting. Finnbarr deflected Carlo's sword-thrust into the floor of the platform instead of into Miranda's flesh. Carlo pulled it out and held it up defensively, as the Fianna circled around him. They landed swords, spear shafts, and flying kicks on Carlo's body, pushing him just enough out of the way that he could not quite reach Miranda. As Carlo rolled away to create more distance, Síle stabbed at his wings with her spear, hoping to pin him down. But Carlo proved nimble with them, and leveraged their strength to roll faster and stand again sooner. First one, then two, then all three of the angry Fianna fighters engaged Carlo in sword combat. Each attack they made was met with a deft defense; each thrust and slice was dodged or deflected expertly. Flames from Carlo's sword scorched their faces. Surprise attacks to Carlo's blind side were rebuffed with a smack from one of his wings. But the melee was quickly decided: as each Fianna fighter was kicked back or disarmed by Carlo, a squad of nearby Centurions would pull the contender out of the fight. First Finnbarr, then Síle, then Ibrahim found themselves held down by four, five, or even six Centurions each.

Their effort gave Miranda time to recover. She was on her feet again, sword in hand, interposed between Carlo and the door of the temple.

"Out of the way, Cartimandua!" he commanded her. "You are defeated, and you know it."

More of the Fianna warriors arrived at the scene, although they struggled with the soldiers to get close to Carlo.

"Fianna: Weapons down! I did not come here to kill," Miranda called on them.

The warriors lowered their weapons, though they wrestled to free themselves from any soldiers who immediately tried to grapple them.

Miranda turned back to Carlo and said, "But nonetheless, I will not let you in the temple."

Carlo kept his burning sword trained on Miranda's heart. "But this is our chance to break the spell!" he howled at her. "We might not get another chance like this for a century! Cartimandua– Queen of the Brigantians– there, you heard me address you properly– you are one of the oldest of our kind. You command respect even among your enemies. I simply cannot understand why you wouldn't want this! The end of the shadow spell will benefit everyone! And elders like you, most of all."

"But it doesn't have to be like this. There is another way," she insisted. "Do you remember your own awakening?"

"What? What about it?" Carlo questioned her.

"Think back," she told him. Then she lowered her sword as she spoke. "Deep down in those little boots of yours, you still remember what it was like the first time you entered the Hidden World, and touched something unassailably sacred. Remember– the sound of the roar of the earth. The cool clarity of your newly Awakened mind. The light from heaven. Remember those things? We get so caught up in our fears, and our politics, and our loneliness, and our pride– all the grind-wheels of life– that we forget how simply glorious it is just to be alive. Carlo, I know you: I know you're a man of faith, God-fearing and proud. Can you get out of your own way for this one moment, and remember what it was like the first time you heard the sound of the divine?"

Carlo glared at Miranda, and shook his head. He lowered his sword. Then he sharply raised it again, and said, "No. No, you can't trick me like this. I am a descendent of the Father of All. I do not take orders; I give them. Now get out of my way!"

He flung himself on Miranda, with a roar of undisguised hate.

His attack was too angry to be effective. Miranda disarmed him.

His sword bounced off the wall of the temple, and clattered to the ground near a bed of flowers. The flames on its blade extinguished.

Carlo's eyes were now fixed on the tip of Miranda's sword, pointed at his heart.

Then she turned her sword point-down, and thrust it into the ground beside her. She stepped toward him. "I did not come here to kill you," she told him again. "I came here to remind you of something you've forgotten."

She opened her arms. Her hero-light brightened. Her feet left the earth. Flames licked up from her flying red hair. She floated backward, toward the temple, and its doors opened to admit her. Carlo struggled to shake off the fascination-effect that Miranda's revelation was having upon him. He saw that inside the temple, the brazier had been broken at the base, uprooted, and pushed down. Its load of burning firewood was splashed across the floor. Where it once stood, a hole had been dug. Beside the hole sat Eric, who looked rather surprised to have been found. Eric pushed a handful of berries into the hole, and covered them with soil.

"The Rabbit!" Carlo said, when he recognized Eric. Then he saw the condition of the brazier. He looked to Miranda and said, "What has he done?"

Eric scuttled away, behind the fallen brazier. As he did so, a small green shoot grew from the hole Eric made in the temple floor. The light of the sacred sun rained down in a glorious curtain upon it. Yet the growing shoot also glowed with a light of its own, which grew steadily warmer as the tree itself grew. In only a few heartbeats it had become a fragile sapling, then as a sturdy youth, then a full and stately tower of green and golden life.

The windows in the temple shattered, as the warmth from the tree radiated out to the world. Everyone who felt it, all across the DiAngelo empire, whether Fianna or DiAngelo or Outsider, held their breath in awe. Some fell to one knee; some felt tears in their eyes.

Carlo himself, held in awe, felt his angel wings grow. He stumbled back, away from the temple.

"What is this? What's happening? I don't understand!" he cried.

His white feathers spread across his back, and over the muscles on his chest, and down his legs. He tried to rip them out. His flesh tore, and blood flowed. New feathers grew to heal his self-inflicted wounds. He turned to face his soldiers. Some of them were changing as well. Armour and helmets and weapons dropped to the ground, as the soldiers found leaves sprouting from their fingertips and hair, or fur and feathers and scales emerging from their backs and arms. Some glowed with hero-light; some laughed or sang with pleasure; some covered their faces and wept.

Síle grabbed Finnbarr and Ibrahim. "We have to get out of here!"

"You said it!" Finnbarr agreed. The three warriors jumped and ran, followed by as many other fighters of every flag, as heard Síle's warning.

Carlo tried to shout something, but an eagle's beak emerged from his mouth. A hood of white feathers cowled over his head.

His feet cracked out of his shoes and became yellow claws. He struggled to stand; he slipped and skidded around the platform, and fell to the flagstones of the avenue. Then his wings grasped the air, and he took off, haltingly at first, then straight up to the swirling clouds. His eagle voice kept crying, until the glare of the sun hid him, and a cloud enveloped him.

Eric stepped out of the temple, fearful that it might collapse around him. He took in the view of the crying, grasping, panicking host of soldiers, whose bodies were transforming into birds, trees, and wild animals. Some soldiers who still had command of their hands leveled their rifles and fired; Eric ducked, and took shelter in the arch of the temple doors. Their aim was poor, as they were covering the glare from the tree with their hands. If any caught the light from the tree in his eye, he stood and dropped his weapon, stumbled forward, and started to change.

Other soldiers, Captain Pollux among them, looked at each other with the wonder, as if newly discovering their own eyes and ears. They dropped their weapons and helmets and breast-plates; some hugged each other, some fell to their knees and prayed for forgiveness. Algernon and Morningfrost and the other Fianna rear guard emerged from hiding. The light of the tree touched them, and they glowed with hero-light of their own. Pollux approached them, hopefully, but warily. Algernon stepped closer, and shook his hand.

As Síle and the Fianna's warriors leapt over the ridge and escaped to the outside world, a darkened head peered out of the cleft in the ridge below. Ildicoe Brigand stepped gingerly into the field, her face open with wonder, but her hands shivering with worry. She quickly saw the light from the temple, and ran toward it. She saw Eric, taking cover from the last bullets from the last capable soldiers. She disarmed them easily, threw their rifles away, and ran to her lover, and swallowed him in her arms.

Eric kissed her, and held her face in his hands. Then he pushed her away. "Ildee! Go home– go home right now!" he warned her.

Ildicoe saw the tree growing in the temple; it was now almost as tall as its steeple used to be, and its branches were curling through the windows. Some of the pillars and bricks were falling off. She saw the light from the core of the tree, pulsing like a breath; she saw the spring robins and goldfinches flitting among its branches. Then she turned around, and saw the field that once hosted Carlo's army now teemed with new oaks and ashes and thorns.

She understood why Eric told her to go home.

She took his face in his hands and said, "Eric, I love you. Do you understand me? I love you."

Eric kissed her and said, "I do understand you. I know you're not a spy. And I–"

Ildicoe pushed him into the temple and shut the door on him. She wedged Miranda's sword through the door handles to hold it closed.

Inside, Eric tripped on some bricks, and fell backward. When he got to his feet again he pulled on the doors, but they opened only a crack: enough for him to see the sword jammed in the way. He rattled the door enough to throw the sword off-balance, although it took time, and Eric had to dodge pieces of the falling temple. When the sword clattered to the ground, he threw the doors open, and shouted for her.

On the stones of the avenue, he saw her clothing scattered around, some of it torn. When he looked around for her, he saw a great raven flying into the new forest.

He ran toward it for a few steps, but then stopped, and slumped down and sat on the ground. His eyes stayed fixed on the place in the forest where the raven disappeared. He raised his hands to his mouth, but they trembled; his fingers curled and gathered over his heart.

"Oh love! I lost you again! I lost them all!"

~ 85 ~

Brother Aidan watched from a perch on the ridge of Fellwater Grove. When the light reached him, its glare was soon matched by the hero-light that shone out from his face and hands. He smiled, closed the battle-book, and sat on the ground. He opened his hands and faced the tree. Its light washed over him. A moment later, all that remained were his clothes where they had fallen, empty, on the ground.

*

Raj Purana was among the DiAngelo centurions who had been chasing the Fianna as they escaped. When he was almost close enough to grapple one of them, he tripped. He attempted to stand again, but found he could not. He tore off his shoes and found tiger's paws had replaced his feet. Then his hands were similarly transformed. He looked to the tree, and understood why Miranda had warned him away. It was the last human thought to enter his mind.

*

Hannah Garvey, the singer from Heathcliff's rally, saw the glowing of the tree through the canvass of her tent. She stepped outside, took off her sunglasses, and saw the tree burst through the spire of the temple, and throw its bricks and stones away. She began to spin in a circle, her arms outstretched, her head thrown back, her face glowing with love. The soldier stationed to guard her dashed over, but had to shield his eyes from the glare of her hero-light. When the light diminished enough for him to look again, he saw a cloud of butterflies flitting away.

*

At Brigantian Farm in Nova Scotia, Devon Willowtree was brushing one of her horses when Neachtain came running in. "Something's happening to the banner!" he said. Devon followed him outside to look. The banner on the roof of the barn was shining almost as bright as the sun; she had to look at it between her fingers. She asked Neachtain what he thought it might mean. Neachtain, however, was unable to reply. His hero-light was shining. Leaves and branches were emerging from various tears in his clothes, and from his ears and nose and eyes. Then she saw that the same was happening to some of the other witnesses. She turned on her heel and ran.

*

In Eric's former apartment, Paul stirred on the floor, then pulled himself into a chair. He looked out the window. Sunlight was streaming into the room. He rubbed his forehead and found a bruise. He looked at his hands and arms. "Nothing's changed," he muttered. He left the apartment and walked down to the one-lane stone bridge nearby. Some ducks floated along the river. City park workers planted flowers in a nearby bed. "Nothing's changed!" he exclaimed again. He began to laugh. His hero-light glowed. A pair of joggers passed him by, and did not appear to notice. He laughed louder, and happier.

*

Shinobi awoke in one of the grove's boat houses. He checked the door and found it locked. Then he saw the light streaming in through the spaces between the door and its frame. Next he noticed his own hero-light glowing in his flesh, although he had not called upon it. For a moment he marveled at the sight of his own hands, warming with a cherry-red luster. Then he used the opportunity to kick the door down. He saw the light in the sky, coming from the tree. Almost involuntarily, he staggered toward it. Then he realized what he was looking at. He shook the hypnotism off, and shielded his eyes, and tottered toward the river. He swam to the opposite shore, then sought shelter behind some trees. When he felt enough time had passed, he risked a glance back where he came from. He could see the top of the tree, still growing, and still throbbing with light. He looked away again, and shook his head. From his pocket, he took out an *omamori* of his own, hung it over his head, and walked away.

~ 86 ~

Quiet returned to Fellwater Grove. Bird calls; wind in the leaves; waters flowing over shallow riverbeds and rapids. The Druid's tree was now as tall as the tower had been, and its branches reached far, each as thick and long as a tree in its own right.

Miranda's voice reached Eric from the remains of the temple. "Eric? Anyone? Please?"

Eric found Miranda curled in the small space that remained between the trunk of the tree and the crumbled foundation walls of the temple. Chunks of the building were still falling away. Eric hurriedly lifted his friend in his arms, and carried her out to safety.

"Is it over?" she whispered to him.

"I think so."

She curled her arms into her breast, and clasped her hands over her heart. "Eric, I think I cannot walk anymore. Can you take me home?" she whispered. She was barefoot now; the flesh on her feet and legs was the same rough grey texture as the bark of the tree.

Eric nodded. He carried her down the avenue, now lined and shaded by red maples and white birches, to the cleft in the ridge that led to the world beyond.

~ 87 ~

Síle, Finnbarr, and Ibrahim were waiting at Miranda's house when Eric arrived, tired and worn. Miranda stumbled rather than walked, and leaned on his shoulder.

"I'd like to sit in the garden, close to Old Hobb; can you help me there?" she asked him.

Eric gently and dutifully sat her down at the foot of her garden, next to the grandfather tree.

"Can I get you anything? A blanket? A cup of tea?"

"Just let me sit here for a while. I need to be alone; I'll be with you again soon."

Eric held her shoulders and admired her for a moment. Then he rose, and joined the others in the living room of the cottage.

Finnbarr had removed his shirt and was admiring his arms, which had grown a thick mane of striped black and silver fur.

"Look, Eric! I'm turning into a badger!" he grinned, when Eric returned.

"Put your shirt back on," Síle chastised him.

Ibrahim said, "I seem all right, except I have no hair anywhere on my body anymore."

"He's turning into a fish," Finnbarr joked. Ibrahim glowered at him, then grinned and messed the fur on his arms.

Síle's hair had turned more golden, and the tips of green thorn stalks and red rose petals peeked out between the curliest of her locks.

"It's very pretty, Síle," Eric complemented her.

"Thanks," she answered quietly.

Eric noted her demeanour. "I take it you don't like it? Ildee didn't like her feathers, either."

"I'm fine with it," she said. She got up, and went to see Kuvira Bhattacharya, who was sitting by herself on the kitchen counter, and hugged her.

"You saw how Síle was being mentored by Satya and Ramu?" Ibrahim explained. "They're still at the grove; the revelation took them. They didn't make it."

Eric looked at the two women, and saw them differently. He approached them and said, "I'm so sorry."

Kuvira nodded, and smiled to him, but said nothing.

"Light up a fire, will you please?" Síle asked him. Eric nodded, and dutifully gathered a stack of kindling sticks to put in the woodburning stove.

"Who else didn't make it?" he asked.

"Algernon, and Morningfrost, are both unaccounted for," Ibrahim reported. "One of our flying boats is missing, they might have taken it. But we haven't heard from them yet."

"What about Ildicoe?" said Finnbarr. "I thought I saw her there, just as we were escaping."

"She was there," Eric confirmed.

"Well? Did she make it?"

Eric closed his eyes and whispered, "No."

Finnbarr looked away. Ibrahim patted his shoulder, and offered to take over the job of building the fire. Eric dropped the kindling sticks on the floor. His shoulders trembled; his voice failed him. Ibrahim gently took his arms and lowered him into a nearby chair.

"What will you do now, Eric?" Síle asked him. "Do you still want to be part of our world? Or do you want us to– leave you alone? For a while?"

Her voice trailed off when it looked like Eric wasn't listening.

"There was good that happened today, too: we have our Fellwater Grove back," Finnbarr said, trying to be cheerful.

"What happened there today," Síle told him. "happened in every place that was joined with Fellwater, through the ley lines. Thousands of Hiddenfolk changed."

"How do you know?" asked Ibrahim.

"Something's different, in the shape of the world. I can feel it. Can't you? It's like a river with not enough water. We here in this house might be among the last of our kind."

"There must be some who escaped," said Eric. "Not all of you live in secret places. Some of you live in houses. Basement apartments. Retirement condos. College dorms. Some of you go to school, and have jobs, and friends, and lives. Your people could be anywhere. And any*one*. There may even be a few sacred *places* out there still to be discovered. Or to be created."

"Sounds like we have something to do, once we finish cleaning up the grove," said Ibrahim.

Finnbarr smiled at Eric. "For all your skepticism and doubt, Eric, you *do* want to be part of our world, don't you?"

Eric looked out to the back garden. "I want to *understand* it. I want to know what happened today. I want to know what else is out there."

"Glad you're still with us, buddy," said Finnbarr, as he clapped Eric on the shoulder.

"Let's bring Miranda her tea," Eric suggested.

The Fianna followed Eric to the foot of the garden. At the place by Old Hobb's side, where Eric last saw his friend as he knew her, there grew a tall new tree. Grey was her flesh, long were her many evergreen fingers, tall and tapered her stature. A few reddish cones grew in the thicker branches, where the boughs drooped down but the tips turned upright.

Seen from a certain angle, the lower trunk might have resembled a woman, sitting cross-legged on the earth, her hands touching the ground, her hair spread out among the branches.

Old Hobb's eyes were still closed, as always, but he was smiling.

"Oh, we've lost her too!" Síle shrieked, when she realized what she was seeing.

"No, we haven't lost her. She's right here," said Eric. He sat by her roots, and placed her teacup in her hands. He closed his eyes.

A raven settled on a branch on the tree, and watched over him.

~ Elderdown: Author's notes ~

Every author writes in the hope, perhaps the faint hope, of being read. Therefore, I thank you, friend, for reading this series all the way to this conclusion.

As with the previous titles in the series, I wanted to play with the literary themes that appear in mythology and folklore, and bring them into a modern setting. Among those themes one of my favourites is transformation, metamorphosis, and disguise. A kitchen maid becomes a princess. An ugly monster becomes a handsome prince. Gods of mythology transform themselves in order to interact with mortals, for better or worse: Zeus, Athena, and Loki, for instance. Sometimes people are transformed against their will as a form of punishment for some offense: Actaeon, a man transformed into a stag; Tiresias, a man transformed into a woman; Arachne, a woman changed into a spider. Transformation is a theme in all three of the previous novels in this series, but I wanted to bring it into more prominence in this final story. Who we are, who we want to be, who we don't want to be, and what we imagine others to be, are important philosophical forces surrounding identity and human relations. Mythic transformation seemed to me an interesting way to think about them.

The Hidden Houses series also attempts to bring Celtic myths into a present-day setting. We've already seen things like the Well of Wisdom, the Cup of Cormac, and the names of the gods from whom the heroes claim descent. Ibrahim's statement during the planning of the battle, "All those things that each of you said you will do: I will do them all myself!" is an homage to Lugh Lamh-Fada's similar statement before the Second Battle of Magh Tuireadh. The Druid's tree at Rath Manannan is based on one of the old literary triads from early Irish texts, which says the psychological condition of *imbas*, or 'poetic frenzy', must lead to inspiration, or madness, or death.

Yet aside from these artifacts, the outstanding thing which, to my mind, makes Celtic myth distinct from Classical Greek and Roman myth, is the way that Celtic stories end in tragedy more often than in victory. Celtic heroes do not come from empire-minded, conquering civilizations. They come from low-tech, agrarian tribal chiefdoms, whose ambitions usually involve just getting by in a world full of hostile natural forces, hostile gods and spirits, and hostile neighbouring tribes. It's not that Celtic heroes lack the agency and glory of their Classical counterparts. And it's not as if Classical heroes don't wrestle with the gods or with their fates. The Greeks invented tragic drama, after all. But in Celtic stories, bad things happen, sometimes for no easily discernible reason at all. The heroes can do little more than make the best of whatever follows. This stands in deep contrast to the numerous Classical heroes whose paths more closely follow the pattern of Joseph Campbell's "Hero's Journey". Celtic heroes, when they win, also usually lose. I'm well aware this is not the Hollywood happy ending many people expect from fantasy fiction. But I think this is more honest and true-to-life; or, at any rate, it's more true to *my* life.

Moreover, it isn't normally a supernatural force that obstructs the Celtic heroes. Rather, it's often a *social* force which produces the tragedy. The Children of Lir are transformed into swans by a stepmother's jealousy. (Transformation again!) The sons of Tuireann are sent on a suicide mission as punishment for killing the man who killed their father. Goll mac Morna resented being Fionn MacCumhall's second in command, so he defected to the enemy in Fionn's final battle, which brought about the end of the Fianna. The most important social force in Iron age politics was the blood feud. To explain: iron age politics was inherently tribal. Therefore when someone committed a crime, the victim's whole family felt victimized, and the offender's whole family was treated as guilty. Some incident might be resolved in a way that everyone finds agreeable. But it's not long before someone lets his rage, or pride, or misplaced loyalty, or jealousy, get the better of him. Then the original problem returns, worse than before. Someone almost always ends up dead. The result is the trap of mutual hatred between two families who continually punish each other for real or perceived crimes, in an ever-escalating and endlessly-repeating cycle of violence. Sometimes an arranged dynastic marriage would bring a blood feud to an end: Goll mac Morna was invited to marry Fionn MacCumhall's daughter, for instance. But this solution tended to be fragile. The tragedy was not just the killing, but the near-impossibility of finding a way out of the killing.

The tribal nature of Celtic politics also sets up another tragic situation called the 'kin-slaying'. If someone kills a member of his or her own tribe, then everyone in the tribe becomes both victim and offender, and the crime cannot be punished. Cu Chulainn, for instance, killed his only son, Connla, a son he didn't know he had. Later, Cu Chulainn found himself trapped in the same tragedy a second time, when he was forced to kill his foster-brother Ferdiad, who had joined the opposite side in a war. It is precisely this situation where Miranda found herself, as you have now seen. Historically, the problems of kin-slaying and blood-feud were ultimately resolved by introducing a new social order and a new religion: Christianity. The solution that Miranda discovers in this novel is another option: a transformation, attending upon a changed relationship with the world. But I leave it to the reader to decide what that means.

Every Hidden House novel shifts my attention to a different lead hero. Fellwater was mainly about Katie; Hallowstone about Eric; Clan Fianna was an ensemble cast story; and Elderdown mainly followed Miranda. (Elderdown also moved some of the action to west Quebec, and the cities of Ottawa and Gatineau, where I live now.) At the same time, every Hidden Houses novel introduces new characters. This time our newcomer is Shinobi, the ladder-climbing infiltrator from House Kami. Originally I was planning to fill this role with a minor character from a previous novel. However, I was intrigued by a conversation I had with Ezekiel Zong-Han Azib, one of the financial contributors to the fundraising campaign which paid for the production of the previous novels in the series. He noted an unnamed character from House Kami, mentioned only in passing in Book Two. We decided that character might be a ninja; that is, a warrior involved in a contract-like arrangement with a peasant community, and who fights that community's oppressors using stealth. I thank Ezekiel for the initial idea.

Even before that conversation, I decided it was important to show that the Hidden World has the same cultural diversity as our real world. That was hard to do, as the main characters in the first novel were Celts and Italians, that is, Europeans. Characters like Satya, Ramanujan, Ibrahim, and George, were only minor parts, but I wanted to treat them with respect. This is why Ramu quotes from the Bhagavad Gita, for instance. (It's verse 3:35, in case you want to look it up.) Also, Miranda's presentation of tobacco to George Medewiwin comes from the customs surrounding the treatment of Elders in the Ojibway and Haudenosaunee traditions. George also paraphrases the argument of Guujaaw, a young Haida man from the island of

Haida Gwaii, who was asked by television host David Suzuki what would happen to his people if the rainforest on his island was logged away. "Well, we'll probably end up the same as everyone else, I guess," he replied. There's something in this statement I find very potent. I invite you to think about it for yourself, as well.

Carlo and Heathcliff, by contrast, quote Machiavelli.

On a lighter note, some occasions of "art imitating life" happened as I wrote this series. For example, I found a satellite photo of Elora, the real town on which my fictional town is based, showing the location of the Brigantian's magical grove concealed under clouds. Perhaps there is a Shadow Spell after all! But more ominously: in early 2015, Nestlé corporation submitted a proposal to extract and bottle water from the aquifer that feeds the village. I shall assume that Nestlé's interest in the water is less political than the DiAngelo's. But I'm keeping an eye on them, nonetheless.

Fellwater began ten years ago, as a tribute to a dear friend, and as a means of preventing intellectual lassitude during a ten-month stretch of unemployment. It has now grown into this four-part series, with multiple spinoffs published and planned. I think it may be the most personally expressive and revealing work of art I have created so far. Every character in my books is real to me; I hear their voices and see their faces as I write them. Yet every character here is also a self-portrait. Every crisis in their lives happened to someone I care about, if not myself as well. And every moment of beauty and peace they find is something I wish for you, dear reader.

Alas, the Great Work of telling their story is done. Yet I do plan to continue writing about the Hidden World. Following precedents like Terry Pratchett's Diskworld and Charles de Lint's Newford, there shall be more stories in the same universe, but with different characters, different questions, and different adventures. Some of these may feature characters who were only peripheral in the main series. (I believe that every character, no matter how minor, should have a story.) Some may feature entirely new characters, and new settings. Two spinoff stories are already published at this time: "A Trick of the Light", and "The Seekers". But with this core series now complete, I have fulfilled most of the ambitions I once had for writing a big-canvass, philosophically-influenced, multi-volume fantasy fiction series. I may someday let someone talk me into into writing Book Five. Indeed, in a late-night corridor of sleeplessness, I wrote a beat-sheet for it. But for now, I shall let these characters rest.

At least for a while. We'll see.

Brendan Myers
Gatineau, Quebec, Canada
May 2015.

~ About the author ~

Brendan Myers loves fairy tales and space exploration. He lives in a library, next door to a forest.

Brendan is a TED speaker, a successful Kickstarter, and the author of sixteen books in fiction and nonfiction. He earned his Ph.D in philosophy at the National University of Ireland, and now serves as professor of philosophy at Heritage College, in Gatineau, Quebec. This is his sixteenth book.

Find him on the web at brendanmyers.net

Follow him on Twitter @Fellwater